THE MAGICIANS OF VENICE, BOOK 3

THE KING'S SEAL

AMY KUIVALAINEN

bhc
press™

Livonia, Michigan

Editor: Chelsea Cambeis
Proofreader: Jamie Rich

THE KING'S SEAL

Published by BHC Press

Library of Congress Control Number: 2020940645

ISBN: 978-1-64397-242-8 (Hardcover)
ISBN: 978-1-64397-243-5 (Softcover)
ISBN: 978-1-64397-244-2 (Ebook)

For information, write:
BHC Press
885 Penniman #5505
Plymouth, MI 48170

Visit the publisher:
www.bhcpress.com

BY AMY KUIVALAINEN

SPECIAL ACKNOWLEDGMENT

I want to acknowledge the excellent works of Professor Dame Averil Cameron, especially her translations of Eusebius's *Life of Constantine*, and Professor Meredith K. Ray's *Daughters of Alchemy*. Without their incredible historical research, this book would never have been written.

The
King's
Seal

PART ONE

THE LOST EMPEROR

*"For in much wisdom is much
grief: and he that increaseth
knowledge increaseth sorrow."*
— Ecclesiastes 1:18 —

PROLOGUE

MILOS WAS A small, picturesque island surrounded by the Aegean's topaz blue waters, and Kreios hated every moment he had to spend on it. Out in the world, he was able to move about; he could go into a café and pretend for a few precious moments that he wasn't bound, body and will, to a madman and a demon.

Milos was the monster's lair, and every step he took, Thevetat's presence pulsed like a toothache. The locals had learned to look the other way, dismissing the opulent mansion, its owner, and the constant stream of visitors as the lifestyle of a man with too much money. Kreios made sure that the visiting priests, acolytes, and vessels that frequented the island supported the locals and behaved themselves. Those that didn't behave were dealt with severely by Kreios, and they were not tempted to step out of line again.

Kreios stepped into the produce store that was also a post office and tourist gift shop, and grabbed a handful of postcards. He greeted the owner, Rhea, with a cheerful smile before pulling out his pen.

After what happened in Venice, Kreios had convinced Thevetat that they needed to limit their digital communications—Galenos was far too skilled in tracking them—and had presented the idea of sending cryptic instructions on the back of postcards. No one ever paid much attention to the scribbled messages, especially if they were written in a dead language.

Kreios hummed to himself as he jotted down the latest orders, the addresses known by heart. Thevetat would never bother to check Kreios's memories of such a mundane task, but he hadn't survived as long as he had because he was careless. He couldn't risk using shielding magic, not when Thevetat was so close, so he chose the simplest way to cover his tracks. He shut his eyes, wrote the one-line message on the postcard, and slid it in amongst the others before opening his eyes again. When he was done, Kreios handed the pile of cards over to Rhea with some euros and left the store.

Kreios had long stopped believing in hope, but something akin to it flickered in the pit of his guts. Whether death or freedom met him first, he didn't really care. All he knew was that within a month, the nightmare he'd endured for the last ten thousand years would be over.

ONE

EVER SINCE DOCTOR Penelope Bryne had met the magicians of Venice, she'd been forced to believe more impossible things by breakfast than Alice in Wonderland. That was why when they said things like, "Constantine the Great is still alive," Penelope had learned to pause, take a breath, and then ask her follow-up questions. Sometimes, the answers she received were more confusing than the impossible thing itself.

It had been a month since Penelope returned from Israel, and she was still having trouble reconciling everything that had happened there. Some days, her grief for Tim was like being pulled to the bottom of the Grand Canal by her ankles. Most of the time, her anger lay like a sleeping serpent in the pit of her stomach, and she did her best not to disturb it. She had work to do; the seal ring of King Solomon wasn't going to find itself. But first, Penelope needed to find Constantine.

It didn't matter how much research she did or how many time periods and historical figures she identified in the record of Tim's visions; she needed a proper starting point. Most of all, she needed to know if the ring actually *worked*.

Penelope was willing to allow some of the legends to have elaborations if the core truth was that the seal ring of Solomon could exorcise a demon. But they couldn't waste time searching for a trinket based on some kind of allegory when they could be using their resources to track down and destroy Thevetat by other means.

Besides, if Constantine was alive, what was to say he hadn't tracked the ring down to get it back?

Alexis understood, but there wasn't much he could do to assist Penelope in locating the emperor's whereabouts.

"I haven't spoken to Con in centuries, *cara*. Aelia will be able to help. From what I can tell, she has always kept tabs on him."

"That's great, but she won't tell me. Every time I approach her about it, she walks away. I tried asking Phaidros, who grunted at me, and as for Zo? All he did was blush furiously and say he couldn't help either." Penelope threw her hands up in the air. "You're all impossible. Can't you use some of that Donato charm on Aelia and get her to spill?"

"I'm surprised you believe Aelia would be susceptible to my charm at all. I'm still holding out hope that we won't need to involve Constantine. I doubt any good can come of it," Alexis replied without looking up from his book.

"Fine. I'll force it out of Aelia myself." Penelope stood from her office chair.

They had gone back and forth on the matter for three weeks, and Penelope's mind remained unchanged; they needed to talk to Constantine. They could research until Thevetat had a new body and sank Venice into the sea, and they would still be no closer to finding the seal of Solomon if it adorned Constantine's finger. Alexis was being stubborn because he was still hurt over what had passed between them centuries beforehand—yet another thing he refused to elaborate on.

Alexis held out his hand to Penelope, and she moved to his desk, letting his arm curve around her waist.

"Careful with Aelia. Constantine has always been a delicate subject," he said, his lips against her shoulder.

"Alexis, if I tried to dodge every sore subject with you magicians, I'd never get a chance to talk at all. I'm going to get her to tell me, or I'm going to make her life difficult until she does."

"Poseidon save me, you sound so much like Nereus sometimes. It's like she's found the perfect way to order us about from beyond the grave."

Penelope bent down so she could kiss him lightly, the soft stubble of his beard tickling her lips. "And yet, you still love me, Defender."

Alexis's indigo eyes glowed hot, and she knew she had to get away before her self-control went out the window.

"I do love you, *cara*. Now, go and talk to Aelia before I find a way to keep you down here," he said, a hint of her favorite wicked smile lingering at the corner of his mouth.

MOIST, SALTY air hit Penelope as soon as she stepped out of the Archives elevator. April had come and gone, and with May, the sticky promise of summer had arrived. Penelope knew where Aelia would be without having to ask. The magician had claimed a stretch of the garden that overlooked the Grand Canal. In the past few days, she had nearly caused two boating accidents by strolling too closely to the stone retaining wall in her bright orange bikini.

Currently, Aelia was sunning herself in another barely-there swimsuit, her hair caught up under a matching pink turban, with a sweating pitcher of spritz positioned on a small table beside her.

"Ah, Penelope, pull up a sun bed and take off those clothes. The weather is far too pleasant to waste."

Penelope dragged another sun bed over to the shade of an umbrella but kept on her top and the jeans she'd cut off at the knees. Aelia lowered her sunglasses and gave her a critical once-over.

"Are you here to ask me to come shopping with you?" She eyed Penelope's improvised summer wear with distaste.

"No, I'm here to ask you about Constantine."

"Oh." Aelia repositioned her sunglasses.

Penelope reached for the pitcher and poured herself a spritz. She had a feeling she was going to need it. "I'm never going to understand your reluctance to find him unless you talk about it."

"You are young, Penelope. I doubt you'd understand even if I did explain it to you."

"Then you need to weigh up whether you want revenge on Thevetat and Abaddon more than you want to protect your own pride as far as Constantine goes."

"That was a horribly low blow."

"I don't care. I've tried to be patient, but I've had it with all of you. I need the ring to stop Thevetat. Abaddon killed Tim. I know he wasn't the greatest of friends in the end, but he was still my family, and I want payback. I'll bug you until my dying breath if I have to."

Aelia moaned. "Poseidon save me, you are a pain in the ass. Drink a spritz and calm down."

Penelope leaned back in her chair, drank, and watched the ferries drive slowly past. When Aelia was still silent five minutes later, she said, "It's okay, Aelia. I'll ask Phaidros. I know he won't hold anything back."

Aelia bit her lip and looked away from her. "Please don't. It will only antagonize him, and we've been getting along so well."

"Then spit it out. I'm not asking any of you to make a phone call or come with me to see Constantine. I'll do it myself. I only need to know where he is."

Aelia's laugh tinkled across the canal, and the ferry load of people turned toward the sound. "Sweet, darling *bambina*, if you think the Defender will let you anywhere near Constantine without him, you are sorely mistaken."

"And if you think Alexis will be able to stop me, then *you* are sorely mistaken. Constantine is just a man. I don't know what the problem is."

"You say that because you've never met him." Aelia sighed and mumbled something under her breath.

Penelope cupped her hand around her ear. "*Scusi?* I missed that."

"Dubrovnik," Aelia repeated. She sat up and refilled her glass.

"The city? What about it?"

"The last time I saw Constantine was in Dubrovnik, 1998. We had been to his villa in Niš."

Penelope waited, but when Aelia didn't elaborate, she asked, "It ended badly?"

"If by badly you mean I drove his Maserati 320S into the ocean, then yes, it ended badly. It always does; that's the problem."

"Dare I ask why you drove his car into the ocean?"

Aelia lifted a shoulder in a lazy half-shrug. "He wanted me to marry him; I said no. He got insistent, so I drove his car into the sea. It happens."

Penelope wanted to point out that such a thing would only happen if you were Aelia, but she didn't want to piss Aelia off when she was talking for the first time in weeks.

"You think he might still be in Niš?"

"He could be anywhere. He has always preferred the east to the west."

"You don't have a mobile number for him?"

"We fought. The number I have, even if I could find it, would be over twenty years old."

"Fair enough. I'll ask Zo if he's heard from Constantine since '98. As you said, it's been twenty years. I'm guessing if he wanted to talk to you, he would have reached out by now."

"Hmm, you would think, wouldn't you?"

Broken hearts are not your forte, Bryne. Back out while you still can. Penelope downed the rest of her spritz. "Thanks, Aelia. I promise not to bug you about Constantine anymore. I'll understand if you don't want to come with us when we go and see him."

"I never said that."

"Why would you want to come along if you two have been fighting for the last twenty years?"

"It might be a good chance to catch up, let him know the world could be ending—you know, that kind of thing."

"Uh-huh," said Penelope, not buying her act for a second. "Maybe you should stay here. I don't want you starting arguments before I can get any useful information out of him."

"All depends on how we decide to argue." Aelia's lips curled into a smutty smile.

"You know what? I don't want to know." Penelope got to her feet. "I'm going to talk to Zo. Enjoy the sun."

"I'll make a few calls and see what I can shake loose. No promises," Aelia called as Penelope walked away.

PENELOPE FOUND Zo in the sprawling entertainment room, fighting Phaidros on the PlayStation.

"Aelia knows where Constantine is. She's hesitating because she's fighting with him," said Phaidros.

Zo punched the buttons on his controller with fervor. "You want to go and meet Constantine? Alexis is going to hate that."

"So everyone keeps telling me. It doesn't change the fact I still need to talk to him." Penelope flopped down on the couch between them and watched as Zo's character dodged the arrows Phaidros was firing at him.

"Alexis is smart. He's stayed away from Constantine because he's poison," Phaidros said. "Now you're going to force him to break his promise to never see Constantine again. Alexis will do it too. As much as he'll hate doing it, he'll hate the idea of you alone with the emperor even more." He cursed Zo in Greek and threw his remote at the other magician.

"Don't be a sore loser," Penelope said.

Zo roared with laughter. "Oh no. You've hit the metaphorical nail on its head there, Penelope. Phaidros is a terrible loser; that's why he hates Con so much."

"Screw you." Phaidros stormed from the room.

"That reaction seemed rather extreme."

"You should know by now, *sorella*, that Phaidros is always going to be extreme when it comes to his Aelia."

"That's so stupid. They aren't even together! Neither are Aelia and Constantine. Why is everyone acting like this? I feel like I'm living in a crazy house."

Was one straight answer too much to ask for?

"Penelope, you are living with magicians. Of course it's like living in a crazy house. As for Aelia and Constantine—that's complicated. It's what happens when those blessed with an abundance of life fall in love, and make no mistake, Aelia is in love with Constantine. She'll always be in love with him."

"Then what's the problem? Why not be with him if that's how she feels?"

"Because she's also in love with Phaidros. She doesn't dare admit it to herself or to him. As for Constantine…well, he's Constantine. It's hard to explain until you meet him for yourself. *Everyone* is in love with him, even Alexis, the straightest man the gods ever created. Why do you think he hasn't talked to him in so long? He's heartbroken, *bella*." Zo leaned back into the cushions beside Penelope and took her hand. "We are hard to live with, I know. There is too much history between all of us to ever be able to wrap your head around, so it's better if you surrender to the flow and don't become too frustrated with us when you don't understand."

"You seem to be the most levelheaded at the moment. Maybe you should be the one to come with me to meet with this paragon of virtue I keep hearing about."

"Absolutely not. Constantine. He's…" Zo placed a hand over his heart with a sigh. It said it all.

Great, another one in love.

Zo smiled as if reading her thoughts. "It's so unrequited it hurts. If Alexis is the straightest man created, then Constantine comes a close second, but I can't help but be in love with that man. You should read his poetry. *Dio mi salvi!*" Zo sighed dreamily.

"He writes good poetry too? Is there anything he's not good at?"

"Not much. Constantine's not a paragon of virtue, so you should dismiss that idea at once."

"I wasn't serious," Penelope said.

Zo gave her hand a quick kiss. "Good. Because he might be a saint, but he's certainly not virtuous."

TWO

MARCO COULD TELL that Adalfieri was pissed off by the way he chewed the corner of his mustache as he read the form in his hand.

"Four weeks is a lot of time, Dandolo," he said when he finished reading.

"I know. However, I do have ten weeks owed to me. I haven't taken time off in nearly three years," said Marco. He didn't want to antagonize the older man any more than he had to.

"What brought this on? I know you've been busy since the bombings—we all have—but it's a part of the job."

"It's not about the bombings or the workload. I need a break, that's all. Isabella and her wife, Guilia, have been trying to get pregnant, and it's taking a toll on the family. I need to give them some space. And I need space myself."

It was a lie, but one that Adalfieri would believe. All things considered, Isabella had been amazing as she coped with IVF and the storm of emotions that came with it. Adalfieri was old-school in that he was a chauvinistic patriarch, and Marco could imagine all of the objections the older man had to a gay couple trying to start a family. Adalfieri was also a politician, however, so he wisely kept his mouth shut.

"Are you going anywhere nice, at least?" Adalfieri asked.

"The Bahamas."

"With a woman? It's a shame that pretty doctor ran off with Donato. She would've been good for you."

"I'm going with a few friends. It's the Bahamas; there will be plenty of pretty women to meet there." Marco gave the other man a wink. He didn't want Adalfieri prying, and if he chose to believe Marco planned to get caught up in the uncomplicated arms of some anonymous women, so much the better. It was easier to explain than, *I'm going to join a group of vigilante magicians on a demon hunt.*

"By friends, do you mean *Signore* Donato?"

"No, but we have a few of the same acquaintances."

"Be careful, Marco. There's much that is a mystery about that man and his circle of influence."

"You don't have to warn me, sir. I might be in need of a holiday, but I'm not about to stop being a policeman. If I see something worth investigating, I'll look into it."

"Good man. You take after your father in some ways at least, even if he never asked to take holidays," Adalfieri said.

Marco stifled an inward groan. It wasn't often that Adalfieri brought up his father, Pietro. They had been friends through the force, right up until Pietro got drunk, went out in his boat, and was never seen again. Marco's mother, a staunch Catholic, had never allowed the word *suicide* to be mentioned in her presence, even if that's what it had been. Marco had moved back to Venice from Padua to be there for his mother and sister. Eventually, laughter returned to the palazzo, and they rarely talked about the drunk man with his hard fists and worse temper. It was only the old men, who never knew what Pietro had actually been like, that ever talked about him with any fondness.

An hour later, Marco breathed a sigh of relief as he stepped out of the police station. He lit a cigarette and got one sweet lungful before it was whipped out of his mouth and crushed to pieces in the hand of the fiercest woman he'd ever met.

Lyca stood proud, like a modern Zenobia, dressed in combat boots, jeans, and a singlet that showed off the impressive white tattoos inked on her black biceps. Her long silver hair was a mass of tiny braids and pulled back in a ponytail. She looked ready for action, as she always did.

"No," she said firmly, holding out her hand until Marco relinquished his packet to her.

"I don't know why I can't have just one."

"Because you need to quit. I won't have some wheezing human giving my position away and unable to keep up. You wanted to join us in this fight. It's my job to make you useful. Don't bitch about my methods." Lyca gestured toward her boat. "Get in. I'm driving."

Ever since the night in Cannaregio, when he'd met the Serpent of Venice, Marco had struck up an odd friendship with the warrior. It was clear Lyca saw Marco as a special project, and he was spending almost as much time at the palazzo on the Calle dei Cerchieri as his own house. It was one of the reasons he wanted to take annual leave from work. Juggling his day job and the investigation into the priests of Thevetat had begun to take its toll. And that was before the grueling workouts Lyca had been putting him through. Giving up cigarettes once and for all had been a part of the agreement.

They pulled into the small wooden dock on the Grand Canal, and Marco tied the boat off. Lyca smirked. She'd already explained that the magic of the palazzo would deal with the boat, but it went against every Venetian bone in Marco's body to leave a boat unsecured.

"Back again, I see," said Phaidros as Marco walked through the door.

"I missed you." Marco offered him a sweet smile. Phaidros snorted and walked away. "What's his problem?"

"What it always is—Aelia. Penelope is pressing them to find Constantine, and nothing pisses Phaidros off quicker than Aelia's lovers," said Lyca with disgust.

Marco knew better than to push for more information. He liked Aelia's company, even if she was extra flirtatious at times to get a reaction out of Phaidros.

Why Aelia and Phaidros didn't get together was beyond him. The one time he'd mentioned it to Penelope, she laughed and said it was because it would make too much sense. Marco had learned to deal with Phaidros's snide comments once he realized there was no real malice in them, and generally, counteracting them with kindness resulted in the magician leaving him alone.

They found Galenos in the library and attached to a laptop, trails of light emanating from him. The first time Marco saw him connect to technology with his magic, it had freaked him out entirely. It was like the magician synced with the machine and became a part of the system. It was easily one of the strangest things he'd ever seen, and that included Alexis pulling the MOSE gates from the sea. Galenos blinked a few times, code racing over his eyes, before he let the magic go. The cords of magic receded back into the magician, and then he was suddenly present and smiling at them.

"*Buongiorno,* Marco. How was work?" Galenos asked.

"Over for the next month, thank God. Did you find anything new?"

Galenos had been using the laptop from the safe house to trace where it had been and what it had been used for—a meticulous task that included studying every time one the priests of Thevetat had logged on to watch porn or transfer millions of dollars between accounts.

"Nothing of interest at this stage." Galenos got to his feet and crossed an item off a list pinned to the wall. He'd made a quick recovery after being fitted for his new arm and leg, and Lyca was working him harder than Marco so he was fighting-fit. They made an odd pair, but Marco had never seen two people so in love with each other.

"Thank God, my sanity has arrived. I thought I heard your voice," Penelope said, coming in from the gardens to kiss Marco's cheek.

"I've never been considered someone's sanity before. How are you, *amica*?"

"Frustrated. Trying to get information out of magicians has become my full-time job."

"Where is your shadow?"

"If you mean Alexis, he's in the Archives." Penelope turned toward the wall of information. "Quickly, tell me something to take my mind off the emperor."

Marco frowned at her tone. Since her return from Israel, there was a spike of iron in her eyes that hadn't been there before. Marco understood the reasoning behind it, and yet it worried him. She should've grieved longer instead of throwing herself into work.

It's how she processes things, Alexis's voice reminded him. Marco had spoken his fears aloud to the magician, knowing that if anyone could get through to Penelope, he could. He trusted Alexis's judgment, but it didn't make him worry about his friend any less.

THREE

---

*A*LEXIS PLACED HIS book down on his cluttered desk and leaned back in his chair. Alexis could feel when Penelope was gone, just like the Archives could. Without the vibrant hum and warmth of her presence, the pressure growing inside of him became almost impossible to ignore. He didn't want to keep her locked to his side, even if he was tempted to. The tide was creeping inevitably higher, and they were no closer to finding the ring of Solomon.

Perhaps it was a fool's hope to think it would work on Thevetat anyway. The collapse of Atlantis didn't slow the wicked old snake down; what hope did they have with a ring? A ring that, in all likelihood, was still in Constantine's possession. Alexis got up with a frustrated grunt and headed deeper into the Archives. It had changed to suit Penelope, but there were still chambers she didn't know about.

Nereus may have shown her the laboratory made of hematite stone, but none of them had mentioned the prisons.

Over the years, they had all gone mad at least once—from magic, grief, or the depression of having a life so long and never seeing an end to it, unable to know why they had been cursed with it. Nereus had to ensure there was a place they could be held that would null the flow of magic inside of them, a place in which they could remain calm enough to recover from whatever ailed them without their magic reacting to every emotion. With the high tide looming and his mind on fire, a cell was the only place Alexis might be able to think straight.

Alexis opened the doorway hidden in the rock and found Phaidros sitting in the room of stone with his back against the wall. Waves of energy and magic rolled off him like a nuclear reactor and were absorbed into the stone around him. Unlike Aelia and Zo, who could control their magic with words, Alexis's and Phaidros's power had a habit of leaking out when they least expected it. If they were emotional, it was harder to control. One look at Phaidros, and Alexis knew he was more than a little emotional.

"What are you doing here?" Phaidros asked.

"The same thing as you, I imagine." Alexis slid down the wall beside him and breathed a sigh of relief.

"That bad?"

"My head is splitting. How about you?"

"It's so bad, I feel nauseous. Fucking high tides. I forgot how awful they are until you get used to them."

"And then once you do, they are gone again, and you have to live with that," said Alexis. They had been through it many times over the centuries. This was going to be the biggest high tide since Atlantis fell—who knew what would happen to them.

"I thought you would be with Penelope." Phaidros glanced at him sidelong with his golden eyes.

"She needed a break from studying the ring of Solomon."

"She's upstairs studying the priest's movements with Marco. She never stops working. Have you noticed that?"

"I have."

"I know you can be just as bad when you're onto something, but she's still mostly human, Alexis. This whole business will chew her to pieces if she's not reminded what's worth fighting for."

"She's coping with her grief the best way she can, Phaidros. I can't interfere with that. I don't know what she needs. I'm trying to support her while she figures it out."

"Do something to get her out of this palazzo. You're both so close to everything happening that you won't be able to see the answers even if you find them. You need a break."

Alexis stretched out his long legs. He *was* feeling claustrophobic. "Perhaps there is some merit in what you are saying."

"I'm sorry, did you just agree with me?"

"There are occasionally pearls of wisdom amongst the muck." Alexis smiled, and Phaidros burst out laughing.

"I suppose that's fair. Honestly, I'm happy that you've got Penelope. Jealous as anything, but happy nonetheless." Phaidros's body grew tense, and Alexis couldn't resist reaching out to touch his shoulder.

"Phaidros, don't you think it's time you tell Aelia? This high tide could be the end of our world as we know it. Stop torturing yourself like this and take the chance." Alexis had promised long ago to never interfere when it came to Aelia, but Phaidros was his oldest friend, and he hated to see him so miserable.

"Aelia isn't ready for me to love her."

"She's never going to be unless you tell her."

"She won't *let* me love her, Alexis. Even Constantine, prick that he is, has only ever tried to love her. She allows it to a point, but when it gets too serious, she does something stupid to push people away. She doesn't want to be loved."

"We all want to be loved. Aelia's afraid. Love and fear go hand in hand. You've lived long enough to know the truth of that."

"We need her for this war against the priests. If I spook her now, she'll run. If she runs, she'll be alone and vulnerable and easy for Thevetat to pick off. I won't risk her life like that."

"I understand. I only want you to stop wasting the time you have with her."

Phaidros laughed. It was a bitter, heartbreaking sound. "All we've got is time."

"For now. This high tide might be the thing that breaks this curse of immortality."

"How is Penelope dealing with the tide? Can she feel it yet?" Phaidros changed the subject too fast for Alexis to carry on about Aelia.

"I'm not sure. Penelope hasn't said. Her magic is unique in that both parts of it originally belonged to other magicians. I don't know what to expect from it."

"Do you think the magic will absorb and become hers? Maybe she'll start demonstrating abilities like yours and Nereus's?"

"The Living Language from my tablet seems to have become her own. I've often thought of it as a proto-language—maybe not the first language, but certainly the oldest—so perhaps that's why it's helping with the translations. All language has its roots in it. Nereus's power came from Poseidon, so who knows what it will do. Penelope can balance my power like Nereus could." He hadn't told anyone about it, and after it happened in Israel, he and Penelope hadn't spoken of it either.

Phaidros raised his eyebrows. "If she can do that, why are you here? Can she do it to anyone else?"

"She only did it once, and it was while…"

"While you were fucking?"

"Gods, you're vulgar. Yes, it happened then. You can see why I wouldn't want her testing it with anyone else."

"It could've just been triggered that way because it was instinctual. If she tested it in other ways, I'm sure she could do it to anyone." Phaidros had a gleam in his eye that Alexis knew far too well.

"I will hit you." Alexis recalled how intimate it was when Penelope drew on his magic, and he'd lock all the other magicians in the prison before he'd let any of them share that with her.

"Okay, okay, but you need to try to get her to explore her abilities. Otherwise, the tide will be here, and she won't know how to cope with any of the side effects."

He was right, and while Alexis secretly hated it, it was enough to give him an idea. "I'm going out for a while. Try not to stay in here too long, or it will sucker punch you as soon as you leave."

"Yes, yes, I know. Go and make love to your lady, Defender," Phaidros said, then shut his golden eyes once more.

Alexis found Penelope upstairs in the library, exactly where Phaidros predicted she would be.

"You can't stop working for five minutes, can you?" Alexis kissed the top of her head.

"Marco turned up, and I got distracted."

"Come for a walk with me, *cara*. They can manage without us for the afternoon," he whispered in her ear.

Penelope looked up at him curiously before smiling. "I should go and get changed."

"Don't. You look perfect as you are."

Aelia snorted from the other side of the room but managed to keep her mouth shut.

"I'll text you if we find anything," Marco said without looking up from the laptop screen.

"You will not. We'll be back soon enough. The world can wait." Alexis placed his hand at the small of Penelope's back and steered her toward the library door.

OUTSIDE, THE sun hung low in the sky, and the sea breeze was cooling off the sticky streets.

"What's brought this on?" Penelope looped her fingers around his.

"I'm tired of being inside the palazzo with all of the squabbling magicians. We need a walk and time away from the search," Alexis said as they moved through the narrow streets of Dorsoduro.

They passed the Accademia Bridge. Alexis gave some euros to Maria, the homeless widow who favored the Campo della Carita. Dodging a crowd of art students outside the Peggy Guggenheim Collection, Alexis bought a bottle of wine and focaccia before they crossed the bridge to the Punta della Dogana. The tourists had cleared out for the afternoon, so they sat down next to the lamppost at the very point, with a perfect view of the light shining on St. Mark's Square across the canal.

"This was an excellent idea," Penelope said before sipping her Chianti.

"You can thank Phaidros. He reminded me that we shouldn't have our heads stuck in books all the time."

"Dates with handsome men are all well and good, but Solomon's ring needs to be found. The fate of the world and all that."

"*Cara*, there is always something threatening the fate of the world. The search for the ring has distracted us from something equally important, and that's your magic," said Alexis.

Penelope looked away from the water and down at the silver rings shining on her hands. "I don't know what you all expect me to be able to do."

"The tide is growing. It's starting to affect Phaidros and me more every day. It won't be long before the others feel it too, and that includes you. I only want you to be ready for it. It's a part of you, and it will grow into what it needs to be. Pretending it isn't there won't make it go away."

"Poseidon's power from Nereus—whatever that means. With any luck, I'll get abilities like Aquaman and will never have to worry about drowning again," she said with an awkward hitch in her voice.

Alexis shifted so he could put an arm around her. "I don't want you to worry unnecessarily. Just be aware of anything…out of the ordinary."

Penelope reached up to brush her fingers against his jawline. "Alexis, I live with magicians. Everything seems out of the ordinary to me, but I promise I'll try to be more aware of it. I wonder if there is anything in the Archives about Poseidon's abilities. I might be able to come up with a list of things to watch out for."

"That's a good idea. I'm sure Nereus will have something. Although many of her books that I *know* I've seen seem to be missing." It was bothering him more each day. *Why would the Archives hide them?*

"Kreios said that Abaddon wanted Nereus's books on the experiments to bring Poseidon back to life. I've looked for them, and they aren't there."

"Maybe the Archives destroyed them when the office was remade for you. Nereus felt strongly that those particular experiments shouldn't be repeated under any circumstances."

"Why didn't she destroy them herself?" Penelope asked, then shook her head. "Nope. Never mind. Magicians are academics; book burning isn't in their nature."

They sat in silence, watching the light begin to fade. In Alexis's arms, Penelope let out a contented sigh. "Maybe we should've disappeared for a hundred years while we had the chance. I could get used to lazy sunsets and wine with you."

Heady magic coursed through Alexis like quicksilver, calling out to him to do just that. "You would miss Venice too much," he said, swallowing the impulse.

"Very true. I don't know what it is, but I feel so at ease here. I don't feel like a tourist. Instead, Venice feels like the home I was looking for but could never find."

"Venice has a way of doing that to people. In a time that was full of mistrust, Venezia threw her arms out to the world, and anyone could live and make money here. Time has changed her in many ways, but not in the ones that count. It doesn't matter where you were born, if you arrive and she invokes fierce love in you, she will never let you go." Alexis's own deep history with the city could never alter his love for it.

"You're going to have to teach me all of Venice's feast days. I don't think I'm ever going to remember them all. We missed Saint Mark's Day when we were in Israel, which sucks, because I love roses."

Alexis frowned at the wistful note in Penelope's voice. "I'm going to have to find a way to make it up to you. Our courtship needs more afternoons like this one."

"I'm really glad I remembered who you are," whispered Penelope.

Alexis's heart expanded as she leaned farther into him to watch the stars come out.

As they wended their way back through the dark streets of Dorsoduro, Alexis asked, "Did you have any luck getting information out of Aelia or Zo about where Constantine might be hiding?"

"Aelia said she will ask around, whatever that means. It surprises me that Constantine didn't keep in touch with any of you. Being long-lived and alone would make me want to reach out to others like me—or at least send a Christmas card."

Alexis stopped walking. "The letters," he murmured. He pulled Penelope to him, and they disappeared in a shower of black-and-silver sand.

FOUR

THEY LANDED AMONGST Alexis's stacks of books. His tower was still warm, the heat of the day trapped in the marble columns and rich wood. The cinnamon scent of his magic was strong, permanently seeped into every piece of parchment and surface. His rooms were secretly Penelope's favorite place in the palazzo; they were the physical embodiment of his personality.

"What's wrong?" she asked. Alexis rarely portaled anywhere unless he was in a hurry, and especially not from a public street.

"Nothing, apart from me being a complete idiot at times. I can't believe I didn't think of it before. It's been so long…" He crossed his rooms and rummaged in a sandalwood box so big that Penelope could have climbed inside with plenty of room to spare. Alexis pulled out a smaller box and placed it down on his workbench.

"I forgot all about these. Time does strange things to memory. I was so focused on placing Solomon's ring at different periods, not wanting to think of Constantine at all, that I missed probably the best clue we have," he said. His ringed fingers danced over the carvings in the box's surface. "It wasn't until you mentioned letters that it clicked."

"Constantine has been writing to you?"

"He was after the third fallout. I placed magic on the mailbox and redirected all letters from him to this box instead. I doubt they will be helpful; they're so old. He would've stopped writing once he realized I was ignoring him." Alexis's expression grew foggy, lost in the river of memories. After a few moments of waiting, Penelope moved to join him at the bench.

"Would you like me to open it?"

"No, it's fine. I'm fine," Alexis said quickly, his eyes refocusing on the box.

Penelope had learned to be patient with all of the magicians, so she kept her questions about the "third fallout" and magical mailboxes to herself. Alexis's fingertips glowed gold and indigo, and the magic sealing the box melted away like mercury. The lid flew back, and hundreds of letters poured from the box, spewing out over his workbench and fluttering to the floor. Alexis looked astonished as his hands moved over them.

"I don't think Constantine realized you were ignoring him." Penelope stepped back, careful not to tread on what looked to be hundreds of years' worth of correspondence.

There was a sharp tang of firecrackers, and the letters sorted themselves into piles. How the letters were folded and sealed seemed to change with time until envelopes became commonplace. There were four letters to every year, and the academic side of Penelope burned to read every one of them for historical references, but she knew it was inappropriate to even ask. The letters had the feel of intimacy about them, and she didn't want to develop any preconceived notions about Constantine's personality before she had a chance to meet him herself.

"I don't know what to say." Alexis stared at the piles.

"Aelia said she stayed with him in Niš ten years ago, and then they went to Dubrovnik. Maybe he gave you an address?" Penelope suggested. She kissed his cheek and left him to his thoughts.

Hours later, Alexis crawled into bed with her, and she drew him close. She didn't need Phaidros's gifts for reading energy and auras to feel his distress. She wrapped her arms around him and moved in, so her chest was flush against his. The inferno of his magic burned inside of him. In her dreamy state, the raw, mysterious, new part of her flared to life in response to it, and then, like it had in Ein Karem, her magic drew on his with a rush that made her skin crackle as she balanced his power.

"Penelope?" Alexis whispered, breathing ragged.

"I'm okay, and now you are too. You should've said something, Alexis."

He took her face in the darkness and covered it with soft kisses. "Thank you, *cara*. Thank you."

"No need to thank me. You said I should be exploring my magic, and balancing the flow of the new magic running into you is just that." She hated the way he seemed to believe he had to suffer in silence and carry everything on his own.

Says the woman unable to process her own grief or allow people to see how much she's hurting.

Alexis's arms tightened around her, his long legs tangling with hers, until there was no space between them. He rested his cheek atop her head. "You are one of the most intuitive people I've ever met, Penelope. Whatever you end up using your magic for, it will be uniquely yours. Your first instinct is to help people. You flew halfway around the world to help the police solve a murder. I'm not worried about what you will do with whatever abilities you possess, because your heart is good. Thank you for balancing me. It's become a problem lately. I feel like I can finally think clearly again."

"You should've said something."

"You've had enough to worry about. I wanted to be the steady part of your life while you accepted what happened in Israel."

"You can be the steady part and still be honest with me about how you're feeling. You can't hide the oncoming tide from me. Don't forget, I have an astrolabe that tells me everything."

"Be patient with me, *cara*. I haven't had anyone in my confidence for a long, long time, and those kinds of habits are hard to break. You know, you haven't mentioned Tim or Carolyn for weeks. We both are very independent, as well as uncomfortable talking about what's on our minds."

"I'm not talking about it because there's no point. It's not going to change anything, and I still don't know how I feel about it. I will ramble in circles if I try to talk about it now. I need to stay focused, not fall apart and have panic attacks because I can't control my anxiety." Penelope's voice hitched.

Alexis stroked her hair. "We all grieve in different ways, so if you need to work, then work. You don't have to speak about it until you want to; just know that you can come to me when you're ready."

"Deal," she whispered, before burying her face into his chest and finally going back to sleep.

THE NEXT morning, Penelope found Marco, Galenos, and Lyca in the kitchen eating breakfast and brewing coffee. The three had become unlikely and inseparable companions in the past few weeks, the terrifying warrior magician taking Marco under her wing as if he were a baby bird who needed to learn how to kill a possessed priest of Thevetat with one shot.

"I'm starting to think you live here, Marco," said Penelope. She yawned and helped herself to the pot of coffee.

"Lyca is a very strict taskmaster. Aren't you, *maestro*?" Marco said affectionately.

"I have to be. I intend to make you useful, even if you are *polizia*." Lyca was peeling an apple with her dagger, carving the green rind into intricate patterns.

"She won't let me have a cigarette with my breakfast. A man needs his morning tobacco to function!"

"A man needs to be seen and not heard. I won't have you wheezing so hard that you give your position away to the enemy. Or worse, *my* position."

"I don't know why you think you can succeed where two doctors and three hypnotists have failed."

Lyca's silver gaze narrowed, and her knife flicked elegantly between her fingers. "They wouldn't cut off a finger for every cigarette they catch you sneaking."

"Oh, dear," said Penelope. She smiled at Marco, who was grumbling in Venetian under his breath. He gave Penelope a secret wink before going to sit next to his would-be mutilator.

"How are your plans going for the Bahamas mission, Galenos?" Penelope asked. The magician had been watching the banter between Lyca and Marco with an amused smile on his face.

"Very well. Once Marco and Lyca start their sabotage of the construction site, I'll crash the accounts of Duilio's company, as well as those of all their shadowy investors and shell companies."

"What's going to happen to all of their employees? They hired a lot of locals to do the work, didn't they?" Shutting down the priests of Thevetat was one thing, destroying innocent people's financial lives in the process was another.

"Don't worry, Penelope. They will all receive their promised wage for the life of the job plus a bonus, all thanks to the money that will be taken from the priest's accounts," Galenos assured her.

"You really are a master magician." Penelope made a mental note to have Galenos do her taxes in the future.

"Where is the Defender this morning?" asked Lyca.

"Archives, probably." Penelope helped herself to the pastries Zo had baked the night before. She had woken up alone. Both Alexis and Constantine's letters were gone from his rooms. He was somewhere in the palazzo—of that she was sure. She could feel him through their *moíra desmós*, the metaphysical and ineffable connection that bound their fates together.

"I wanted to ask him why you're glowing today," said Lyca.

Marco sniggered and waggled his eyebrows. "Why do you *think* she's glowing, *maestro?*"

Lyca flicked him in the back of the head. "*Idiota*, not that kind of glowing. Glowing *with magic*."

"Have you been practicing with your power?" asked Galenos.

"I'm trying to figure out how to balance Alexis's magic like Nereus used to do with other magicians. I want to be able to help as the tide grows higher." She took the astrolabe out of her pocket and popped open the latch so she could study the ticking dials.

"That's what it is. You're still carrying the aftereffects of Alexis's magic on your skin." Lyca clicked her tongue and shook her head. "Be careful you don't bite off more than you're capable of chewing, Archivist. Nereus had many, many years exploring her own power before she attempted experiments with the magic of others."

"Do you think she wrote any of those experiments down?" Penelope hoped they hadn't disappeared like Nereus's other journals.

"Not every answer in life can be found in your beloved books," said Lyca.

"The important things usually can. I want to find Nereus's books, and the Archives won't produce them, no matter how many times I ask."

"Maybe because they aren't in there," mused Galenos, his eyes thoughtful.

Penelope's coffee paused halfway to her lips. She hadn't considered that Nereus wouldn't have kept them below the lagoon.

"You should do a search of her rooms, see what she's got locked up," Marco suggested.

"You are assuming the palazzo wouldn't keep her secrets as its master. She helped create not only the building but the magic; she would've found ways to protect her treasures," Lyca said.

"It's not surprising that you wouldn't want other people to touch her things, but I don't see a way around it. I can't find the books anywhere and they could be in there."

"You're her heir, Penelope. What was hers is now yours to do with as you wish. I only meant to manage your expectations because if Nereus didn't want the books found after her death, you won't find them. I know you'll be respectful with whatever you may find."

The astrolabe hummed ominously in Penelope's hand, making her wonder what other magical items she'd inherited...and how to find them.

FIVE

PENELOPE FOUGHT THE urge to head straight to the Archives. If Alexis was still reading his way through the letters from Constantine, she didn't want to intrude. She couldn't imagine what he was feeling, knowing that Constantine hadn't given up on him. Penelope thought of Carolyn, and a sharp pain low in her ribs reminded her that she could no longer pick up the phone and call her friend.

Blinking back unexpected tears, Penelope shut her eyes and focused on Nereus. Letting the palazzo guide her, she placed one foot in front of the other, maintaining a steady stride and doing her best to ignore the walls moving around her.

She walked down hallways and up staircases she'd never seen before. They were decorated with less artwork and felt far older and stranger. The walls changed from elegant wallpaper to plaster, to polished wood, marble, and rough stone.

When she came to a long tunnel of slick, dripping stone walls, the hair on the back of her neck rose. She stepped forward and all but ran through the subterranean crypt, the air heavy with the smell of stagnant brine and decay.

"I hope these are safety measures, Nereus, and that you didn't have a full *Phantom of the Opera* fetish going on." Penelope laughed nervously in the darkness. She pushed through a rotting wooden door and stepped into a foyer of speckled marble. It was bare except for an elaborate set of wooden doors painted in shades of indigo, purple, and green, the engravings flecked with gold leaf. The doors looked like they belonged in a temple or palace, not a bedroom.

Penelope rested her hand on the brass handle, which curled around her wrist like a hot, greedy tongue.

She shrieked as the grip on her hand tightened. Light flared under her skin as the metal tongue sucked, tasting her magic. When it released her, the door swung open. Penelope checked her hand over. Her arm ached, and she was grossed out, but other than that, she seemed unharmed.

Holding her hand to her chest, Penelope crept through the doors, fearing what piece of furniture would attack her next.

"Oh, wow." Her jaw dropped. She had expected Nereus's rooms to be beautiful—everything in the palazzo was—but she hadn't expected *this* suite of rooms, which opened out to views of a vivid blue sea. A sea that was definitely *not* the Venetian lagoon.

Murals in ochre, blue, green, and purple covered the walls. They reminded Penelope of the palace at Knossos. She was certain they were scenes of life in Atlantis: racing horses, fantastical sea creatures, fishermen hauling nets, arguing scholars, and wildly chaotic markets. On one wall was a tall, elegant spike of a building; she recognized it from Alexis's books.

"The Citadel of Magicians." Penelope stroked its shimmering beauty with her fingertips, then approached the open window and stuck her hand outside. It was warm, the crashing of waves on the beach below whispering to her. She wasn't foolish enough to think that she could climb down and swim in the waves. She had seen Alexis play with the weather often enough inside the palazzo to know not to trust the view from any window.

Penelope opened another door. Inside was a wooden dresser covered with small boxes. Rings, bracelets, cuffs, and necklaces were arranged carefully, all items of strange beauty that Penelope couldn't resist running her fingers over. A cuff made of fiery golden metal drew her eye almost immediately. A symbol combining a trident and open book was engraved into it and inlaid with a dark blue stone.

"Poseidon's insignia?" Penelope guessed and picked it up. The metal wasn't gold or bronze. *Orichalcum. It's made of orichalcum.* The knowledge rose to the surface of her brain, and she had to sit down on a nearby chair before her legs gave way. Both Pliny and Plato had spoken of the legendary metal. Overwhelmed, Penelope closed her eyes as she clutched the cuff to her chest and tried her best to keep her breath steady. She was holding a relic of Atlantis in the palm of her hand.

Despite living with the survivors of the legendary country, Penelope still hadn't lost her ache to know more about Atlantis. Stopping Thevetat had taken over as her first priority, but her yearning for the place that no longer existed would always be there. One day, she would write the truth of it all, even if it only ended up on a bookshelf in the Archives. She understood Alexis's and Nereus's need to write, to process all that they were living through, even if they could never share it with anyone.

When Penelope opened her eyes, there was an envelope on the table in front of her. On the envelope, her name was scrawled in handwriting she was now familiar with.

"Nereus?" She half-expected the older woman to appear, cackling at Penelope for being stupid enough to believe she was truly dead. It wasn't like this was the first time a letter had appeared inexplicably. Penelope picked it up and opened it.

> *So you made it here at last, did you, Penelope? I'm sure it's taken you long enough. To answer the most burning question in that brain of yours—yes, they are modeled after my rooms that were once in the Citadel of Magicians. Can you blame an old woman for being homesick? I understand that part of you always longs to know more about Atlantis, so I decided to allow the rooms and magic to remain once I was dead, so you would have somewhere to go and be near it.*

Everything in here is yours, but the real gift is that you now have a peaceful place that will not admit the others if you don't want them to enter. No doubt, you have realized that living with magicians is complicated, and you were fool enough to fall in love with the greatest of us.

Your magic will be starting to come through by now, and you might have found the truth of its original owner, but there is something you must understand— it is your *magic now. It doesn't matter who it has been passed through. Know that it will help you if you let it. It's a part of you as much as your kidneys are, not something to fear and hide from. No more hiding, Penelope. You are the Archivist now. I'm counting on you to watch over them and make sure they don't do anything particularly foolish.*

The astrolabe holds the answers to all of your questions; ask it what you need, and it will guide you. There are only two things I will ask of you: light the incense for Poseidon and kiss Alexis for me. He likes to hide his grief almost as much as you do.

—Nereus

"Holy crap." Penelope lowered the letter to her lap. She was never going to get used to magic messages popping out of thin air. How many more had Nereus hidden about? Penelope placed the orichalcum cuff over her wrist, unable to part with it.

What had Nereus meant by lighting the incense for Poseidon? Penelope hung on to the letter as she strolled about the bedroom, finding a stunning bathroom made of tiny aqua and gold tiles. "Extra" didn't even begin to cover the opulence of the design.

Penelope peered into a wardrobe, finding what looked to be the fashions from the past ten thousand years, then came upon a pair of wooden screen doors. She thought it might have been another wardrobe but instead found a funerary stele carved from driftwood. It had been mounted on the wall, and in front of it was a low table covered in copper bowls of herbs, shells, and stones, and pyramid-shaped incense burners. Nereus's instructions suddenly made sense as Penelope looked up into the carved likeness of Poseidon. He held a trident in one hand, like many surviving likenesses of Poseidon, but that was the only similarity. He wasn't the typical muscle-bound god or the old man of the sea. He was tall, like all of the Atlanteans, with long, curling hair and a patrician's nose, and from the angle she was standing, she felt like Poseidon was looking down it at her. In his other hand, he held a book, the trident-and-book symbol carved upon the cover. He had the bearing of the scholar-king that he was and would've been damn imposing in real life.

"You look like a hard guy to impress, but I fear Nereus's ghost more than yours." Penelope reached for some matches that had been left by a bottle of wine and wooden goblet. She struck the match and held the flame to the incense. The room filled with the ancient smell of forgotten things. Penelope tried to identify what it was, but it came to her as feelings: cold ocean waves between her toes, the tingle of spring coming, a flower she'd never smelled before, the first taste of new wine, a lover's caress in the darkness.

"Hello, Poseidon. I'm Penelope," she said and touched the book in the magician's hand. She didn't even have time to scream as the rooms dropped away. In an instant, she was standing on a beach, the night sky ablaze with stars above her.

Poseidon stood in front of her, arms folded and looking down at her. If Penelope thought the stele had looked imposing before, nothing could've prepared her for the real thing.

Tall and lean with broad shoulders and long black hair, Poseidon wore a blue tunic and a kilt of dark leather, painted with gold and buckled with a sword belt. Magic radiated off him in potent waves that made Penelope want to turn and run the other way.

"W-What the hell is going on?" she whispered.

"So, it will be you then," Poseidon said in a voice as deep as the ocean they stood beside. He had the most brilliant aquamarine eyes, and Penelope found she was afraid to look away from them.

"It will be what?"

"You're the one that is meant to stop Thevetat." His tone revealed his skepticism. "The heir. *My* heir. I thought I would get some kind of warrior, at least. You look like a scared little girl."

"You would too if you were ripped back through time and space to a doomed island to talk with a god." Penelope scanned the empty beach; this had to be some kind of illusion or a trick to mess with her. "You've had your fun, Nereus. Let me wake up now!"

"Who is Nereus? What are you raving about, woman?"

"Nereus. Your heir, Nereus," Penelope explained.

Poseidon frowned, and the air crackled around him. "If what you say is true, I haven't met her yet."

"What do you mean? She's the one who told me to light incense and now I've apparently time traveled!" Penelope said, her frustration overriding her fear.

"Explain," he demanded, and his power sizzled in the air. Penelope opened her mouth and the story of how Nereus found Poseidon and he taught her his magic came tumbling out. Poseidon's frown deepened with every word.

"In case you're wondering, I'm *her* heir. Or I'm meant to be," Penelope finished explaining. "I lit incense and here I am."

"You are a magician?"

Penelope laughed. "Um, not exactly, though people keep telling me I am."

Poseidon grabbed her arm. "I can feel…" He closed his eyes for a moment. "You have some of my magic." He twisted the cuff on her wrist. "And you wear my insignia to show your allegiance. What you're raving about is the truth."

Oh boy, did she need to snap out of whatever this magic was. "Why am I here? Why would Nereus send me here?"

"I don't know. This magic that binds you must belong to your master, but you have a link that is tied to another magician. How did such a binding occur?"

"No idea, but his name is Alexis. Nereus said my fate is tied to his."

Poseidon rubbed his chin and muttered something under his breath that Penelope didn't catch. "You are going to stop the demon and the priests of darkness I keep seeing in my visions, aren't you?"

"His name is Thevetat, and I'm certainly going to try."

"How many warriors do you have in your army?"

"Eight," Penelope said, raising her chin. "So far anyway."

"Eight! Surely you jest."

"Seven magicians, including myself. And a human."

To Penelope's surprise, Poseidon laughed. "You must be quite a capable eight."

"We are."

Poseidon raised an eyebrow at the confidence in her voice. It was confidence she didn't always feel, but she wasn't going to let some dead magician king mock her either.

"There's a fire in you, woman. I like that. Tonight, I did a ritual to see the one who would save us all from Thevetat, and here you are. I'm not going to question it. The magic in you says you are my heir, so I will believe what you say. Well met, Penelope." He offered her his hand, and Penelope took it. He kissed the back of her wrist, and strange magic filled the air, along with the scent of horses, the sea, and a hint of something floral Penelope couldn't identify. When Poseidon stepped back, his insignia was left glowing on her skin, and then it faded to a dark blue tattoo. It pulsed with his power as Penelope pulled her hand away.

"What did you just do to me?" she demanded.

"I gave you my blessing, magician, and because you're untrained, I'm going to send you a protector—someone whose devotion to me will be the key to finding you. I see the magic that is connecting us through time is fraying. Go now, my heir. Make me proud."

Poseidon kissed her forehead, and Penelope was thrown off the beach and back into Nereus's bedchamber. She slumped to the floor, fear and adrenaline pumping through her veins as a panic attack swept over her. The *moíra desmós* inside of her throbbed, and the silvery black sand of a portal shimmered in the air.

"Penelope!" Alexis's voice roared from the other side. He forced his hand through, but whatever magic Nereus had over her rooms would not let him any farther. Penelope grabbed his hand and pulled with all of her might.

"Let him in! I give permission!" she shouted at the room. Penelope jerked backward as Alexis hurtled through the portal and caught her as they both crashed to the floor.

"Are you hurt?" Alexis checked her over, his eyes wild.

Penelope trembled as the panic attack dragged her down.

"Look at me, Penelope. Focus on me. You're okay. You're safe. Tell me what you need."

"Hold me as tight as you can," she managed.

Alexis pulled her to him, resting her back against his chest and wrapping his arms around her. "Breathe with me, *cara*."

Penelope held his hand over the pressure in her chest and focused on matching her breath to his until the pain eased. Alexis's heat and scent surrounded her, and the feeling of safety slowly returned.

"Thank you," Penelope said finally. She blinked back tears.

Alexis rested his face in the groove of her shoulder and froze. "What happened, Penelope? You smell like—" He inhaled, burying his nose in her hair. "By the gods, you smell like Atlantis. The flowers that used to grow there…the scent is caught in your hair. What happened?"

Penelope took a deep breath, then told Alexis everything that had happened since breakfast. He stared around the rooms like he was lost in time, his eyes filling with tears that he refused to let fall.

"I've never been in here," he admitted. His eyes lingered on the murals before he went to the window. "It looks so much like home. This magic is like nothing I've ever seen. The letter is right. This is exactly how her rooms were at the citadel."

Penelope followed him to the carved stele of Poseidon. He sniffed the incense and shook his head.

"This is definitely Nereus's magic. She used to make this incense to make magicians' visions clearer. She clearly wanted you to meet Poseidon. I can't imagine the complexity of magic she used to make it happen." Alexis turned Penelope's wrist and ran a thumb over the book and trident. "There is magic bound up in this mark. Protections that I don't understand—powerful protections."

"Great. Something else for me to stress about."

"It used to be the symbol for the Citadel-trained magicians. Poseidon founded us, and this was his personal mark. It's like past and present are colliding." Alexis kissed her fingers before releasing her hand. "Gods, you scared me. I couldn't reach you. The connection between us completely disappeared. It wasn't like when you astral-travel. According to the wards, you were gone entirely."

Penelope wrapped her arms around him, resting her face in the groove of his chest that seemed to be made just for her. "I'm sorry I scared you."

"Don't apologize for something you had no control over. No wonder you had a panic attack." Alexis went to kiss her forehead but paused. "I can feel his power here too. He's done something to your third eye."

"Just what I need. He said he was going to send me a protector. Do you think he meant you?"

"I honestly don't know. If he did, I'm sure I would've received a letter from Nereus too. I suppose we'll have to wait and find out."

"Sometimes I wish magic was less complicated and unpredictable."

Alexis pulled her close. "I'd like to say you'll get used to it, but I never have. Take comfort in the fact that Poseidon's blessing will help you in some way, even if we don't know how yet."

And it's going to be a mixed blessing, no doubt. Penelope took Alexis's hand. "I can't do anything about metaphysical discussions with dead magicians, but I *can* get back to work searching for the ring. Let's go back to the Archives."

SIX

ONCE BACK IN the secure and familiar surroundings of her office, Penelope visibly relaxed, and the frightened wariness in her eyes eased ever so slightly.

You could have broken her in a little more gently, Nereus. Alexis couldn't understand why his mentor would be so reckless. There was an urgency with Thevetat's priests on the move, but traumatizing a new magician was callous, even for her. He tried to consider the implications that Nereus, and now Penelope, had been heirs to Poseidon. Had Poseidon told Nereus of Penelope's visit, and that's the reason she had chosen her?

The feeling of being adrift in a river of time came over him again, and Alexis forced himself to focus on the wall of information in front of him, lest he drown in memory and possibilities and the sheer frustration at other magicians messing with his beloved.

"Tell me what you found in the letters," said Penelope. She was studying the patterns of paper he'd made on the floor.

"As we figured out last night, there have been exactly four letters every year since 1455." Alexis stepped in between the piles.

"And that was when the third falling-out happened?"

"The actual argument occurred in 1452. It took him nearly three years to bother writing, and by then, I'd accepted that reconciliation wasn't worth the trauma of arguing it out with him."

"You say that, but a third falling-out means there were two before that you managed to overcome. Perhaps Constantine was hoping it would happen again. These letters make it clear that he was adamant the friendship could be fixed."

Penelope crouched down amongst the letters, touching the dates but not reading anything more than that. He had to admire her restraint; as a historian with such information literally at her fingertips, it must have been difficult for her. Her respect of his privacy seemed to trump any of her curiosity. It made love for her surge up so quickly he fought not to kiss her.

"Most of the letters are a one-sided argument, Penelope. He was trying to wear me down to see his point of view."

"I suppose when you're immortal, you have plenty of time to try to get someone to change their mind. If it comes to it, can I trust you to put aside your grievances with Constantine to get the information we need?"

Alexis was taken aback that she felt she had to ask such a thing. "Of course I will, *cara*. Never doubt that I will put finding Solomon's ring above all. It's more important than any disagreement. If Constantine has information that can help us, I'll do anything to get it out of him. I might even beat it out of him if he wants to be a prick about it."

Penelope laughed, though they both knew he meant it. "Let's hope it doesn't come to that."

"It won't. Hunting a weapon to kill a demon prince is exactly the kind of thing Constantine loves. He'll annoy us until he knows all the details."

Penelope raised an eyebrow. "Each one of you seems to have a complicated love-hate thing with Constantine. Why did you fall out?"

Alexis sat down on the floor beside her. "Which time?"

"Whichever one is easiest to talk about."

"The last time, I refused to get involved—or let Constantine get involved—in the war with Mehmed II and the siege of Constantinople."

Penelope paused in her shuffling. "Seriously? Why would anyone choose to go into a siege?"

"He couldn't handle the idea of his city falling to the Ottomans. It didn't matter that the Roman Empire was no more and that the siege was on its last gasp. Constantine thought he could save it—with my help and magic, of course. I tried to explain to him that all empires must fall in order for something new to grow, but he wasn't in the right frame of mind to listen to anything I had to say. He wasn't able to live with the idea of losing the dream of Constantinople, but I couldn't live with losing him in some suicidal mission. So I locked him up until it was over."

"That seems a little extreme."

"It was the only way to stop him."

"Was it a high tide?" Penelope asked, a teasing gleam in her eye.

"I suppose, now that I think about it, it was." He didn't like what that connection said about him. Or what it boded for the upcoming months.

"Okay, so you locked Constantine up, and he was pissed about it. I can understand that. What about the time before that?"

"That was when he became…whatever he is now."

Penelope frowned at the letters in her hands. "I have many follow-up questions, but I think I just found something."

"What?" Alexis leaned over her shoulder.

"Look at the top of the letters. They all list a date and a place." Penelope rearranged the piles. "They form a pattern. See? Niš, Dubrovnik, Istanbul, and Badija, then back again."

"He's moving about with the seasons," said Alexis, catching on.

"Exactly. If we're right, Constantine should be in Badija this time of year—or about to head there." Penelope wriggled to pull her phone out of her pocket and started tapping away. "It's a tiny island in Croatia. It doesn't look like there's much there, just a monastery and some tourist places for day snorkeling."

"He could be staying at the monastery. He's always liked going for contemplation a few times a year."

"It's worth checking out. If Constantine's not there, maybe the priests will be able to tell us where he went or have a number for him."

"Constantine is clever, perhaps one of the most cunning men I've ever known. He wouldn't have written the locations on his letters if he didn't want us to find him." Alexis sighed in resignation. "When would you like us to go?"

Penelope smiled. "You're not going to argue about it or try to talk me out of involving him?"

"You say that like I have the slightest chance of convincing you."

Penelope's gaze heated and went from his eyes to his lips, making his heart race. "There are strategies you could use to make me see your point of view."

"I would never resort to such dirty tactics." Alexis raised a hand to his heart in mock offense.

"What a pity."

Penelope squealed as he grabbed her and dragged her onto his lap. He buried his hands in her thick, loose hair and kissed the soft skin of her neck. He could still smell Atlantis on her, the magic of Poseidon buzzing and making her skin glow. It was something he would have to investigate…but not now.

"If you are feeling neglected, Doctor Bryne, you only need to say so."

She wrapped her legs around his waist. "That's all it would take?" She stroked her fingers along his jawline. Before her lips could reach him, a throat cleared in the doorway.

"I'm going to kill her," Alexis whispered.

"I do hate to interrupt all the 'research' that's going on in here," said Aelia, sauntering in.

Penelope narrowed her eyes. "Then why are you?"

"I thought you wanted to know where Constantine was?" Aelia brandished a scrap of paper at them as she sat down on the chaise lounge. "I found the address you wanted. I knew I had it somewhere."

"Let me guess. Badija?" Alexis said.

"If you already knew, what did you need me for?" Aelia huffed. She looked at the scattered letters around them. "Are they from Constantine? Where did you get them all?"

"He sent them to me. Some came from Badija. You only confirmed it."

"Fine. Can you two…detangle? I can't talk to you when you're all over each other like a bunch of horny teenagers. Really, Defender, you're old enough to have some self-control."

Penelope lifted a finger—*just a minute*—then kissed Alexis so thoroughly that he forgot Aelia was even there.

"*Now* I will detangle." Penelope released him and slid from his lap, leaving him slightly dazed.

"I should have brought some money to throw at you," Aelia complained, though she grinned at Alexis when Penelope wasn't watching. In that moment, he knew precisely why Nereus had created such a heavily warded sanctuary.

"Penelope, there's something different about you." Aelia tilted her head. All the teasing was gone from her voice. Her violet eyes rested on the cuff and tattoo on her wrist. "What in Poseidon's name is going on?"

"I don't know what you're talking about," Penelope said, though she looked quite like a rabbit cornered by a wolf.

Aelia stood and made for the door. "Family meeting. Now."

IN THE upstairs library, coffee in hand, Penelope explained what had happened in Nereus's apartments.

"If I had even an inkling that your presence there would cause such a mess, I never would have suggested it," Lyca said, looking troubled.

"It needed to happen. I have to say, Penelope, your energy is like a supernova right now." Phaidros looked her over in a way that made Alexis want to step between them.

"Can you see what Poseidon did?" Penelope shifted the shining cuff on her wrist to reveal the mark. "Why is it always tattoos with you magicians?"

"It's a physical sign of lasting, powerful magic. You act like you haven't seen Alexis naked."

Penelope ignored him. "Okay, so it's some powerful magic. What does it do?"

"Let me have a look. May I touch you?" Phaidros asked. "It will help me get a better read on whatever Poseidon's done."

Penelope held out her hand to him, and Phaidros's golden fingers traced the symbol. Alexis's hands were clutched into fists, and when he realized this, he quickly released them. He couldn't blame his reaction on the high tide; his frustration was a product of watching another magician mess with Penelope's magic. Seeing her pushed and prodded—her destiny trifled with—was fraying his nerves.

Phaidros shut his eyes. "It's definitely protection, almost like a shield covering you. It will help you deflect malicious magic, but I don't know if it would be wise to test that theory. Whatever it is, it has integrated with your other power."

"What about my third eye?" Penelope tapped between her brows.

"He supercharged it. I think he planted some magic in it. It's hard to explain." Phaidros opened his eyes and stepped back from her. "I've honestly never seen anything like it."

"What will it do?"

"Make the obscure a lot clearer? Make magic use easier? I'm not sure."

"Freaking magic!" Penelope threw her hands in the air. "Can't anything be precise for once?"

Aelia and Zo laughed.

"Get used to letting go of that control of yours, *bella*. Magic likes to play by its own rules, and thank the gods for that," said Zo. "Otherwise, we would've all been bored out of our brains for the last ten thousand years."

Marco shrugged. "I don't see why you're so worried, Penelope. Strange things happen to you all the time. If it's going to help you, it's a blessing."

"What if I can't control it?"

"Poseidon wouldn't have given power to you if that was going to happen. You don't give a baby a handgun to play with. If he's meant to be one of the greatest magicians that ever lived, he's smarter than you're giving him credit for."

Alexis had to hand it to the inspector—he was pragmatic enough to get through to Penelope when they couldn't. They had all been around magic far too long to be able to give her satisfactory answers or assurances.

Penelope nodded, her eyes growing resolute as she took this on board like she did with everything else. Alexis had always been surprised how quickly she accepted things. He hoped Marco was right, because at this point, he was unsure how he was going to help Penelope with her magic or how it would manifest.

Aelia sighed. "The Defender is looking like a terrified mother bird, so let's talk about something we *can* control."

"We might have found Constantine." Alexis forced his expression into blank neutrality.

"Where?"

"Badija."

"Ah, the monastery, of course." Zo nodded.

"If you all knew about his fondness for it, why didn't any of you bloody say something?" Penelope snapped.

"Because they are worried Alexis might kill him," said Galenos from behind his computer screen.

"I have no intention of killing Constantine." Alexis folded his arms. Did they think he was that unstable?

"You wouldn't do it on purpose," Zo said. "But you might do it if Constantine flirts with Penelope, and you know that he will."

"You're all ridiculous. Alexis wouldn't hurt anyone for that." She took a breath. "Look, Constantine has the information we need. We're going. I would prefer if we worked as a team, which means no hiding things for personal reasons. Stopping Thevetat needs to be more important than all of your bullsh—" The glass beside her shattered, spraying water across the coffee table.

They all stared at the dripping mess for a silent ten seconds.

"Did she do that?" Marco finally asked.

Alexis moved behind Penelope and placed his hands on her shaking shoulders. "It's okay, *cara*."

"I'm sorry, Penelope. I should've thought of Badija earlier," Zo said.

Phaidros crouched down to pick up the pieces of glass. "I'll come to Badija as backup for you and Alexis in case your power advances." He gave Alexis a knowing look. If Penelope's magic *was* unstable, Phaidros could knock her out before she could hurt herself or anyone else.

Aelia got to her feet. "If you're going, I'm going. If Constantine is in a mood, he's more likely to talk to me than Alexis. I promise to find out what he knows, Penelope."

"I need to go home and see Isabella. I'll be back tomorrow with my bags for the Bahamas," said Marco. He bent down and kissed Penelope's cheeks goodbye, but she was still staring transfixed at the spilled water.

When they were finally alone, Alexis crouched down beside her. "Talk to me."

"I'm scared," she whispered.

"There's nothing to be scared of. We have all gone through what you're experiencing. You are very unique, because your magic was gifted by others, but it's still about learning discipline and control."

"I can't go about smashing things every time I'm pissed off."

"None of us care what you smash. You are more important. And you have the right to be frustrated and pissed off with all of us. You are so…direct. It's because you're young. We're old, cranky bastards that have issues trusting each other half the time."

"You all have to get over it. If we don't stop Thevetat, I'm never going to get closure for what Abaddon did to Tim and Nereus." Angry tears filled Penelope's eyes. The grief she'd been so carefully hiding was open and raw for once, and Alexis drew her close.

"Patience, beloved. I know you're frustrated. We will get them, but we need to be smart about it. One step at a time. We'll go and see Constantine tomorrow, if you like."

"This has been the most exhausting day," she said against his shoulder.

"Then let me take care of you." With that, Alexis scooped her up into his arms, took her back to the tower, and put her in his bed, where he stroked her hair as she drifted off.

She was almost asleep when she whispered, "Alexis, I can feel the sea."

SEVEN

PENELOPE DREAMED THAT she was part of the ocean, floating gently in the gray-blue lagoon, the water alive with energy and magic around her. Then the waves clutched her and pulled her down and down until she woke gasping for air, her fear of drowning shoving her back into consciousness.

Breathe, you're okay. Penelope dragged her palms over her sweaty face and cringed when she realized she was in her musty clothes from the day before. They smelled very faintly of something floral, but with a tart edge like citrus. Alexis had said she smelled like a flower from Atlantis. Overwhelmed by the thought, she hurried downstairs to her bathroom. Standing under the soothing fall of hot water, she thought back on her dream and the ocean that seemed to want to speak with her.

Too much magic for you, Penelope.

The tattoo on her wrist wasn't as easy to dismiss as a dream. It was going to be a constant reminder that she had somehow met Poseidon, however briefly or strangely. The faint buzzing under her skin and pressure in her head from the day before seemed to be gone. She felt remarkably normal.

Remember to focus on the things you currently have control of, she told herself. The letter from Nereus had said the astrolabe held the answers to all of her questions, so what had she missed? She thought all it did was keep track of the magicians and the flux of the tide. What answers could an astrolabe give her on how to deal with emperor saints, hunting for lost relics, and a demon determined to make itself a permanent body?

That didn't even include the new magic settling in her bones. Despite Phaidros's assurances, it felt as if her body no longer belonged entirely to her. Alexis wouldn't let her hurt herself, let alone anyone else, so she had nothing to gain by worrying more than usual. She wished again that she could call Carolyn for the calming advice she used to offer when Penelope was overthinking or stressing about a project. Carolyn was dealing with her own grief. Whatever magic Alexis had done to her memories, Penelope didn't want to risk tampering with them for her own selfish reasons.

Pulling herself together, Penelope dressed and went to see what miracles and drama—as she rarely got one without the other—the day would bring. What she found was Marco coming in out of the early Venetian sun, a small suitcase in his hand. It was one of the few times Penelope had seen him out of a suit. Dressed in dark jeans and a gray V-neck shirt, he looked positively casual.

"You're looking better this morning after yesterday's misadventures. How do you feel?" he asked.

"I'll live. A trip to speak with a dead king is all in a day's duties as an Archivist, didn't you know?"

"It's good practice for when you have to meet sixteen hundred-year-old emperors, I suppose." Marco gave her a teasing grin, and she laughed, the anxiety of the dream easing away.

"What have we gotten ourselves into with these magicians, Marco?"

"Something terrifying and wonderful," he replied without hesitation. Unlike Carolyn, Marco had embraced his new reality without fear or judgment.

"Terrifying and wonderful is the perfect way to put it." Penelope looped her arm around his as they headed for the kitchen. "How is Isabella?"

"Good. She's trying not to show how happy she is that I'm finally going on a holiday."

"And Guilia?"

"Fussing over Isabella every moment. The usual."

Penelope nodded. She had known people trying to get pregnant through IVF, and the emotional burden on a couple could be trying. She was glad they were in good spirits. "And you? Are you ready to commit some international corporate sabotage?"

Marco flinched. "It makes me sound like a criminal."

"Well, what would you call it?"

"Vigilantism," said Zo as he came into the kitchen.

"That sounds even worse." Marco grimaced.

"You can call it whatever you like; it will still equate to the same thing. You're a brave man, going on a mission with Lyca. You better leave your squeamishness here in Venice."

Zo pulled out some mugs and started the coffee while Penelope went through the fruit bowl, looking for the last of the apricots. Living in the palazzo had taught her many things that were missing from her childhood, including that the kitchen was certainly the heart of the home. It was where the magicians seemed to gravitate at all hours of the day and night.

"Have you seen Alexis this morning?" she asked.

"He was arguing with Phaidros about the quickest way to get to Badija about an hour ago. It looks like you will be meeting Constantine sooner rather than later."

"How are you going to handle being the only one here for once?"

"Very well. I'm going to be naked from the moment you leave."

"Just be careful when you decide to cook," advised Marco, which led to much jeering in Italian that Penelope couldn't follow. If she had to guess, she'd say it included a certain amount of male humor and profanity they didn't want to expose her to.

"Keep your dick in your trousers until I leave, okay?" She took the cup of coffee Zo offered her.

Phaidros strode into the kitchen. "You aren't missing much."

Zo huffed. "Like you would know."

"Is there more coffee?"

"Not for assholes. What's made you so grumpy?"

Phaidros shifted Zo out of the way to get to the French press. "The Defender has been trying to talk Aelia and me out of going to Badija, and I'm done arguing with him about it."

"Perhaps it would be better if you stayed. You never did get along with Constantine."

"Alexis needs the backup."

Zo and Penelope shared a knowing look. Alexis was the last person who needed backup. Phaidros was going because he didn't like being separated from Aelia.

Thankfully, the conversation was saved by the arrival of Alexis. He had a severe look in his eyes until they rested on Penelope and relaxed.

"I'm glad to see you up, *cara*." He took Penelope's hand and kissed it. "I've booked us a charter flight to Split that will be leaving in three hours. How are you feeling?"

"Good. Fine. I was exhausted last night, but it turns out I only needed a good sleep. Why are we going to Split?"

"To pick up a boat to drive to Badija. In typical Constantine fashion, he has chosen the most inconvenient location to live."

Penelope stood on tiptoes and kissed Alexis's irritated expression. "Are you going to be this agitated the entire time? Because I'm more than happy to go by myself."

"Nice try, Archivist, but until the priests of Thevetat are dealt with for good, you aren't going anywhere without me." He hooked his fingers around the belt loops of her jeans and tugged her closer.

"I'm going to go and pack and will meet you both at the front door." Phaidros hurried out of the kitchen before Alexis could argue.

"Maybe you should leave him in Croatia," offered Marco.

Zo laughed. "He'll probably suggest the same thing to Lyca about you."

"Are you sure you're going to be okay here by yourself?" Penelope asked Zo. She didn't like the idea of any of them being alone since the attack on the palazzo.

"Are you worried about me, *bella*?"

"I'm worried about my books. I've only just managed to convince the Archives to stop moving all my things about."

Zo gasped in mock horror and looked to Alexis. "Are you going to stand there and let her wound me in such a manner?"

Alexis rubbed her shoulders. "Zo is one of the best warriors I've ever trained with, Penelope. The Archives will be perfectly safe in his care."

When Lyca and Galenos appeared, Lyca eyed Marco. "By all the noise you're making, I assume that means you are ready to go."

"Whenever you are, *maestro*."

Penelope gathered him in a hug. "Give them hell...but safely."

"I'll be fine, *amica*. Lyca will have my back." He released her with a smile.

Penelope hugged Galenos too but hesitated when she got to Lyca.

"I'll watch over him, Archivist," the warrior said with a pat on Penelope's shoulder. Then Alexis and Lyca clasped each other's forearms.

"Happy hunting," he said.

Lyca's eyes filled with gleeful malice. "And you, Defender."

Ten minutes later, Penelope asked, "They're going to be fine, right?" She stood on the terrace overlooking the Grand Canal, watching as Marco helped Galenos load their luggage into a boat.

"Lyca wouldn't be taking Marco with them if she didn't think he was ready for it." Despite Alexis's reassurances, Penelope's chest tightened with worry as the three of them drove away.

BY THE time Penelope arrived in Split, she had shelved her worry for Marco and was focused on the growing tension in the magicians around her. Phaidros was pretending he wasn't bothered by Aelia's dangerously skimpy purple playsuit. Meanwhile, Aelia was distracted and kept checking her hair and makeup, and Penelope had to loosen Alexis's grip on her hand more than once.

Penelope had been on many boats in her life, but none that were driven by a pissed-off magician. Earlier, she'd wondered why they hadn't hired a car in Split and driven down the coast to a ferry. She should've guessed it had something to do with speed limits.

Phaidros's magic was largely energy manipulation, and while Penelope had seen him use it on people before, she'd never experienced the effect it could have on machinery. The air around Phaidros hummed with power. Alexis positioned himself at Penelope's back and instructed her to hang on to a safety bar at the front of the boat.

Once they cleared the harbor, the tightly bound magic fled Phaidros and flowed through the boat's engine and circuitry. Penelope tightened her grip as they surged forward with a burst of speed. Sitting in the back of the boat, Aelia's wild bronze curls streamed behind her as she tilted her head back and laughed. Phaidros glanced at her in his rearview mirror, and his lips twitched in a half-smile.

Penelope closed her eyes and let the salty wind blow away all the fog and anxiety that had been threatening to overwhelm her. She could feel the water around them in a way she never had before, as well as the teeming life it contained. She remembered Elazar's story: Nereus meeting Poseidon while he was standing in the sea doing magic. Could this sudden awareness of the sea be an ability he had passed on to her?

A trip that would've taken them three hours by land barely took an hour with Phaidros at the wheel of the boat. The Franciscan Monastery on the island of Badija was a set of sprawling Gothic-Renaissance buildings surrounded by tall pine and oak trees.

"Can you tell if Constantine is in there?" Penelope asked Alexis as they docked the boat.

"Not yet. If he's not, I'm sure someone will know where he's hiding. If they don't, we can try tracking him with magic. He's got a unique signature that will make tracking easier."

Phaidros huffed. "Everyone's energy signature is."

"But not everyone is immortal," Aelia said. "Even you have to admit that Constantine is unique."

"If by 'unique' you mean 'a cursed asshole,' then yes, he *is* unique."

"You shouldn't have come," Aelia snapped.

"Back at you, Princess."

Penelope took Alexis's hand. "Let's go talk to some of the priests. You two can wait here. We don't need your glowering"—she glared at Phaidros—"or your hemline"—she nodded at Aelia—"frightening anyone away."

Alexis made their inquiries in fluent Croatian while Penelope smiled politely and marveled at the architecture.

Soon, they turned and made their way back out into the afternoon sunshine. As they did, Alexis said, "He's not staying in the monastery, but he's close."

Phaidros and Aelia were looking at their phones, ignoring each other like sullen teenagers.

"Are you sure we can't just leave them?" Penelope rolled her eyes, and Alexis gave her a grin they couldn't see.

"We need to walk the rest of the way." He passed Penelope her battered khaki backpack. Just like before her trip to Israel, before their departure this morning, Penelope had found that the palazzo had packed for her. She hadn't run out of underwear last time, so this time, she'd simply slung the bag over her shoulder and headed out.

Following the instructions given to them by the helpful priest, they followed a neatly trimmed path of white gravel that wended through the gardens and into the trees behind the monastery grounds.

A villa made of brown-and-white stone rose up through a grove of olive and fruit trees. The villa was a converted church, with arched, stained glass windows and facades decorated with the occasional fantastical beast or gargoyle. A large deck made of polished cyprus pine overlooked the water, and steps led down to a pebbled beach.

The ironbound, carved wooden door opened, and a man stepped out. He looked them over with sharp, blue-gray eyes, then folded his arms over his broad chest. He looked about thirty years younger than the memory Penelope had seen of him. His curly hair and clipped beard were now dark instead of gray, and there were fewer lines around his eyes. Despite that, his bearing and frown were unmistakable.

Constantine.

EIGHT

THEY ALL REMAINED locked in a silent stare-off until Alexis stepped forward and held out his hand.

"*Quid agis?*"

"Surprised to find magicians on my doorstep," said Constantine.

Alexis's smile was mocking. "Why? Have you stopped believing in miracles?"

"Only when you are involved, Alecto." Constantine grabbed Alexis's hand and pulled him into an embrace, giving his back a hard thump. "It is good to see you, brother."

Alexis let him go. "We have a lot to discuss."

"I can see that." Constantine's gaze lingered on Penelope before resting on Aelia. "Hello, my love. Come to destroy another one of my cars?"

"I don't know. Have you got any nearby?"

Constantine's serious expression broke into a massive grin, and he opened his arms. Aelia all but flew into them, and he picked her up and spun her off the ground.

"Why didn't you call me, you stubborn bastard?"

"I got the impression you needed some space," he said soundly before putting her down. "I see you've brought your bodyguard with you."

Phaidros rolled his eyes. "You don't know Aelia as well as you think if you believe she needs a bodyguard."

"If *you* don't believe it, why are you here, Phaidros?"

"I came to see if a thousand years made you less of a prick."

"They didn't seem to do you much good." Constantine turned his back to him and took two steps toward Penelope, looking her over. "And who might you be?"

"Doctor Penelope Bryne," she answered, refusing to look away, even under the intensity of his inspection.

"And what is your profession, Penelope?"

"Archaeologist with historian tendencies."

"Excellent. How did you fall into such bad company?"

"A long story. Alexis was going to kill me."

Constantine's dark eyebrows rose. "Is that so? In my experience, when the Defender wants someone dead, they usually end up as such. How did you survive?"

"I frustrated him so much that he fell in love with me."

Constantine tipped his head back and laughed loud enough to scare the birds out of the trees. "I like this one, Alecto. I'm tempted to fall in love with her already."

"Try it, and I'll put your immortality to the test," Alexis said, his tone frigid.

Constantine clucked his tongue. "You still have no sense of humor." Constantine held his arm out to Penelope. "Come with me, Penelope. I wish to hear your story first, and then we will get to the matter of what you want."

"What makes you think I want anything?" Penelope rested her hand on his arm with a sweet smile.

"Well, Alecto wants something. Otherwise, he wouldn't be here with his charming new consort to distract me and Aelia to sweeten my temper. Phaidros has simply followed Aelia because it's his life's purpose."

"Con!" Aelia's face went scarlet.

"What? I didn't say that I wasn't happy to see you all. Even Phaidros's glare is a welcome sight after so long." Constantine turned back to Penelope. "Beer?"

Penelope had never seen anyone but Nereus manage the magicians so efficiently. Far sooner than expected, she found herself warming up to the handsome emperor. "Yes, please. A beer would be perfect."

"Excellent. I brew my own using a wonderful recipe taught to me by a Trappist monk in 1685."

Penelope glanced back at Alexis, who gave her a nod of encouragement.

"There are spare rooms if you intend to stay the night," Constantine said over his shoulder, then he led Penelope into the cool shade of the house. "Don't worry about them, Penelope. They'll find their rooms, and Alecto will check the perimeter to make sure there are no deranged monks or tourists ready to jump out and attack you."

"You tease, but it's happened more than once in recent—" Penelope stopped in her tracks, her jaw dropping in surprise.

Constantine had led her into a hall that had once been the main church, complete with stone pillars to hold up the arched roof. It had been whitewashed, with exposed beams of polished wood, and the stone floor had been covered with Persian carpets. Couches, tables, and wooden shelves stacked with books lined the walls.

What had struck her dumb, though, was the blaze of color and light produced by the afternoon sun streaming through the stained glass windows. The whole room was illuminated and multicolored. She couldn't tear her eyes away from the rainbow of images: lush gardens; mythological creatures; and animals of every sort; long-faced saints; boats on stormy oceans; stars and magi; terrifying angels with flaming swords, all surrounding a magnificent Christ in red-and-purple robes, arms wide as if the beautiful chaos flowed from him.

At least he's not a white guy. Penelope smiled approvingly.

"You arrived at just the right moment, my dear. This is when it's at its most magnificent." Constantine's voice was soft, his eyes turned upward.

Penelope spun slowly to admire the craftsmanship, and it took a few moments to realize what made it different from many of the church windows she'd seen before. "There's no Crucifixion. I thought you Catholics weren't happy unless there was something painful to look at."

"It's true. There has always been an awful preoccupation with the brutality of the sacrifice, which takes away from the entire point of the event itself."

"And that is?"

Constantine looked pointedly at the glorious imagery around him. "*Life* is the point of it all, Penelope. Mankind focuses on the murder but not the miracle because it's the part of the story they can truly understand; it requires nothing of them. That Christ died isn't the wonder of the story. People die horribly and alone every day. He defeated death and was seen teaching by hundreds of people after the Crucifixion—*that* is the wonder, and the meaning of it is what people fear the most. Always, always focus on life, Penelope. It is an ever-unfolding miracle." The passion in his voice was nearly as brilliant as the art around them, and now Penelope's eyes were glued to him instead. Constantine draped an arm around her shoulders. "Come, I promised you a beer."

"That's a good idea, or I'm going to start ogling other things in this room, and we'll never make it out. It's an occupational hazard."

"Once you have your beer, you're welcome to look at anything in this house."

"Thank you. I promise not to touch."

"Why would you promise such a ridiculous thing? Touch whatever you like." He gave her a charming smile, then led her into a modern kitchen with a wide window that looked out over the ocean.

"Zo would love this," she said, admiring the view.

Constantine took tall glasses down from a cupboard. "Where is Zotikos? I would've loved to see him. He always gives such brilliant insight into problems I'm having with my writing."

"He couldn't come. We didn't want to leave the palazzo and my Archives unprotected."

Constantine cocked his head. "*Your* Archives? Where is Nereus?"

"She was murdered," Alexis said from the doorway.

Constantine went pale and gripped the edge of the countertop. He questioned Alexis in Latin, the conversation moving back and forth so rapidly Penelope didn't have a hope of following it. And she didn't need to. The emotion between the two men was telling enough. Phaidros and Aelia joined them mid-conversation but didn't interrupt.

Finally, Alexis moved Constantine out of the way, then took a few bottles of beer from the fridge and poured them into glasses.

Constantine exhaled a long breath. "Dear Nereus. This is a blow."

"She never liked you," Phaidros said.

"Yes, she did. She may have chastised me for being too ambitious for my own good, but she always answered my emails."

"You were emailing her?" Alexis's eyes widened in surprise.

Constantine took one of the beers. "Of course I was. Just because you don't know how to reply to a letter doesn't mean she didn't." He opened a set of glass doors and headed out onto the deck.

Penelope moved so she could brush gently against Alexis. "Are you okay?"

"I will be. Now that I'm here, I'm strangely pleased to see him."

"I was alone with him for ten minutes, and I can already see why you were such good friends." Penelope rested a hand on his back as she took a glass of beer for herself. "You are both deep-thinking, enigmatic warrior types."

Alexis's smile was affectionate. "Is that so?"

"Stop making the Defender look like that. It grosses me out to see him so soft." Phaidros reached over the bench to grab the last two beers. He gave one to Aelia, and they followed Constantine outside. "I suppose we should go and make sure the peace is kept."

"Constantine is more than capable of handling Phaidros." Alexis leaned down and rested his forehead against hers. "I love that you are so natural at this. You aren't intimidated, and you can hold your own in the strange situations I keep putting you in."

"Someone very recently said that life is an ever-unfolding miracle, and I think it explains living with you perfectly."

"Ah, I see Constantine has been teaching you his theology already."

"He has, and he makes a valid point." Penelope tilted her head to the side and kissed him. "We better not keep them waiting."

Alexis ran his thumb over her lip and finally nodded. "A good idea. I find you far too distracting."

Outside, Constantine, Aelia, and Phaidros sat in deck chairs, watching the waves. Aelia was speaking softly of Nereus and the attack on the palazzo.

"I saw news footage of Duilio's death and the bombing. I should've known that you were involved." Constantine gestured to Penelope. "Come and sit beside me, Archivist. I want you to tell me all about how a mortal became Nereus's chosen one."

"Only if you tell me how you're still alive."

"Deal." Constantine held out his hand. It was large enough that it swallowed hers and rough with callouses in the usual spots for regular sword training—the same as Alexis's.

Aelia groaned. "This is going to take hours. I'm going for a walk to watch the sunset, where I don't have to listen to conversation about the damned priests of Thevetat."

"Good idea, my dear." Constantine waved her on. "Take Phaidros with you, and let the monastery kitchen know that I'll have guests for dinner tonight."

Phaidros looked at him and scoffed. "You still don't know how to cook for yourself? Unbelievable."

"I don't cook when I've provided the monastery fish from my day's catch. They offer to cook it for me. Honestly, Phaidros, you're as critical as ever."

"Only because I know what you're really like, little emperor." Without waiting for a reply, Phaidros followed Aelia.

"Alecto, why did you bring him knowing he'd be so disagreeable?"

Alexis's eyes flashed with amusement. "He didn't want to stay behind and leave Aelia to be caught in your wicked web again."

"*My* wicked web? Does he know her at all? Clearly, he's only ever listened to her account of our affairs."

"You use each other and have always done so. Don't pretend otherwise."

Constantine ignored him and turned back to Penelope. "You are a beautiful bloom amongst these thorny immortals. Tell me your tale, lovely Penelope, and make sure you leave in all the sex and violence."

DESPITE CONSTANTINE'S urgings, Penelope left in the violence but none of the sex, her magic, or the literal contents of the Dead Sea prophecy. Constantine seemed to know when she was skipping over parts, based on his teasing side-eyed glances in Alexis's direction, and she did her best not to blush.

"Your demon worshippers are back after all this time. No wonder Aelia is so subdued," said Constantine. *Subdued* wasn't a word that Penelope would ever use to describe Aelia.

Perhaps you need to pay better attention, Bryne. They'd all been upset since Nereus's death and the trip to Israel, and Penelope had been too focused on her own grief to see anyone else's suffering.

"We are all wary," said Alexis. "I thought they were dead. They've managed to hide from me, and that is no easy feat."

"They have played a very long game, Alecto. They will continue to outmaneuver you because they've had so long to prepare. They first struck at your heart—Venice—and then Nereus, to disable you, to make you emotional."

Penelope bristled. "You sound like you admire them."

"Don't confuse admiration with acknowledgment of a well-played move. It's what I would've done. Penelope got away from them and ruined their plan to kill her. Now they know she is a weakness of yours, Alecto. They know the more upset she is, the more distracted you will be, and they killed her friend to make sure of it. Even with Tim's involvement at the Dead Sea, his true value was in being close to Penelope. They will do it to all of your allies. I would make provisions for your inspector's family if he is so determined to help you."

"Zo is watching over them, and the priests of Thevetat have been rooted out of Venice," Alexis said.

"You need to make a plan and stop being on the defensive all the time. Thevetat will do his best to keep you looking the wrong way if you keep running after every disaster."

Aelia and Phaidros arrived with trays of food, and they discussed Lyca and Galenos's plan to cut off Abaddon's resources. Penelope remained watchful, listening to the others talk and interact with each other. As long as they weren't discussing personal history, the peace prevailed, and the sarcastic comments were kept to a minimum.

Later, they sat drinking brandy in the main hall with the stained glass and managed to remain civil enough that Penelope had a chance to really observe the man everyone managed to get caught up in knots over.

Constantine's questions about the hunt for Thevetat since the bombing were precise enough that Penelope caught glimpses of the military genius she had read about in the historical accounts. Physically, he was big, broad, and so masculine Penelope was grateful Carolyn wasn't there to flirt herself to death. He had lines at the corner of his eyes from staring at battlefronts and Holy Land sunsets, and when he smiled, they creased upward in a way that made Penelope want to smile too. There was something about him that could make you believe pleasure was as vital and nourishing to the spirit as Holy Scripture. He was unashamedly equal parts sinner and saint.

In comparison, Alexis had and would always have an intangible air about him, as if he were part of a dream—the subtle whisper of the turning pages of a forgotten fairy tale, with a hint of danger and golden magic lingering in his shadows. Constantine's air was rooted in mud and blood, battle and passion, and if you dreamed of him, it would be a dream of glory and theology and would be entirely of his design and purpose.

"We should pick this up again tomorrow." Constantine set his empty glass down. "I want to go to the chapel to think this through and pray for Nereus. I know you're holding something back from me." He peered at Penelope.

"And what makes you think that?" she asked.

"Because you still haven't asked me what you really want. You're deciding if you can trust me first."

"You're not offended?"

"Not at all. It's a smart move, considering you had no idea your friend Tim was a close associate of Abaddon."

Penelope didn't know if the barb was intended, but the words still stung.

"We all could do with some sleep. Thank you for allowing us to stay under your roof tonight, Constantine." Alexis offered him a short bow.

"I wasn't lying when I said I'm pleased to see you all again. Sleep well." Constantine paused by the door and gave Penelope a provocative grin. "Penelope? Feel free to browse the books if Alecto isn't entertainment enough for you tonight. Otherwise, my door is always open."

Alexis glared. "Pray to your God that I don't smother you in your sleep, Emperor."

Constantine's smile only brightened.

NINE

FOLLOWING CONSTANTINE'S EXAMPLE, they all dispersed to various parts of the villa, but Penelope was restless. The night of conversation had done nothing to empty her mind or put it at ease.

Alexis brushed a thumb across her cheek. "I need to call and check on Zo. Go for a walk, Penelope. I've set wards around the grounds, so as long as you don't wander out of them, I'll be able to find you if you get into any trouble."

"Can you read me so well already?"

"You're wound so tightly that you're making me anxious too. Take some time for yourself. It might calm you enough to sleep." Despite his encouraging tone, there was worry around his eyes.

She kissed his cheek. "I promise I won't be long."

"You say that because you haven't seen all of his books yet."

Despite the temptation of a new library, Penelope needed to be outside. The night was warm, and small solar-powered lights guided her through the gardens. Her mind was exhausted from the churning worries, unanswered questions, and plain frustration. Penelope took three deep breaths and looked up at the stars' burning fire above her. When an eerily beautiful sound drifted through the trees, she abandoned her deep breathing and soon found herself at the side of a small stone building.

Curious, Penelope found an open door and slipped inside to the front of a chapel, hidden in a stone nave behind the altarpiece. It shielded her from view, but she could still see the wooden pews and brightly painted murals, all lit by hundreds of beeswax candles. Constantine stood transfixed as Aelia sang, her voice reverberating so that the very stones seemed to hum in time with her.

With eyes silver with tears, Constantine held his hand out to Aelia, and she let herself be drawn into the circle of his arms. When the song ended, Penelope found her own cheeks wet, even though she hadn't understood a word of it.

"Psalm 53 in Aramaic. You really do know my weak spots," Constantine said.

"I had to do something to get your attention. I swear I was one step away from coming in here naked."

"Come now, Princess. There's no need to be so dramatic."

"Isn't there? I haven't seen you in ten years, and you haven't tried to kiss me once. Have you finally become unattracted to me?"

Constantine ran his fingers through her hair. "Such a thing would be impossible. I'd happily kiss you if I thought it was me you wanted to make love to."

"I'm standing in your arms right now. That should be indicative enough."

Feeling like an intruder, Penelope turned back toward the door, only to find that it had closed during Aelia's song. As quietly as she could, she pushed down on the handle, but it was locked. *Shit, shit, shit.* She was going to be forced to wait them out before she could try the other chapel doors.

"When are you going to stop lying to yourself?"

"What are you talking about? I'm not lying to myself about anything." Aelia stared up at him in defiance. "What's wrong? Has God finally cursed you with chastity?"

"Not yet. Don't be angry. Listen to what I'm saying." Constantine pulled her back to him. "I have loved you since I met you, but you can't return that love in a way I'm willing to accept anymore. I thought if I waited long enough, your heart would change. But it hasn't, and I want all of you or none at all."

Aelia stumbled back like she'd been slapped. Penelope prayed if there was a God, it would teleport her somewhere else. Instead of God, the chapel doors opened, and Phaidros stood like a golden angel ready to smite them all. "You've got to be kidding me. Really, Aelia? How many times does he have to hurt you before you'll stop running back to him?"

Constantine let Aelia go. "Tell him, Aelia."

"Tell me what?"

Constantine straightened his shoulders and strode past Phaidros and out of the chapel.

Phaidros moved to join Aelia where she now stood alone. "What is he talking about?"

"What are you doing here?" she snapped. "It's none of your damn business, and you have no right to interfere."

"I didn't even know you were in here! I was out in the gardens. I saw the lights on and walked in on you making another stupid mistake that will leave you heartbroken."

"It's my heart to break!" Aelia's shoulders shook as she turned away from him. "It doesn't matter anyway. He doesn't want me, and you were right on time to witness my rejection."

Phaidros's fierce expression softened. "I've always said Constantine is a fool, and now here is irrevocable proof."

Aelia turned a tear-streaked face toward him. "Gloat. Now is your chance to humiliate me the way I humiliated you."

"No."

Aelia shoved him hard in the chest. "Do it! Tell me how stupid I am. I know you want to."

Phaidros caught her hands. "*No.* You've been hurt enough for one night."

"Please do it," she begged. "Then I can stop feeling this way, and we can finally be even."

"Even for what? What are you talking about?"

Aelia laughed bitterly. "You really have no clue. Do you have any idea what it's been like to carry this debt around for centuries, and to know I have no way to atone for it?"

"What debt?" Phaidros looked helpless.

"You…asshole." Aelia pushed her hands through her hair and began to pace. "Fine! Here's the ridiculous truth of it all: On Atlantis, I was forced to publicly reject you so my father wouldn't have you killed. I couldn't accept your wish to court me because I was royalty and a high priestess, and you were still a boy from a backwater village, no matter how talented of a magician you were." She released another bout of bitter laughter. "And then, all the princes and honorable sons that were meant to be better than you wouldn't even bother to risk their lives to save me. No, as I lay dying, the world exploding with fire around me, it was the fucking peasant who rushed in to save me, even after I'd been so horrible to him. That is a debt I can *never* repay." Aelia buried her face in her hands and sobbed.

Phaidros hesitated before putting his hands on her shaking shoulders, and when she flinched, he drew her close. "There is no debt, Aelia. There never has been, and you should've known that."

"I'm so, so sorry—"

"You've nothing to be sorry for. I have never regretted saving you, even when you've been a pain in the ass."

Penelope gritted her teeth, uncomfortable to be witnessing such an intimate scene. She pulled urgently on her link to Alexis. He appeared wild-eyed and ready to fight in a cloud of shimmering black sand, but Penelope rushed to clap a hand over his mouth. She pointed at the locked door helplessly and then at Phaidros and Aelia. Alexis took her hand, and they disappeared in a swirl of shimmering black sand.

ALEXIS AND Penelope reappeared on the villa's pebbly beach.

"Thank you. I got locked in." Penelope related the conversation she'd overheard, feeling awkward at witnessing something so private.

"I sympathize with you, my love. On the bright side, they are finally talking it out. Aelia has never spoken to me about this. How terrible to carry that misplaced guilt for so long." Alexis shook his head.

Penelope laughed. "So much for my relaxing walk."

"How about a relaxing swim instead?"

She frowned. "Are you serious?"

"Very. It's a warm night. The water will be perfect." He dragged off his shirt and unbuckled his belt. Alexis had that playful-yet-mysterious look in his eyes that Penelope loved most. It said, *Come with me, and we'll have adventures no one will believe.*

She was weak for it, so she pulled her singlet over her shoulders. "If we give some poor priest a heart attack, you're doing the CPR."

"If it makes you feel better, I'll put a barrier up so no one will see us." Alexis grinned as he waded out into the dark blue water. He turned, watching her undress with an expression that made Penelope blush all over. She'd always been too studious to be one of those teenagers throwing parties and skinny-dipping with boys she shouldn't—something she was embarrassingly aware of as she did her best to appear as unfazed as Alexis did.

She waded out to him, and he held his hands out to balance her. The water cooled her burning core, and the tenseness in her muscles released almost instantly. It was the most relaxed she'd been in the sea since she nearly drowned. Alexis's hands came around her waist and stroked the base of her spine.

"This was a great idea." Penelope draped her arms around his neck.

"Are you feeling any better? Calmer, maybe?"

"Much better. How's Zo?"

"He's fine, as I knew he would be. You're worrying far too much, *cara.* This isn't the first time we've been in a war. We all know what to do."

"I can't help it. Nereus trusted me to be her heir—to look after all of you, not only the Archives." Penelope hid her face against his neck, not one to admit her worries aloud.

"We aren't your responsibility, Penelope. Nereus was our master and our mother. You are not, so don't try to be."

"I don't know what I'm going to do about the Archives, Thevetat, or the magic I'm suddenly supposed to have. I've always had a plan, but now I'm in a situation where I don't know how to help."

Alexis held her close to his chest. "You only need to be yourself. Nereus chose you for your strengths and abilities, for your stubbornness and tenacity, and the compassion and patience you have for all of us. You don't need to be anything else."

Heart burning, unable to find the words to express her emotions, Penelope whispered, "I love you."

Alexis kissed her shoulder. "I love you too, but you need to stop thinking so hard and be kinder to yourself."

"*I* need to stop thinking so hard? That's rich coming from you! You're so caught up in your head, you don't even know what day of the week it is."

"I don't need to know the day of the week, because every day I wake up with you, I count as a blessing."

Penelope laughed. "Smooth, Donato. Very smooth."

"I thought so." Alexis spun her around in the water before sinking down so that he was level with her. "You'll be the one to get the information we need out of Constantine. He already likes you, and that is no easy feat."

"He might kick us out after what I just witnessed. I'd thought that if all else failed, Aelia could use her charms on him."

"You don't need Aelia's charms when you have plenty of your own. He's changed since I last saw him. He's calmer and far more receptive to listening than what I thought he'd be."

"He's missed you. I can tell. You both have fierce intellects and can challenge each other." Penelope had seen how easily they'd fallen back into conversation. The time apart didn't seem to be an impediment, and she hoped that the peace between them lasted.

"Constantine has never had a problem with challenging anyone," Alexis said. "And I'm not interested in talking about him right now." He gave her a heated look, then kissed her.

All thoughts fled Penelope's brain as her body took over. She hooked her legs around him and buried her hands in his wet black curls. The sea, the starry sky, the man in her arms—it all made her feel so alive that her heart pounded and her breath caught.

Alexis broke off the kiss so abruptly that she almost slipped out of his grip. "Penelope, look," he whispered, his voice filled with awe.

She looked down. Small streams of water tangled and wrapped around her arms and chest. "What's happening?"

"Shhh, don't panic. Breathe, *cara*."

"Why are you doing this?" She twisted her arms about.

"I'm not doing it. *You* are. Tell me, what were you just feeling?"

Penelope stared wide-eyed at the liquid lace rising from the ocean to clothe her. "I was feeling…connected to everything."

"And now?"

"Nervous. But not afraid."

"Good. Put your hands on my chest."

As Penelope moved, the water stayed where it was, dancing around her fingers as she placed her hands on his pecs.

He asked, "Can you transfer it to me?"

"How?"

"Focus on what you want it to do. It's okay; you won't hurt me."

For a long moment, nothing happened. Then, ever so slowly, the water trickled from Penelope's hand and webbed over his chest. "It's working." She bit her lip. The floral-and-citrus scent that had clung to her clothes after her vision of Poseidon hung around them. Her throat tightened. "Can you smell that?"

Alexis pressed his nose to the top of her head. "They were called Poseidon's Tears," he said, his voice far away. "It's become the scent of your magic."

Something shifted, and the watery lace splashed apart, making her jump, and Alexis burst out laughing. "Well done," he said between salty wet kisses.

"What do you mean 'well done?' I barely held it for a second. Oh, I feel—" She swayed, and Alexis moved to hold her upright.

"You're okay, Penelope. Better than okay."

She sagged in his arms. "I'm so drained. Why?"

"Magic is energy, and you just released some of that energy. You'll get used to it as you learn to control it. How's your foggy head? Any better?"

Penelope rolled her neck. The pressure that had been wrapped around her head for days was gone. "Yeah, it is. How?"

"I tried to warn you that the magic of the high tide will affect you too. It seems it already has been. After the glass exploded, I thought getting you into water might help, and it appears I was right."

"You don't need to look so smug about it."

"I have you wet and naked in my arms, and your magic just manifested. The night is perfect. Of course I'm going to be smug." Alexis kissed her neck. "You are going to be such a great magician."

TEN

IT WAS STILL the wet season in the Bahamas, and it didn't matter how many times Marco showered, he was still uncomfortably sticky. They had rented rooms in a boutique hotel off the main beach in Nicholls Town and had been careful to avoid the notice of tourists, locals, and the constant stream of Duilio Industries workers. While the company's head office was in Nassau, the construction workers, engineers, and project managers commuted from Nicholls Town to the floating hotel site at the smaller islands of the Joulter Cays.

On the night they arrived, Lyca had disappeared. When she returned, she'd woken Marco with a rough jab and presented him with his new outfit—a light blue worker's uniform stolen from a clothesline—and an access ID, thanks to Galenos. Marco thought going to the site was an unnecessary risk that could explode in their faces.

Lyca, however, was insistent. "We might as well go and see what we're dealing with. I don't care for photographs. I need to see the enemy's camp with my own eyes."

"What if we're recognized?" asked Marco, even as he pulled on the overalls.

"The only people who might know what we look like will be priests in managerial positions, and it's been my experience that no one in that kind of position notices anyone lower than them." Lyca put on a blue cap that hid most of her silvery-white hair.

They were scanned for phones at security before boarding the boat that ferried workers out to the construction site. Lyca stood silent beside him as tall fangs of steel rose out of the ocean in front of them, like an ancient creature rising from the deeps.

"I felt the same way when I first saw it," a man said. "Can you imagine what a monstrosity it will be once it's done?"

"No, I can't," Lyca murmured. "What's holding it up?"

"Each major claw is bolted into the ocean floor, and the support cabling is almost finished being established. From what I hear, once they've finished constructing parts of the hotel's foundation, they will begin bolting them in. Everything else is going to be built on top of them." He shook his head. "I'm just a welder. Fuck knows how the thing even stays in place."

Lyca gripped the side of the ferry's railing and hissed under her breath.

"What's wrong?" Marco whispered.

"Everything. I can feel the magic of this place. The weaving of the traps under the water are holding it in its boundaries, like a massive spiderweb." Her grin was sharp and sudden.

"Is that a good thing?"

"For me, not for them."

The boat stopped at the largest island of the Joulter Cays, which had been overrun as a project site. The workers filed off the boat and went on with their various tasks, while Marco followed Lyca and kept his head down. In a demountable building marked *ELECTRICIANS,* Lyca produced two thin slivers of metal and picked the lock on a large metal cabinet. She pulled out two tool belts and passed him one.

"Try not to look so nervous, Marco."

"I'm sorry I'm not as practiced breaking the law as you."

Her smile was not encouraging. "You'll get used to it, Inspector."

They had expected surveillance, but Marco was surprised at just how many cameras were spread out on the laneways between buildings.

He pulled his cap farther down. "Why hasn't Galenos hacked into these yet?"

"These are all on a closed circuit. Nothing is being transmitted off the island. Don't worry, I have a little present from Galenos to give them."

"Please tell me it's not a bomb."

"Nothing so primitive."

Lyca had memorized the plans of the project site that they'd found in the office in Venice, and Marco trusted her sense of direction as they moved between demountable buildings, workshops, mess tents, and parked plant equipment.

Marco looked about at the city of construction. "This is so much bigger than I imagined it would be." A scent caught in his nose, and he stopped, dread settling in his stomach.

"What is it?" asked Lyca.

"Do you smell that?" It was like church incense with an underlying fug of decay.

Lyca bared her teeth and followed the source of the smell, Marco stumbling to catch up with her. She halted in front of a marquee made of black canvas.

"Keep a lookout," she commanded, then gripped a metal tent peg and, with incredible strength, pulled it out of the ground. She rolled under the flap of the canvas before Marco could even think to tell her to be careful.

Not knowing what else to do, he pretended to tie his boots before he went through his tool belt to "check his equipment." Just when he was about to risk calling out to her, Lyca appeared. He helped her up and brushed fine white sand off her back.

"Fucking priests," she muttered.

"Is that blood?" He snatched at a stained sleeve.

She sneered. "No, it's oil."

"Lyca, we can't leave any bodies for security to get suspicious over."

"There was only one priest, and he was a small man. No one will find where I stuffed him before we bring this place down." Lyca turned Marco around and gave him a small shove. "Move. Stop gawking at me."

They hurried back to the makeshift road. "What was inside?"

"Nothing much. An altar, where he was burning incense, and there was a hand, carved with symbols, but there was no sign of the body it came from or any other sacrifices."

Marco's stomach turned. "Where do you think it came from?"

"I don't know. It was freshly severed, though. Maybe a day old. It's not our immediate problem."

Marco never thought he would see the day a severed hand wasn't an immediate problem, but he trusted Lyca to get him off the island alive, so he followed her without further complaint.

"This is the building," she said a few minutes later.

It looked like the twenty other beige-colored buildings they'd just passed. She pulled a yellow box from her pocket—it looked like some kind of frequency reader—and crawled under the half-a-meter clearance under the building. Marco did his best to ignore the sweat dripping down his back. He smiled at two women in neat skirts and polo shirts, and desperately wished for a cigarette.

Lyca reappeared with a wide smile. "It's done. Galenos will take it from here and access their security feeds. Let's get the next ferry back."

"Just like that?" He'd expected to be there longer than an hour.

"No point hanging around when we'll be back tonight." Lyca dumped her stolen tool belt under the building. Marco followed suit. "Did you see anything of note?"

"Nothing. Everyone seems to be too busy to pay much attention to anyone else."

"Good. The less memorable we are, the better." She looked about at the rushing workers and hooked her thumbs around her overall pockets. "Almost seems a shame to rip it apart." Marco would've believed her if it weren't for the huge grin that spread across her face.

IT WAS almost midnight when Lyca kissed Galenos goodbye. She and Marco climbed into the inflatable dive boat and headed back out to the islands. Lyca seemed to have a sixth sense for sandbanks, because she drove as if she had night vision.

Maybe she does. Marco wouldn't have been surprised. His handguns rested in leather holsters over his shoulders, and two more knives were fixed to his belt. All of the weapons had been gifts from Lyca. Marco still dreamed of Kreios climbing off the ground after he'd shot him. Lyca had assured him that her bullets would be more effective against the priests than his regular ones.

"How can you be sure?" he'd asked her.

"Shoot a priest and find out if you don't believe me."

"Ever the pragmatist."

Lyca beached the boat on the southern tip of the main island. The metal claws of the hotel shone in the light of the full moon, making them look even more like a monster's mouth.

"Search the beach caves," Lyca said. "Galenos spotted another two priests on the surveillance feed heading down to them this afternoon. I haven't forgotten about that hand, and I want to make sure there's no trace of the priests left."

"The island is empty of workers. What makes you think the priests will still be here?"

"Call it a hunch. I don't need you to watch over me, and you can't help in what I'm about to do." Lyca stripped off her hoodie and pants. Underneath, she was wearing a black dive suit, with only a single blade strapped to her calf.

"What are you about to do?"

"Use the magic that Abaddon has so lovingly collected for me." Lyca took two steps into the waves and paused. "If there are more than two priests, wait for me. Don't be a hero and get yourself killed."

"Worried Alexis will get angry if you don't take care of me?"

"Alexis? No. It will be Penelope that will try to kill me." Without a word of goodbye or good luck, Lyca dived under the waves and vanished.

Marco had barely gone a hundred meters when the sand shook underneath him. His eardrums popped as an invisible wave of power pulsed across the island. He'd been warned that high tide made the magicians more powerful. It had been astonishing enough to see what Alexis could do when the tide was down, but nothing could have prepared him for what was unfolding before his eyes.

Penelope had said that Lyca's magic was killing and destruction, that she could travel through shadows and manipulate them. Neither Penelope nor Marco had seen her use her power, and he'd assumed that was because she didn't have the need to destroy anything in Venice. Now, she did.

Black shadows boiled out of the ocean and wrapped around the floating hotel's frame like a kraken's tentacles. Metal groaned as the shadows tightened, ripping the scaffolding apart like petals of a flower, sending a wave of water toward him. Marco turned and ran up the beach, resisting the urge to look back as another earsplitting crash roared through the night. He made it to a scrubby tree line, breathing heavily, when a girl screamed. Marco's hand rested on one of his guns as he crouched down and crept toward the sound.

From an opening in a rock formation farther down the beach came a light. Marco waited, watching for guards. When none appeared, he kept to the shadows and crept toward the opening. The earth shook again, and he managed to dive behind a cluster of shrubs just as someone shouted, "Go see what is happening. We will finish up here and make sure this sacrifice isn't wasted."

Bastards. Marco promised Lyca that he wouldn't hesitate, that he would kill if he had to, but as the priest passed him and headed down the beach, Marco remained unable to move. He was sweating, adrenaline dumping down his spine as he worked up the nerve to follow him. Then another scream jolted him into action.

He moved quickly down into the sandy cave mouth with his gun raised, and headed toward the light. The short trek between rough stone walls soon opened up into a cavern fifty meters wide. A girl that could've been no older than six was strapped to a slab of rock. There was a woman beside her, but all that remained of her was carved and bloody. Marco didn't hesitate again. Gunshots echoed through the cave, and both priests slumped to the sand.

"Don't be scared. I'm here to help," Marco said in English, hoping the girl would understand. He pulled out his knife and cut the leather cords that held her. The ground shook, and a spray of rocks fell from the cavern roof. He bundled the frightened girl into his arms and ran. They made it out and onto the beach just as the cave collapsed in on itself.

A swathe of shadow in the shape of a woman strode toward them, blood dripping black from the blade in her hand. The girl sobbed and buried her face into Marco.

"Who is this?" Lyca asked. Her silver eyes glowed with magic.

"She was in the cave. I killed the men who had her."

"Look at me, girl," Lyca demanded, and she obeyed, her brown eyes wide. "Do you have parents? A mother or father?"

"Mama." The girl pointed at the collapsed ruin of the cave before bursting into tears again.

"Oh, no. She was sacrificed beside her. The girl saw everything," Marco told Lyca in Italian.

Lyca placed a hand on top of the girl's matted hair, and silvery light poured over her like a halo. The girl slumped unconscious in his arms.

"What did you do to her?"

"A kindness," Lyca replied, and they walked back to the boat in silence.

ELEVEN

$\mathcal{A}$LEXIS WOKE WITH the dawn. The villa was suspiciously quiet as he roamed his way through the halls. He wasn't surprised when he found Constantine working out in the gym. It would seem that at least some of the emperor's habits were still the same. Weapons were mounted on the walls, and new equipment was scattered about the room.

"I was wondering when you were going to wake up," Constantine said from the treadmill. "I suppose Penelope would be a good excuse to sleep late."

Alexis smiled pleasantly. "Yes, she is. The villa's empty. Is that your doing?"

"Phaidros and Aelia went back to Venice about an hour ago. They left a note; they didn't want to wake you."

"What did you do to them?"

"I didn't do anything, except tell Aelia a truth she already knew." He gave Alexis a tired look. "You know she's only ever loved Phaidros. Everyone else has just been a plaything, and I'm done with it."

Alexis pushed a hand through his hair and swore. "Do you think she admitted it to him?"

"She admitted enough that he was willing to hurry her back to Venice and risk your displeasure." Constantine slowed the treadmill to a steadier pace. "You brought her here as bait, and I would like to know why, Alecto."

"Actually, I told them *both* not to come. When have they ever listened to me? Aelia said she missed you, and you ran her off because you were jealous that she wasn't fighting with Phaidros. It's always the same with you two."

Constantine stopped the treadmill and toweled down his sweaty face and chest. "I'm not jealous. After sixteen hundred years, I'm *done* chasing that woman. I did us both a favor and let her go."

Alexis's eyes narrowed. "That seems very mature. Who are you, and what have you done with Constantine?"

"Very funny. Even I get tired of some battles. It's better those two are out of the way. Now I can commit all of my energy to wooing Penelope away from you."

Alexis folded his arms. "You don't have enough experience to keep a woman like her interested."

Constantine flashed a charming smile. "I'd rather let the lady decide that for herself."

"She already has. Stop trying to irritate me because you're in a bad mood." Alexis took out his phone and messaged Phaidros: Why did you leave?

The reply was almost instant. Aelia was upset and wouldn't wait. I didn't want to leave her alone when she was so volatile with the tide only making it worse.

I thought you were here to support Penelope if Poseidon's magic spikes?

You're powerful enough to protect her. You won't hurt her, though feel free to hurt Constantine as much as you like.

"They will already be in Split by now. It's too late to call them back," Constantine said.

"I wasn't trying to. It's better this way. Venice will be better protected if Aelia and Phaidros return to it."

Constantine grunted. "You always did love that city like it was your mistress."

"That's rich coming from a man who travels to the same four places every year and will always return to Istanbul like the tide."

"Constantinople," came Constantine's automatic correction. "You got my letters after all."

"I did."

"And you never wrote back to me. Not once." Old hurt and anger burned in Constantine's eyes.

"I used magic to send them out of sight. I thought you would stop writing after I ignored the first few."

"Why would I stop? You are my brother, Alecto."

"You didn't think so the last time we saw each other."

"You put me in a jail cell! Of course I was upset."

"I saved your life, and I won't ever apologize for it."

Constantine shook his head. "You're still as stubborn as ever. I hope Penelope knows what she's in for with you, *praecantator*."

"She does," said Penelope. Alexis didn't know how long she had been standing there, but her mere presence diffused the brewing argument. "If you boys are done bitching at each other, I could do with some coffee."

Even with a frown, Penelope looked beautiful, her hair out in a wild bounce of curls that made Alexis want to bury his hands in it. A faint glimmer of magic tinged her skin, and he felt the vibration of it in her aura. The raw potential of it drew him like an excitable moth to a candle flame.

"I'll make you all the coffee. If Constantine doesn't have any, I'll go find you some," Alexis stammered, unable to look away from her.

Constantine stared at him, thoroughly amused. "There's coffee. I'm not a Philistine. Make enough for me, Alecto. I need a shower, and you need to pull yourself together."

Penelope's frown deepened, as if trying to determine whether or not Constantine was insulting them.

"What was that all about?" she asked once they were alone.

"Nothing. Constantine's building up to an argument with me, that's all."

"Maybe it'll help clear the air, and we can get on with it. Now, about this coffee you're going to make me."

Alexis lowered into a short bow. "I am my Archivist's humble servant."

Penelope smiled mischievously. "Oh, I like the sound of that."

In the kitchen, Penelope made toast as Alexis brewed coffee and told her of Phaidros and Aelia's hasty retreat back to Venice.

"I hope Zo manages to get some clothes on before they arrive. Perhaps we should warn him." Penelope smirked. "Nah, let's let him find out the fun way."

"Wicked girl." Alexis grinned. "How are you feeling after your dip in the ocean?"

Penelope's smile turned brilliant. "Better than I have in weeks, which I suppose means you were right about the tide starting to affect me."

"And the Living Language? Has it given you any strange messages?"

Penelope looked at her hands, turning them over. "Not as yet. I haven't had a chance to use that little piece of you since I left the Archives."

"The little piece of you," Constantine echoed from the doorway. "What does she mean by that, Alecto?"

"Here it comes…" Alexis whispered.

He and Penelope shared a look. With that look and without words, she asked for his permission, and he reluctantly nodded his head.

"Yesterday, I told you I found Alexis's tablet," Penelope began. "I didn't tell you what happened when we put it back together… A part of the Living Language jumped into me."

Constantine's expression darkened. "You shared your magic with her—this woman, that you barely know—yet you refused it to me after everything we'd gone through?"

"I didn't share my magic with her, Con. The Living Language is exactly that—living. It chose to gift itself to Penelope. The magic—"

"If it was your tablet, it was your magic. Don't you dare blame this incident on an inanimate object."

Penelope stepped between them. "That's enough. You weren't there. Neither one of us had any control over the magic transfer. Even Nereus didn't understand why it happened."

Constantine looked her over, eyes narrowing. "Why you? What's so special about you that an ancient, magical language would give itself over to you?"

Alexis's temper flared, but Penelope was quicker.

"I'm not an arrogant asshole, for starters. If you want to hear the full story, I suggest shutting up long enough to let me speak." They eyed each other. Alexis had seen Constantine cower the most seasoned generals with his imperious stare, but Penelope only raised her chin higher.

"Please, Constantine. Sit down," she said, and to Alexis's surprise, he did. Penelope set a cup of coffee down in front of him. "As I was saying, the Living Language has given me the ability to translate languages…"

Penelope explained how Nereus had gifted her with a piece of her magic in order for her to take on the mantle as Archivist. Constantine looked as if he were going to explode but managed to keep quiet as Penelope related the words of the Essene prophecy, the Atlanteans' part in it, and the weapon that could banish Thevetat forever.

"You're the first magician with Atlantean magic since it fell. No wonder Alecto is so obsessed with you. You're something new in a world that has long stopped surprising him," Constantine said once she had finished.

"I was obsessed with Penelope before she had anything to do with magic."

"The high tide is a poor time to fall in love, Alecto."

"How do you know it's high tide?" asked Penelope.

"Aelia told you? Of course she did," Alexis replied.

"Perhaps she was concerned that I'd do something you disagreed with, and you would lock me up again."

"And here we go." Alexis sighed.

"What's the matter? Are you afraid Penelope will see past this perfect Prince Charming persona you've crafted and glimpse the beast within?"

Alexis bristled. "You had no problem with my beast when it profited you."

"Why do you think I call him Alecto, Penelope? It's because he used to be my Fury. He was so feared that men would whisper his name around the fires." Constantine's smile turned vicious. "Every emperor needs a servant like you to keep their hands clean."

Alexis's laugh was a dark, bitter sound. "Your hands aren't clean, Constantine. They are dripping in the filth you've waded through. Even the God you love has cursed you."

"So, your immortality is the result of a curse? You did promise me that you'd explain how you came to be alive." Penelope tried to diffuse the tension in the air the best way she knew how—distracting Constantine into talking about himself.

"I promised that on the proviso that you're honest, and you still haven't told me what you really want."

Penelope stood firm. "The ring of Solomon."

Constantine choked on the piece of toast he was eating. "And what makes you think I have such a relic?"

"Don't try to lie, Constantine," Alexis said. "You had it on the night I tried to convince you not to go after Shapur."

"I had many rings, some ancient, but I think I'd remember a ring that could command demons and djinn."

Penelope wasn't going to be dissuaded so easily. "Perhaps it didn't want to work for you, so its origins remained unknown to you."

A muscle feathered in Constantine's jaw. "And how do you know it would work for you?"

"Because it started to translate in the memory I saw of it. From what I understand, you have to be able to read and say the word that's engraved on it in order to use it. My magic was already doing it, I just need to find it to be sure. I know you have the ring—or should I say *had* it? Tim's visions revealed that it's passed hands since you, but I wanted clarification on who it went to after you."

Constantine stood to make more coffee. "I don't know how much help I can be with that."

"You lost it, didn't you?" said Alexis.

"I didn't lose it. I knew exactly where it was." Constantine let out a sigh of resignation. "It was stolen."

"Do you know when?"

"April 1204."

Penelope frowned. "Why does that date sound familiar?"

"Fourth Crusade, *cara*."

"Fucking Enrico Dandolo, may his name be forever cursed," Constantine hissed through gritted teeth.

Penelope crossed her arms. "Easy there with your curses. One of my good friends is a Dandolo."

Constantine raised an eyebrow at Alexis. "How times have changed that you would allow your woman to associate with such a person."

"His woman has a name, and she'll associate with anyone she likes." Penelope had to restrain herself from strangling the emperor. "I knew Marco before Alexis, and he saved our asses, so be careful what assumptions you make about my friends."

"Mia culpa." The note of sarcasm in his voice made Penelope's nostrils flare.

Alexis spoke before she could say something to inflame the conversation further. "Tell us what happened, Con. Where was the ring stolen from?"

"Where do you think? I didn't build the Church of the Apostles to house only my bones, Alecto."

"What else was there?" Penelope was nearly at the end of her rope with Constantine, but the archaeologist within overpowered her frustration.

"The most valuable objects you can imagine." Constantine joined them back at the table. "Holy relics, saints' bones, and treasure from all corners of the world, and other items that needed to be hidden away and protected, not unlike your Archives. I saw and approved every stage of the design plan in order to have a holy place where the apostles themselves could be housed, honored, and protected."

Alexis narrowed his eyes at him. "And that's why you built a space for you too? To honor the apostles?"

"Well, he did end up becoming a saint," Penelope said.

"The both of you are wrong. I built my tomb there because, at the time, there was nowhere in Constantinople that rivaled its beauty or was more guaranteed to stand the test of time. I'm not a saint, Penelope. I'm cursed. I'm surprised Alecto didn't tell you that much, at least."

Alexis shrugged. "I've learned that being 'cursed' is a matter of perspective."

"A perspective of yours that changes whenever you have a new consort."

Penelope rubbed at the space between her brows and then dropped her hand away. "Can you two please stop arguing with each other? We are meant to be friends, remember?"

"Tell her the full story, Constantine, and then we can leave you alone to enjoy your holiday." Alexis had warned Penelope that once the initial pleasantries were over, all of the niggling old grudges would come out. Alexis looked torn between happiness to see Constantine in a good frame of mind—something he obviously hadn't been in when they had last seen each other—and wanting to yell at him.

"You did promise. I told you what I want, so my half of the agreement is honored." Reaching over, Penelope took Constantine's hand. "I'm only trying to understand you better, and I want to hear it from you. These magicians won't tell me anything about you; you know how cagey and secretive they can be."

Constantine, ever the lover of flattery and the attention of a beautiful woman, visibly softened all over. His expression transformed to indulgent and charming. "They would undoubtedly get it wrong anyway, my dear. Magicians are terrible for exaggeration."

Alexis rolled his eyes. "Magicians aren't the only ones. Every time I hear Con speak of his curse the story changes."

Constantine held onto Penelope's hand, and she gave it an encouraging squeeze.

"Tell me your story. I promise neither Alexis nor I will interrupt. It's not every day an archaeologist gets to hear the greatest Roman emperor in history explain how he conquered death itself." Alexis smiled at her audacity. Penelope couldn't believe her sweet-talking actually worked.

Constantine kissed her hand. "As the lady commands…"

TO FULLY understand the uniqueness of my affliction, you must first know that my life has been filled with the miraculous.

My mother, Helena, was a barmaid from Bithynia, and while the nobility of my father cannot be denied, the elevation of my mother and the infant growing in her belly was the first miracle of my life. From a young age, I felt the hand of the divine doing its best to guide my way despite the faults of my character.

When I first heard a supernatural voice speak to me, I believed in my pagan heart that it was one of the pantheon. I had searched for a god worth worshipping, but once I found them failing to give me what I needed, I moved to another, always searching and never being fulfilled.

I won't bore you with information you already know well enough, but this might help you understand that when I realized it was not Sol Invictus guiding me, I moved on again.

Finally, when the supernatural voice revealed itself to be a messenger from the Christian God, I did not hesitate to do as it instructed, and much was given to me in return. I was triumphant at the Milvian Bridge, and Rome was mine, even though my knowledge of this God was little to nothing.

My mother, who had always known of my experiences with this divine voice, was also converted, and being the person I trusted most, I sent her as my envoy to Jerusalem. Once there, she was guided by a seraph to find the sacred objects that had been lost in time. My father might have been a Caesar, but Helena was not a weak woman to be denied when she had fixed her heart on something. She had the temple to Venus that Hadrian erected over Jesus's tomb pulled down so it could be a holy place once more and set men to work finding the relics she'd been shown.

These incredible treasures she found—I knew no regular vault would do to store them. They had to be protected in a place of reverence and beauty, and in a dream, I was shown the Church of the Apostles.

Constantinople was to be the center of the world, and I wanted to ensure that it would be a place of the future—unlike Rome, which had already begun its descent into a decaying pit of vipers, where old tradition and bureaucracy hung on and refused progress at every turn. There was no place in Rome for a church like the one I saw; it had to be Constantinople.

I oversaw every part of the plan, starting with the most crucial part of all—a vault built deep into the rock. The surface structure had yet to be fully completed when I died, but the secret chambers had been filled with all of the items Helena and others had found.

The only treasure that remained out of the vault at all times was a ring my mother believed to have been worn by Solomon himself. In a dream, she was directed to where the Second Temple had been destroyed by Titus. It had been built over the foundations of Solomon's Temple, and within the rubble, she found it—a ring of carved carnelian and bronze. It was a plain thing compared to my other riches, but I wore it proudly,

Despite Helena's assurances that it was indeed King Solomon's seal, I was only able to see it cure a few fevers, not exorcise demons. That's not to say it hadn't in the past.

When I traced its history, I managed to place it in the hands of an exorcist that was brought to Vespasian's court. Josephus wrote about the incident in *Antiquities*. He and the emperor had witnessed a man named Eleazar use the ring to pull a demon out of the nose of a possessed man. What happened to it afterward, I could never discover for sure. I only know that it was Vespasian's son Titus that destroyed the Second Temple in Jerusalem. It was sacked for its riches, and yet it was the exact spot that Helena dug up the ring.

I was wearing the king's seal the day I died. I'd postponed my Persian campaign, Alecto's warning weighing as heavily on me as my own failing health. I went to my villa in Nicomedia to celebrate Passover, thinking that a break at the hot springs would be all I needed to recover.

When I woke on the morning of the 21st of May, I knew deep in my soul that it would be my last day. I gave the instructions for my body to be taken back to my beloved Constantinople, and finally, I allowed Eusebius to baptize me. I died, my heart at peace, knowing I had made many mistakes but willing to surrender myself to God's mercy.

Over the centuries, I've tried to remember what came next, but there's only darkness. I do know that my son and priests escorted my body back to Constantinople. I was carried in a golden coffin draped in purple, and the priests performed their vigil after I was placed in my mausoleum in the Church of the Apostles. My secret and final request to Eusebius was to bury me with the piece of the True Cross that Helena found so that I could protect it in death.

I don't know if it was this final act or the combined holiness of the relics in the earth beneath me, but I woke in the darkness of my tomb, the heavy golden lid of my coffin open. It was Eusebius who found me, frightened and raving in the vaults. He helped me out of the mausoleum and had me placed in a monastery where I could recover my senses. I could be emperor no more; my old life was a thing to be forever cut from me. It took me almost a year of seclusion to regain my mental stability. Resurrection was not meant for mortal men, and there was a price to pay for it.

The years passed, and I did not age. I wandered the earth, feeling as cursed as Cain. I always knew I was alive for a reason, but to this day, I am still searching for the reason I came back.

The holy relics remained safe under the Church of the Apostles until Enrico Dandolo let his men loose. They sacked the church treasure and tombs, including the ring of Solomon, which was locked in my coffin. The crusaders never found the entrance to the vault. It was why I wanted to return to Constantinople before Mehmed II's army rampaged through it. I wanted to empty the vault, not fight them.

The city was lost, and because Alecto prevented me, the vault of relics was too. The Fatih Mosque now sits over the site. I can still hope the precious treasures are safe—that they remained hidden by some miracle—but it makes no difference either way. If they are still locked in the vault, I can't retrieve them. If they were pillaged and are now lost to the world, God help anyone who mistreats them.

TWELVE

PENELOPE'S COFFEE HAD gone cold. She rubbed at her forehead. Every time she touched the center of her brow, the air around Constantine shimmered like a heat wave. *What's wrong with me now?* She drank some water to clear her head. Maybe it was a migraine coming on.

"Maybe not as much was lost as you suppose," Penelope said. She shifted her gaze to Alexis. "The Turkish corsair pirated a few of the crusader's boats during the Fourth Crusade to rescue what they took from the Imperial Library of Constantinople, and I'm guessing you did so again when Mehmed II arrived on its doorstep."

Constantine's eyes narrowed. "So that's where you ran off to. You locked me up and set Phaidros as my keeper, then vanished for three months while you went and did the very thing you imprisoned me for? You really are a bastard."

"You never specified your proper intentions for going back to Constantinople. You never mentioned your vault of relics. If you would've been honest, perhaps you could've joined me. As it was, I picked the ships off once they were well away from the city." Alexis was unapologetic.

Constantine looked even angrier, so Penelope reached for another subject. "Do you still think you're cursed?"

"Some days are easier than others. The Eastern churches still have me sainted, but I am clearly no saint. Sometimes, I've been in the right place, where I've been able to help make a difference. Perhaps one day, I will have atoned enough for my great sins that I'll be able to die peacefully. In the meantime, I do my best to keep busy. It's the key to keeping madness at bay."

Constantine and Alexis shared a long, knowing look. There was a tiredness and a timelessness in it, a shared grief in having a life without a foreseeable end.

Will I be like that one day? It was something Penelope wasn't even remotely ready to consider. She had inherited a few pieces of power; that didn't make her a magician, especially not one that could be tied to whatever held the Atlanteans' body clock in check.

"Do you really believe the ring can stop a demon prince?" asked Constantine.

Penelope nodded. "Yes, if it will awaken for me when I need it to."

"The Essene prophet believed it would." Alexis leaned his arms against the table. "Back on Atlantis, we tried killing off Thevetat's vessels, thinking that if he had no bodies to jump into, he would be forced to return to wherever he came from. Our last mission was not only to free prisoners and find Aelia, but to do whatever it took to kill Abaddon and Kreios. The volcano erupted, and we thought the job was done."

"Ten thousand years is a long time to be wrong, Alecto."

"I searched for survivors and traces of their bloodlines but found none. Kreios and Abaddon knew us—our magic and methods. They kept themselves hidden from view."

"And now they've revealed themselves when they are most powerful, and you don't know how to fight them."

"I wouldn't say that," said Penelope. "Lyca and Galenos are striking a blow to them as we speak."

"Good. I hope you are prepared for the priests of Thevetat to retaliate, because it won't take them long." Constantine gnawed on his bottom lip. "I don't like this. You're on the defensive and haven't had the time to prepare. You're relying on a two thousand-year-old prophecy and Kreios being a traitor to his master instead of playing you like a fool."

"We don't have much choice. I saw the ring in Alexis's memory," Penelope said. "The words on it began to translate for me. This will work."

"You don't know the Defender very well if you believe he's going to let you get close enough to kill a demon." Constantine frowned at Alexis. "I thought you loved this woman."

"I do. That doesn't mean I'm going to stop her from doing what she needs to. I'll always stand beside her, but I'm not the heir of Poseidon. Penelope is."

Penelope found his hand under the table and squeezed it. God, she loved it when he talked about supporting her and staying out of her way.

Constantine shook his head, then returned his gaze to Penelope. "You may live to regret that. I don't know where the ring is. Where will you look for it next?"

"First we'll figure out when it went missing: possibly the Fourth Crusade. Tim mentioned crusaders in his visions, but I didn't know what time they slotted in to."

"If you had that information already, why come to me?"

"I wanted proof that the ring's power is legitimate—which it is, because you used it to heal people—and I needed to know that Tim's visions were definitely rooted in reality. After learning that you were still alive, I also wanted to make sure that you hadn't managed to get it back. The visions seem to show where the ring has been, and I didn't want to waste time only to circle back to you."

"I did try to find it again," Constantine admitted. "I've recovered barely a third of what was lost. The ring I never heard of again."

"Do you have any of the relics here? I'd love to see them. Magical artifacts are kind of my thing now." Penelope smiled.

"Only one travels with me at all times. The rest are in a safe place."

He didn't elaborate on where that safe place might be, and Penelope couldn't blame him. She couldn't imagine losing the Archives to thieves or war like he'd lost his treasures. He waved her along to walk with him, and Alexis followed, giving them plenty of space to talk.

"I have never seen him so concerned about a woman and yet be so willing to allow her to risk her life and fight beside him. The Defender has a mortal heart after all," Constantine whispered with a charming grin.

"I'm a lucky woman, just like all of Alexis's friends."

"Be careful, Archivist. You haven't seen his bad side yet. When you do, know that you can always talk to me."

Penelope raised an eyebrow. "I don't know if you mean that genuinely or if you're only saying it to piss him off."

"Can't it be both? Love him dearly, not blindly. All men have secrets they wish to forget, and he has darker secrets than most. I love him too, even if I want to punch him in the face at times."

"I'm sure he feels the same way about you."

Constantine laughed. "He's welcome to try. He never could beat me in an honest wrestle."

Constantine unlocked a wooden door, and Penelope's senses were overcome with the smell of books: leather, paper, dust, dye, and inks. Bookshelves in neat rows filled the large room, and situated at the far end was a work desk and cabinets for tools. All of the books were covered with dark green, red, or blue leather, the titles and decorative borders embossed on the spines in gold.

Penelope gaped. "Did you make all of these yourself?"

"This's my scriptorium. I like to keep busy, and I enjoy writing."

A half-finished page rested on a sloped wooden desk, brushes and inks arranged beside it. The borders were a mass of fantastical creatures and vines.

"This is beautiful," she said.

"I lived as a monk through most of the medieval period, moving cities and sects often enough that my lack of aging didn't arouse too many suspicions." Constantine touched the edge of the parchment fondly. "As I said before, nothing keeps away madness like work and routine. Why do you think Alecto never stays still? He needs to be moving forward, searching the world for different types of magic, so he doesn't go more insane than he already is."

"That sounds awfully critical coming from a man who runs about to document mystical experiences and writes his own," Alexis said as he scanned the shelves. "How many books of mad monks' testimonies do you have now?"

"About five thousand. It's important to preserve the flame; you know that better than anyone. I'll have you know my *Cloud of Unknowing* still sells very well."

"I thought the Christian mystics were a medieval movement," said Penelope. "Didn't they have crazy visions of Christ's wounds and such?"

"Crazy is a matter of perspective. The mystics study the mysteries of God, Penelope. They haven't disappeared, despite the Church's determination to discount anything they can't explain. It's like they want to take all of the joy and—dare I say it?—magic out of the Bible, from Ezekiel's angels to Jesus's miracles."

"Which church?"

"*All* of them," grumbled Constantine, and Alexis laughed.

"Oh, Constantine. Why are you still so surprised by that? How many times have I told you that whatever small men's minds can't comprehend, they brush away from fear or lack of imagination?"

"I can't help it. They have turned a rich, miraculous heritage of faith and grace and wonder into a bare and bland facsimile of what it is meant to be and slapped their own prejudices on top of it, and then they have the balls to say it's in His name." Constantine's shoulders tightened. "Their lazy faith is insulting, and it grinds my nerves."

"Now, now, don't work yourself up. You are meant to be showing Penelope your relic, remember?"

Alexis managed to smother Constantine's fire long enough that Constantine unlocked a drawer in the wooden cabinet and took out a small glass-and-bronze box. Inside the box was a piece of wood, as long and thick as Penelope's pinkie finger with one end bound in gold.

"What is it?" she asked.

"This is a piece of the True Cross that Jesus was crucified on." Pride filled Constantine's voice.

Penelope frowned as she stared at it. "How do you know that for sure? It could be any old piece of wood."

"You think I would lie about such a thing?" He straightened, and Alexis hid a smile. "This piece was tested by Helena after she found three crosses on a dig in Jerusalem. A woman, close to death, was brought to her, and the first two pieces did nothing to help her. The third piece—*this* piece—healed and restored her to full health. Since then, I have used it to heal people."

Alexis opened his mouth, but Constantine raised a hand. "Save your lecture on magical objects not being magical at all but merely conduits to channel the user's magic. I know, Alecto. I still maintain that holy relics are divine—not magical—objects and are therefore not subject to your conjectures."

Alexis shrugged as Penelope bit the inside of her cheek to keep from laughing.

"Don't mind Alexis. I like your relic and what it means to you," she said as Constantine locked the box away once more. "What else do you have?"

"Plenty. I'll tell you one day once your spat with Thevetat is over. I don't like the idea of you being tortured for information and giving up my collection after you reveal your own."

"Thevetat isn't interested in holy relics. They know where the Archives is, and it will always be the desire of Abaddon's shriveled heart," Alexis said. "He wants books, not treasure."

"Men like Abaddon want *power*, Alecto—in any way that they can get it. Even false relics have power over a person who believes in them." Constantine went to a shelf, took down one of the books, and began to wrap it in brown paper. "A gift for Zo. Tell him I want to know what he thinks." Constantine handed the package to Penelope.

"I'm sure he'll be delighted. He did tell me how much he loves your writing."

"Zo is the kindest of the magicians, if you hadn't already noticed, and he always gives the best feedback."

Alexis rolled his eyes. "Oh, please. Zo would love it if you wrote a book of haiku about laundry detergent. He's never been able to criticize anything you do."

"Good Lord, Penelope. How do you put up with his miserable attitude? Perhaps you should stay here with me. Let these magicians clean up their own dirty mess as they failed to do last time." With his charming smile at full force, Constantine kissed the back of her hand. "It would be my pleasure to host you here. Or I could take you to my mountain villa in Niš, where I could make love to you under the summer stars in a field of wild fl—"

Alexis crashed into Constantine, tackling him to the floor. Penelope jumped out of the way with a surprised gasp.

"There is my Fury that I know and love," Constantine yelled, his fist hooking Alexis in the jaw. Alexis slammed back into a bookshelf. "Be careful of my books, you clumsy bastard!"

"They aren't worth reading anyway," Alexis hissed through his teeth, and they collided again in a pile of fists and abuse.

Penelope stood back, torn between wanting to step in and letting them sort it out on their own. She settled with the latter, leaving them in the scriptorium to curse in Latin and beat the crap out of each other.

PENELOPE HAD finished packing their things by the time Alexis appeared in the doorway looking bloody, tousled, and sheepish.

"I'm sorry," he said.

She arched a brow. "Feeling better now that you got it out of your system?"

"Yes," Constantine called out from behind Alexis before they both started laughing.

Penelope shook her head. "Boys."

A few hours later, they were out in the gardens, bidding Constantine goodbye. He crushed Penelope in a bear hug.

"It was good to meet you, Archivist. Call me if you have any more questions about the King's Seal or if you want some better company." He slipped a card into her back jeans pocket.

"Thank you, Constantine. It's been…strange."

"You're welcome here anytime. Be better than the priests of Thevetat when you fight them. Remember, it is the grace we show our enemies—those who are weaker and different from us—that proves who we really are." Constantine kissed her forehead and let her go, grabbing Alexis into a hug before he could stop him.

"Good luck in the war to come, Alecto. There has to be more to Thevetat's plan than getting himself a body. Be on your guard, and if you need help, I'm always in the mood for a fight against a demon prince."

"I will, though you'd better start practicing with a sword again."

"I never stopped. Go, before I hit you again." Constantine pushed him toward Penelope. "Answer my letters sometimes."

"I will." Alexis wrapped his arms around Penelope, and magic roared around her. When she opened her eyes again, she was standing inside the palazzo in Dorsoduro.

"I thought I felt a disturbance in the wards," said Zo, a sword resting flat against his shoulder.

Penelope let Alexis go so she could give Zo a kiss on his cheek. "I have a present for you."

"So do I." He waved them toward the kitchen after placing his sword down on the dining table.

Penelope dug out the brown parcel from her bag and offered it to him. He opened it, saw the cover of the book, and blushed as red as the leather that bound it.

"You should let me read it first to see if it's worth your time," said Alexis, but Zo snatched it out of his reach.

He held it protectively to his chest. "Back off. This is my gift."

"He's teasing you, Zo. Now, where's my present?"

Zo pulled a postcard off the fridge and passed it to her. "This arrived for you," he said. And with that, he hurried out of the kitchen with his book.

The postcard featured a picturesque island surround by aqua waters. *Greetings from Milos* was printed over the image in a clashing red font. She flipped it over to find a series of messy symbols scrawled across the glossy paper. The Living Language shifted inside of her, and the symbols changed. Penelope's stomach clenched as she read aloud: *"Wish you were here. —K."* She passed it to Alexis. "Why would Kreios send me a useless postcard?"

"Because it's not useless. It's a message," Alexis said. "This is where Thevetat is hiding."

PART TWO

THE KNIGHTS, THE PRIESTS & THE TIGRESS

*"It is strange to observe how the
gift of healing can be granted
to one, and yet have a miracle
denied to another. What makes
the suffering of one soul more
unbearable than another's?
And how is it measured?"*
— Excerpt from the lost
pages of *Experimenti*
by Caterina Sforza —

THIRTEEN

MARCO HAD BEEN back in Venice for only a day when Penelope received the message to meet him at a café at the Campo Santo Stefano. She'd been following the reporting on the destruction of Duilio Industries' prototype hotel in the Bahamas and the resulting crash of all of their stock. She had to hand it to Galenos—he'd known exactly where to hit Thevetat's investors. It was like he'd lit a foxhole on fire, and the shady investors were now scrambling out into the light.

Penelope didn't try to hide her relief when Marco came strolling toward her in the Venetian sunshine. *He's not hurt. You can relax now.* The tightness in her stomach left her as she hugged him.

"If pretty women threw themselves at me every time I came home, I'd leave Venice more often."

Penelope laughed and held him tighter. "Shut up. I'm just happy to see that Lyca kept you in one piece. Your sister is scary; I didn't want to have to explain all your injuries."

"Well, I don't have a scratch on me, as you can see. You need not fear Isabella's wrath." Marco gave her back a pat. "Really, Penelope, I'm okay. If you keep hanging on like this, Alexis might show up to murder me in my sleep."

Penelope let him go and looped her arm around his. "You know he'd never wait until you're asleep. I'm allowed to be happy that you're not injured. I've seen the news and what's left of the site. I didn't realize the destruction was going to be so extensive."

Marco huffed. "You and me both. Let's get a drink. The wine outside Italy is awful."

"I don't doubt it. I had a beer in Croatia that has ruined me for all other beers."

Settled in a small wine bar, Marco told Penelope about what really happened in the Bahamas and the ferocity of Lyca's magic.

"She did warn me she was going to use the cache of magic they had already trapped within the foundational construct, but nothing could've prepared me for that. That place was huge, Penelope, and she ripped it apart like it was paper." Marco drained his glass and refilled it from the bottle.

"I've always wondered what she could do with those shadows. I guess now we know," Penelope said. "What happened to the little girl?"

"It turns out she and her mother had been snatched from a resort playground in Nassau. We told the police that we found her wandering the beach. She's with her father now, and they are still looking for the mother." Raw guilt flashed over his face. "Lyca wouldn't let me tell them about the mother. She wiped the little girl's memories. I don't know how far back, but enough. Lyca told me she isn't as good at it as Alexis, but it will be enough that the girl will never remember her mother's death. The police will put it down to shock, and that will be that. Then they'll keep searching for a dead woman."

"That's awful. These fucking priests, Marco. At least you were there in time to save the girl. That's a victory." Penelope squeezed his hand.

"I know. I still felt helpless watching what Lyca could do. How can a normal human compete with that?"

"You don't need to have magic to be amazing. That little girl isn't going to remember the magical, scary woman from the night that terrified her. She'll remember the man who looked after her until her father arrived. Your compassion is its own kind of magic."

Marco smiled shyly. "If you keep talking like this, I'm going to have to try to steal you away from Alexis."

"Ha!" Penelope topped up her own glass. "Good luck. Believe me, with all the weirdness that's starting to happen, you're not going to want me."

Marco's expression went from playful to serious in seconds. "What's happened now?"

Penelope told him about the visit to Badija, including the spark of magic she'd used to manipulate the water during her swim with Alexis.

"So you did break the cup that day," said Marco.

"Lost my temper and caused it to smash without being anywhere near it. I could turn into a walking disaster."

"You're currently living on a series of islands. Is this going to be a problem for you as the magical high tide rises? Because Venezia doesn't need a flood every time you get pissed off at the magicians."

Penelope shook her head. "I'm not that powerful, even with the high tide coming up. I made some water shapes for about thirty seconds, and that was it. All it really did was help clear my head a bit."

"For now. Who's to say what you'll be able to do once you learn how to control it and become a magician yourself."

"I can translate languages and control a little bit of water," Penelope said, ticking her abilities off on her fingers. "That doesn't make me a magician. And if it *did*, I would be the most useless magician of all. Books and water don't mix. It's the stupidest combination to have in a fight."

"You don't know that, *amica*. If Nereus and Poseidon gave you these abilities, then you can bet they saw a reason for them. These are gifts, and you owe it to yourself to use them. You can read anything in the world and understand it. You aren't a warrior like Lyca, but you're just as important in this fight."

Penelope swallowed the ball of unexpected emotion caught in her throat. "Thank you, Marco. I'm really happy that you're here with me and that you aren't scared by all of this."

"You give me too much credit. I'm fucking terrified, but I'm not going to run from a fight. Those bastards hurt my Venezia. They don't get away with that. As for you? If I left you alone with those magicians, you'd be bound to go crazy and swamp the city."

Penelope grinned over the top of her wineglass. "Keep it up, Dandolo, and I'll train the canals to splash you every time you get too cheeky."

"Such threats don't frighten me." Marco grinned. "So, your lost emperor didn't have the ring. Where will you look next?"

"The Fourth Crusade and the sack of Constantinople. Constantine assures us that that's when his tomb was robbed and the ring was taken. He didn't have many nice things to say about your ancestor."

"Enrico? I'm not surprised." Marco made a dismissive gesture. "With a name as old as mine, you get stuck with more than one crazy person in the tree. Did Tim say anything about Enrico specifically in his writings?"

"I'm going to go back and read everything pertaining to crusaders." Penelope pushed a hand through her loose hair, her curls a riotous tangle thanks to the humidity. "It's hard for me to read through them. I need to find a way to separate my feelings about Tim from the document, because it's our treasure map to the ring. The biggest problem is the visions aren't in a sequential timeline. He wrote about the crusades, but it wasn't until we talked to Constantine that they could be connected to the Fourth Crusade specifically."

"Well, you're one of the smartest people I've ever met. You love this puzzle, despite the circumstances. This is what you're good at. You'll figure this out." Marco refilled her glass. "Saints save me, you found a piece of Atlantis when everyone has discounted it as a myth. This is factual history you're dealing with, not theoretical. You're going to unravel this in no time."

Penelope shook off her melancholy and lifted her glass. "You're right. I'm awesome. I've got this. Cheers to finding a mystical ring and kicking a demon's ancient ass with it."

Marco laughed. "I'll drink to that."

TWO HOURS later and still buzzing from the wine she'd drunk, Penelope leaned against the wall of the glass elevator and let the view of the Archives take her breath away. She was glad to be back in her office, despite the Archives' bad habit of rearranging her desk when she wasn't looking. Slouching back in her chair, Penelope looked over the glass wall that had become their timeline for the ring.

Alexis had added notes and a number under *Constantine*. They had numbered each of Tim's visions in order to reference them in a way they both understood, and the number Alexis scrawled under Constantine's name was a reference to Tim's vision of the emperor. Penelope had never worked with a partner on a personal project before, and Alexis was careful of treading on her toes as they tried to unravel the visions.

Penelope turned on her laptop and opened Tim's document. He'd mentioned crusaders more than once, but now with Constantine's part of the story, she had a decent spot to start at. She scrolled through the document, doing her best to ignore the sick feeling she got whenever she read it.

"I thought I felt you return to the palazzo," Alexis said as he came through the door. "How was Marco?"

"Disappointed in the wine in the Bahamas," Penelope said. "Don't worry. I helped him make up for it."

Alexis chuckled and kissed the top of her head. "Is research and wine a wise mix?"

"Very wise. It's my most guarded essay-writing secret of all, and it will keep me focused on one thing instead of the usual ten."

Alexis sat down at his own desk. "Hunting crusaders?"

"I'm trying to find the part where Tim mentioned the burning city…" She shifted her attention back to her screen.

Alexis flipped open his printed version of the document. It had color-coded tabs that Penelope tried not to make fun of. She'd never color-coded her research in her life.

"Check page four, about halfway down." Alexis read aloud: *"The city of water and spires and golden domes was burning black. Allies killing allies. Men in armor and crossed surcoats, storming into their own holy places to pry jewels and sack gold as punishment for the emperor.* It has to be Constantinople. A city of golden domes burning could be mistaken for Jerusalem, except for the mention of water. Tim most likely saw the Bosphorus."

Penelope created a comment and linked it to the passage in her document. "And this is why I love you and your beautiful, big brain."

"That's all?"

"Don't worry. I appreciate all your other big, beautiful body parts too." Penelope smiled.

A touch of color pinked Alexis's cheekbones. He cleared his throat. "Moving along from the attack on Constantinople, Tim says: *The chest in my hands was small and bound with leather straps, and when it was placed as tribute at the bald man's feet, my name was struck off a list. The man nodded in acknowledgment, but I wanted to stand out to him, so I took the ring from my finger and offered it to him. 'From one emperor to another, I give you a gift taken from the great Roman saint's hand. It is said to hold mystical powers that made him invincible in battle. May it bring you the same blessing in the wars to come.' The bald man wouldn't have the ring long, and despite his wizard's experiments, the ring never revealed its secrets. Even at the moment the emperor's blood came from his mouth so red and he placed it into the hands of another, the ring didn't change. It was never seen again by the red emperor destined to rot in his red tomb."*

Penelope spun the astrolabe on her desk as she thought. "We could make a list of emperors at the time of the Fourth Crusade and work through it?"

"It depends on how many years had passed since the crusader helped sack the city. He could have been an old man when he passed it on. It was definitely tribute or taxes he was paying, so he was noble. This line about great wars to come...a red tomb for a red emperor.

I know I'm missing something." He got out of his chair and paced. Penelope opened a new document to begin working on her list while Alexis struggled with his memories.

"It's on the tip of my brain." Alexis cursed and stopped pacing. "Make your list of kings and emperors, *cara*. I need to work this riddle out where I won't irritate you." He walked across the room to give her a swift parting kiss. "I'll be back when I have an answer for you."

He disappeared amongst the stacks, taking all of his wound-up energy with him. With a rapidly fading wine buzz, Penelope went back to work.

FOURTEEN

$\mathcal{A}$LEXIS STARED AT the slab of marble on his workbench for a good thirty minutes before he picked up one of his tools. *Stop stalling.*

Nereus deserved her funeral stele and to have the proper rites performed. He'd put it off. With hunting the priests of Thevetat and Tim's death, this duty had slipped lower on his to-do list than it should've.

As he stood unmoving, the grief Alexis had buried for his mentor and friend rose to the surface. The magic in his blood throbbed. Very slowly, he rested his chisel against the stone and began to work, his mind pulling him out into the deep river of his memory.

The first time Alexis had seen Nereus was at the Temple of Poseidon in the capital city of Atlas. Her hair had been dark then, her brown face only lightly lined. Abaddon had stood beside her, already a man past his prime, full of open and obvious distaste for the Matriarch of the Citadel of Magicians. It had already been twenty years since Poseidon had passed his mantle to Nereus, but the old elites and patriarchs of the city still struggled to believe it. Nereus was always more than a match for the court dramas she was forced to participate in.

Alexis had never dreamed of becoming a magician. He was the son of a stonemason, and his highest hope for the temple visit was to receive a few well-paid commissions as a sculptor. Instead, he'd ended up with a whole new profession.

Nereus had taken one look at the tablet he'd carved and claimed him before anyone else could. No amount of protesting from Abaddon—or Alexis, for that matter—was enough to change her mind. Alexis's family was compensated for the loss of the extra pair of hands that turned normal work beautiful, and he'd been relocated to the Citadel of Magicians that day.

Did you see Penelope in my future even then? He had to wonder. If Penelope's vision of Poseidon had been true, Alexis might've been put on this path to her. Had Poseidon done something to ensure that Nereus found Alexis and subsequently Penelope? Alexis didn't want to even begin to contemplate that. Instead, he focused on what Nereus had told him during their first lesson together:

"Magic is an unknowable force that moves through the foundations of the world. It can be found in the most unlikely places, and the magician cannot hope to understand it, only to respect it. It will shape who you are, pull your life apart only to rebuild it once more, and tie you to people in ways you can't imagine. Your fate will change and change again, because ultimately, you are its servant, not its master. We are keepers of the flame, not the flame itself."

His life changed the day she'd taken him as an apprentice.

Poseidon had seen a vision of the rise of Thevetat and the fall of Atlantis—and the time it would take for Penelope to arrive to stop the demon prince once and for all. The *moíra desmós* between them proved that magic had joined their fates together, but it didn't mean they had no choice but to love each other. Alexis smiled wryly; even Poseidon couldn't have made that happen. Nereus and Poseidon put them on their paths toward each other, which he would always be grateful for, but Nereus had also seen her own death at Abaddon's hands and hadn't said anything to him.

"I'm so angry at you for that," Alexis muttered to the cold marble. "We could've changed that fate if you hadn't been so damn stubborn."

She'd wanted to finally die. He could understand that; he'd contemplated destroying himself more than once over his long life. But if it had been as simple as that, Nereus would've committed suicide. No, she had to die by Abaddon's hand as a catalyst for the final battle with Thevetat in the hope of ending him once and for all. What a burden to carry.

Alexis's back prickled with sweat. He pulled off his shirt and kept carving. It had been a long time since he'd carved—especially a funeral stele—but his hands remembered, the picture in his mind's eye growing with every tap of his chisel and hammer. The physical work felt good, his muscles stretching as the old craft came back to him. As always, sculpting allowed him to move into an almost meditative state, and his mind opened up to other things.

The visit with Constantine had been eye-opening, though Alexis still didn't know how he felt about seeing his old friend again. Constantine, despite his many flaws, had never given up on him, and something akin to guilt had been sitting uneasily in Alexis's stomach ever since. Constantine's God preached forgiveness, and maybe after hundreds of years, the unyielding emperor who never forgot a slight had finally learned how to do it. Penelope's words about how lonely immortality must be stuck with him the most. Alexis had always had the other magicians, whether he wanted them or not, but Constantine had no one.

If Abaddon was as connected as he seemed, would he know of Constantine's continued existence? Maybe he should invite him to stay at the palazzo until this was over. On the other hand, if he did that and Abaddon didn't know about Constantine, he would be painting a target on his back.

"Constantine has stayed alive this long. He can take care of himself. He's not an idiot," Alexis said aloud as he reached for a different sized chisel. If things became too dangerous, he'd extend the invitation, even if he doubted Constantine would willingly subject himself to any kind of protection or cohabitation with Phaidros and Aelia—which was another problem he didn't know how to solve or help with.

Perhaps keep your big nose out of it? Nereus's voice said in the back of his mind. She was right, as she always was. When they arrived back in the palazzo, Alexis had checked on Phaidros and learned that Aelia had closed herself off in her wing. He hadn't pushed her to come out. In a day or so, Aelia would emerge and pretend that whatever had happened in Badija didn't bother her in the slightest, and everyone would pretend along with her to keep the peace.

"Oh, Nereus, how did you put up with us for so long?" Alexis murmured to her shade. A cackle of amusement came in reply.

Alexis turned his thoughts away from the never-ending emotional saga of Phaidros and Aelia and focused on getting the edges of his border just right.

The lines of Tim's vision unfurled in Alexis's mind: *From one emperor to another, I give you a gift taken from the great Roman saint's hand.* There were many self-styled emperors during that time, from England to Jerusalem and back again. Penelope would find them all, her intrepid mind not resting until it was done.

...despite his wizard's experiments, the ring never revealed its secrets. Which wizard? There weren't many that would've been bold enough to use such a title during the thirteenth century and not be branded as a heretic. Maybe that had simply been Tim's interpretation of the figure he'd seen. At the time, there were many alchemists, and the studies of the sciences were becoming more active through Europe in some courts that embraced the practical knowledge to explain the mystical phenomenon. Science and magic were yet to be mutually exclusive practices.

It was never seen again by the red emperor destined to rot in his red tomb.

A red tomb—that was something unique if it wasn't a metaphor. Alexis reviewed the facts: a bald, red emperor with a red tomb, who had a wizard in his court to do experiments.

Alexis's chisel slid off the edge of the marble in surprise. "Fucking Frederick."

THAT EVENING, the magicians and Marco met in the floating courtyards for dinner. It was the first time they were all meeting
together since their separate adventures, and Zo's hosting flare was in
full force.

Alexis sat next to Penelope, fondly remembering the last time
they'd all eaten there. He'd already been half in love with her. His heart
had nearly stopped when he saw her in the gorgeous green dress Aelia
made her wear. That night, Penelope had kissed him with so much
passion, he'd almost given in and begged to spend the night with her.
He was glad his self-control had held out. Penelope was worth court-
ing properly, and every day she made him want to be a better man to
deserve her.

Alexis listened with only half of his attention as the trip to the
Bahamas was discussed in detail and Penelope spoke of their visit to see
Constantine. Phaidros and Aelia were careful not to look at each other,
the latter wedged in between Zo and Marco. Alexis tried not to sigh in
frustration; whatever was happening between Aelia and Phaidros was
still unresolved.

"You seem unusually quiet, Defender," Zo said as he refilled Alexis's wine.

"That's his plotting face," said Lyca, looking at him over her plate
of spit-roasted lamb.

Phaidros smirked. "No, that's his *thinking about Penelope naked*
face."

Aelia shook her head. "I'm pretty sure it's both."

"You're all ridiculous." Alexis shook his head.

"And wrong," Penelope interrupted. "That's Alexis's *I've solved a
mystery, and I'm waiting for everyone to shut up so I can tell them* face."

Alexis kissed her cheek. "You are right as always, *amore.*"

"I hope I get a prize." She winked.

"Out with it, Alexis. What have you learned?" asked Marco.

"With Constantine's help, we figured out the ring was stolen from his tomb at the Church of the Apostles during the Fourth Crusade, and that it came back to Europe," Alexis explained. "One of Tim's visions spoke about the crusader then giving it to a bald emperor."

Penelope reached for more bread. "There were also lots of weird references to wizard's experiments and red tombs."

"With a bit of time to think, I figured out that there's only one bald emperor whose court had a wizard and ended up in a red tomb," said Alexis.

"Michael fucking Scot." Zo glowered from the other side of the table.

"And his myopic, heretic master Frederick II of Sicily."

The magicians let out a collective groan. Marco gave Penelope a puzzled look, but she only shrugged.

"Okay, so who are they?" Penelope looked at Zo in alarm. "You know there's not a lot past the Peloponnesian War that has ever held my attention for long. Wasn't Michael Scot in Dante's *Inferno*? You put him in Hell?"

"He put himself there," muttered Zo. "*Dio*, this conversation is going to give me indigestion; I just know it."

"You'll be fine," Penelope said before giving Alexis's knee a squeeze. "Tell us."

"Frederick II was the king of Sicily from about AD 1198 to 1250 and was even the Holy Roman Emperor for a time," Alexis said. "Think of him as a somewhat madder Rudolf II. He was fascinated with mysticism and the sciences, and his court welcomed leaders in such fields."

"Crazy people and heretics, he means," said Phaidros.

"Like Michael Scot." Alexis gave Zo a warning look not to interrupt before continuing. "Some people claim Michael was the greatest of polyglots, astrologers, and intellects of his day. He was about fifty years old by the time his travels landed him in Sicily and got Frederick's attention."

"A union of reprobates," Zo added.

Alexis threw up his hands in defeat. "You tell the story if you're so determined to interrupt me."

"Well, you're taking too long. Michael Scot thought himself a genius and had Frederick believing his bullshit to the point that they began their experiments."

"Experiments?" Penelope's voice was unsure, as if she could already sense the horrors coming. Alexis curled a comforting arm around her.

Zo nodded. "It started with calculating the distance between heaven and Earth, writing astrology charts for members of the court, and discussing mathematics with Fibonacci."

"Right up until Frederick started to get really fucking weird," Aelia muttered.

Zo clinked his glass to hers. "Exactly. The questions he put to Scot took a dark turn. How much does a soul weigh? What does it look like? It seemed innocent enough, until they decided to lock a prisoner in a wine cask with a hole in the top, so that when he died, they could see if his soul escaped through it. He also liked to send his prisoners to do various tasks, like hunting and eating and sleeping, and then have them disemboweled to see who digested their food better."

"That was nothing compared to the children." Phaidros's eyes darkened. "Frederick somehow got it in his head that if an infant were raised without human interaction, they would revert to the proto-language that was first spoken in Eden. He wouldn't allow their poor nurses to speak to them or suckle them or even let them be bathed. Without that love and nurturing, the babies died, but Frederick only cared that his experiment didn't work. If I had known about them before they were all dead, I would've killed the monsters who did that to such innocents."

"How awful." Penelope rested a hand on her neck, visibly uncomfortable. "I'm glad the ring of Solomon never woke for such horrible men."

"It's a mercy," Alexis said. "Both Frederick and Scot were too puffed up for their own good. The ring, however, must've passed from Frederick's hands before his death."

"You don't think he would've given it to Scot?" she asked.

Alexis shook his head. "No. Remember, when he gave Frederick the ring, the crusader said, 'May it bring you the same blessing in the wars to come.' Frederick wouldn't have parted with any mystical talisman if he thought it would help give him victory in Jerusalem."

"Another crusade?" Marco guessed.

"The sixth to be precise. When he was crowned, Frederick promised the pope that he would take back the Holy Land, but he dragged his feet in fulfilling that promise. The Fifth Crusade got as far as Egypt and then completely failed. The next time he tried, he legitimized his claim over the Holy Land when he married Isabella II, heiress to the Kingdom of Jerusalem."

"Did he make it to Jerusalem?" asked Penelope.

"No. It went better than the first try, but Frederick got sick in Brindisi, and Hermann von Salza, Grand Master of the Teutonic Knights, made him return to the mainland to recover."

"Tim did reference he saw the emperor coughing up blood, and he put the ring in the hands of another." Penelope's face lit with excitement. "There were references to knights in the manuscript. Do you think he could have given it to this grand master as a good luck charm before they pressed on without him?"

Alexis narrowed his eyes. "It's absolutely possible. Even if the ring never changed for Frederick, he knew it was a holy relic, and the crusaders needed all the help—real or imagined—that they could get."

"I could go down to the Archive—"

"No." Zo shook his head. "That's something to check tomorrow. For now, let's focus on finishing this wine and enjoying the rest of the night without worrying about insane men doing ridiculous things in the name of power."

To that, Alexis could only lift his glass and agree.

FIFTEEN

PENELOPE WOKE FROM a restless night's sleep to a velvety touch along her bare collarbone. She frowned, sleep struggling to hold onto her as the soft touch moved over her shoulder and down her arm. Scents were now creeping in: coffee, cinnamon, and...roses? She opened an eye and beheld a glorious sight. Alexis was lying on his side, naked except for an ostentatious royal blue robe embroidered with golden Venetian lions and red roses. He had a rosebud in one hand and was gently caressing the folded petals against her bare skin.

"*Buongiorno, mi amore,*" he purred, a pleased smile on his face.

"You're up early this morning." There was already a blush creeping up her bare chest.

"How could I sleep when you're next to me, all languorous and deliciously free of clothing?"

"And that's the reason for the rose—" Penelope looked about the room. It was *full* of roses—all red and perfect in vases of every shape and color. "Am I missing something, or is there a theme this morning?" She pushed her wild hair from her face and found he had entwined her curls with tiny buds. Penelope raised an eyebrow at him in surprise. She'd never been with anyone remotely romantic, and she didn't think she would ever get used to Alexis when he was feeling extravagant.

"Last night, you said wanted a prize."

"A room full of roses is a pretty over-the-top prize."

"As you pointed out on our walk, we also missed the Feast of San Marco while we were in Israel." Alexis's smile warmed as he moved the rose in his hand to caress the side of her cheek. "This is me making up for both things. Would you like to hear the story of why we give roses on the feast day?"

Penelope moved to take a sip of her coffee and got comfortable. "Tell me, magician."

Alexis propped his head up with one hand. "The day is the Feast of Saint Mark, but it is also the *festa del bócolo* that celebrates a very tragic Venetian legend. Once upon a time, a man of low birth was cleaning fish at a dockside when a black-and-gold gondola came to dock at the market. Two maids appeared from the cabin, and then stepped out a woman so beautiful he thought an angel had been given human form."

Alexis tucked the rose he'd been holding into the waistband of her underwear before making another appear in his hand. A smile spread across Penelope's face. Even small acts of magic still delighted her whenever he decided to do them. She wanted to kiss him but held off; his story wasn't over.

"This man fell in love with the nobleman's daughter so completely that he knew he'd never want another. Then the impossible happened: the daughter saw him, and she fell in love with him right back."

"The scandal," Penelope whispered, earning a raised brow of warning for interrupting.

"At the time, Venice was open-minded, but there was no chance one of the Libro D'Oro patriarchs would let his daughter leave the family to become a fisherman's wife. He didn't care about the name, but that name had to have money." Alexis resumed his slow exploration of Penelope's skin. Where his touch went, a rush of heat followed. He seemed determined to make her burn.

Penelope would've never allowed a previous lover such a long and close inspection of her body, but all of those self-conscious hang-ups had been done away with in the past few months, because when Alexis looked at her, he wore an expression of such delight and lust that she'd never felt more beautiful.

Alexis's rosebud stopped its journey on the soft underside of her breast. "Are you listening to me, *cara*?"

"Trying to. Someone is driving me to distraction." Penelope bit her lip.

Alexis's indigo eyes zeroed in on her mouth, and he cleared his throat. "Stop that, or I'll never get this story finished."

Penelope swallowed her laughter. "Apologies, my love. Please continue."

"The man knew that he must make his fortune, and in those days, the quickest way was to fight in a war. In secret, he met with his love one last time before boarding the ship, determined to win money and glory. For two long years, he did just that, and it seemed as if luck and all the blessings of the saints were on his side. In the final battle before he was due to return home, he was struck down with a mortal blow right through his chest."

Alexis ran the rose in a long line over her chest and heart.

"As he lay dying, he plucked a single rose from a nearby bush and gave it to his closest companion. His last request was that it be delivered to his Venetian love." Alexis kissed the rose and passed it to Penelope. "Since then, it has been customary for Venetian men to give their lovers a single rose on Saint Mark's Day."

Penelope took the rose from him and held it to her heart. "You clearly ignored the part of the tradition where only a single rose was required." She edged closer to him.

Alexis ran his hand over the curve of her spine, then eased her back onto the pillows. "I am not Venetian," he murmured, bringing his lips to hers.

Penelope's mind emptied until there was only him, her hands roaming over his hot skin covered in the tattoos of old magic. She groaned as his mouth moved to her neck, the soft stubble of his beard making her tingle with goose bumps. She pushed the robe off his broad shoulders. "This is lovely but not as lovely as you naked."

"You're delightfully impatient." He laughed, freeing his arms from the swathes of fabric.

"You've only got yourself to blame—waking me up and driving my body insane." Penelope reached up to touch his black curls. He really was the most perfect specimen of male beauty. Knowing that his looks came third after his brain and heart, which he'd given to her, made her ache with happiness.

"Saints save me, I love it when you look at me like that." He bent to kiss her collarbone, then moved slowly down to her breast. Penelope gasped as he reached a nipple and teased the hard little peak until it ached and her core grew hot. Alexis whispered Atlantean words against her skin, and his fingers dipped under the lace of her underwear. Magic sizzled in the air, and the underwear vanished.

"Where did they go?" Her small laugh turned to a groan as he massaged her.

"Who fucking cares," Alexis growled. "There is only one thing that matters right now, and that's the most perfect rosebud of all."

With that, he lowered his mouth to her, and she almost fell off the bed. One large hand moved to her stomach to pin her down as he worked her. Only when she was trembling and whispering his name like a prayer did he ease up and move above her. His indigo eyes were burning with barely restrained lust and magic.

"More?" he asked.

Penelope locked her legs around his hips. "God, yes."

He thrust slowly inside of her, and a fine tremor ran through him as he allowed a moment for her to adjust. "I could die a happy man right now."

"Don't die, and don't hold back." Penelope thrust her hips up and raked her nails down his back.

The tether that was holding Alexis's patience snapped, and he gripped her wrists, pinning her down as he moved inside of her.

Penelope met the intensity of his passion with hers until the maddening rhythm and sensation sent her over the edge again, taking him with her.

Magic was thick between them, racing as quickly as their heartbeats. Alexis rested his forehead on top of hers as their shallow pants mingled. They were joined in every way they could be, their bodies and magic and hearts so intertwined that she didn't know where he started and she finished. And then she heard it—that indescribable melody she'd heard only once before. His heart song.

His eyes opened in wonder. "Can you hear it too?"

She nodded. He rested his ear against her chest, and they lay there listening until the magic faded and it was only their rapid heartbeats once more. Alexis rolled off her and pulled her close to rest with her head on his chest.

"God bless Saint Mark and his feast day," Penelope whispered, making Alexis laugh. She sighed happily as he kissed the top of her head, and the magical tension that hung in the air finally broke, showering them in a soft rain of rose petals.

PENELOPE TOOK one look at the wall of research in her office and turned around and walked back into the Archives. She was still trying to process the previous night's revelations about Michael Scot and Frederick II. Her dreams had been filled with prisoners screaming in wine barrels and sad, mute children crying.

Alexis had managed to scare away the fear that morning with his stories and his body, and she had no intention of letting the slimy horror of her nightmares return.

There were other tasks to do besides throwing herself back into the horror of Tim's manuscript. She wanted—*needed*—to learn more about the two magical abilities she'd inherited. She had meant what she'd said to Marco; as far as usefulness in a fight, she didn't think she'd be able to help at all. Still, she had these abilities for a reason, and she was determined to find out what that was.

Penelope knocked on the door of Galenos's computer lab and gave him a wave.

He sat behind his desk. "Good morning, Archivist. What can I do for you?"

"I want to use the database to find books on Poseidon."

Galenos pointed at a spare laptop. "Go for it. Nereus had a copy of his book of stories. It was passed around schoolrooms and scholars' houses on Atlantis to teach children about our founder."

"That sounds perfect. Let's hope it hasn't disappeared with all of her other journals."

"It doesn't surprise me that they did. Nereus was an extremely private person who wouldn't have liked the idea of her journals being read by anyone."

"She could have left me instructions on how to use the astrolabe, at least."

Galenos laughed. "I helped her build the thing, and even I have no idea what it really does beyond tracking us and the magical tides."

"You think it does more than that?"

"I have my suspicions. Nothing was ever as it seemed with Nereus. She was the Matriarch of the Citadel of Magicians for almost a century before Atlantis sank. She knew more about magic than any living being, and she loved to use it." Galenos gave her a sad smile. "I miss her."

"Me too. Though some days, I want to strangle her," admitted Penelope.

"I bet." His eyes crinkled at the corners. "Let me know if I can help."

Galenos went back to staring at his screens, and Penelope sat down at the laptop. She opened the database search forms and wrote *Poseidon* in the main field. A long list of books and their locations came up, and she printed it out. "Well, that was easy for once."

"Just remember the books like to move," said Galenos, dousing Penelope's confidence. "They'll be somewhere down here though."

It took thirty minutes of searching, but Penelope managed to find one book on the long list.

"There you are!" she all but shouted as she removed the book from where it was wedged between a block of volcanic rock and a treatise of the stars written by a Babylonian mage. *Stories of the King* was pressed into the pale blue leather, and Penelope held onto it tightly, lest it decide to disappear again.

She was searching for a reading nook when she heard the unmistakable sound of Alexis humming. With a smile, she followed the sound and found a workshop, carved into the rock. There were blocks of stone of all shapes and sizes, and at the center was a worktable. Alexis had his back to her, leaning over a slab of white marble.

"I didn't know you had a workshop down here." Penelope sat down on a three-legged stool.

Alexis lowered his tools. "There are still many parts of the Archives you haven't explored. You always get stuck amongst the books," he said, flashing her a teasing smile.

"Who could blame me?" She brandished her book at him. "I have had a minor success this morning."

"Poseidon research?"

"You know it?" Penelope asked in surprise. Surely he couldn't remember every book in the Archives...could he?

"I know it very well. Tell me how you like it." He turned his attention back to brushing stone dust away from his work.

"Can I ask what you're making?"

"A funeral stele for Nereus." He rested his hand lightly on a long slab. "It's overdue."

"I can't wait to see it. I'm sure it's going to be as lovely as all your other works."

"There's a spot in the gardens she liked. I'll have it placed there, and we can do the proper rites for her. She would be mad to learn we haven't done them yet."

"I'm sure she would understand, Alexis."

"She would understand, but she would still lecture me about it," he said with a fond smile. "I've meant to ask if you'd like one for Tim."

Penelope's stomach turned. It was one thing to hold his memory close; it would be quite another to walk past a marble stele of him every day, his features perfectly rendered.

"It's an amazing offer, and one day I might take you up on it, but I'm not ready yet." She held the book tighter to her.

Alexis moved so he could bend down and kiss her forehead. "When you are, you let me know, and I'll do it."

"Thank you." Penelope changed the subject as she swallowed her tears. "Something you can help me with now is telling me how to convince the Archives to stop moving books around so I can find them."

"Nereus used to just ask the Archives for the books she wanted."

Penelope huffed. "Really? Simple as that."

"I swear she did. She would say what she wanted out loud, and they would appear in her office. You know the Archives is sentient. It has the ability to hide books, which means it can also find them when they are needed. You are the Archivist; this place belongs to you as much as the rest of us. Tell it what you want and let it work for you."

Penelope got back to her feet and reached up on tiptoes to kiss the edge of his jaw. "I will. Thanks for the idea. I'll let you get back to your carving."

"Don't get into any trouble." There was a knowing look in his eye.

"You know me—I wouldn't know how."

"I'm sure I have at least two more gray hairs since I met you. Do you know how hard it is to give an immortal gray hairs?"

Penelope blew him a cheeky kiss before leaving him alone in the workshop in search of a cozy study area. She sat cross-legged on a plush couch and placed the book in her lap.

"Okay, Archives, listen up," she whispered. She shut her eyes so she didn't feel so utterly ridiculous and took a deep breath. "Please. I need you to give me Nereus's books about Poseidon." She waited for a long minute before she heard a rattle. She peeked one eye open. The astrolabe was now sitting on the coffee table in front of her. She let out a frustrated groan.

"Come *on*. You give me this thing nearly every single day. Learn a better trick."

Maybe it was her. Nereus possessed an unknowable amount of magic, and Penelope had barely a drop. Perhaps the Archives responded to Nereus better because of that?

"Please…" She shut her eyes again.

Penelope let herself fall into deep, meditative breaths, reaching out to touch that new and strange part of herself. There was a slight tingle in her fingertips, and then she was suddenly sitting at a bar. "What the hell?"

"Hello, Doctor Bryne. I didn't know we had a date."

Kreios was sitting beside her, dressed in an elegant black-on-black suit, a wide smile on his handsome face.

SIXTEEN

PENELOPE GLANCED AROUND. A glass of wine sat in front of her, and a wide bay of windows revealed a square and the magnificent facade of the Duomo.

"We're in Florence?" she asked uncertainly.

"Well, I am. You're only here to interrupt the first peace and quiet I've had in a month," said Kreios.

"How are you doing this?" She looked at her bare hands. She'd left her rings, including the one Alexis had given her to stop astral projecting, on her bedside table. *Shit.*

Kreios folded his long legs. "I've been trying to contact you for weeks, and finally, you've responded—at the most inconvenient time."

"You killed Tim, you asshole. He had no memory. He couldn't have been any threat to you—"

"Let me stop you there." Kreios's black eyes filled with anger. "Abaddon killed Tim, not me. I saved Carolyn's life by getting her out of that room. Don't think for a moment I wasn't punished for that. Tim was dead from the moment he agreed to go on the Cave 12 dig organized by Abaddon, and you know it."

Penelope swallowed the words of abuse she wanted to hurl at him. "Thank you...for Carolyn," she managed, her mouth filled with ashes.

Kreios made a dismissive sound. "Don't bother. I'm not going to fool myself into thinking we are polite people that thank each other and will one day be friends. Did you get my postcard?"

"I did. Is that where he is?"

"It's where they are all going to be. Why haven't you done something about it yet?"

"We need to find something that can stop…our enemy forever." Penelope didn't know if saying Thevetat's name would summon him to them.

"Have you found Nereus's books?"

"Not yet, but I'm working on it."

"Work faster. Abaddon risked going to your palazzo to find them. They are the most important books in your precious Archives."

"He won't be able to fuse demon and body together without them. We have time—"

"We don't." Kreios took a sip of the amber liquid in his glass. "After Abaddon failed to retrieve Nereus's notes on the rituals, Thevetat pulled Abaddon's memories apart to find the night they tried to bring Poseidon back from the dead. Thevetat knows the ritual to perform it, but he doesn't know how Nereus sabotaged it. If she ever wrote that information down, you *must* find it. You delayed them by destroying the web in the Bahamas, but it only slowed them down a little and pissed them off a lot. They are just waiting for the high tide to be at its peak. You have a month at the most before Thevetat is in his body and trying to release a demon horde to help him take over the world."

"What? I thought you said he only wanted a body!" He'd mentioned nothing about Thevetat trying to release more demons.

"He needs a body, and so will all the rest when he summons them. Humans burn out too quickly and won't be able to contain the power they'll be able to wield," Kreios said and then added, "The last time we met, I didn't know he'd planned to summon more of his kind. Abaddon finally told me because he needs someone else to help him during the ritual."

Penelope's stomach filled with ice. "Tim knew. I thought it was the curse messing with him, but he said something about demons being released from the sky." He'd sounded so scared on the message he left on Carolyn's phone. He'd seen it, and they all had ignored him, discounting it for madness. Of course they wanted more than a body for Thevetat. That was only the beginning of what they were planning.

"It changes nothing. If you stop Thevetat before he can fuse into his body, we'll never have to worry about whatever else he plans on summoning. The high tide is coming in faster than I thought. You need to move faster, Penelope."

"I've got a way to track the tide. I'll make sure we have what we need by then," Penelope said with a dose of courage and conviction she didn't feel.

Kreios narrowed his black eyes. "There's something different about you. You've got a touch of...something new."

"That's none of your business."

Kreios cocked his head, his gaze going to her third eye. "Oh, Doctor Bryne. You really are full of surprises. I bet Alexis is at his wits' end worrying about what you'll do next." He chuckled.

"Are we done?"

"We are. Get your magicians moving. Find the books, and get to Milos before we're all fucked." Kreios took her hand and kissed it. "Until next time."

PENELOPE JOLTED awake, gripping either side of the couch and gasping for air. She vowed then and there to never take Alexis's ring off, no matter how much the heat swelled her fingers. She clung to what Kreios had said so she'd be able to tell Alexis word for word. Penelope snatched the astrolabe off the desk and opened it to the back. The dials were glowing an ominous blue.

"Not peak high tide," she said. She twisted it and spotted a flash of red. "Hello, what are you?" She lifted it closer to her face so she could get a better look.

There was a new twisting glyph, and it was glowing. Without thinking, she poked it. Air rushed about her like a cyclone, and she screamed as her hand was sucked into the astrolabe. Alexis came rushing around the stacks, reaching for her as the world darkened and closed in around her.

Penelope landed heavily on a mound of pillows. Dazed, she lay still, trying to get her bearings and ensure nothing was broken.

"Don't panic, don't panic, don't panic," she whispered like a mantra as her eyes refocused. Alexis's fear and alarm were radiating through the *moíra desmós* and making her chest hurt. She tried to focus on sending back that she was okay, then sat up and looked about.

The roof above her glowed faintly blue, and strange shadows marked a pattern along it. She stilled. It was the same blue as the astrolabe. She was *in* the astrolabe. Her heart raced. She climbed out of the pillows—pillows that had been stacked on top of a wide reading lounge, almost as if designed to break a fall. *Her* fall.

"God damn you, Nereus!" Penelope kicked a cushion because anger was always better than fear.

The wide circular space she found herself in was piled floor-to-ceiling with books. Chains held them in place on the bookshelves, and they hummed with magic. She freed one and opened the cover. It was handwritten in Atlantean, the words shivering and moving under her touch.

"Oh shit," she whispered, suddenly realizing she'd had Nereus's secret library all along. "That's why the Archives kept giving you the astrolabe. God, Penelope, you're so dense."

Although how Nereus thought she'd be able to figure out the astrolabe's secret storeroom was anyone's guess.

More and more things fell into place the longer Penelope thought about it. Nereus had been on a mission with Alexis and the others when Atlantis sank, and yet she had her books with her. Carrying a library onto a battlefield was impractical...unless she had a device in which she could carry a whole library with her wherever she went. The astrolabe had remained in Nereus's possession at all times and was protected because of it.

A surprised laugh escaped Penelope's lips. Abaddon had killed Nereus in a fit of anger and hadn't even bothered to check her pockets. Even the Archives was a glorious decoy.

Penelope didn't know how long the magic would last, so she started scanning the book titles. Most of them were journals and research notes of projects, lists of war supplies, and detailed descriptions of experiments being performed at the citadel. She was going to need Alexis's help if she was going to get through it all. Penelope tucked a book that mentioned Poseidon in the first few pages under her arm.

Okay, Nereus, how do I get out of here? Not knowing if the astrolabe was as sentient as the Archives, Penelope added out loud, "I'd like to leave now, please."

For a moment, nothing happened. Then, without warning, her body was stretching in a way that *definitely* wasn't normal. She screamed as she was pulled through the ceiling and back into the Archives. Phaidros caught her before her legs gave way.

"Easy, I have you," he said, then helped her into her office chair.

"Oh God, that was the worst." Penelope put her head between her knees to fight off the rush of nausea.

"Here, drink this." Phaidros passed her a glass of water. "You've been in that thing for five hours. You're going to be dehydrated."

"Five hours? It felt like only an hour to me." She rubbed at her chest. She couldn't feel Alexis. "Where is Alexis? What's happened?"

"He's okay, Pen—"

"Don't lie to me! I can't feel him anymore!"

"He's fine! Drink the fucking water, and I'll take you to him. Just breathe."

Penelope's heart was pounding, but she did as she was told and drained the glass.

"I swear, you two are as insane as each other. If something happens to either of you, the other just automatically assumes the worst."

"You don't understand. It's like my lifeline is completely gone." Penelope's heart stuttered.

"It's probably a good thing. That tie of yours has just driven Alexis half-mad because he was unable to get to you. I've been guarding this damn astrolabe for hours. I knew you'd turn up eventually, and I told him as much, but when it was clear he couldn't settle down, I put him in prison."

Penelope gripped her empty glass to keep from dropping it. "You did *what*? What prison?"

"You really need to get your head out of your books, Pen. The Archives is a lot of things. It's not only a library."

"Show me."

Leaning on Phaidros's arm, Penelope shuffled through the stacks until they came to a bare stretch of the cavern wall. Phaidros placed his hand on it, and a golden sigil appeared before a door slid open.

"I wouldn't have been able to find that!" Penelope protested.

"Apparently Alexis didn't bother to show you either."

"Maybe because he knows I'll never need it."

"You might not, but every one of us has had our time in here— Alexis most of all." Phaidros pointed to a door with a small window slot in it.

Penelope stood on her tiptoes to look through it and gasped. There was Alexis, cross-legged on the floor amid a storm of blue light-ning. The black stone walls around him sucked the crackling energy in, and yet more and more flowed out of him.

"What is it doing to him?"

"Absorbing and neutralizing his magic. When you got sucked into the astrolabe, Alexis was worried he would lose his temper and acciden-tally break you in an attempt to free you from it. I convinced him to go for a time-out. After an hour in a cell, I'm exhausted. He's been in there for three." Phaidros looked in through the slot. "Remember this moment, Penelope. This is what he really contains under his skin, and we haven't even reached peak high tide yet."

"He is…incredible." Penelope gazed in at him in sheer awe. "Kreios made contact again. Thevetat knows the ritual and is going to perform it as soon as the tide peaks. I need Alexis to store some of that power, because if Thevetat gets into his body, he's going to summon more of his kind."

"Poseidon save us…" Phaidros sighed. "Tell Alexis the news while he's still in there. We don't need him blowing up the palazzo."

ALEXIS WAS lost in a storm of magic and memory. It was his own helplessness that had driven him into a cell, not Phaidros's coaxing and thinly veiled threats. Alexis released his frustration out and into the walls around him, a part of him wondering just how much they could take before they cracked.

Penelope's fearful face kept playing over and over in his mind. She was sucked into the astrolabe like a frightened djinn. If he couldn't protect her from a dead magician's trinket, how was he going to save her from Thevetat's wrath? If it weren't for the *moíra desmós* telling him that she was still alive, he would've lost his mind completely.

Penelope is clever. She found her way into the astrolabe, and she will find her way out again. His voice of reason was having a hell of a time fighting off the other voice, which told him he should've taken the time to study the damn device before letting Penelope carry it around like an accessory.

It was yet another worry atop his ever-increasing pile. Alexis wished that the destruction of the cache of magic in the Bahamas would leave Thevetat and Abaddon licking their wounds for months, but he knew it was foolish to hope. Constantine was right; Thevetat would retaliate, and they had to be ready for it. Ancient rage and hurt filled him, and he forced more magic from the deep well inside of him.

In the early days, when Alexis had been unable to process the irrevocable loss of Atlantis, he'd devoted himself to time magic. He'd created theories on how to project his consciousness back to his past self in order to warn of Thevetat before Abaddon could summon him, or even to send his physical self back in time permanently. Any idea he presented to Nereus had been shut down and absolutely forbidden. Playing with time was too dangerous, and they had all suffered enough. It had taken a hundred years for Alexis to let the ideas go, mainly because their lack of aging was becoming a concern. As magicians, they'd expected to live longer than other humans, but not by centuries. Nereus had convinced him to give up on the time projects and work on finding the answer to their immortality.

Based on Penelope's dream trip to see Poseidon, perhaps Nereus already knew time magic, thanks to her old master. Poseidon had seen Thevetat's rise and Atlantis's destruction. Had Nereus known their first war against them would fail all along? She'd let Alexis go half-mad trying to find a way to go back and stop it. How much had Poseidon told her of the calamity to come? According to her letter to Penelope, Nereus had a vision of her five years ago and knew she'd be the one to take over the Archives and be an asset in the fight to come.

I'm sending you a protector, Poseidon had told Penelope. If he'd meant Alexis, then Alexis had failed twofold.

Alexis... A voice called through the storm of magic around him. He opened his eyes just as Penelope walked through the wall of his magic and knelt down in front of him.

"Are you in there, Alexis?" She rested her palm against his cheek.

Half-dazed, he reached for her, pulling her into his lap and holding her tight until he was convinced that she was really there.

"I'm okay. I'm not hurt," Penelope assured him. "Let the magic go so I can talk to you."

"I couldn't reach you," Alexis croaked.

"I was here all along, only smaller."

"It doesn't matter. I couldn't stop it happening to you. I couldn't protect you."

"I don't need you to protect me, Alexis. I need you to love me."
Penelope kissed him, and the warmth of her lips pushed back at the
cold darkness inside of him. The magic flowing about them stilled, and
the walls pulled the rest away until they were only Alexis and Penelope
once more.

"What happened to you?" asked Alexis.

Penelope let out a low whistle. "Where do I start? I think we
should've stayed in bed this morning."

Alexis held her incrementally tighter as she told him first about
Kreios drawing her to Florence and then what she'd found inside the
astrolabe. Alexis groaned once she was finished. "Oh, my Penelope,
why are you so impossible to keep safe?"

"It was scary, but it's all good news. We can figure out what's in
the books that are locked in the astrolabe for a start."

"I'm tempted to throw the damn thing into the canal for all the
trouble it's caused today."

Penelope pressed a kiss to the frown line between his brows. "Stop
it. You'll do no such thing."

"You were gone for *five* hours, Penelope."

"Next time, come with me if you're too impatient to wait for me."

"It's not about impatience. It's fear. You're so new to magic, and
I worry that you're going to be hurt by your own curiosity. You didn't
stop and question why a new glyph would appear on the astrolabe.
Instead, you poked it without a second thought."

"What was I meant to do?"

"You should've shown me first. I could've told you it was a sigil
used for openings and that touching it would activate it." Alexis bit
down his frustration. "And you should be wearing the ring I made you
so your body stays together."

Penelope took his face in her hands, forcing him to look her in the
eye. "Stop trying to control everything. You are the one that has always
said magic is an unknowable force. You were scared today; that's why
you're pissed. But guess what? Because I pressed the sigil, I managed

to find the books we've been looking for for months. Because I forgot to put the ring on, I saw Kreios, and now we know what our enemy is planning. Deal with things not going your way, Alexis."

"I can't lose you."

"You will if you don't let me make my own mistakes, because sometimes, those mistakes give us the answers we need. I'm a newcomer, but I'm linked to all of this just as much as you." Penelope pushed her hands through his hair, and he rested his head against her chest. "I love you, Alexis. I'm sorry I scared you."

"I'm sorry that I can't keep you safe."

Penelope laughed. "Oh, magician, I knew I was never going to be safe again as soon as I walked through the palazzo door. Still, I'd choose to do so again and again."

"I love you, Penelope. I can accept you doing crazy things like getting sucked into astrolabes if you promise you'll always find a way back to me." Alexis tilted his head up, and she brushed her nose against his.

"Of course I'll come back. You're my home."

SEVENTEEN

FROM THE OTHER side of the cell door, Phaidros watched Penelope calm Alexis faster than he ever thought possible. After waiting a few minutes to make sure she wasn't in any danger, Phaidros walked away, the intimacy of the moment too painful to watch.

Zo almost crashed into him coming out of the elevator. "Have you seen Aelia?"

"No, I was in the Archives. Why? What's happened?"

Aelia had kept to herself since they'd arrived back in Venice. The emotional upheaval between them in Badija had been powerful, and they both needed time to process it.

"I don't know if anything is wrong yet, but she isn't in the palazzo. I thought she might be with you. She must have gone out shopping or something." Zo didn't have to say that he was worried. His harried energy was enough to put Phaidros on edge.

"She should've told someone that she was leaving. We don't know if any of Thevetat's minions are about, and Penelope just had a conversation with Kreios. He's in Florence. That's close enough to worry about."

Zo pushed his hands through his dark hair. "Damn it. She's not answering her phone. We have no way to warn her."

"It's okay. I'll track her. Stay here in case she comes back." It took effort for Phaidros not to let his own fear and worry show.

"She told me what happened on Badija. You've got a right to be upset, Phaidros, but please don't antagonize her. Just bring her home."

"I've no intention of making her angry."

Zo managed an amused smile. "If she's out drinking and flirting about, try not to kill anyone either."

Phaidros opened the door to the palazzo. "You know I don't make promises I can't keep."

OUTSIDE, THE weather was warm, and the sea breeze kept the humidity from being too oppressive. Phaidros closed his eyes and did the one thing he never liked doing; he reached out with his magic and found the ghost of Aelia's energy. It glowed like a trail of fuchsia and gold, and his magic hummed as soon as he brushed against it.

"At least you're on foot," Phaidros murmured.

She had gone to a small wine bar in Dorsoduro before walking across the Accademia Bridge. Her erratic pattern in the Campo Santo Stefano told him that she'd danced to whatever the violinist busker had been playing. Then she'd headed to another wine bar for a stop before winding farther through the streets.

During summer, there were always street festivals, markets, and the occasional party in a square, but it was a private party that Aelia's energy led to. The bodyguards in front of the gated palazzo in San Marco barely looked at him as he threw up a glamour and walked right in.

The beautifully restored palazzo was filled with celebrities and socialites, and melodic dance music played low enough that people could talk just below shouting level. In the ballroom, dimly lit chandeliers cast the guests in shadows as they danced. The side of the room opened out to a long balcony on the Grand Canal. The cool night air drifted in.

There were so many people and so much energy in the room that Phaidros's senses where overwhelmed. He was just about to close his magic off when he saw her.

Aelia was dancing with a group of handsome young men, her dress a red, glittery handkerchief that caught the light. Her golden-bronze hair was a loose tumble of wild curls that swayed with every movement of her body. Like always, Phaidros was momentarily struck dumb by the sight of her. He understood the pained, entranced looks on her admirers' faces better than he'd ever like to admit. Aelia herself looked lost in the music, like she had surrendered to her magic and let it take her to a place where only the music mattered.

Phaidros didn't want to be the one to wipe that look off her face— he could've watched her forever—but Kreios being as close as Florence kicked his protective tendencies into overdrive. As he approached, the men around Aelia took one look at the feral, predatory gleam in his golden eyes, and their energy shuddered with fear. They disappeared into the crowd before he was even close enough to touch her.

Aelia's eyes were shut. While she moved in her own world, Phaidros's heart slammed in his chest. He let his energy twist into hers and pull him into the music with her. She turned and smiled at him, so he moved behind her, slipping an arm around her waist. She leaned back against his chest, her head resting against his shoulder.

"You took your time," she said.

"If we were playing hide-and-seek, you should have hidden better, Princess."

"Who said I was hiding?" Aelia laughed. "Spin me."

Phaidros obeyed, taking her hand and twirling her before bringing her close again. "You know that dress is dangerous enough to be considered a war crime."

Aelia ground her hips back against him, giving him a full view down at her beautiful breasts. "I'm so glad you noticed."

"Everyone in Venice has noticed. Is there a reason you're exposing yourself like this tonight?"

"Are we still talking about the dress?"

"Kreios is back in Florence, and I doubt that he's there without priests. None of us should be outside of the palazzo alone."

Aelia reached her arms around the back of his neck, and he fought down the desire that rushed through him. "But I'm not alone. You're here with me." Her lips brushed his ear. "Exactly where you should be."

"Look, I know you're upset about Badija, but if you're out looking for a rebound, I'm not it." Phaidros had to say it, even if it made her furious and ruined whatever this moment was. Aelia had damaged his heart enough over the years. He didn't want to be a temporary lover while she got over Constantine rejecting her for the first time in their long lives.

"I don't need a rebound. I need you to dance with me, because no one dances with me like you do." Aelia's grip on his hair tightened. "I can feel your magic brushing against mine."

Phaidros flushed. "I'm sorry. It's an energy thing—"

"I can always feel it when it lightly touches mine. It's as shy as you are," Aelia teased. "Let it *out*, Phaidros."

His heart stopped beating, and he froze. Aelia continued to move against him as she started to hum. Her power curled around him, coaxing him back into the dance. "You don't know what you're asking."

"Yes, Phaidros, I do." She released him so she could curl about in his arms and face him. She pulled him close. "Stop being so afraid and come play with me."

Her magic tugged at him again, and knowing it was probably the most self-destructive thing he'd ever do, Phaidros released his magic. She gasped. Her face lit up in surprised joy as his magic joined her energy. He opened his mouth to say something, but she placed her fingers over his lips.

"Shhh. Just dance with me," she said, then turned in his arms once more.

So he did, their magic and energy so caught up in each other that nothing else existed. Phaidros couldn't have imagined a more unlikely scenario when he woke up this morning, but he was too far gone in the moment to question it.

Aelia had always fucked with his head, and no matter how many centuries passed, she always made him feel like the inexperienced youth, one that had fallen so hard in love with the girl that he'd never be capable of letting her go.

Aelia might never let him hold her in such a way again, so he was going to make the most of it. His magic licked against her skin, and she trembled as he moved his hand down her hip to where the hemline of her dress met skin. Throwing all caution to the wind, he pressed his lips to the back of her neck and breathed in the rose-and-sex scent of her skin.

"Tell me to stop," Phaidros begged.

"No." Aelia pressed her glorious ass against him, and his grip on her thigh tightened. She took his other hand and guided it across her rib cage, trapping it over her breast and pressing it there so he couldn't move it away even if he wanted to. Phaidros had had too many lovers to count over the centuries, but he suddenly felt like a trembling virgin who couldn't believe his luck.

His lips against the shell of her ear, he asked, "Why?"

"Because I want you, and nothing else I've done has made you see it. Stop being such a chickenshit, Phaidros. If you want me, then *prove* it." Aelia pulled out of his arms and strode off through the crowd.

Anger and confusion and desire swirled hot through Phaidros as he followed her up the winding staircase, pushing past the other party-goers. He caught the gleam of her red dress as she bewitched the security guards, who were responsible for making sure the guests didn't get into the private parts of the house. They didn't stop him as he followed after her. He was furious at himself for letting her walk away from him in the first place. As soon as Phaidros stepped into the dimly lit room, Aelia's magic was around him. She stood there with a challenging glare on her face.

"I don't think we're meant to be up here," he said, his hands tightening into fists so he wouldn't reach for her.

"Does it look like I care?"

Phaidros's heart rate was erratic again now that they were alone. His energy still pulsed with hers, refusing to detangle. "What do you want from me, Aelia? I told you I won't be your rebound—"

"You're so frustrating. Your magic is connected to mine; can't you feel what I want?"

Phaidros *could* feel it—lust and anger and want and need all churned up. He didn't know what was hers and what was his.

"We need to go back to the palazzo. The others will be worried—"

Aelia picked up the decorative vase next to her and threw it at him. He dodged it, and priceless porcelain shattered against the wall. "I'm not going anywhere!"

"What was that for, you psychotic woman?" He closed the space between them. "Are you going to trash this person's house because I'm trying to keep you safe?"

"You're not trying to keep me safe. You're scared of *us* more than you are of Kreios. I might have carried guilt over you coming to save me, but I've been right here for centuries, and you've been too much of a coward to admit what you want."

"I'm not the only one," Phaidros hissed. His temper flared, finally getting the better of him. His magic roared over her, making her gasp. "I can feel your desire right now, and you still don't want to make the first move? You're angry because it's your decision to make, as it's always been. You're too frightened to take what you want, in case I reject you." Phaidros bent down until he could see the fire in her violet eyes. "I won't be the one to grovel to taste you, Princess. I'm not just another one of those powerful men you make beg for that piece of heaven between your thighs. You want me? You respect me as an equal, or leave me the fuck alone."

They glared at each other for a long, charged moment before Aelia launched herself into his arms and pressed her mouth urgently against his.

Phaidros gripped her to him and held her up as she ripped open the buttons of his shirt. He placed her down on a side table so he could free his arms from the torn fabric. Her hands were back on him in seconds, an appreciative sound coming from the back of her throat as she explored the planes of muscle. Her legs locked around his hips, bringing him close so she could undo the buckle of his belt.

Phaidros ran his hands up her bare arms, then slid the thin straps of her dress down. His mouth broke free of hers, and he dragged his teeth down the side of her neck to the thin black lace of her bra. Aelia cried out as his mouth found her hard nipple.

"Phaidros…" she whimpered, and the ache in it sent him wild.

He dragged her off the table and carried her over to the bed. Her clothes were off in seconds, and he was almost undone by the sight of her naked on the sheets. A whisper of a melody escaped her, and magic shivered over her. The smooth, bronze surface of her skin melted to reveal the dark tattoos over her scarred chest and stomach. Phaidros let his eyes drift over the marks on her forearms and curved thighs. Panic flashed across Aelia's face, but he reached down to stroke her cheek.

"Sometimes, I hate the gods for making you so fucking beautiful," he said, because there was not a single part of her he didn't want to worship. Phaidros didn't give her a chance to hesitate. He lowered his head and licked the scarred glyphs between her breasts. Her hands tightened in his hair as his mouth reached her stomach. He ran a hand down the curve of her hip and dipped his fingers into the silky wetness between her thighs.

She groaned as he explored her. "You're killing me."

"We could be in this room for the next century, and I still wouldn't have done half the things I've imagined doing to you, Aelia."

Her aura exploded with light as her orgasm raged through her. She gripped at his shoulders, pulling him up and kissing him so fiercely she was almost biting him.

She ripped open his jeans. "Play games later," she said and gripped him so tightly he almost lost control. He removed her hands so he could kick his jeans to the ground.

Aelia stared at him. "And you say I'm beautiful."

"You are when you aren't arguing with me."

Her hands glided down his spine, her sharp nails digging into his hips as he moved slowly inside of her. She reached up to kiss him with soft lips. Her gentleness lasted for a moment longer before she bit his bottom lip hard enough to draw blood.

"Stop acting like I'm going to break and fuck me," she growled.

"You're not the boss of me," Phaidros hissed, but he slammed into her, all pretense of gentle lovemaking gone. Just when he sensed her energy spike toward another orgasm, he pulled out. She let out a cry of outrage, and he only laughed.

Phaidros flipped her over, dragged her hips up, and thrust back inside of her. Aelia cried out in pleasure, pushing back against him, meeting his furious need with her own. He braced himself over her and licked the sweat off the curve of her backbone, making her tremble. Aelia gasped as he fisted her hair and forced himself deeper inside of her.

This time, when her orgasm flared, his own roared with it, until they both collapsed onto the bed, sweating and shaking. Phaidros didn't know how long he lay there, a dazed mess, but Aelia's warm lips brought him back to the present. She brushed the damp curls from his face and kissed him again. His arms came around her, unwilling to let the dream of her go just yet.

She ran her fingers along his chest. "What was it you were saying about Florence?"

"Kreios is there, too close for comfort. He got a message to Penelope, and Alexis almost blew up the palazzo."

"Sounds like I missed an eventful afternoon." She propped her head up on her hand. "I suppose we should get back before Zo works himself up too much."

She was right, even if his hand tightened on her. "Whose house is this?"

"I have no idea, but they aren't going to be impressed when they find the state of this room." They both laughed wickedly.

Phaidros brushed his knuckles against her cheek. "What does this mean, Aelia?"

"For once, I have no idea, but it will either be the death of us or make us into something else entirely." She brushed her lips against his. "And isn't that just a wonderful thought?"

"It is, even if you scare the shit out of me." Phaidros tangled his fingers in her hair.

Aelia's face lit up in delight. "Good, that means you want it as much as I do."

"And may the gods have mercy on us both."

EIGHTEEN

THE NEXT DAY, Penelope eyed Alexis over the top of her book. He sat at the other side of her office, busily scribbling notes onto his copy of Tim's manuscript. Alexis seemed to be back to the normal, academic version of himself as opposed to the sheer vortex of a magician from the day before.

They had told the others about Penelope's visit with Kreios. They all agreed that Kreios could've manipulated the dream space to show Florence, just as he had shown Penelope his palace in Atlantis, and it didn't necessarily mean the priests were active so close by. None of them seemed surprised that Thevetat was planning on summoning more demons.

"I hate to say it, but Kreios is right. It won't be a problem if we can stop him from getting into a body of his own," Phaidros had said.

They all were taking it better than Penelope was. She was terrified at the thought of more creatures out there like Thevetat.

As a precaution, Alexis requested that no one go anywhere alone until they were positive Kreios and the other priests weren't trying to get back into Venice. He'd been rippling with so much magic and authority that not one of them had dared to question him—not even Aelia, who looked like she'd been out partying for hours.

"What's the matter, Penelope?" Alexis asked without looking up from his work.

"Nothing."

"And nothing involves staring at me?"

"It's my favorite way to do nothing." This earned an amused lift of his eyebrows.

"Is that so? Have you found anything interesting?"

"As a matter of fact, I have." Penelope put her book down and reached across her desk for her laptop. "I did some digging into Frederick II's involvement with the Teutonic Knights, and it looks like he sponsored them quite extensively. His buddy Hermann von Salza was the Grand Master of the Teutonic Order at the time of the Sixth Crusade and even helped him out with the pope when Frederick was excommunicated. If Frederick did give Solomon's ring to Hermann as a good luck gift, we could safely assume it reached Acre and the safekeeping of the Teutonic Order's headquarters there."

"It makes sense. The Order was founded in Acre in 1192, and he may have seen it as the safest place to house and protect a relic of Solomon," Alexis said. "Tim did mention a set of black-and-white heraldry in his other crusader's reference."

Penelope scrolled through the document on her screen. "Exactly, and the mention of Acre got me thinking, because Tim also talked about a city preparing for a siege."

Penelope found the passage she was looking for and read aloud:

"The city was afraid after they received the message of no mercy or quarter to be given. They had to try again, talk their way through it, and save those living in the city. There was a room full of men arguing, black-and-white crosses mixed with other insignia on soldier's uniforms. They didn't think talking with the sultan would fix anything. They were willing to wait until reinforcements arrived, and they would do everything to hold out until then. Sir Philip would go to Cairo and beg if he had to. I watched his group ride out from the city, banners raised and horses proud, despite the fear that they left behind. It was on the following day that the priest arrived in his rough brown robes. He was a Florentine and was determined to study in Baghdad despite the danger. I told him to rest and plan to leave the city, for by the end of the year, we'd surely all be dead.

"I don't know if it was days, months, or only hours that passed, but I was suddenly in dark tunnels built under the Order's chapel, shoving a small, olive wooden box into the priest's hands. By dawn, I had smuggled him out of the city. Then there was only blood and screaming and fire; the walls were surrounded by the enemy. There would be no peace. Frightened people were slaughtered, and the city's buildings were reduced to rubble. I was dying of a gut wound, but I'd done my duty. The priest had gotten out on time, and he'd keep the ring safe."

Alexis had risen from his chair as Penelope talked and was placing neatly written sticky notes on their timeline. "So this puts the ring definitely in Acre in 1291, but it was gone before Sultan Khalil arrived with his soldiers. The priest was lucky to get out when he did, assuming he managed to successfully sneak past the army."

A certain tone in his voice made Penelope glance up from her computer. "You were there?"

Alexis shook his head. "Not when it happened. I was living in the East at the time, so I saw what remained afterward. A siege is horrific enough when it ends peacefully, let alone when the invaders manage to get in, and it's always the innocents that suffer the highest price. There was barely a city left once they were done."

Penelope got out of her chair and went to stand beside him to look at the wall. She wanted to comfort him, knowing there was a deeper pain in Alexis's memories than she could ever begin to understand. Constantine's advice was that work was always the best thing to keep Alexis's melancholy at bay.

"1291 is the latest time period we've managed to nail down so far," Penelope said. "Between the two of us, we are going to find Solomon's ring in no time."

"We have a lot of time to get through between 1291 and now."

"Then I suppose I'll have to tolerate you taking up my space a little longer."

"Are you trying to get rid of me already?"

"I suppose you're not the worst study partner I've ever had."

Alexis's eyes gleamed with amusement, and he lifted her chin with his finger. "I can ask the Archives to make me an office, but who would you stare at when you're doing nothing?"

"You make a valid argument, although I could convince the Archives to make a kitchen and get Zo to come down—" Penelope didn't have a chance to finish the sentence before he was kissing her.

"If a kitchen turns up in the Archives, I'll turn it to rubble before Zo even has a chance to try to redecorate it."

Penelope screwed up her nose. "Why would he want to redecorate a brand-new kitchen?"

"Zo has never met a kitchen he didn't try to redecorate." They were still sniggering when the man himself pushed open the office door. "Speak of the devil, and he'll appear."

"Have you seen the news?" Zo asked, and Penelope's smile froze.

Alexis's tone turned urgent. "What's happened?"

"Florence has been attacked."

Alexis didn't wait for further explanation. He took their hands and portaled them upstairs.

In the entertainment room, Phaidros was paled-faced, watching a news stream. Aelia was beside him, holding his hand as they watched Florence burn.

"Tell me," Alexis said impatiently.

"Two attacks—small bombs inside trucks that were driven through crowds in the Piazza della Signoria and the Piazza del Duomo," said Phaidros. "Emergency services are on scene, but they aren't yet reporting how many are dead or injured."

"And they're blaming us." Aelia pointed at the screen. There was a smoking truck crashed into the side of the Duomo, and on its side was the unmistakable trident-and-book insignia of the Citadel of Magicians.

"It's a message, not blame. This is for the Bahamas," said Penelope. Her hand automatically moved to cover the same symbol tattooed on her wrist.

"I knew I should've gone to Florence as soon as Penelope saw Kreios there," Phaidros said, voice ragged with guilt.

Zo reached for the remote and turned up the volume.

"The exact motivations of the attackers are unclear," the reporter said over the roar of sirens. *"The drivers of the vehicles died in the initial blasts, but a video manifesto by the New Atlanteans was published on You-Tube only an hour before the attack. They are claiming to be the lost bloodline of Atlantis and are rising up to take back their authority as the 'First Men.' They also claim that the recent discovery of a stone tablet in Crete was the sign they were waiting for to make their presence known."*

Penelope swore, and then her phone started ringing.

"Don't answer it," Alexis said before turning his attention to Phaidros. "Go and get ready. We need to get to Florence and investigate this ourselves."

"I'm coming." Lyca emerged from the shadows. "I haven't killed enough priests to cool my anger."

"Zo and Aelia, I want you to check in with Gisela Bianchi. DIGOS will be all over this." Next, Alexis turned to Penelope. "Text Marco and tell him to get ready for the media. It won't take them long to link the tablet script from the Duilio case to the diatribe in the You-Tube clip. Don't talk to the media until I get back."

"Okay." Penelope nodded, already halfway through her text to Marco when Alexis vanished, Phaidros and Zo hurrying out after him.

"Those fucking animals." Aelia's eyes were still glued to the screen as the camera panned over the horror. "They did this on Atlantis too."

"The priests? Why?" Penelope asked, though she knew that inciting fear was always the goal of such attacks. She had watched 9/11 on her TV as a horrified teenager and saw the world change from that moment. The scenes of terror and war had become painfully common, from the invasion of Iraq to the London Bridge attack and Christchurch shootings. She'd stood numbly by, watching as Palmyra, Aleppo, and so many other cities had been looted and bombed, their people killed.

"The priests wanted to turn people against the Citadel of Magicians and Poseidon," Aelia said. "The priests would go into a town, take the magically gifted for their sacrifices, and then they would destroy everything else. They would leave the insignia of the Citadel of Magicians on any wall that remained, so that when the magicians did turn up to help, they would be attacked, or the people would run in fear of them. It took months for word to spread that magicians weren't the ones responsible for the atrocities, and by that time, many innocent magic users had been slaughtered by common people."

Aelia's expression saddened even further. "Phaidros's sister and little brother were killed by their own village council. It's good he's going to Florence with Alexis. It would kill him to sit here and do nothing."

Alexis, Phaidros, and Lyca appeared soon after, all wearing pieces of armor and weapons that they would glamour to look like normal clothing.

"Leave your phone on. We'll keep each other updated. Let us know if you learn of other attacks." Alexis still had that cold calm about him even as he kissed Penelope.

She hid her surprise as Aelia came forward to help tighten one of Phaidros's vambraces.

"Don't do anything stupid that will get you killed," she said.

Phaidros gave her his sharky, zero-fucks smile. "Is that an order, Princess?"

Aelia flicked her hair over her shoulder. "Fine. Go ahead and die then, but I'm stealing all of your stuff if you do."

"We don't have time to flirt." Lyca gripped Alexis's shoulder.

Alexis locked his hands around Phaidros's forearm, and they disappeared.

"I don't think I'll ever get used to seeing that," Penelope admitted.

"It's a sign of how strong Alexis is getting. Only a few months ago, it was a stretch for him to come to me in Vienna. Now, he's taking more than one of us across the countries. This high tide is going to be terrifying." Aelia sat back down on the couch and tucked her legs underneath her.

Penelope sat down beside her, not wanting to be alone while she waited to hear from Alexis. His hunt across Italy had been enough to make her realize it would be the waiting, not the danger, that would be the hardest for her to cope with.

"They've done this too many times to count, Penelope," Aelia said softly.

"And that thought is supposed to comfort me?"

"No. You're too in love for anything I say to bring you comfort. It was merely to point out that they aren't going to do anything stupid."

They sat in silence, watching the endless news footage and some of the recovered YouTube clip rife with neo-Nazi propaganda. The attackers claimed to be lost descendants of Atlantis and the heirs to the earth through their Aryan heritage.

"Fucking Nazis. Those monsters just never seem to die, no matter how many we kill," hissed Aelia. "If I could travel back in time, I would kill Edmund Kiss before he could ever publish his stupid book. Alexis thought Kiss's theories were so ridiculous that no one in their right mind would believe them. He had no idea how deep Kiss was in with the Schutzstaffel, and by the time he did, Kiss's poisonous theories were already rooted."

Nazis and their fascination with Atlantis was one of the hurtles Penelope had to struggle over in her own research. Helena Blavatsky's tales of Thevetat, however skewed from the truth that Penelope now knew, weren't the most dangerous theory that had come from her fantastical writings. Her idea of Root Races, especially the Aryans, was twisted up for even darker purposes when they got the attention of pseudoscientists doing their best to place Atlantis in Northern Europe. In 1922, it began with Karl Georg Zschaetzsch's *Atlantis, The Original Homeland of the Aryans, With One Map*, which sought to reinforce the theory of Atlantis being the true Gothic homeland, but it was Edmund Kiss's *The Last Queen of Atlantis* and his pseudo-archaeology that worked to support the dangerous and racist theology that the Germans were the master race.

"What did Alexis do when he found out? Kiss got off at Nuremberg because he was only an archaeologist." Penelope half-dreaded the answer.

"Kiss was an idiot, and the rest of the scientific world knew it. Without his supporters, he was just another nutcase and was ignored. He wasn't really the problem; Himmler was. He was the one who funded Kiss and any archaeologists that could tie the Germans to the advanced Aryans and Atlantis. That's also how the likes of the Institute of Ancestral Heritage got their money." Aelia suddenly broke into a dark and vicious smile. "Don't you worry. Alexis got his revenge on Himmler."

"I thought Himmler committed suicide while he was in custody."

"Do you think a vain, self-important man like Himmler would've committed suicide? Especially when he knew the British and Americans would keep him alive as long as he kept giving them information?" said Aelia. "It may have looked like poison to humans, but what do they know about what magic can do to flesh? Alexis always said it was one of the most satisfying kills of his life."

"Did he get Hitler too?" Another suicide shrouded in mystery.

"Oh, no. Zo and Phaidros got that little weasel." Aelia's attention turned back to the TV. "Their ideology is like cancer. No matter how many times it gets cut out, it always seems to resurface."

"Maybe Hitler really was possessed by the devil." As Penelope voiced this other conspiracy theory, she realized what she'd said. "You don't think…"

"That he was supported by Thevetat? It would make sense. There was so much about that rise of power—the cruelty and horror of what they did in the camps—that was so similar to what Thevetat's followers did on Atlantis. We never even considered that Abaddon could've still been alive and spreading his lies." Aelia wrapped her arms around herself. "It doesn't matter now. We can't change the past. Only stop them in the here and now."

Penelope stared at the fire engines hosing down the Duomo and police spreading tape around the site to keep the public out. "I feel like such an idiot. I saw Kreios in Florence. I should've realized he was trying to tell me something."

"You can't blame yourself for this, Penelope," Zo said. He carried in a tray of glasses and a bottle of scotch. "Kreios is a master manipulator, and if Thevetat is in his mind as much as we can assume, there isn't anything he could've said as a warning. He might not have even known what Thevetat was planning for Florence until after he spoke to you."

Aelia scowled. "Are you seriously taking that animal's side right now?"

"No, but we don't know the truth of it either. Kreios saved Carolyn from Abaddon. I think he would've warned Penelope if he knew about what was going to happen."

Aelia started hissing at him in Atlantean when Penelope's phone rang. She hesitated; she didn't recognize the number.

"Don't answer it," Aelia said.

Zo jerked his head at the phone. "She has to. Alexis could be using a burner."

"Both of you shut up." Penelope put the phone on speaker. "Hello?"

"P-Penelope Bryne?" a woman's voice asked in a strained British accent.

"Yes? Who is this?"

"My name is Suzie. A man told me that I needed to ring your number and give you a m-message, or he'd k-kill me." She sniffled. "He said to tell you that F-Florence isn't the real attack; it's only so you don't look back to Israel."

"Suzie! What else—"

The phone went dead.

"Elazar," whispered Zo. His glass fell to the floor as he searched his pockets for his phone.

Penelope pulled hard on the *moíra desmós* as she rang Alexis's number. "Pick up, pick up, pick up," she chanted, and on the fourth ring, it finally got through.

"Penelope, what is it?" Alexis shouted over the wail of sirens and screams in the background.

"Florence is a distraction! They're going after Elazar!"

The phone connection crackled and died.

NINETEEN

I N FLORENCE, ALEXIS placed them a few streets back from the Duomo and out of the way of any spectators or police. Phaidros's expression hardened as his gaze focused on the plumes of black smoke billowing over the tops of the terra-cotta roofs. Alexis's phone flashed with Gisela's number.

"Pronto."

"Alexis, where are you?" Gisela asked, never one to waste time on pleasantries.

"Firenze. This attack is Duilio's followers' doing, and I need you to find out what kind of presence DIGOS has on the scene."

They hurried through the streets and toward the Cathedral of Santa Maria del Fiore. He really hoped that the terrorism branch of Italy's police would be out in force in case Kreios had any other surprises planned.

"I've already been contacted by our Firenze branch about the attacker's video. I should warn you: they are going to investigate Penelope's involvement with this group."

"I thought she was cleared after the Duilio investigation in Venice."

"She was. That was before a terror group cited her discovery as motivation to commit mass murder. There's something else you should know. They are keeping it out of the media for the moment, but DIGOS has removed bombs from underneath the Ponte Vecchio and the Ponte Santa Trinita."

Alexis swore colorfully. Kreios had warned Penelope about retaliation, but he'd barely given her enough time to prevent any of it from happening.

"Thank you, Gisela."

"Let me remind you that you aren't police and shouldn't be interfering in investigations."

"Consider your legal obligations to warn me covered. I'll let you know where to look if I find anything." Alexis hung up before she could lecture him about being a vigilante, then turned to Lyca. "I need you to get over to the Piazza della Signoria and see if you can pick up a priest's trail. There have been other bombs found, which means we don't know how many more have been planted."

Without a word, Lyca turned and walked into the shadowy alcove of a building and was gone.

"I'll never stop being jealous of her ability to do that," Phaidros said. "Where were the other bombs?"

"The bridges. It might have been an attempt to prevent emergency services from getting to the Duomo."

Phaidros shook his head. "It's because those bridges will have loads of tourists on them. Thevetat doesn't care about taking buildings, only lives."

The square was packed with emergency service crews and police, all trying to help the wounded and keep spectators out of their way. A large delivery truck was still smoking as firefighters doused it and the side of the cathedral.

"We need to get inside and check for damage," Phaidros said. "If the truck hit it hard enough, it could've shifted or cracked the structure. The last thing we need is for Brunelleschi's Dome to come crashing down on the crowd."

"It will be full of police checking for bombs. Stay here. I'll check it myself." Alexis's magic sizzled as a glamour settled over him, rendering him invisible.

"Show-off." Phaidros huffed with an impressed grin. "Let's hope everyone is too busy to notice an extra shadow that shouldn't be there."

Alexis ducked under the police tape and hurried toward the wall of the cathedral the truck had crashed into. He rested his hands against the stonework, sending his magic through it. It was a different kind of healing or mending magic. Alexis sought any weaknesses in the cathedral's structure. He'd be damned if he lost the Duomo the same year as the Notre Dame fire.

Small cracks sealed, and the building stabilized from the thousand small mendings. Six months ago, holding a glamour and doing such work would have drained his magic dry. With the high tide, the exertion was equivalent to that of Alexis making a cup of coffee.

Once he was satisfied that the building wasn't going to collapse, Alexis moved quickly back to where Phaidros was waiting. He gasped as Penelope pulled on the *moíra desmós* so hard his vision swam. He shed his glamour and stumbled into Phaidros, who steadied him.

"Something's wrong." Alexis fumbled for the phone in his pocket just as it began to ring. "Penelope, what is it?" he all but shouted over the noise around him.

"Florence is a distraction! They're going after Elazar!" Penelope was able to say before their reception scrambled.

"Go. We'll take care of Florence," Phaidros shouted.

Alexis shoved his way through the crowd, crashing through the lobby of the museum and into the public bathrooms. Finding them mercifully empty, Alexis focused on Ein Karem, his heart pounding. He plunged through the portal and had just enough sense to pull up a shield before landing in Elazar's burning lounge room.

"Elazar!" He moved into the kitchen. Fire licked up the walls and curled along the ceiling. Alexis tried to pull the oxygen from around the flames but felt nothing. This was no ordinary fire. *Thevetat's magic.* He didn't have time to hunt the grounds for priests. He needed to find his nephew before the house came down around them.

"Elazar! Can you hear me?" Alexis shouted, inhaling smoke as the fire ate through his shields. His armor heated enough to burn his skin underneath, and agony screamed through him. He shoved his pain aside and searched the rooms. Blood stained the carpet in Elazar's bedroom. Panic rushed through him. "Elazar!"

The paintings on the walls bubbled, and the books on the shelves were crinkling to ash. *The books.* Alexis went to the metal door to the underground library and found it glowing hot. The roof above him cracked and began to cave. Burning debris struck him in the shoulder. Alexis jumped through another portal into the genizah as it all came down, then brushed the burning coals caught in his clothes.

A pain-filled wheeze stopped him dead. "Uncle?" Elazar was propped up against a shelf, one hand clutching at his bleeding side, the other with a handgun trained on him.

"Elazar!" Alexis rushed to his side. "How badly are you hit?"

"It's just a graze, but it won't stop bleeding. Those bastards broke through the wards. I couldn't stop them. They did something… It was like the house was hit with a wave of darkness. It killed my phone, so I couldn't call for help."

Alexis hushed him. "Tell me later once we get out of here. I can't put the fire out. I tried. The house will be gone in minutes. I'm sorry, Elazar, but we need to go. There's nothing I can do."

"Don't be sorry. At least you're here." He looked around at his collection. "Upstairs wasn't where I kept the true treasures, but all of this? It can never be replaced."

Alexis helped Elazar to his feet, the burns on his shoulders screaming as he lifted the older man up. "It's high tide, so I'll see what I can do, nephew."

With one arm around Elazar, Alexis closed his eyes and let his magic roll out of him. Elazar gasped as the room filled with blue light and a wide portal opened up beneath them. Alexis held tight to Elazar as they fell through nothingness and then crashed into the upstairs library of the palazzo in Venice. Zo and Galenos were there in moments, and through a daze, Alexis said, "He's hurt. Help him first."

"Alexis!" Penelope rushed to him, her face pale and terrified. "Oh my God, you're burnt."

"Help me move him," Aelia said, and between them, they got Alexis to one of the couches.

Penelope looked like she would faint. Alexis couldn't focus on anything but her and the pain hammering through him.

"Get her out of here, Aelia. She doesn't need to witness this."

Penelope shook her head in protest. "I can help—"

"You can help by leaving right now, Penelope," Alexis snapped, and she reared back like he'd struck her. Penelope turned on her heel and bolted, the hurt in her eyes striking him like a blow. "Fuck."

"She'll be fine, Alexis. She's a lot better off than you are right now. She'll only get in the way."

He was barely conscious as Aelia sang a pain relief charm onto his burnt skin and then removed the breastplate he wore. "Elazar…"

"Zo has him. Don't worry, Alexis. You saved him…and all of his books by the looks of things." Aelia pulled a face of disapproval. "We really need to have a conversation about your priorities, Defender."

Alexis bit down a cry as she removed scraps of his shirt from the wounds. "Your bedside manner is terrible, Princess."

HE DIDN'T know he'd fainted, but Alexis came to hours later. Aelia sat hollow-eyed in a chair opposite him. His chest and shoulders were wrapped in bandages that smelled like they'd been soaked in lavender and honey.

"How are you feeling?" Aelia asked.

"Like I've had a burning house dropped on me." He attempted a smile and looked around with bleary eyes. Elazar's library was crammed in piles around them. "How is Elazar?"

"He had a bullet graze along his right ribs and is covered in bruises, but Zo got the smoke out of his lungs. He'll be okay with plenty of rest. I think Zo is more upset about it than he's letting on." She lifted the edge of the bandages across Alexis's chest. "You're almost done. I healed them, but the new skin is going to be sensitive and a little red for a day or so. I don't have your and Nereus's healing abilities."

"You've done more than enough. Thank you, Aelia." He shifted his arms experimentally. "Do you know where Penelope is?"

Aelia pushed her hair from her face. "I tried to find her, but she wasn't in the usual places. She's still in the palazzo somewhere; I'm sure of it."

"She's in Nereus's rooms." The warding would keep the other magicians from finding her. He tried to feel her out through the *moíra desmós*, but she'd closed him off.

"You should rest before you have wild makeup sex."

Alexis sat up slowly. "Have you heard from Lyca and Phaidros?"

"The situation in Florence has settled, as much as it can. Everyone is scared and in shock. Phaidros went back to his palazzo in Santa Croce. Everything still seems to be in one piece. His housekeepers are fine and well. Small mercies." She twisted her phone about in her hands.

"He's going to be fine, Aelia. Phaidros is more than capable of fending off priests when he needs to."

"Not if they firebomb his house with him inside of it. Elazar said that your magic couldn't put the fire out, and you know what that means—"

"It means that Thevetat is sharing power, or Abaddon was in Israel. It would take a powerful priest to get through the warding, for a start. Don't worry about Phaidros. He'll be home soon."

Aelia bit her lip. "Alexis, I love him."

Alexis softened, surprised that she'd finally said it aloud. "I know. That doesn't mean he won't be able to handle himself if they are attacked by priests. You need to have faith in his abilities."

Alexis pulled at the soaked bandages across his chest. "Help me get rid of these. I need to find Penelope and apologize to her." He didn't want to get stuck talking about Aelia's emotions, which were tricky to navigate at the best of times. Alexis was feeling guiltier every second he was awake and not talking to Penelope. She'd been afraid for him, and he'd made it worse.

"Sending Penelope away was the right thing to do. She'd have gotten in my way, and seeing you that wounded would have traumatized her. She hasn't seen this kind of life before, Alexis. I worry she won't be able to take it by the time we've seen this through."

"She's stronger than you give her credit for. I was a horror of blood and charred skin. If our positions were reversed, I wouldn't have been half as calm as she was."

Aelia helped him remove the bandages and carefully inspected the new skin, not letting him leave until she was satisfied that he'd healed enough. "Go and find her." With a wrinkle of her nose, she added, "Maybe find a bath first."

Alexis bowed to her, placing a kiss on her hand. "My thanks, Princess."

"Yes, yes, I'm a wonder and a miracle. Now get out of here, and don't trip on any of Elazar's books on the way out."

ALEXIS RESISTED the urge to portal into Nereus's rooms. The last time he tried, he'd been stuck in the warding like a fly in a web, and if it weren't for Penelope pulling him through, he was sure he'd still be there. The palazzo was determined to take him the long way round, even though the rooms were firmly in his mind.

"I can't make it right with Penelope if you don't let me near her," Alexis said after he was led through the main foyer for the third time in twenty minutes. The next door he went through dumped him into a subterranean stone tunnel, the walls slick with wet algae and smelling like an estuary.

"I'm almost too afraid to ask where this is," Alexis muttered.

The tunnel ended and he found himself standing in front of two very familiar double doors. As a young apprentice, he'd stood outside of them many times while waiting for either a lesson or a chastisement. There was even the overly friendly brass doorknob that tasted his magic before allowing him to pass. Whatever permissions Penelope gave the last time he'd visited must have still held true, because the rooms let him enter without having to fight through the warding.

In the sitting room, he found an unfinished glass of wine and a pile of open books around Penelope's journal. Some books he knew were from Atlantis without touching them. They'd sat on shelves behind Nereus's desk at the citadel. He remembered staring at their spines, tuning out as she lectured him about using too much magic too quickly, going too deep into the citadel library, stirring up the chimera, racing horses with Phaidros through the gardens. The astrolabe sat on one of the titles, and for a gut-wrenching second, he wondered if she'd gone back inside of it. He picked it up tentatively.

"Penelope?" he whispered to it. After a moment, he heard a splash of water from the other rooms and put the astrolabe back down again.

The bedroom layout had changed since he was last there, the palazzo making personal touches to accommodate the new Archivist. The bed was still a carved wooden four-poster, but the sheets had changed from yellow and red to sea green and purple, and he noted with some amusement that there was now a phone charger on the bedside table. Penelope would drag even the palazzo into this century, whether it liked it or not.

Alexis tapped on the bathroom door before edging it open. The room was still covered in tiny indigo tiles, but now the ceiling was painted with golden astrological symbols, and there was a shower with a brass head and a sunken bath big enough for five people. Penelope was submerged, sitting on the stone seat, steaming aqua water to her shoulders. Her hazel eyes looked red, and her gaze flicked over his bare chest and shoulders.

"I'm sorry," he said, knowing that he couldn't ease his way into conversation. "You were scared for me, and I yelled at you. I'm a bastard. You didn't deserve it, no matter how much pain I was in."

"You seem to be healing quickly."

"Aelia's magic. She's getting better at it."

"Still sore?"

"Not really. It feels more like a sunburn now." Alexis touched the pink skin on his shoulders.

Penelope rested her chin in her hand. "So what you're saying is, you have no reason not to get in here with me."

"Only if you're inviting me."

"Hurry up, or I'll change my mind and stay pissed off at you."

Alexis didn't need to be told twice. He kicked off his boots and pants and climbed into the hot water. He stayed on the other side of the pool, allowing her space. "Gods, this stings and feels so good at the same time," he said to break the silence.

"Are you going to tell me what happened?"

And so Alexis told her everything, from Gisela's warning that the police would be investigating Penelope again, to the Duomo and the cold fear of not being able to find Elazar.

"I haven't felt that kind of terror in a while. Zo is going to be beside himself."

Penelope held out her hand to him, and he moved across the bath, taking her in his arms. She twisted her fingers in the damp ends of his hair. "They killed all those people in Florence as a *distraction*. Fucking bastards. We need to keep Elazar here until they are stopped."

"Agreed, though Zo is unlikely to let Elazar out of his sight for a while. He loves him dearly, and he hates being reminded of Elazar's mortality." Alexis rested his forehead against Penelope's. "I'm so sorry about before. I was out of line."

"Alexis, your skin had melted away. I've never seen anything so painful-looking in my life, and it scared the hell out of me. You were right to send me away. I would've been panicking the whole time.

It's taken me four hours to calm down enough to realize that, so let's not talk about it anymore. You're here, and you're safe, and that's all I care about." She sniffed, and he kissed the tears that tracked down her cheek.

"I'm okay, Penelope. Remember, I'm going to get damaged occasionally, but I'm always going to recover."

"I think I prefer it when you're stuck in the Archives as my study partner," Penelope said miserably.

"I saw the books outside. Were they in the astrolabe?" Alexis hoped to move her mind away from the horror of his burnt body.

"Just a few that I grabbed, and most of them I don't understand because it's magical theory. I was reading about weather magic—at least that's the gist of it. There are at least another hundred books inside the astrolabe that I could use your help with." She gave him a smile and then a kiss that made the horrors of the day feel a bit farther away.

Alexis pulled her closer. "Anything for my Archivist."

TWENTY

PENELOPE WOKE WITH her lips pressed to Alexis's shoulder. He was sleeping deeply and didn't wake when she moved out of his arms and off the bed. She was tired from the emotional upheaval of the previous day, her shoulders aching from how tightly she'd held herself.

In the bathroom, Penelope washed her face and wrangled her curls into a braid. She'd dreamed of burning cities, magical spells in books, and corridors in a tower she'd never been in before.

The rooms around her had changed a little—the new bed had been a welcome surprise—but it still felt like she was in an ancient city every time she looked out at the sea and the city of Atlas. Her mind boggled at the combination of magic and memory it would've taken to create.

These rooms were starting to feel more and more like a haven, tucked away from the horror and noise of the world, which was why Penelope had to get dressed and go see how things stood in the rest of the palazzo.

In the walk-in wardrobe, she found a clean pair of khaki pants and a floaty black singlet that fit her and then shut Alexis in the bedroom. He needed to heal and restore his magic, and this was the only place none of the other magicians could get to. She would have nightmares about his burnt shoulders and chest for as long as she lived.

After Alexis ordered her away, Penelope barely made it to Nereus's rooms before she vomited up the contents of her stomach from the visceral horror of his injuries, the sight of Elazar bleeding, and the gruesome images from Florence, all of the innocent people mowed down in the streets. She'd climbed into the bath, the water instantly calming her and the strange magic that had awoken inside of her. She never would've dreamed that being in water would comfort her, but it did, pulling her to a place where she could think clearly again.

The attack on Elazar made her worry for her parents and Carolyn, not to mention Constantine, and she contemplated how to contact Kreios to make sure he warned her if Thevetat decided to go after them.

Eat something and then figure out the next steps. Her appetite was usually the first thing to go when her anxiety ramped up, so she would have to force herself to eat, even if her stomach protested every second of it, and she also needed to get Aelia to do some yoga with her to calm down. Most pressing of all, she needed to figure out which books in the astrolabe were going to be most useful to them. By the time Penelope had reached the kitchen, her to-do list was so long she wanted to cry.

After turning on the hot water kettle, she opened the fridge doors to hunt for something to eat.

"I was about to make some eggs for Elazar if you want some," Zo said behind her.

"You know I'm never going to say no to your cooking." Zo looked haggard and sleep-deprived. She wrapped her arms around him. "Are you okay?"

"No. I want to rip Thevetat's priests apart with my bare hands. H-He's an old man now. What threat could he have been to them? The fucking cowards." If Zo hoped to hide the tremor in his voice, he was unsuccessful.

"Hey, he's okay. Alexis got him out, and he's safe here with us." With that, she let him get on with cooking—the one thing that always seemed to comfort him.

"I can't believe Elazar was bleeding to death, and yet he made Alexis bring those damn books with them." Zo beat a bowl of eggs with ferocity.

Penelope cradled her hot coffee. "I can't believe Alexis had the magic to bring all of it with them. It must've been so draining."

"That's nothing. You need to ask him about the time he moved the whole Spartan army during the Peloponnesian War. I don't think even Alexis knows the limit of his magic on a high tide."

"Maybe it's a good thing if we're going to have to get past all of Thevetat's priests on Milos." Penelope fiddled with the orichalcum bracelet on her wrist, thinking of Poseidon's wry smile. *You must be quite a capable eight…*

"Zo? Do you think I should warn my parents and Carolyn that Thevetat might send people after them? I don't know what to tell them just yet, but I'm sure I could make something up. I'm worried about them."

"Don't be. Alexis has had private security watching over them since Israel. Elazar, however, objected to anyone watching over him, and we thought the warding on the property would be strong enough to keep everyone out. We didn't predict Thevetat himself would turn up in a vessel to break through them." Zo tipped the scrambled eggs onto two plates and passed one to Penelope.

"Maybe Thevetat went after Elazar not only because he's your son, but because his knowledge could help us." If Elazar was going to be staying in Venice, she'd be asking for his help to search for Solomon's ring as soon as he was well.

"I don't care why they went after him, only that they did." Zo set up a tray of food and tea and headed for the door. "I won't lose my son to a fucking war the way I lost my wife."

Penelope took a bite of eggs, even though she didn't particularly want to. Alexis hadn't told her that he had people watching over her parents. *Probably because he didn't want you to worry about their safety any more than you already are.* Halfway through her breakfast, she pulled out her phone and found Constantine's number. She'd programmed it in after their trip to Badija, and even though Alexis probably wouldn't agree to it, she gave him a call.

"Doctor Bryne, what a pleasant surprise." He didn't actually sound surprised at all. "Seen that bad side of Alexis, have you?"

"I didn't call to talk about Alexis. I'm calling because I—I think you should come to Venice, for your own safety." She was trying not to think about what effect his presence would have on the palazzo, which was why she wasn't asking anyone before inviting him.

Constantine laughed a deeply rich sound that made Penelope's lips twitch. "What makes you think I'd be safe sleeping under the same roof as Aelia and Phaidros? Have they agreed to this visit?"

"I don't need their approval to extend an invitation to one of my friends."

"Is that what we are? Friends? Does Alexis know you've called me?"

"I don't need his permission either." Penelope tried to keep her temper in check.

There was a long silence, then Constantine asked, "What's happened to spark this concern for my well-being?"

"The attack on Florence was Thevetat's doing."

"I'm nowhere near Florence."

"They used the attack to distract us while they went after Elazar."

"Dear God." Constantine's tone had gone from amusement to despair in seconds. "Please tell me he's—he's not—"

"Elazar is wounded but not fatally. They burned his house down with him inside, but Alexis got there in time to rescue Elazar and his books."

"Is Zo okay?"

Penelope put her fork down, thinking of Zo's furious cooking. "He's devastated. Angry in a way I've never seen before—"

"I'll come. Zo needs to talk it out with someone who knows what it feels like to be a father. Alexis and Phaidros lack the experience to understand what he's going through. I'll settle things here and leave in a day or so. Those fuckers went after that sweet boy to pick a fight? Fine. We'll give them one." Constantine hung up before Penelope had a chance to respond.

Penelope finished her eggs, wondering if she did the right thing and what would be unleashed when Constantine arrived. Her phone pinged, and she read through a message from Marco. He was checking in on her and the others. It seemed he and his family were enjoying his unexpected holiday. It was good to hear but also a reminder of her own predicament. It was only a matter of time before the police dragged her in for questioning about the Florence bombings.

"One day at a time, Penelope," she whispered and hoped Gisela Bianchi could hold them off as long as possible.

IN THE library, Elazar's books had been left where they'd fallen. Penelope considered how horrified Elazar would be to see them that way and began to sort them into piles and take them down the elevator to the Archives.

"If you could make a spare shelf to store them, I'd really appreciate it," Penelope whispered to the Archives. She still didn't exactly know how the magic of the Archives worked; she simply asked and hoped for the best. On the third trip down, the Archives shuddered. Penelope carried an armload of manuscripts through the stacks. Instead of a few new shelves, she found a completely new room, filled with shelves, desks, and lamps. The books she'd already carried down were now arranged in a way that made sense to the Archives, if no one else.

"Thank you. I'm sure Elazar will be very happy to have his books stored here." Penelope brushed her hands against the olive shelves. She carried on, and each time she returned with more books, the previous ones had placed themselves neatly away.

As Penelope worked, her mind pulled at the Gordian knot that was the past few weeks. They needed to find out who the priest was that the Teutonic Knight smuggled out of Acre. She needed Alexis's help to go through all the books in the astrolabe in order to find out how Nereus's experiments worked and how she'd managed to stop Poseidon from being raised from the dead.

If she hadn't seen Nereus bring the hit man who attacked her back from the dead for questioning, Penelope would have scoffed at anyone for suggesting such a resurrection was possible. There was a part of it that made Penelope's skin crawl on a visceral and ethical level. Nereus had known how to do necromancy and had sabotaged the process somehow without anyone else knowing. As always, Nereus had been the smartest person in the room, and the men around her hadn't known any better to question why the experiment had failed; though Abaddon had suspected enough to risk an attack on the Archives to get the information.

Once all the manuscripts, jars, and scrolls had been safely stored, Penelope took some photos of the organized shelves and went in search of Elazar. She'd never been to Zo's part of the palazzo. The magicians were protective of their space, and Penelope had gone out of her way to respect that. It was hard enough for all of them to live under the one roof—something that hadn't happened since they'd left Egypt—and as Alexis explained, magicians were as territorial as cats and would fight anyone with the least provocation. It made Penelope wonder how the Citadel of Magicians had operated.

The palazzo didn't seem to have a problem showing Penelope to a set of dark gray doors with maroon trim. She knocked tentatively, feeling like a ten year old waiting to see if her friend could come out and play.

Zo opened the door. "Penelope? What are you doing here?"

"I wanted to see if Elazar is awake. I thought he might like a visitor."

Zo looked like he was about to say no when Elazar's strong voice called, "For the Almighty's sake, let her in, Abba."

Zo gave her a stern look. "Try not to work him up. He's meant to be resting."

"You look like you need a rest too." She felt Zo's wards release and grant her entrance. "I'll stay with him if you'd like some sleep."

Zo's rooms had a neat kind of chaos about them and were filled with lifetimes' of mementos. Art hung from the walls, stuffed bookshelves lined the rooms, and wherever there was space, small scraps of paper with poetry written on them were tacked into place. Elazar was propped up on a high-backed day lounge, a small table beside him with steaming tea and books atop it.

"You're going to have to forgive my father. He's acting like an overprotective lioness," he said as Penelope bent down to kiss his cheek. "He's already healed all my wounds, but still he won't let me move."

"You're my son. I have a right to be upset," Zo snapped.

"Go and sleep, Abba. I want to talk to Penelope. I'm not going anywhere." Zo mumbled something but headed for his bedroom. "*Ani ohev otcha,*" Elazar called as the door closed. "I swear, Penelope, he's driving me insane already."

"He was frightened he'd lost you, Elazar. Surely you can understand that."

Elazar patted his shoulders and chest. "But I am here, and I'm well. He can stop being so upset now. I'm far too old to have my father hovering around every second to make sure I'm still breathing."

"You know what these moody magicians are like better than anyone." Penelope took a seat opposite him. "Stay in bed for the day, and let Zo sleep. I'm sure he'll ease up tomorrow." She didn't want to point out that it was precisely because he was an old man that Zo was so panicked. Being mortal and having a mortal son would be hard enough. Penelope couldn't imagine what Zo was going through.

"Let's hope so. I'll go mad if he tries to make me sit still for days." He settled back amongst his pillows. "It is nice to be back in Venice. It's been too long."

Penelope pulled her phone out and passed it to him. "Here, I wanted to show you that your books aren't scattered all over the floor anymore."

"Would you look at that? The Archives has made space for them. Do I have you to thank for this?"

"I helped. You know me—I can't handle improperly stored books either."

"Thank you, Archivist. As much as it pains me, my house can be rebuilt, the books replaced, but these were the treasures, the irreplaceable things." He passed Penelope's phone back to her. "Where is Alexis? He's the one who saved them when he didn't have to. I've never seen him use magic like that. It was an inspiring sight. I've spent my entire life around these Atlanteans, and I've never gotten used to the wonders. I suspect you will be the same way."

"Oh, you know, if I don't smother them all in their sleep before then." Penelope smirked. "I don't know how Nereus did it. I now understand why she made a haven for herself that's impossible to enter without permission."

At the questioning look in his eye, Penelope updated Elazar on inheriting Nereus's rooms, the astrolabe library, tracking down Constantine, and Kreios's visit.

"I'm exhausted just listening to all of this. Constantine is a remarkable man. It doesn't surprise me that he'd have a storehouse of relics hidden away. By now, you should realize that immortals are pack rats who hoard their treasures like demented old dragons." Elazar laughed.

"I could really use your help finding Solomon's ring. Zo isn't going to let you return to Israel until this mess with Thevetat is over, and I need all the help I can get. I'm split between finding the ring and trying to undo the magic Thevetat is going to use to fuse himself with his new body. I'm not too proud to admit I need help." Penelope ran a frustrated hand down her face. "That's not even mentioning this magic inside of me that I have no idea what to do with."

"These things have a way of becoming clear in time. If you find the ring, you might not need a way to sabotage the magic as Nereus did."

"I can't rely on the ring actually working for me. Constantine confirmed that it *does* work, but he never performed an exorcism with it. If he, an absolute believer, couldn't get it to work for him, I can't expect it to work for someone like me."

"The prophecy said that it would, so I suppose you'll just have to have faith—in yourself more than anything else. Find the way to unravel the magic. It's always better to be overprepared than underprepared when going into battle." Elazar took her hand and gave it an encouraging squeeze. "I'll help you in any way that I can, Penelope. We're family now, and I'm eager to get back at the bastards who burned my house down."

Penelope looked over her shoulder to make sure Zo's door was still closed. "We'll start tomorrow."

THE SUN was setting when Penelope put together a plate of croissants, fruit, and coffee and went back to the citadel rooms in search of Alexis. She couldn't think of them as *her* rooms—though she was becoming more inclined to stay there for the lack of disruptions—and they had changed too much to be called Nereus's rooms anymore, so she'd started referring to them as the citadel rooms.

Alexis was awake and wrapped in a purple robe with golden Byzantine embroidery. He was studying the books she'd been puzzling over, and he'd taken over her journal, writing down notes like he couldn't help himself.

Penelope placed the tray on the table. "I thought you'd still be asleep." She kissed the back of his exposed neck.

"I was coming to see you, and then a diagram caught my eye. I thought I'd see what it meant and became a little stuck," Alexis said. He looked at his watch and cursed. "That was two hours ago. I'll get you a new journal."

Penelope smiled at him—her crazy, book-obsessed magician. She passed him a croissant. "Here, eat this and tell me what you've been reading. I couldn't make sense of it, even with the Living Language to translate."

"This is how the citadel's magic was contained within the walls and prevented from leaking out into the rest of the city. I'll admit, I never gave it much thought as an apprentice, but it really is ingenious what Poseidon came up with. Nereus figured it out. It seems like much of this book is focused on how Poseidon did things."

Alexis flicked through the pages, showing Penelope the complex wardings. Once again, most of it sailed over her head, but she didn't interrupt because Alexis nerding-out over magic never failed to cheer her up. After ten thousand years, he still loved magic with a wild, child-like innocence.

"You said there are more of these books, didn't you?" he asked, eyes bright.

Penelope spun the astrolabe on the tabletop. "Enough to keep you excited for the next hundred years. You need to stay focused. We need to figure out the details of her resurrection experiments, remember?"

"Yes, of course. I can't help but be excited. Nereus kept all of these to herself and probably wouldn't have guessed her old experiments would be of interest to anyone. It's like I'm a student all over again—a heady thought for someone as old as I am." Alexis smiled.

Penelope kissed him soundly. "Okay, magician. Let's go through this pile first, then I'll show you the rest."

TWENTY-ONE

ZO MANAGED TO keep Elazar bedbound for a whole day before Penelope found him out in the center courtyard drinking coffee with Alexis.

"I see you've sprung the prisoner," Penelope said as she joined them.

Alexis's eyes glinted with amusement. "I sent Zo to the markets to distract him for a few hours."

"Thank you for your intervention, Uncle. I don't know what he healed, but I haven't felt this good in years." Elazar breathed in the salty summer air. "It's good to be back. As much as Israel has my soul, there's nothing quite like Venice."

"We'll have to go on some walks together. There's still so much I haven't seen." Penelope reached for Alexis's coffee, and he relinquished what was left to her.

Elazar rubbed his hands together. "An excellent plan. First, I'd like to see my books."

"Of course, and I'll have to show how far we've gotten in deciphering Tim's visions."

Alexis chuckled. "Be careful, Elazar. She'll recruit you into the hunt before you know it, and you won't get to see any of Venice at all."

Penelope whacked him on the arm. "Hey! You're meant to be on my side. I've lost you to Nereus's Atlantis books, so I need a new study buddy."

"There will be plenty of time for me to do both. Searching for a mystical Near Eastern relic like King Solomon's ring would be hard for any scholar to pass up. Especially when the search is being led by a beautiful woman." Elazar winked in Penelope's direction.

"Be careful of his charm, Penelope. He learned all his best tricks from me."

Penelope rolled her eyes. "I'll have to keep that in mind when we're discussing wandering priests—the sexiest topic I know." She was less concerned with charming men and more concerned with running out of Tim's clues before they reached the last hundred years. That morning, she'd been alarmed with how many parts of his manuscript were left unhighlighted.

"Have you heard from Phaidros and Lyca?" asked Elazar.

"They're on their way home. Lyca found the apartment where the bombs were made, but it had been abandoned, much to her disappointment. Gisela texted me this morning to say they hadn't found any more bombs, so let's hope that Kreios will back off for the time being." Alexis frowned. "Despite his warning about the attack on Elazar, we can't see him as anything but a threat."

They all knew Kreios wouldn't stop, especially with Thevetat controlling his movements, but Penelope breathed a sigh of relief to know that Florence was safe for the moment. She twisted the silver-and-lapis lazuli ring on her finger, wondering if she'd be able to connect with Kreios again. Maybe she could get some insight into where they were going next.

Alexis's long fingers closed over hers. "Don't even think about it, *cara*. If he's as much of an ally as he claims, he'll find a way to get a message to you."

"Alexis is right. Don't borrow trouble, Pen. You have enough worries." Elazar drained his coffee and got to his feet. "Now, let's go and see my books."

"**THIS VIEW** never gets old, no matter how many times I see it," Elazar said as they gazed out of the glass elevator at the Archives beneath them.

"As much as I hate the circumstances, I'm glad you're here, Elazar. These magicians are so jaded when it comes to the wonder around them," said Penelope.

"They've lived very long lives of incredible wonder and loss. It takes something truly unique to get them excited. Like Alexis and the intensity of his love for you. The poor old bastard never saw it coming. You've woken him up, and it pleases me greatly." Elazar patted her shoulder. "You're going to be good for all of them."

"I'll try my best, though I think they'll get sick of my enthusiasm sooner or later." Penelope laughed. She led him through the twisting paths between the stacks to where the Archives had constructed the new office.

"Ah, my babies," Elazar crooned. He ran his fingers over the spines and checked for damage.

"They're all here, although I can't tell you how the Archives chose to arrange them."

"That doesn't matter. I'll move them about to how I had them at home."

Penelope bit down a laugh. The Archives had its own ideas about arranging books, and she'd given up trying to move the ones in her office. It took Elazar half an hour before he was satisfied that all his treasures were stored correctly. He looped his arm around Penelope's, and she took him to her office.

"Dear Lord, you've been busy." Elazar stared at the windows covered in their makeshift timeline of quotes, historical figures, sticky notes, and maps.

Penelope grinned. "Sit down and get comfortable. I'll run you through it."

BY THE time Penelope got around to explaining the fall of Acre and the escaping priest, she and Elazar were back upstairs, making spritz in the kitchen.

Elazar tipped the slices of orange he'd been cutting into a pitcher of ice. "You've done exceedingly well to get so far so quickly."

"There are benefits to living with immortals. They've all been involved in courts and wars over the years, and Alexis has investigated anything even remotely magic-related."

The kitchen door burst open, making them both jump.

"What's going on here?" Zo demanded, his arms laden with shopping bags. Penelope flinched at the anger in his gaze.

"Penelope and I were discussing her hunt for the ring, Abba."

Zo dumped his bags on the counter. "I need to speak with you a moment," he said, taking Penelope by the arm and dragging her out of the kitchen.

"Hey! Let go," Penelope snapped and shoved him off.

"What do you think you're doing? Elazar is meant to be in bed. He was shot and nearly burned alive two days ago, remember?"

"Zo, you healed him. He's fine."

"He's an old man! Even with the healing magic, his body will take time to recover. You've lured him out to help you without thinking how it will hurt him."

Penelope had never seen Zo so angry and distraught, so she bit her tongue to keep from lashing out at him. "I didn't *lure* him anywhere. Elazar wanted to see his books, and we got to talking. He says he feels fine, and you treating him like a little kid won't help the situation."

"Don't you dare tell me how to look after my son."

Penelope was about to lose her temper when the blue front door opened with an excited flourish and an unmistakeable bulk filled it.

"Con?" Zo's face turned from anger to shock in seconds. "What are you doing here?"

Constantine dropped his bags onto the speckled marble floor and dragged Zo into a bear hug. "I came as soon as I heard what happened. It's going to be okay, Zotikos."

Zo seemed to struggle against the embrace for a moment before bursting into tears, and sobbing into Constantine's chest. "They almost killed my baby."

"I know. Don't worry. We'll get justice for what they did to him." Constantine looked over Zo's shoulder at Penelope. "I've got this, Doctor Bryne." He dismissed her with a small wave, and Penelope backed away, relieved to no longer be the target of Zo's anger anymore.

"God, I need a drink." She made for the kitchen, hoping Elazar had poured her a big enough cocktail.

"Please don't take his anger to heart, Penelope," Elazar said as she sat down at the bench.

"What's all the noise about?" Aelia came into the kitchen through the back door. "Oh spritz! Good idea." She kissed Elazar and helped herself to a glass.

"Constantine is here," Penelope said, bracing herself for the onslaught of abuse.

Aelia lowered her glass. "I can't say I'm surprised. With Thevetat coming after the things we love, it makes sense that Alexis would summon him. I should probably text Phaidros and warn him."

"You're not mad? I thought after Badija…"

"I was upset, and I'm not anymore. Con was right about a lot of things—not that I'll ever admit that. You can assure Alexis that I won't try to murder Con in his sleep."

Penelope bit her lip. "Alexis didn't ask him to come here. I did. Actually, he made the decision for himself when I told him about the attack on Elazar. He was worried about Zo."

Aelia and Elazar shared devilish smiles, and Aelia looped an arm around Penelope's shoulders. "I'm sure the Defender won't stay mad at you for long. It's good to see you aren't waiting for his permission like an obedient little woman."

"What about me has ever given you the impression that I'm obedient?"

Aelia's phone beeped, and she took it out of her shorts. Roses bloomed in her golden cheeks as she typed back. "Phaidros and Lyca have arrived at the train station. They'll be here soon," she told them.

"You seem pretty pleased by that, Aunty. Something you're not telling me?"

"It's better that we are all together under one roof so we can protect each other, my little bird."

It was clear neither Penelope nor Elazar believed her. Alexis's voice joined Constantine's in the next room, and Penelope steeled herself for hot tempers. Instead, when Alexis came into the kitchen, he bent down and kissed her.

"Thank you for convincing him to come," he said, stroking her cheek with his thumb.

"I don't know how much convincing I had to do." Penelope looked up at him, her mouth dry. He smelled of sandalwood and cinnamon and burning power, and there was a glimmer on his skin that told Penelope he'd been doing magic. Whenever he looked like that, she struggled to keep a straight thought in her head.

"I've warned Phaidros," Aelia said.

"Constantine has offered to stay in a hotel if it's going to be a problem."

Aelia shook her head. "It won't be." She moved out the door with a small skip in her step.

"Something's going on. That response was too optimistic." Alexis frowned.

"Aunty is a woman of many secrets. It's good for all of us if she's happy," Elazar said, then followed after her.

Penelope eyed Alexis. "What have you been up to this afternoon? You're...shimmering."

Alexis smiled as he reached for the half-empty pitcher. "I've finished Nereus's funeral stele."

TWENTY-TWO

Penelope watched as the sun went down across the Grand Canal. Aelia interrupted the peaceful moment by pushing another bottle of wine into her hands. She had another three in her own, and Lyca was coming up behind her with even more.

"Do you think we have enough wine?"

"It's going to have to last us a whole night, Penelope. It's bad luck to pause the lamenting to go get more," Aelia told her.

With Alexis's pronouncement about the finished stele, the palazzo had become a flurry of activity. Zo got himself together and had since been criticizing Alexis for dropping funeral food preparation on his hands. All worry and anger over Elazar's attack seemed to have been pushed down in the face of Constantine's arrival and the amount of cooking he needed to do. Penelope had a strong suspicion that Alexis knew his news would be the very thing to shove Zo toward recovery.

When everyone else went to greet Phaidros and Lyca, Zo had taken Penelope's hand and kept her in the kitchen. "I'm sorry. I shouldn't have ever spoken to you like that or grabbed you in anger. This whole business has driven me mad."

Penelope had wrapped her arms around his waist, pulling him into a hug. "I know, Zo. It's okay. We're okay."

Zo kissed her forehead. "We are. Well, for the moment at least. You, on the other hand, are about to be introduced to Atlantean funeral rites."

"Should I be worried?"

"Yes. Lyca and Aelia are going to keep you up all night drinking and singing and other mysterious rituals unknown to us menfolk."

"In my day, women used to rend their clothing in grief," Constantine had said. He'd managed to sneak in behind her wearing a hopeful grin.

"Yes, but in your day, women also used to curtsey whenever you entered a room, and that's not about to happen either." She'd yelped in surprise when Constantine hugged her from behind, Zo and all, and squeezed.

"Oh, Doctor Bryne, I do enjoy that sharp tongue of yours. I can see why you love her so much, Zo."

"And I love to breathe," squeaked Penelope, though she was woman enough to admit that being sandwiched between two very handsome, brawny men wasn't the worst experience she'd ever had.

"If you guys are going to have a threesome without inviting me, I'll be so offended," said Phaidros.

Penelope reached out to him. "Help!"

"All right, off the Archivist so a real man can hug her." Phaidros shooed at them. "Back off, you miscreants."

Penelope let out an exaggerated sigh as Zo and Constantine dropped her and Phaidros caught her up.

"Nice to see you causing as much mischief as you can in my absence. Calling Constantine was particularly cheeky."

"She missed me. Poor girl is only human." Constantine winked.

Penelope rolled her eyes. "He wishes."

"Well, I hope you slept well last night, Pen," said Phaidros, giving her back an encouraging slap. "Because you're about to be more shit-faced than you've ever been in your life."

Phaidros's ominous words came back to her as she eyed the bottles they carried through the gardens. Alexis had told them he placed the stele in Nereus's favorite spot. This instruction must have made sense to Lyca and Aelia, leaving Penelope to follow them deeper into the gardens than she'd ever been before.

Like the rest of the palazzo, the gardens and grounds seemed to change with the season and the palazzo's whim. So little of it was seen from the Grand Canal side that Penelope had no way of judging where its solid perimeter lay.

"Should we be getting drunk so soon after an attack? What if something happens?" She couldn't help thinking that a night off to drink, even in memory of a friend, was an extravagance and a risk they shouldn't take.

"Nereus's shade has waited long enough to be honored," Lyca said sharply. "If we stop respecting our dead, drinking, making love, celebrating life, then Thevetat and his horrid followers have already defeated us."

"What Lyca means is, think of tonight as lifting the middle finger in Thevetat's direction," Aelia said. "Besides, the men aren't allowed to get drunk, so if another attack happens, they'll be able to go and save the day without us."

"Oh, please. It would hardly be the first time I've gone into battle drunk." Lyca snorted. "'Leave the men to save us!' Ten thousand years, and I've still not managed to break you from thinking that bullshit."

Aelia stuck her tongue out at Lyca's back. "We'll be fine, Pen. Lyca knows what I mean, and she's also full of shit. She barely talked to me for the first four thousand years."

"It took that long for you to become interesting. Ah, there is the stele. Well done, Defender." Lyca stopped walking and pointed.

In a small grove of blooming orange trees was a marble stele that stood three meters tall. Sitting on the ledge of the marble base was a goblet, flowers, a bowl, and a glass, pyramid-shaped incense burner. Penelope almost dropped the wine she was holding when Lyca stepped out of her line of sight and she saw the details of the carving. Nereus was depicted sitting on a bench and passing a handful of flames to Penelope.

"But…that's me! Why am I on her stele?"

Aelia and Lyca both looked at her like she was an idiot.

"You're her heir. She is passing the flame of her knowledge, magic, and authority onto you," Aelia explained. "Usually, funeral steles show the dead with their relatives, but magicians are always with their apprentices."

Penelope stared at her face depicted in stone. The expression of calm as she accepted the flame was something she'd never felt in life. There were other objects carved around Nereus: an open astrolabe, books, a globe, a small statue of Poseidon, candles, and a pair of curved daggers that must've been her weapon of choice.

"It looks so real, like she's going to stand up from her stone seat and ask me for some wine." Penelope's fingers itched to touch the stone.

"Alexis has always done excellent work." Lyca popped the cork on a bottle of wine and filled the goblet that sat on the altar. "There you go, you grumpy old bitch." Lyca took a swing from the bottle and passed it to Penelope.

"It's bad luck to speak ill of the dead."

"It's worse luck to lie. Nereus *was* a grumpy old bitch, but that doesn't mean I didn't love her all the same."

"I can't really blame her after living with you magicians for ten thousand years." Penelope took a big mouthful of the wine. There was no label on the bottle, and it left a weird taste in her mouth. There were familiar flavors—dark grapes and honey—but also the bitter aftertaste of salt and ashes.

Aelia seemed to read Penelope's expression. "Funeral wine. Zo made it for the occasion." She filled the bowl on the altar with grain, then arranged fruit and shells on top of it. She passed Penelope a box of matches and pointed to the incense.

Penelope drew out a match and hesitated. "The last time I lit magical incense, I ended up falling out of time and having a chat with Poseidon."

Lyca and Aelia both were nonplussed.

"If you see Nereus, tell her she left behind a damn mess." Aelia took the bottle of wine from Penelope and pointed to the burner. "Go on. It's not going to light itself."

Taking a deep breath, Penelope lit the match and held it to the incense. It was almost disappointing when nothing happened. "Well, that was anticlimactic," she said as it began to smoke.

"I could've told you Alexis made this batch of incense," Lyca said. "He wouldn't have trusted any of the stuff Nereus left behind."

Out of the bags they'd brought along came a blanket and pillows for them to sit on. It wasn't until Aelia started pulling out hummus, olives, freshly baked flatbread, honey figs, pomegranates, and more that Penelope realized one of them must have enchanted the bag somehow. No way could it have held so much otherwise.

"Why aren't the guys allowed to be involved in this?" she asked.

"Because men only get in the way. Women are the gatekeepers of life and death; we're there when you are born, and we are the only ones strong enough to be there at death. Dying can often be a messy, heartbreaking business, and most men don't have the strength to guide people compassionately to the next life." Lyca lay down on the pillows, stretched out on her side, and opened another bottle of wine. "Aelia will sing the lament at dusk and the life at dawn, and hopefully, Nereus will be at rest and not haunt the palazzo. She deserves to move on and find her love."

"Does everyone have a bottle of wine?" Aelia asked, and Penelope sat down next to Lyca on the big blanket. Once they were settled and the sun began to dip down into the lagoon, Aelia started to sing. Penelope, who was determined to pace herself, found that within thirty seconds of the song, every heartache she'd ever had bubbled to the surface. She didn't worry about getting too drunk after that.

The strange funeral wine was becoming better with every mouthful, especially as the hidden traumas of her life rose up and assaulted her: the barbed comments from her father, the way her mother never defended her, how other academics had treated her when she told them she was going to find Atlantis. She relived the crushing fear of drowning and the panic attacks that had crippled her. The few men she'd allowed space in her life had all gone once they saw the real her, all of them growing frustrated and intimidated by her and her ambition.

Penelope wanted Aelia to stop, but she kept singing. In the song, she heard Thevetat's taunts and Abaddon's laughter, Tim's cries as the fear and madness ate away at who he was. Worst of all was Carolyn's accusation: *You knew they were coming for him!*

Penelope wasn't aware that Aelia had stopped singing—only that by the time she came out of the horrors inside her, the sun was down and torches had been lit around the orange grove. Her face was damp with tears, and the bottle in her hand was empty. She placed it on the growing pile of empty bottles and reached for another.

She sniffed. "You could have warned me."

"No point. It wouldn't have made it easier," said Lyca. She pointed to where Aelia sat. Her eyes were glazed as her tears continued to fall. "It's hardest for her. The song and the magic take a big toll. You've only got thirty years of pain to deal with—you're blessed."

"You seem to be holding up well despite your age."

"I don't love easily or as hard as Aelia. Great love, great grief. All of my pain at the moment is caught up in losing Nereus, and that's why we are here tonight."

Minutes later, Aelia escaped her stupor. "Gods, I hate doing that." She wiped her face and nose on a handkerchief and spat next to a tree. "Damn grief magic in my mouth. I'll be tasting it for days. How did you go, Pen?"

"Fuck you."

Aelia laughed. "Eat something. You'll be fine. In a few days, when the hangover has worn off, you're going to feel more unburdened than you have in your life."

Penelope reached for a block of dark chocolate and stuffed a piece in her mouth. "I'll take your word for it, because right now, I want to push your perfect ass into a canal."

Still laughing, Aelia sat down next to her and kissed her cheek. "I'm glad you're sharing this moment with us. Nereus would've known who you were as soon as Alexis dragged you out of the canal, but she never let on. It makes me wonder about all the other secrets she kept."

"Like who was the favorite child?"

"Alexis," Lyca and Aelia said at the same time.

"Doesn't surprise me. He's my favorite too."

Lyca scowled. "You two are so disgustingly in love. It still bothers me to see the Defender so soft."

Aelia took two big mouthfuls of wine. "I slept with Phaidros."

Penelope choked on the chocolate she was chewing, and Lyca sat up. "What did you just say?"

"I. Slept. With. Phaidros."

Lyca's eyes widened. "I honestly don't know what to say."

Penelope went with: "Finally?" Aelia turned as red as their wine. "When did this happen?"

"A few nights ago, when I went out. It kind of just…happened."

Penelope doubted that. She'd been waiting for some kind of reaction after Badija, like fireballs and black eyes—not sex. "And how have things been between you since then?" Penelope gestured to Lyca for a fresh bottle of wine.

"Fine. Nice," Aelia replied shyly.

"And are you two together?"

"I don't know. It's weird. I don't know how to do this with him. He's not some random one-night stand. It meant something, but neither of us knows what." Aelia sighed and collapsed backward onto her pillows. "I don't know what to do."

"Fuck him again," said Lyca, and Penelope shoved her. "What? She should. It's been a long time coming. Why make it complicated? Or was the sex terrible?"

Lyca and Penelope looked at Aelia, eyebrows raised. She covered her burning face with her hands. "No, it was really good. It would be easier if it were bad."

"Then I don't see a problem." Lyca's eyes glittered. "I always thought he would be good in bed. I'm pleased he didn't disappoint you after so long."

Aelia groaned. "Shut up. I wish I hadn't told you."

Penelope gave Lyca a sly wink. "But you *did* tell us. That means we need details now."

"Oh, yeah? And are you going to spill all of Alexis's bedroom secrets?"

"We aren't talking about Alexis and me. You brought this up, so you've got no one to blame but yourself. When Phaidros didn't have a meltdown over Constantine being here, I knew he was in too good of a mood… It's all coming together."

"It's because there's no more competition. Now he can act like a human and not a lovesick puppy," said Lyca.

Aelia made a frustrated sound. "This is the worst timing for a relationship."

Penelope shrugged. "If I can get used to it, you can too. At least you're not dealing with new magic at the same time."

"New magic that'll grow with the tide." Lyca changed the subject, much to Aelia's apparent relief. "What are you doing to manage it?"

"Trying to manipulate water. I did it on Badija but haven't really tried it since. I don't know what I'm supposed to do with it all. The Living Language makes sense with my background and new position as Archivist. Doing water tricks in the ocean seems pretty useless."

"Are you kidding me?" Aelia sat up again. "You have no idea what Poseidon could do with those 'water tricks.' He controlled the seas, calmed storms, destroyed ships. You could use it to protect Venice or send a tidal wave to destroy Milos and Thevetat's base."

"If I were Poseidon, maybe. I can't do any of that."

"Yet," Lyca said. "You need to use it more. Practice in the canal entrance. No one will see you, and the palazzo will ensure you don't damage it. Take Alexis if you need to, though I doubt you do. Magic can only be guided, not taught. You need to find out how it works for you and what you want to do with it."

"I'll try. I've been so caught up in hunting the ring and Nereus's books that I haven't given it much thought."

"You'd better start," Aelia said. "Delegate, Penelope. Elazar and Constantine can help with the ring. Alexis can look through Nereus's books and free you up to study magic. It won't go away, no matter how much you ignore it."

"Okay, okay. I will. Now let's talk about something else. You're killing my buzz."

They changed the subject, but the thought of being able to control a tidal wave didn't leave her.

Lyca and Aelia told Penelope about Nereus and their time in Egypt, the arguments they'd had with her, and the firm hand she used to keep them together, no matter how much they fought. She never stopped being the Matriarch of the Citadel. She'd been their home and their steady head during the times the world was burning around them or when their long lives and magic had driven them to madness. Penelope listened, and her own heart was saddened that she never had enough time to learn from Nereus. She did have her books, and perhaps one day, she could understand her through them.

At dawn, when she could barely keep her eyes open, Alexis appeared through the trees with Phaidros, Zo, Elazar, Galenos, and Constantine.

"No rending of garments?" Constantine frowned.

"You first," Penelope slurred.

Alexis glared as Constantine gripped his T-shirt. "Do it, and I'll make you regret it." He sat down beside Penelope and took the bottle of wine from her hands. "Did you leave any for me?"

Penelope didn't answer. She was too focused on the shape of his cheekbones to form words. He took a mouthful of wine and winced.

"I forgot how terrible this wine is."

"Shhh, you'll offend Zo." Penelope placed her fingers over his lips. He smiled underneath them. "You're very handsome, Alexis."

"Stop making sexy eyes at each other. You have an audience," Zo said.

Phaidros hushed them. "The dawn is coming, so everyone shut up."

Penelope may have been wasted, but she still noticed that Phaidros had sat down next to Aelia, the tips of his fingers very subtly twisting in the ends of her bronze hair. Aelia swayed as she sat upright, then broke into song.

Penelope half-expected the horror of the lament to come back to her, but unlike the first time, this song was lighter and infinitely more beautiful. Alexis pulled her close as the magic in the song stirred her emotions.

It was like the sunshine that spilled golden over the lagoon—full of life and warmth and promise. It was a burden put down; it was the hope of new love and the burning flames of faith. It was a song of deep love and loss and every kind of joy bound up inside of it. Penelope started crying again, but they were the healing kind of tears, and she wasn't alone. There wasn't a single one of them with dry eyes, and by the time Aelia finished, her voice was barely a crackle. That didn't stop her from joining in with Constantine for a Latin hymn that Nereus had loved.

Penelope swayed unsteadily as Alexis helped her to her feet. After a few jolting steps, he lifted her up in his arms, carrying her through the early morning light. Her last thought was that she finally had somewhere she belonged.

TWENTY-THREE

ALEXIS KNEW WHAT it was like to have a lamenting hangover, so when Penelope didn't move throughout the day, he was smart enough to lower the curtains and use healing magic to cure her nausea and headache as she dozed.

It was the first day in a long time where Alexis could work alone in his tower. He was still reading through the small pile of Nereus's books, and he'd filled half a journal with notes and diagrams as he sought to understand her theories and experiments.

There were enchantments that represented the whimsical side of her nature, like how to make a seashell tell you all it had seen, and then there were the boggling, complex workings, such as manipulating the energy of a crowd to stop events like riots...or start them. The books seemed to date back to before she was made the Matriarch, when she'd been an apprentice working under Poseidon. Nereus had always been private about that part of her life. As a typical student and surrogate son, Alexis hadn't given it much thought, but looking back, he should have pressed her more.

Nereus had been a brilliant magician, but still, the complexity of the magic she'd wielded under Poseidon's tutelage was mind-blowing. Even with his knowledge and experience, Alexis sometimes struggled to follow the thread of her thoughts and the reasoning behind her experiments. So far, he hadn't come across anything surrounding resurrection and necromancy. He needed to go into the astrolabe to study its contents, but it wouldn't work without Penelope.

Alexis's phone vibrated, and he was surprised to find a text message from Constantine: Pen's office in the Archives. E & I have found something.

"How did they get in there without her?" He hoped they hadn't messed up the order of notes on his desk.

Outside the tower, Alexis wasn't surprised to find that the sun had set again. When he was studying new magics, marking time became irrelevant. He'd expected to be fascinated by Nereus's books, but he hadn't planned for the waves of acute homesickness that they caused. Perhaps it was time to let the world know the truth of Atlantis's existence, even if they never revealed the magical history. *That would certainly make Penelope happy.* But Atlantis would have to wait a little longer. They had a war to win first.

Constantine, Elazar, and Zo had made themselves comfortable in the Archives. Another table had been moved into the office, and the three of them sat clustered together, talking and pointing at book pages and a laptop screen.

"Where have you been all day?" asked Constantine.

"I was studying in the tower. What trouble have you three been up to?" Alexis folded his arms.

"You needn't look so disapproving, Uncle," said Elazar. "I was thinking of the priest who escaped Acre before Khalil's arrival."

"Which started Con off on a debate." Zo sent a fond smile in Constantine's direction.

"One of the sources for the fall of Acre and its repercussions was a Dominican priest called Riccoldo da Monte di Croce, who was a missionary *and* from Florence." Constantine took control of the laptop. "Most of his letters have now been digitized by academics. The internet has been a blessing for information sharing."

"Riccoldo had been in Acre only weeks before the siege and wrote letters about it from Baghdad," said Elazar.

"That would've been a hard place for Christians to live, let alone a traveling monk," Alexis said. "He must've had a good reason to want to risk his life in such a manner."

Elazar nodded. "Exactly. He composed quite long-winded apologetic writings about Islam and Judaism, as well as multiple travel letters from his time at the court of Arghun Khan. When he settled in Baghdad, he started studying the Quran and other Islamic theology texts."

"It makes sense. If Riccoldo was given Solomon's ring in Acre, he could've been curious about it and wanted to see if any of the Islamic and Jewish traditions spoke more about it. If the ring has any protective properties, it could explain how he managed to survive."

"The papal bull he carried wouldn't have hurt either," added Constantine, referring to documentation issued by a pope. "Riccoldo was a Florentine, so he would've brought the ring back to Italy with him."

"I have to admit, I'm impressed. I should let you argue amongst yourselves more often." Alexis wrote the information down on a sticky note and stuck it to the glass wall under the *1200-1300* section. "How do we find him now?"

"So glad you asked," Elazar said. "Riccoldo returned to Florence and died in 1320. He was a Dominican at the Santa Maria Novella, so I have to wonder if he bequeathed all of his possessions to the Church."

Constantine made a doubtful noise. "Something as important as the ring of Solomon should have been sent to the Vatican. If he had concerns for its safety, he wouldn't have left it in the hands of any old church administration, especially if he had enough Vatican connections to have a papal bull."

"Why not give it back to the Teutonic Knights?" suggested Zo. "They were the original keepers after all."

"The knights had been kicked out of the Holy Land, and Hermann von Salza was long dead. The knights in Germany might not have had knowledge of the ring. Constantine is right," Alexis said. "The Vatican would be the obvious bet, and Tim's document does mention popes, so this a viable guess as to how it ended up in their hands." He tapped his fingers against his chin. "We'll need a way to prove it, and I doubt the Vatican would be willing to share the full catalog of their relics."

"You never know. They've been digitizing their archives, and Riccoldo would be a figure of interest not just to theology students, but also anyone researching medieval China." Constantine pulled out his phone. "Let me send some emails. I have a contact that may know something, including whether they have Riccoldo's documents or if they're tied up in private collections."

"Penelope will be relieved to have one less person to identify," said Zo. "The sooner we find the ring, the better. We need to see if it awakens for Penelope or one of us."

"If it does, I'm going to be pleased and pissed at the same time. When my mother or I wielded it, I never saw it perform an exorcism, only some healings," said Constantine. "What if we do find it and it doesn't work at all?"

Alexis was reluctant to even consider it. "We try to sabotage the ritual that will bind Thevetat to his new body. I know Nereus wrote about a similar experiment that Abaddon was present for. I need to find her book—"

"And if you can't find it? Alexis, you need to start thinking like my general again. Too much of your plans rely on equipment you don't have yet."

"I know that, but I don't see us being able to defeat him without them."

"From what Zo has said, Kreios told Penelope that they are going to be on Milos for Thevetat's ceremony. What do you know about the island? Have you studied its defenses? Do you know if he is in a mansion or a camp?" Constantine asked. "For God's sake, don't scowl at me, Alexis. I'm only asking the questions you should've been all this time."

"Alexis can't do everything, Con," Elazar said. "Perhaps you should talk to Lyca and Phaidros about planning a campaign. Galenos can find some maps of Milos that could help us locate Thevetat's base."

Alexis shot Elazar a grateful look. Constantine was right. He'd been too hopeful that magic would prevail instead of a head-on attack.

Constantine said, "I suppose I'll have to. Someone has to prepare for a fight."

Alexis was about to defend himself when the *moíra desmós* shuddered. He clutched at his chest, sensing strange magic inside himself. *What are you doing now, Penelope?*

"Alexis? What is it?" Elazar rose from his chair.

"I don't know. My connection to Penelope is playing up. I should go see if she's okay. Con, please let me know if you hear back from your contact so I can plan a trip to Rome if needed." Alexis's magic beat in his chest, and he hurried through the Archives to the elevator.

Once upstairs, he whispered a spell, and silvery lines of unfamiliar magic revealed a trail through the palazzo. He followed the trail and found Penelope sitting on the top step of the sheltered canal entrance, her loose yoga pants pushed up to her knees and her feet in the water. She was wreathed in silver power, and a meter-high wave of water was frozen in front of her.

"Penelope?" whispered Alexis, afraid to scare her and cause the stagnant wave to rush over them. She was deep in a meditative state and didn't reply. Alexis sat on the stone walkway behind her and created a barrier so that if she did lose control, the water wouldn't rush in and flood the palazzo. Shutting his eyes, he focused on the shape of the magic in an attempt to figure out how she was holding it. What he found almost shocked him enough to lose hold of the barrier.

Penelope was holding the wave in place by sheer stubbornness and determination of will. There was no structure to it—no understanding of the energy and matter or the reversal of natural gravity to hold the magic in place. It had taken Alexis years of training to master the ability to manipulate matter. She was doing it because she wanted to. *How is this possible?* What had Poseidon unlocked in her?

He didn't have long to wait before the wave wobbled, and he rushed forward to grab Penelope as she cried out in alarm. The wave crashed over them. It hit his barrier and sucked back into the canal, taking them with it. Alexis held onto Penelope, keeping her upright as his hands found purchase on a metal ring in the side of the entrance wall.

"Penelope? Are you awake?" As the water finished draining out into the canal, Alexis's feet found the stone floor, and he dragged her toward the stairs.

Penelope spat out a mouthful of salt water and pushed her drenched hair out of her face. "Well, that backfired." She looked up at Alexis, soaked and alarmed, and laughed.

He sat beside her on the steps. "Would you mind telling me what that was all about?"

"Aelia and Lyca said Poseidon could make a tidal wave."

"And you thought trying it out in the middle of Venice was a good idea?" Alexis struggled to believe the other magicians would encourage her to be so reckless.

"I wasn't trying to make a *tidal wave*. Just one wave. When a little one rolled toward me, I tried to hold it up," Penelope explained. "Don't look so mad. You're the one that said I had to start using my magic before the high tide peaks."

"I didn't mean by practicing alone, Penelope. You could've been hurt. It's why magicians become masters and have apprentices, so they can guide their students and ensure they don't hurt themselves."

"I'm not your apprentice, and you are certainly not my master."

Alexis rubbed a frustrated hand over his face. "I *know* that, Penelope. What I'm trying to say is that you need to have one of us near if you want to practice. You do need to learn how to control your magic; I'm only asking you to do it safely."

The anger in her eyes softened. "I scared you."

"Yes." He pulled her to him and kissed her wet cheek. "You were holding a damn wave up by yourself. Of course I was scared. You have no idea the complexity of the magic you were working. Tell me how you managed it."

"I didn't really think about what I was doing. There's a note in one of Nereus's journals about water and weather magic—a comment written in the margin that says it's easier to reach out into the water with mind *and* touch. So I tried it. I put my feet in the water and reached out into it with my mind, like I would in a meditation. I know that doesn't make sense, but the way water feels has changed since I met Poseidon. It's so *alive*, Alexis. If I concentrate, I can feel it like I can feel you."

Alexis wanted to find a way to meet Poseidon and shake him for tangling her up in his revenge on Thevetat. He smothered his anger and ran a hand over Penelope's back. "I don't understand it, but magic is strange. If that's how you access your magic and get it to flow, then go with it. We won't be able to teach you the way we were taught, but we can be here to look after you as you learn. You and I can look at the journals together and find the parts that do work for you. But promise me you won't try anything like this again without one of us near to protect you."

Penelope gripped his sodden shirt. "I promise. I honestly didn't think it would work. You know I'd never do anything that could harm Venice or us."

"I know, *cara*. You are too talented for your own good sometimes."

TWENTY-FOUR

$\mathcal{A}$FTER THEY'D SHOWERED and dressed in dry clothes, Alexis told Penelope about Elazar and Constantine's discovery.

"I sleep off a hangover for one morning, and this is what happens. Constantine could've told me he had Vatican ties. I would've asked him about the pope references in Tim's manuscript," Penelope said while combing out her damp curls.

"Constantine funded the building of most of the first churches in Rome. He was never going to let those ties slip, even if he was fluid about which denomination he was worshipping in. It's good that he and Elazar are working on it and freeing you up to come with me." He was smiling, but his eyes were still troubled. Penelope couldn't blame him for being concerned after almost getting washed out into the Grand Canal. If she had known that she was going to be even remotely successful at creating a wave, she would've waited for him to be there.

"Where are we going?" She took his hand.

"My tower, so you can show me the note you found in Nereus's journal, and then we're going to try to get back into the astrolabe. I need to see what I'm dealing with. I might be able to find an order to her catalog that you might not be able to."

"I was more concerned about finding a way out than searching for a system. Here's to hoping the astrolabe will let you inside of it."

Upstairs in the tower workroom, Penelope studied the pages of the open journals spread about. "Wow, you've been busy."

"I'm hopelessly fascinated. Nereus never talked about any of this magic. There are a few things that I recognize—like how to navigate your way through a desert when you lose your direction in a sandstorm, how to make it rain, wards to protect against illness—but there is so much she never taught me." Alexis was unsuccessful at hiding the hurt in his voice.

"She probably thought you were too advanced and had no need to learn it. She was always very proud that you were her student, and I'm sure if she felt you needed to know this stuff, she would've taught you."

Alexis's brows lowered. "Like the fact that you were her heir or that lighting the incense would make you have a vision of Poseidon? Honestly, Penelope, I feel like I didn't know her at all."

Penelope lifted his hand and kissed his knuckles. "She had her secrets for a reason. You can't control everything, my love. Now, let me find this book for you so you can see the note I found."

After digging through his pile of notes and books, Penelope found the slim volume she was searching for. It was bound in dark blue leather that was starting to crack, and the pages were soft from being handled often. "It was in here somewhere. I found it the night you went to Florence. I needed a distraction after Aelia told me you killed Himmler."

Alexis let out a noise of frustration. "It's like a man can't have any secrets at all anymore. They turn into such gossips as soon as I leave the room. God knows if they're even telling you the right version of the stories."

Penelope raised a quizzical brow. "So, you didn't kill him?"

"Yes, I did, and I'd cheerfully do it again, and I'm not ashamed of that. I'm only irritated that they like to tell you these things behind my back to goad me."

"Probably—oh, here it is!" Penelope gave him the open book and showed him the scrawled lines in the margin. "I couldn't make sense of the diagrams or any of the theory. Whoever wrote this note seemed to have figured it out and decided to include a simpler explanation."

Alexis frowned at the scribble. "I can't even read this. This isn't Atlantean."

"Maybe the Living Language is translating it for me. It says, 'Reach out your mind to the water, and it will listen to you. Touch it with your magic, and it will obey you.' It's a bit vague, but it worked."

Alexis flicked through the pages. "This is one of Nereus's earlier journals from when she was just beginning to learn magic. The notes aren't written in her hand, so perhaps they are Poseidon's comments on her experiments with water. She never taught this to me, but perhaps she taught the magicians who had an affinity for water."

"I suppose I could go through each one, search for his notes, and see if they work for me." Penelope took the astrolabe out of her pocket and placed it on the workbench. "But hunting Poseidon's notes can wait until after we find Nereus's necromancy experiments."

"Another part of magic she abhorred but seemed to practice when convenient."

"You know Atlas made her do the experiments to bring Poseidon back. She risked her life and position to sabotage the experiment so they'd believe it impossible." Alexis's grief for Nereus and confusion over her actions was like a raw wound. Penelope put her arms around his waist. "Forward, not backward. Don't be angry at Nereus. It'll mess with your perception, and I need you too much to lose you to past hurts you can't change."

Alexis wrapped himself around her, bringing her close and resting his cheek on the top of her head. "I know, *cara*. I'm sorry. I miss her, and that's why I'm angry at her. It's stupid reasoning."

"No, that's grief. I want to kick Tim's ass at least once a day, but mostly, I just miss him." Penelope tilted her head up. "Are you ready to search through a bunch of amazing magical books with me?"

Alexis's smile was sly. "I love it when you talk dirty to me."

Penelope freed one hand, picked up the astrolabe, and flicked it open. The red sigil was pulsing with light as if it were waiting for them. "Hold tight, and don't let me go."

"Never," Alexis said and gripped her tighter.

Penelope pressed on the sigil, and they were sucked inside the device.

THIS TIME, Penelope was more prepared for the fall. Alexis caught her as the astrolabe's interior materialized around her, then lowered her to her unsteady feet.

"I don't think I'm ever going to enjoy that," she said.

"You've had your body changed by magic. It should never feel natural." Indigo eyes scanned the haphazardly stacked books around them. "The Archives must have hidden these after the attack on Nereus. Many of these bindings seem familiar." He ran his fingers over the chains that secured the books to the shelves.

"I told you there were at least a hundred of them." Penelope studied the shelves. Last time she was there, she was too panicked to think clearly. "How are we going to tell if the books we're hunting are even here?"

"We'll have to go through them. But we're going to make it a bit easier with magic. The books we need are from Atlantis, so if we start with the oldest of them we might have a better chance of locating them."

The feel of Alexis's magic crept over Penelope's skin as he raised his hands, made a series of small movements, and whispered something in Atlantean. The scent of firecrackers and spice filled the room as the magic rushed out of him and danced along the shelves in a streak of pale blue light. As the light traveled over the books, some began to glow with different colored auras.

"The warmer the color, the older the book." Alexis reached for a glowing red book on a high shelf.

"Okay, but we can't forget that time works differently in here. We don't want to cause a panic if the others can't find us," Penelope said, then joined his search.

"I'm hoping that they're too busy to notice we're gone. Constantine was getting in contact with the Vatican to inquire about any trace of Riccoldo da Monte di Croce, as well as organizing the rest of them to start planning an invasion of Milos." Alexis was nonchalant as he browsed through a notebook.

Penelope paused, her stomach flipping. She hadn't thought far enough ahead to consider how they were going to get close enough to use the ring on Thevetat. Kreios had said they were all going to be on Milos. Just how many people had Thevetat recruited to his cause?

"I'm happy he's here to do it," Penelope said. "I remember studying his campaigns as an undergrad. I suppose if I were going to choose a general to plan a battle for me, it would be him or Alexander the Great." She didn't add that their army was only nine people with Constantine, and she didn't really count herself as any kind of a fighter. *Six of those people are the strongest living magicians on a high tide,* her mind clarified. "Alexis?"

He didn't look up. "Yes, *cara*?"

"How do the priests of Thevetat get their magic?"

Alexis put the book he was looking at back on the shelf and reached for another. "All of their power comes from their worship of him. The sacrifices feed his power, and then he shares that power with them."

"So they aren't like magicians that have acquired their own individual magic through study and practice. What magic they have comes solely from him?"

"That's right. Why do you ask?"

"If Thevetat is going to be using the tide and all of his power to bind himself to a body and give it life, he won't be focused on sharing it with all of his followers at the same time. It won't matter how many of them there are because they won't have access to their power source."

"Which means they'll only be humans during the ritual," Alexis said, finishing her train of thought. "It will be an edge but not necessarily an easy win. They will have numbers and plenty of weapons.

Thevetat and Abaddon know they'll be vulnerable while completing the magic, which means they will surround themselves with guards. Humans are still plenty vicious without adding magic to the mix."

"Still, it'll be something else for Constantine to consider—whether he's planning to meet a bunch of magic users or machine guns."

Alexis gave her a long, unreadable look, and the hair on her arms rose as his magic leaped up. "I hate that you even have to consider such things, Penelope—that you need to think in this way. Bringing you into this war is the most selfish thing I've ever done."

Penelope fought the urge to throw a book at him. "Alexis, stop pretending like it was your choice. Can you read the script of an ancient ring? No. Are you Poseidon's heir? No. You need to accept that I was always meant to be a part of this. Our fates are *literally* tied together. You didn't have the power to keep me out of this."

"Knowing the truth doesn't make it any easier. You don't like it when I leave for a dangerous conflict, so don't ask me to be fine with you doing the same. I love you too much not to be afraid to lose you."

"Our fates are tied together. You couldn't lose me even if you wanted to," she tried to joke. He didn't smile. "Alexis, stop thinking about locking me in a tower or I swear—"

She didn't see him move, but he was suddenly in front of her, pressing her back against the wall and kissing her. His magic was a roar in her ears, and she tried not to let the sensation of it overwhelm her. In her mind, she saw it as an ocean of power, and she focused on calming the storm-tossed waves. Alexis groaned and pulled back from her.

"Thank you," he whispered against her mouth, hands still tangled in her hair. "I'm sorry."

"I love you, but you need to accept that we're in this together. However horrible and terrifyingly wonderful." She gripped the sides of his entari robe and held him to her.

"I do accept it. I just fear what I'll do if anything happens to you."

"I know. Help me kick Thevetat back to where he came from, and we won't have to worry about any of this ever again. We're after the red books, right?" Penelope said, trying to move his focus from his anxiety to the task at hand. Dealing with her own was trial enough.

Alexis kissed her forehead and stepped back. "Yes, *cara*. Anything red or orange is a sure bet."

When they had uncovered all of the oldest books, they placed them into two small stacks. "I suppose we should see it as a blessing that there are less than twenty of them." Penelope piled them into Alexis's arms.

"It will keep us busy enough." He peered at her. "I'm sorry, for... before."

Penelope hugged him, books and all. "It's okay. I think I've freaked out enough in the past few months to make us even. Okay, astrolabe, return us."

"That's all you need to do?" Alexis managed to ask before they were dragged back to his tower.

TWENTY-FIVE

PHAIDROS AND CONSTANTINE were sitting at one of the worktables arguing.

"Finally! You two took your time." Phaidros turned to Constantine. "I told you they would turn up."

Alexis placed his armload of books down on the table. "What are you two doing here?"

"Waiting for you! You could have left a note saying that you were going to Alice-in-Wonderland yourself into a magical device." Constantine folded his arms in annoyance.

"I told you they would figure it out and complain," said Penelope.

"He worried all the same." Phaidros nodded at Constantine. "They're back now. You can stop pouting and tell them."

"Tell us what?" Alexis asked.

"My contact in the Vatican Secret Archive got back to me. There is a letter from Riccoldo to Pope John XXII asking him to guard his most sacred relic—a ring that was given to him during his time in the Holy Land."

"Does the Vatican still have it?" Alexis asked.

"Remember Tim saw the ring getting passed from a pope to someone else?" Penelope reminded him.

Constantine nodded. "Exactly. Elazar has been looking into those passages, and he believes it might have been Pope Sixtus IV in the vision."

Alexis spared an uneasy glance in Phaidros's direction. The golden magician looked unusually still and guarded.

"What is it?" asked Penelope.

"I had a complicated relationship with that particular pope," Phaidros said.

That was a surprise. "Complicated how?"

"Phaidros was in love with his nephew's wife." Alexis's disapproval was still evident, though Phaidros didn't look an ounce remorseful.

"Sixtus was responsible for the building of the Sistine Chapel as well as the Vatican Secret Archive," Constantine said. "That he had knowledge of such a relic in his vaults isn't a surprise. He would've been curating what was placed under the Archives' many locks and protocols."

Phaidros's cool demeanor vanished. "Sixtus was a grasping, political despot whose machinations almost destroyed Florence because of his vendetta against the Medicis."

"Focus, please." Alexis shot him a look. "Sixtus had the ring and gave it to someone. Who would he care about enough to give them such a powerful relic?"

"Girolamo. Who the fuck else would he give it to?" Phaidros spat the words out like poison.

"Who's Girolamo?" Penelope asked.

"He was Sixtus's nephew." Alexis ran a hand over his face in frustration. "It seems this journey is going to unearth every ghost we have."

"Because it's a damn prophecy," muttered Phaidros.

Penelope turned to him. "What do you mean by that?"

"Prophecies are tricky and often weave people, events, and time together. This ring of Solomon has been chasing us through the centuries because we're all tied to the prophecy: Constantine was our ally; Alexis and Zo were at Frederick's court; Alexis arrived at Acre not long after the sacking and would've been in Baghdad the same time as the priest; the priest was a Florentine and lived there when I did; the Vatican connection links us back to Constantine and now bloody Girolamo and Sixtus. You see? We're woven through time together, chasing each other back and forth. And you're the key to the prophecy, Penelope. That's why it was Tim's destiny to find the scroll and bring you into it."

"Not to mention Poseidon's meddling premonition of the war against Thevetat that predates even Solomon's trinket," added Alexis.

"The Fates and their games nor God's providence change the fact that we are all bound together in this matter." Constantine's gaze settled on Alexis. "It could very well be one of the reasons I've not been given the release of death. It could be the key to all of your long lives. Once this final hand is dealt with Thevetat, we could all go back to being mortal."

"If that's the case, you'd better get ready for another dip in the baptismal font," Phaidros said, with only a little sarcasm.

Penelope dropped into one of Alexis's reading chairs. "This is a lot to take in. I knew all of you related to the different periods identified in Tim's writings, but I thought that was the result of living for so long, not because a prophecy has been making you chase an object you didn't even know about."

Phaidros pursed his lips, then nodded. "If you want to get *really* meta about it—you could've been drawn to Atlantis because of your link to the prophecy. You knew deep in your guts that Atlantis was real, and you wanted to be the one to find it, and that obsession forced you onto this path. I imagine it was the same for Tim and his irrational love for the Dead Sea."

Penelope's heart raced. She put her head between her knees as the room spun. "Oh my God."

"That's enough, Phaidros." Alexis's warm fingers came to her neck, and he massaged the tense muscles there. "Breathe, Penelope. It's going to be all right, *amore.*"

Phaidros shrugged. "It doesn't change the fact that I'm right. I'd know—I've been caught up in more prophecies than any of us."

"Probably God's way of punishing you for being such an asshole," Constantine muttered.

Penelope sat up as her breathing evened out. "Enough arguing. We can't do anything to counteract the mystical complications of prophecies. We *can* find this damn ring. Tell me about Girolamo and Sixtus."

Alexis nodded, getting back to business. "They were responsible for stirring up the Pazzis in their conspiracy to wipe out the Medicis and take over Florence. Girolamo was Sixtus's right-hand man in Rome, especially after Girolamo's brother, Pietro, died."

"He wouldn't have been half as successful politically if it weren't for Caterina. He was a ridiculous ass of a man," said Phaidros.

"And that was a good enough excuse to kill him?" Constantine asked.

"Spare me your judgmental tone. You've had men killed for less. If I didn't kill him, his bullshit would've gotten Caterina and the children killed. I only regret not doing it sooner." Phaidros gave an unapologetic shrug. "Forli was always going to be better under her control."

"Forli? Wait, Caterina…as in Caterina Sforza?" Penelope gaped at him. "You were having an affair with *La Tigre*?" She couldn't believe it. *"You?"*

"Oh good, you've heard of her."

"Of course I have! She's only one of the most badass women in history." Penelope gave him a long, careful look. "Keep this up and I'm going to have to start respecting you."

"Don't be too rash." Phaidros winked.

"Getting back to Girolamo," Alexis prompted. "If Sixtus did give him the ring of Solomon, how long was it in his possession? In Rome, his property was sacked after Sixtus died."

"If it stayed in the family, wouldn't there have been some form of will or bequeathment?" Penelope asked hopefully.

Phaidros frowned. "It would've gone to his children and Caterina. So many of her belongings ended up in the hands of the Vatican after she was imprisoned by Pope Alexander in the Castel Sant'Angelo.

Fucking Borgias." He was about to spit, but the look Alexis gave him warned him not to dare.

"The hatred burned twice as hot because Aelia supported them," Constantine whispered to Penelope.

"Please don't start," Alexis begged as Phaidros reddened.

"She was only fucking Cesare because she was jealous I was in love with someone other than her."

Alexis tipped his head back in exasperation. "Another war instigated by your quarrels. I'm surprised Europe remained as unscathed as it did between your arguments."

Penelope was beginning to have a whole new appreciation for why Aelia and Phaidros finally getting along was such a big deal. She dug about in her memories of undergrad Renaissance History.

Caterina Sforza made a big impression on her and Carolyn. Not only had she outlived three husbands, including a Medici, but she also gained her own political power at a time when noblewomen were treated as pawns with wombs. She refused to surrender Forli to Cesare Borgia's forces, knocking back their offers of peace, and once their army finally breached the city, Caterina, armed and angry, fought them off until they overpowered her and took her back to Rome.

"Didn't Caterina get released from the Castel Sant'Angelo? Surely they gave some of her possessions back."

"What little they did return Caterina spent on fighting the Medicis to get her son back from them. Lorenzo was a hard man, but in the end, giving Caterina what she wanted was easiest," Phaidros said. "If the Vatican recognized the ring's origin, they would've kept it and anything that pertained to it."

Constantine nodded. "Good point. You don't hand a relic like that back to a woman who's already been a thorn in the side of three popes by that stage."

"Could you ask your Vatican contact what he knows?" Penelope asked.

"It's a she, but I'll ask. Whether or not she admits to it will be another matter. The Vatican is comfortable withholding information for the perceived good."

Penelope smiled. "A good day's work all round. I'll check through Tim's notes, but I feel like we're closing in on the ring's last location."

"Good luck getting the manuscript off of Elazar," said Phaidros. "He's quite fascinated with the idea that the Essene scribe managed to imprint his prophetic visions onto a consciousness nearly two thousand years later. If nothing else, it's keeping his mind off his destroyed home."

Elazar was in his new office in the Archives, the printed version of Tim's manuscript in front of him. He looked up guiltily when Alexis and Penelope walked in.

"I'm sorry. I couldn't help myself."

"As long as you keep producing such excellent leads, you can have it as long as you like," Alexis replied. "We're after the passage you found about the pope and any other passages we haven't identified already."

Elazar flipped through the document. "Now that we've found Riccoldo and his journeys, there isn't much at all. Here's the paragraph about Sixtus: *There was a guy sitting on a throne of gold. He wore white priest's robes, a red cowl, and a cap. He was talking about Florence and revenge on someone he referred to as 'the deceitful banker's son.' A younger man stood obediently in front of him, and then the posh pope guy pulled a ring from his finger and gave it to him and said, 'Subdue Florence, and I'll give you whatever glory you wish.'"* Elazar passed the manuscript over to Alexis. "Not much of a creative writer, that Tim, but he managed to get the important details. Phaidros guessed it was Sixtus and Girolamo in the blink of an eye."

"Old wounds are like that. You're right—there's only one passage left."

"Read it to me? My head is spinning." Penelope sat down on a spare chair.

"Dressed in a plain dress, the sick woman wrote page after page in her cell. She twisted the ring between her fingers, whispering to it over and over like a prayer. She was dying, and it refused to save her. She would take it to her tomb, for no man deserved to wield it."

"Caterina?"

"Perhaps," Elazar said. "We would need to check with Phaidros. There's no point making assumptions until we have definite confirmation that it was in Girolamo's possession and then passed on to her."

To pass the time, Penelope told Elazar about the contents of Nereus's secret library until Constantine found them again.

When he did, the foreboding look on his face worried her. "What did she say?" she asked.

"There are boxes of Girolamo's and Caterina's documents in the archive, but she doesn't have clearance to access them." Constantine tapped his phone against his palm. "There's only one way I can think of getting our hands on them, and you probably won't like it." He shared a look with Alexis and laughed.

"We go to the Vatican," Alexis said with a devious smile, "and we steal them."

TWENTY-SIX

*A*LEXIS HAD PREDICTED an argument the next day, but it didn't come from the quarter he'd expected.

"I don't want to leave Elazar." Zo folded his arms across his chest after finding Alexis drinking his morning coffee in the courtyard and cornering him.

"Zo, you are the best at magically counterfeiting objects. We need you."

"Take Phaidros. It's his dead girlfriend's documents after all."

"That's exactly why he shouldn't come. I need someone steady, who's not going to get emotional over familiar handwriting." Alexis checked that no one else was around before adding, "Aelia admitted to me that she loves Phaidros. They nearly destroyed Italy over Caterina and Cesare. I don't want their chances together to be derailed or soured by old animosities."

"If Aelia loves him, they'll get over it. Caterina and Cesare are long dead. Whatever they have going on hasn't been affected by Constantine's presence here. *Constantine*. If they can tolerate that old flame living with them, they can handle the matter of Phaidros's dead lover."

"Elazar will be safe here with or without you. You can't hover over him forever." Alexis's effort to remain calm slipped away as his voice rose.

Zo took a deep breath, seemingly readying himself for another spat when Constantine found them.

"What are you two doing hiding out here?"

"Trying to convince Zo that he needs to come to Rome to leave perfect copies of whatever we're going to take."

Constantine turned his stern gray gaze on Zo. "Elazar doesn't need you, Zotikos. I do. Stop arguing about something so ridiculous. We are battling an army of darkness. That takes priority. You are coming." Zo flushed and tried to respond, but Constantine held up a hand. "No. Stop it. There's only one man I trust to do this with me, and it's not Phaidros. Go on. You need to pack. We're leaving in two hours." Constantine gave him a charming smile.

Zo huffed in defeat. "Fine, but I'm driving."

"Yes, of course you can."

"I hate you so much."

"Don't lie," Constantine called to his retreating back, then turned back to Alexis with a satisfied smile. "You see, Alecto? You needn't turn everything into such a drama. Sometimes a firm hand and no room for protest is all that's needed."

"We both know Zo can't deny you anything, so there's no room to criticize me."

Constantine sat down at his table and took one of his papers.

"Are you sure you're going to be okay stealing from the heart of Catholicism. Won't your God get upset at you for taking his things?"

"The Church took them first. What is it you like to say about stealing? Acquiring it for preservation purposes?" Constantine's relaxed, charming smile returned. "Besides, it'll hardly be the first time I stole something from the Vatican."

"You're incorrigible."

"It's what you like about me the most." Constantine looked at him over the edge of the paper, his clever eyes missing nothing. "What's wrong? You've been in a mood since your trip into the astrolabe. Did you and the lovely doctor have a fight? If so, I really should be giving her my shoulder to cry on and not you."

"We're fine. I overreacted a little," Alexis admitted, adjusting the rings on his fingers.

"Did you hurt her?"

"No!" His eyes widened. "I'd never do that."

"Then what's upsetting you?"

Constantine would be relentless, so Alexis told him about going into the astrolabe and the spill of magic when it had reacted to his fear for Penelope. "I don't want to be a controlling partner, but there are parts of me that wish she'd never found her way back to the palazzo. She'd be so much safer."

"But you'd be miserable. Penelope's presumed safety would also be debatable. You said yourself that Thevetat tried to kill her even before you revealed yourself to her. Alecto, my dear friend, you must stop trying to control all of this. You are the Defender; I understand that is a part of your duty, but Penelope is here by divine appointment. Even you cannot fight against that."

"You know that doesn't make me feel any better."

"The truth usually doesn't."

"Penelope mentioned something else you should factor into your plans."

"Oh, praise God, she wants to have an open relationship."

"No, you idiot. She pointed out that it doesn't matter how many men Thevetat has protecting him. Once he starts his ritual, they are all going to be reduced to humans because he won't be sharing his power."

"Clever girl." Constantine rubbed his chin. "This is good news."

"There are still only nine of us, including you and Marco."

"I have some mercenary friends that wouldn't turn down the work."

Alexis could see the military wheels of his mind turning. Parts of the upstairs library were now covered in aerial shots of Milos and the surrounding islands, and Constantine and Lyca had their heads together to not only find Thevetat's base, but to discover the best way to approach it. Milos was no deserted island, and the last thing Alexis wanted was tourists and innocent locals getting caught in the cross fire

of a magical battle—or worse, recording it on their phones and upload-
ing it to social media.

"Let me worry about it, Alecto. You need to focus on the ring and
the magic and your lovely Penelope."

Alexis leaned back in his chair. "Thank you, Con. I'm glad you're
here."

"Of course you are. I'm delightful, and I have the way of getting
into the Vatican. Let's pray you find your answers there."

TRUE TO schedule, Alexis, Pen, Zo, and Constantine left Venice for Rome. They picked up one of Zo's cars from their garage on the
mainland, and soon Alexis and Penelope were tucked up in the back
seat.

"We'll only be gone a night or so," Alexis had assured Phaidros
before they left.

"Don't get caught," he'd replied.

Alexis hadn't seen Aelia, but he felt her magic in the palazzo, so he
knew she was haunting her wing. "Take care of them."

Phaidros rolled his eyes. "Worry about yourself and what the
Swiss Guard will do to you if you're caught."

In the past, Alexis had come and gone from the palazzo without a
care, knowing that Nereus had enough magic to protect it and whoever
was sleeping under its roof.

"I haven't been to Rome in years." Penelope gazed out the back
seat window.

"I'll bring you back for a visit once all of this is over," he promised. He needed to focus on the future, despite what they would face
on Milos. He was trying desperately not to get lost in his memories
of the war on Atlantis. What would they find in the middle of Thevetat's compound? They'd raided many camps in the old days and
what they'd uncovered…

Penelope's hand wrapped around his, snapping Alexis back to the present.

"After all of this is over, I intend to take you up on your offer to stay in your tower for a hundred years."

Alexis laughed.

"A hundred years with only Alexis for company? You'll be trying to murder him within the first year," Constantine said from the passenger seat.

"I don't think so." Penelope's eyes were hot as they slid over Alexis.

His smile grew wider, and he lifted her hand to kiss the soft inside of her wrist. "I'd do my best to keep you occupied."

"If you two start making out in my back seat, I swear to all the gods that I'll kick you out onto the street," warned Zo.

"And you'll have to deal with me watching." Constantine shot a wink in Penelope's direction.

Alexis narrowed his gaze. "Do it again, and I'll take that eye."

"Don't listen to him, Penelope. He has missed me immensely."

"I can't see why, no matter how pretty you are," she said.

"Constantine is not pretty," said Zo.

"That's right. I'm too ruggedly masculine to be pretty, right, Zo?"

"Absolutely. And I only compliment people who I intend to sleep with. Isn't that right, my beautiful Penelope, light of my life?" Zo laughed when Penelope leaned forward to tickle his ear.

"You wouldn't be able to handle me, sweet poet."

Alexis smiled where Constantine and Zo couldn't see. He loved watching Penelope go toe to toe with the other magicians, putting them in their places while making them fall in love with her at the same time. They'd all had spouses and lovers over the long centuries, but those companions hadn't always known their secrets or been introduced to the other magicians, and it had been a rare thing for them to be unafraid and accepting when they did. It felt like Penelope was always meant to be with them. It wasn't just her magic—they'd met plenty of people with gifts—it was because she was like them. She loved them all fiercely, no matter how much they pissed her off.

Alexis drew her to him, and she placed her arm around his waist, her head finding its place on his shoulder. She belonged not only to him, but to all of them. His heart swelled with even more love for her.

They were both asleep by the time they arrived in Rome four hours later. Penelope's hand had found its way through the buttons of his shirt, her palm resting against his heart. Even months after the night at the Lido, she still needed the reminder that it was still beating.

I'll stand by you, and we will face Thevetat's defeat or our death together, Alexis silently promised her. Constantine was right; Alexis had to believe this was a part of her destiny as much as his. It didn't matter what gods or magic, prophecy, or higher power had forced their paths together. She was his partner in all things—death included.

"I love you," Penelope murmured in her sleep, as if she'd somehow heard him. Then her green eyes fluttered open, and she smiled. "We're here." She looked around at the city streets Zo navigated through.

"You slept through the whole trip, and it was incredibly boring." Constantine sighed. "I was going to wake you up, but then I thought sleep might be a good thing, considering what we're going to be up to tonight."

When in Rome, Constantine lived in Monteverde, on the Via Calandrelli near the Villa Sciarra park. Zo wove expertly through the tight lanes and passed the brick retaining walls as they wound higher up into the hills. The buildings glowed with warm shades of sepia, ochre, peach, and terra-cotta. Penelope made happy little sighs as she gazed out at the streets lined with poplar and pine trees.

They pulled into the drive of a three-story, terra-cotta terrace house surrounded by a high, vine-covered wall. "Have you changed your code since last time?" Zo asked, reaching out of his open window to the gate's keypad.

"No," Constantine said, and Zo punched in a number. If nothing else, that proved Zo had been in contact with Constantine more that Alexis and Aelia had realized.

"Very trusting of you to give him that," Penelope said as the gates slid open.

"Zo is the one magician I trust implicitly. He's probably stayed here more than I have in the past fifty years."

"It's in a good spot—that's why," said Zo. "Plus, you hate Rome. It seemed a shame to let it go to waste."

Penelope leaned into the space between them. "A Roman emperor who hates Rome? That doesn't sound right at all."

"By the time I became emperor, Rome was a cesspool of vipers and strategically irrelevant in running the empire. Why do you think I built a new capital in Constantinople?"

"Because if you had stayed in Rome, you would've been assassinated within the year?" Alexis was teasing him, but that didn't mean it wasn't the truth.

"The assassins certainly would've done their best. Constantinople was a much-needed clean slate."

"And it had absolutely nothing to do with it being a city-sized monument to your ego?" Penelope asked with a raised brow.

Constantine chucked her under the chin. "You need to stop reading all of those misguided historians and listening to Alexis's lies, my dear."

Alexis scoffed. "I'm sure you did your best to trash all the historians of your time because they had you all wrong."

"That was to cover up the secret of my resurrection, and you know it." Constantine unclipped his seat belt and swiveled around to give him an infuriating smile. "You can hardly chide me for ruining historians' careers when you're sitting beside a victim of your own sabotages. Not to mention the unfortunate ends of the past nine thousand years' worth of historians who weren't pretty enough to get past your defenses."

"*Mio Dio*, you all carry on." Zo parked in a courtyard next to a classically carved stone well.

Penelope took in the gardens and the wrought iron touches to the building's smaller balconies. "This place looks lovely, Con."

"As pleasant as the gardens are, Penelope, I have a feeling you'll love what's inside even more." Constantine wrapped her arm around his and led her up the stairs to the door. "Grab my bag too, please," he called before disappearing inside.

"Remind me again why we like him?" Alexis reached for Constantine's bag in the boot of the car.

Zo took it from him and hefted it over one shoulder. "Because we have a weakness for beautiful, bossy people," he said. "You'd better hurry before he shows Penelope his collection and she falls in love with him."

Alexis only rolled his eyes. "She wouldn't fall for his charm as easily as you."

TWENTY-SEVEN

PENELOPE KNEW THAT she shouldn't be surprised by the contents of Constantine's house—or the houses of any of the magicians—by now. They were always full of things that should be in museums or galleries, and yet her jaw dropped once inside Constantine's house. For one, most of the walls were painted in vivid frescoes, each one a scene of something significant that had happened in his life. Penelope recognized some, like the Battle of the Milvian Bridge and his coronation as emperor. Others were more recent, like a scene from Jerusalem and snowcapped mountains. There were more images that resembled his stained glass windows on Badija: the apostles, Biblical stories, and Christ. There were also paintings and old photographs of artists, writers, and theologists, weapons, statues, books, and tiny stone tablets.

"You immortals are such hoarders." She squeezed Constantine's arm.

"You can't help it after a while. Why do you think we end up with so many houses? We don't all have a magical palazzo that will make us more space at the snap of our fingers. You know you can read and touch anything in the house, Penelope."

"Thank you, Con. I'll be careful not to break anything. These frescoes are amazing. Can I ask who did them?" She stepped closer so she could study one of Constantinople.

He offered a self-conscious smile. "Isn't it obvious?"

Penelope jerked back in surprise. "No! You? Really?"

"It's not so surprising," Zo said. "You have to keep yourself busy somehow when you have all the time in the world."

"Constantine likes to be surrounded by the thing he loves most, which is himself." Alexis looked around at the walls with a frown. "Honestly, your ego is astounding."

"Don't listen to them, Penelope. It wasn't my ego that fueled these paintings." Constantine's voice was strangely soft. He waited until Alexis and Zo had moved to other parts of the house before continuing. "There were times I thought I was going mad, like I'd disconnected from who I was, my memories becoming more like a dream. Painting the memories helped ground me and remind me who I really was. It's easy to lose touch with yourself and reality when you're immortal. Alexis won't admit it, but he's been lost more than once in the same manner. It's why everyone is so happy that you're with him—you'll help keep him grounded."

"I hope so. Sometimes, I think I brought Alexis's world down around him."

"It would be best to let go of that guilt right now, Pen. This war would've come with or without you. I, for one, am glad you're on our side." He kissed her hand. "Come, let's see where the other two have gone to. We have until six o'clock before the Vatican Secret Archive closes for the night."

"I still don't know how you expect us to get in there without being spotted, considering all of the security cameras and guards they have."

Constantine laughed. "Don't you worry, Doctor Bryne. They still won't see us coming."

AFTER A hasty meal of pasta, Penelope dressed in black jeans, boots, and a cotton T-shirt. It was a warm, humid night, and she was sweating before she finished pulling her boots on.

"Remind me why I have to wear jeans and boots in this heat?" she asked.

"You'll thank me for it when the time comes." Constantine passed a garment bag to Alexis. "This should fit."

Penelope sipped on cold water in the kitchen until the three men appeared—dressed identically as priests with black shirts and pants and pristine white collars.

She swallowed her water as her cheeks reddened. "You know, I had a dream like this once."

Alexis hid a smile while he pulled his tangle of black curls into a bun.

Constantine reached out to adjust Zo's collar. "You'll have to tell me all about it when we return."

"I'd love to, but I'm going to be too busy playing 'confession' with Alexis. I've just got so many sins. I'm a sinner. Sin all over," she said, straight-faced. Alexis gave her a promising smile in return.

Constantine sighed. "Some people get all the luck. Get your game face on, or I'll leave you behind." He passed Penelope a black satchel bag. Inside, he'd packed a flashlight, water, snacks, and mercury-filled glow sticks.

"Why am I suddenly concerned?"

"No need to worry, *cara*. I won't let you get lost," Alexis assured her.

Appropriately geared up, Penelope followed Zo and Constantine down into the cellars.

Constantine took out a bundle of iron keys. "I hope you don't mind small spaces," he said, then opened an ancient-looking door. He turned on a battery-powered camping lamp and disappeared inside.

Zo followed. "Make sure you knock down all the webs as you go. God, I hate spiders."

Penelope stepped into the cool, earthen tunnel, and realization dawned on her. "We're in the catacombs?"

Alexis stuck close behind her. "We will be. Constantine created this tunnel to join up to Rome's underground necropolis."

Penelope was familiar with the kilometers of catacombs under the city, dating back to the Etruscans. As Christians settled in Rome during the second century, the need to bury instead of burn the dead had arisen, and the catacombs expanded even farther.

"How far is it to the Vatican?" she asked just as the tunnel began to widen.

"About a two-kilometer walk," Alexis said.

"And we can trust that Constantine knows the way for sure?"

"Absolutely. He's smuggled in many popes and assassins over the years."

"Not to mention he funded most of the earliest churches in Rome, including St. Peter's, and ensured he had a hand in all of the designs, which always included multiple escape routes," Zo said over his shoulder.

"Clever."

"As a fox."

"And twice as handsome," Constantine called back to them. "Stop talking about me when you think I can't hear. You know these walls echo."

"We know," Zo said. "We just don't care."

The tunnels opened out, and chills swept down Penelope's arms. On all sides were niches carved into stone and earth, and each one held human bones. Shining her torch around, she saw that some were bigger than others, and the stone lining them was decorated with painted pictographs, figures in robes, pagan and Christian iconography combining together. Penelope tried not to get distracted, but she was overcome with the awe that always came with brushing against something so ancient.

"Does anyone know about these?" she asked.

Alexis shook his head. "No one has been in these particular catacombs for centuries, except Constantine."

"As much as I respect your profession, Penelope, sometimes it's better to let the dead be," Constantine said.

The archaeologist and historian sides of Penelope rose up. "Can you blame us young ones for wanting to know about our origins or hoping for a glimpse of the past to see where we came from and how people lived and loved?"

"If you don't mention my catacombs to any of your grave-robbing friends, I promise I'll tell you anything you want to know about life as a Roman and Byzantine."

"Be careful, Con. She'll hold you to that promise. Trust me. I speak from experience." Alexis lightly touched her lower back, diffusing her anger at being referred to as a grave robber.

Penelope took a calming breath and changed the subject. "Stop me if this is a dumb question, but why don't we use magic to portal ourselves into the Vatican Secret Archive? Why go through these catacombs at all?"

An amused chuckle burst out of Constantine. "Because Alexis can't get through."

"That's not entirely true," Alexis said. "The Vatican has certain... protections. There must've been a priest or two over the years holy enough to have the ability to do proper warding. Out of respect, I haven't tried my hand at breaking through them. There's never been a need to tamper with them because of Constantine's back way in."

"Seems fair. I get why Con insisted on the priest's attire in case we get spotted, but I don't get why *I* didn't get any."

"The Vatican is still on the fence about women being priests, and it would raise too many questions to see a woman dressed as one. It's not because I don't think women should be priests. Jesu save me, there were women priests in Paul's day, so I don't know why it became an issue later on."

"The damn patriarchy, that's why," Penelope whispered.

"And before you ask me, Penelope—no, I didn't purposely convince the Council of Nicaea to leave all the female apostles out of the

New Testament, and no, I wasn't responsible for making the Roman Empire Christian. All I did was sign an edict so that everyone would stop killing them."

"Poor Con has had to deal with some damning rumors over the centuries. As you can tell, he's still a little sensitive about them," Zo whispered, clearly trying not to laugh.

"I feel your pain, Con. If you think you've had it bad, try being an Atlantis expert and watching the crazies swarm with excitement." Penelope's amusement died as she remembered the Florence bombers citing her discovery as motivation to kill people. Even knowing Thevetat was behind it didn't make her feel any better. Gisela was still managing to keep the media and police from involving her in their investigations, but Penelope knew it was only a matter of time before she would have to go in for an interview.

Seeming to sense the change in her energy, Alexis found her hand in the darkness and gave it a gentle squeeze. No matter what happened, Alexis would be there.

Ten minutes later, Constantine said, "Not far now. This used to be the outskirts of the necropolis used by the Circus of Nero. Most people think I had these sections filled in when the basilica was commissioned, and I was content to let them keep believing it."

They came to a wood-and-iron door, and Constantine pulled out his bundle of ancient iron keys. "Be ready to take out the security cameras if we need to," he said to Alexis.

"Wait, I have something better." The scent of Alexis's magic filled the tunnel, and a second later, his magic settled over her skin.

Penelope shivered. "What was that?" He hummed with power, and her heart did stupid things when she looked up at him.

"It's a glamour to hide us from electronics, both recording devices and sensors. To any technology, we're invisible."

"Nice. When did you learn this?" Zo asked.

"It's something Galenos and I worked on a few years ago. I'll teach you later. Shall we go?"

The hinges groaned as Constantine unlocked the door and pulled it toward them, revealing wooden paneling. With a gentle shove, the wall slid forward.

"Doors hidden by bookshelves? I *love* this." Penelope tried to supress her enthusiasm.

Constantine went first and gestured to them that the coast was clear just as a woman appeared. Penelope froze, thinking they were busted before they'd even begun. The woman—tall, dark-haired, and stunning in a neat suit—all but launched herself at Constantine, kissing him with a violence that would've shocked Penelope had she not been trying not to laugh.

"Jesus Christ, we're on a time frame." Zo cursed under his breath, and Penelope elbowed him.

"Of all the places to blaspheme." Alexis merely shrugged, as if all heists with Constantine went like this.

When the couple finally came up for air, they exchanged hushed words in Italian too quickly for Penelope to follow. Constantine gestured at them. "This is Chiara. She's going to show us the way."

Chiara straightened her blouse, though she didn't look even a little bit embarrassed.

Penelope stepped out of the secret tunnel. "That's a lovely shade of lipstick on you."

"Jealousy is a curse," Constantine replied with a wink.

Penelope struggled to remain focused as they followed Chiara through metal shelving crammed with manuscripts. The Vatican Secret Archive had over eighty kilometers of shelving and contained over six hundred years' worth of letters, documents, papal bulls, and family histories. The conspiracy theorists loved it almost as much as they loved Atlantis, speculating what secrets were housed in the archive, from the true history of Jesus Christ to evidence of aliens. She would've liked to dig around for any mention of Atlantis, though she had a feeling that if they ever had anything, Alexis would've relieved them of it centuries ago.

Chiara stopped in front of a security door. Behind the wall of metal caging were hundreds of archive boxes. Chiara whispered to Constantine, passing him a piece of paper. He kissed her again, then she hurried away through the stacks.

Constantine held up the sticky note, which had a series of numbers written on it. "Location of what we're after."

"She didn't want to stick around?" asked Penelope.

"She's a busy lady, and I don't want to get her into any unnecessary trouble. Staff need to be out of the archives in twenty minutes. I don't want to give the guards any reason to come looking for anyone." He gestured to Zo. "I believe this is your area of expertise."

Zo made a noise in the back of his throat. "You wouldn't know what my expertise is." Regardless, he crouched down near the swipe card panel. Fascinated, Penelope watched as Zo sketched an invisible sigil on the keypad and whispered under his breath. His magic flared, and the door unlocked and swung open.

He shook out his hand. "You have to love a high tide."

"Any more magic and you would've blown the door off its hinges," Alexis said sternly.

"Everyone's a critic." Zo sighed. "Lead the way, Con. You know this storage system better than anyone."

In the end, they split up, Penelope and Alexis going one way and Constantine and Zo another, as they searched through the shelves.

"I'm extremely impressed with your self-control right now, Doctor Bryne," Alexis whispered.

"After the Archives and your Atlantis room in Venice, it would take a lot to impress me. That's not even mentioning Elazar's or Constantine's books." She'd been exposed to more rare collections in the past few months than she could've imagined. It wasn't as if she didn't have enough reasons to defeat Thevetat, but having the time to go through all of the Archives was high on her motivations list.

"After this mess is over, the Atlantis room is yours. Any questions you have, any memory you want to look at it, you need only to ask."

"You sure know how to charm a girl, Alexis Donato." Penelope pulled him closer.

He rested his hands on the shelves behind her, caging her in. "I did the research." He lowered his head so that she could reach up and kiss him. Penelope was dimly aware that it was probably a mortal sin to make out in the Vatican, and she counted her blessings that she wasn't Catholic.

"That's disgusting," Zo said. "Are there pheromones in the air down here that aren't working on me? Hurry up. We've found it."

"We'll discuss the list of Atlantis secrets I want to know later," Penelope said, and Alexis gave her a secret smile.

"If you're finished, come this way." Zo snagged Penelope's hand and pulled her out from under Alexis's arms.

"You're so pushy."

"Because I don't want to get caught—something you all should be concerned with instead of grinding up against each other."

"She can't help it. Books turn her on," said Constantine from a row over.

Penelope shrugged. "Guilty as charged."

They waited as Zo unlocked another cage. It contained at least another fifty archive boxes.

"Which one is it?" she asked.

Constantine opened the first box. "Chiara wasn't sure. She doesn't have that level of access and only knew the cage number. We're going to have to search through them."

Twenty minutes later, Penelope reached for another box, and her hands tingled with a flush of magic. The Living Language flashed words along her arms, too rapid for her to follow. She tipped open the lid and drew in a breath. Inside were bundles of letters and a thick leather book crammed with pieces of paper and held together with string. She looked at the contents list that had been pasted under the box lid. Magic hummed inside of her, and the typed Italian shivered and altered to read, *Correspondence of the Riario and Sforza families,*

Last Wills and Classified documents seized Pope Alexander VI, 1477-1509, "Experimenti" Ed. 1. 1509.

Unable to contain her excitement, Penelope said, "I think I found something." She passed the cardboard box lid to Alexis.

"Thank God. This was taking far too long." Zo inspected the contents of the box. His hand paused on the bound leather book. "Strange. I can feel the faint hum of power coming from this."

Alexis passed back the lid. "Let's take it. We can confirm its contents once we get back to Constantine's house. You know what to do, Zo."

"Yeah, yeah," Zo muttered as he leafed through the other documents, checking the box's entire contents. He spoke Atlantean under his breath, and for the hundredth time, Penelope wished she knew it. Zo used words to harness his magic, and after seeing his poetry, she had no doubt that they would be beautiful. The air beside her shivered like heat waves. Piece by piece, a box appeared, and the contents spun to life out of magic.

"So that's how you replicated my piece of the tablet in Greece. No wonder no alarms were raised."

Alexis picked up the original box, and Zo finished and slid the counterfeit back in its place.

"Not a bad night's work," Constantine said before they hurried through the dark archives and back to the secret door.

"Let's just hope it's what we're looking for, and you and Phaidros haven't made the wrong guess on where to look."

"Have faith, Penelope. It was prophesied that you'd find Solomon's seal ring. I might even let you keep it when we're done."

"Good luck getting it from her," said Alexis, with only a touch of a threat.

Penelope tuned them out as they headed back into the catacombs, her mind and the magic under her skin still racing after their brief contact with the box's contents. It held secrets, and she couldn't wait to get her hands on them again.

TWENTY-EIGHT

MARCO COULDN'T REMEMBER the last time he'd had so much time on his hands. He'd spent the last few days working for Isabella, doing all the odd jobs that maintaining the family palazzo demanded. He'd played host to the flurry of guests, tightened door hinges, cleaned rooms, polished furniture, and did whatever else Guilia instructed him to do. They were both determined that Isabella do as little as possible after the recent round of IVF, and while she hated the coddling, she had kept herself to the kitchen, cooking for the guests and their little family.

Despite the physical labor, Marco was bored. It wasn't a bad thing. He'd been working like a madman for years now. Maybe if he'd learned the value of slowing down earlier, he could've kept one of his girlfriends over the years. The work had always been a bigger issue than personality clashes. He wasn't sure if he liked this sudden introspection that this time on his hands afforded.

When Lyca turned up, Marco sent a prayer of thanks up to San Marco and hurried to greet her.

"What's happened? Has there been another attack?"

Lyca stepped out of her boat and gave him an incredulous stare. "Why do you assume the worst when I turn up to visit you? Are you that bored?"

"Yes." Lyca would've known he was lying if he said otherwise.

"Too bad. I've come for your sister's coffee and biscotti, not to free you from the confines of your holiday."

"Lyca! *Buongiorno!*" Isabella appeared and took the terrifying assassin into her arms, kissing her cheeks warmly. Isabella was the only person Marco had ever seen be game enough to embrace Lyca apart from Galenos. She had a warmth about her that obliterated any objections.

"It is good to see you, Bella. How have you been feeling?"

Isabella took Lyca's arm and led her toward the kitchen as they chatted like old girlfriends. Marco had introduced them in the weeks after their discovery of Thevetat's safe house in Venice. It had been Alexis's idea. If there was any chance that Thevetat could target Marco and his family, he wanted to ensure that Lyca's presence around them didn't raise any red flags. Marco often wondered if Penelope knew just how much Alexis took care of things under the radar.

Alexis had not only sponsored the reconstruction of the bomb sites, but funded restorers and builders to ensure that Venice was put back together exactly as she had been. One night, he'd shown up at Marco's house and demanded that he drive him around the whole lagoon. He'd done magic—something Marco still couldn't get over no matter how many times he saw it. "Venice needs more than just me protecting it," Alexis had said, and his body glowed with blue light as he created warding around the whole city.

Marco had wanted to argue that there were also the *polizia* to do their part, but the words died on his lips. His fellow officers had no fucking idea what really attacked them during Carnevale. Gisela knew something didn't entirely add up, even if she did agree to let Alexis be an informant of sorts. She'd questioned Marco on where Alexis had gotten his information, and he'd done his best not to relinquish any of the magician's secrets.

In the kitchen, Isabella set out pretty coffee cups and placed a tray of freshly baked pastries in front of Lyca. "How did you know I've been baking this morning?" she asked with a smile.

"Magic." Sugar dusted the smarmy grin Lyca gave Marco.

"Is Penelope still in Rome?" He sat down and took one of the almond treats before Lyca cleared the entire plate.

"You don't need to look so worried. She'll be home soon enough, and she has three big men to protect her."

"Marco is always worried. That's his magic." Isabella kissed the top of his head before pouring his coffee. "I haven't seen my brother this much in years."

"Don't pretend you won't be happy to see me go back to work."

"Of course I will. You're constantly under my feet." Isabella chuckled. "I'll go find Guilia. She's due for a break too." She left them alone in the kitchen.

"I worry about Penelope because there are psychopaths hoping she gets the blame for the bombings in Florence. I fear her being attacked by upset citizens more than Thevetat's people." Marco let the words tumble out, knowing they only had minutes alone.

"They won't be going out in public, and don't forget she's sleeping with the biggest psychopath of us all. They're currently robbing the Vatican and will be home before you know it."

Marco crossed himself. "God have mercy on you all."

Lyca only smiled. "God will understand. It's Aelia and Phaidros I'm worried about."

"Why? What's happened?"

"The documents Penelope has gone to get—they belonged to Caterina Sforza. She and Phaidros were lovers for most of her life. Aelia sided with the Borgias in their wars, mainly because she was jealous."

"And bringing up such love and war is going to reopen old wounds? That was a long time ago."

"Not so long when you're as old as us." Lyca sipped her coffee. "Plus, they slept together a week or so ago."

Marco choked on his biscotti. "What?"

"Surprised me too. You didn't think you had a chance, did you?"

"No. Nothing like that. To be honest, Aelia is too much drama for me. I couldn't keep up with her. I'm only surprised they finally went through with it." Marco stared at Lyca curiously, and her visit suddenly made sense. "You're hiding from them."

"The argument kicked off about an hour ago. I decided to make myself scarce." Lyca shrugged. "Also, I wanted to eat some of your sister's baking."

"At least you're honest. Here I thought you wanted my company."

Lyca was still laughing when Marco's phone rang. As he went to silence the call, he paused at the name. Gisela Bianchi. "I need to take this."

Lyca dismissed him with a wave. "More pastry for me."

"*Buongiorno*, Agent Bianchi." Marco stepped out of the kitchen and into their gardens.

"Hello, Marco. How's your holiday going?"

"Very well. Calm. Relaxing. Lots of family time."

"Sounds horrendously boring."

Marco laughed. "It is. What's wrong, Gisela? I know you're not ringing me because you miss me."

"And what if I am?"

He could almost see that frown line between her lovely brown eyes. "I'd be flattered, but you don't want to hear about my holiday. Spit it out."

"Where's Penelope?"

"Rome, with Alexis. A short visit. She'll be home in a day or two."

"Can you please talk her into going in to give a statement? I can't hold them off any longer, Marco. I gave them everything in the Duilio case. They've combed through all of the public research on her discovery and the internet forum chatter around it. There are a lot of crazy Atlantis believers out there. I had no idea how many people see Penelope as their hope to find it."

"I'm not sure she'd be pleased to hear that. She's dealt with many intense fans over the years."

"There are some crazy conspiracies, and the authorities want to make sure she's not secretly stirring these people up. The attacks in Florence were well coordinated, and no matter how many times we take the terrorists' manifesto video down, another one pops up."

"I've got someone I can talk to about that. He'll be able to trace where they're coming from." Marco made a mental note to bring it up with Galenos.

"I have a team for that."

"The more people on it, the better. I don't want anyone blaming Penelope for this atrocity."

Gisela made a sound of frustration. "They already are, Marco. That's what I'm saying. She needs to submit herself to questioning before they drag her in. Please, you're her friend. Talk to her before it's too late. It will be worse for her if it looks like she's being arrested, and I don't want to think about what her overprotective boyfriend will do to a protestor."

"You're right. I know. I'll talk to her as soon as she gets back."

"Use your policeman tone on her and get her to listen. I have to go. Let me know when she's going in so I can make sure they don't botch the interview."

"Thanks for the call, Gisela. It was nice to hear from you."

"Try not to get too fat as you lounge about all day."

"Try not to be too jealous that I got approved for holidays."

He almost dropped the phone in surprise when he heard her laugh on the other end of the line. "I'm so tired, Marco," she admitted, the exhaustion in her voice audible.

"You're welcome to come stay in Venice if you want a break."

"I might just take you up on that one day." She hung up before he could reply.

"What did Gisela want?" Lyca asked, appearing out of nowhere.

"*Dio!* Would you mind not sneaking up on a poor man?" Lyca stared at him expectantly. "She wants me to convince Penelope to go give a statement to prove she had nothing to do with the attacks. We also need to ask Galenos to wipe that video off the face of the earth."

"Consider it done. I'm glad you're still on friendly terms with the agent. We might need her before the end." Lyca sat down on a stone bench.

"What do you mean?"

"Milos. That's where Thevetat's lair is, and it's where we will attack him. I've been going through it with Constantine—the best ways to approach the island, etcetera. There is going to be a moment—a window of time when Thevetat is going to remove his power from his priests. That's when we'll attack."

"Will you let me help?"

"You want to? We will be vastly outnumbered, and they might not have magic, but they'll have weapons. It will be messy and not at all legal. Are you really willing to risk your life like that? You have a family that loves you." Lyca's fierce expression left no doubts about the seriousness of the coming fight.

"I know, but you're my family too. I need to see this through, Lyca—no matter how dark or messy. I need to know in my bones that it's over. I love my family, but they gave up on me being the one to carry on the family name long ago." The thought still pained him a little, even though he'd accepted that he wouldn't be the one married and surrounded by children. He'd never admit that he was also secretly relieved the pressure had been taken off him, and the fear that he'd become his father as soon as he had children of his own was something he no longer had to worry about.

"I won't let you be on the front line, so you can forget about that. You can still help. I want you stationed at Milos as a tourist, so if we can't stop Thevetat, you can call in backup. You need to be able to get the word out to another team, and they will bomb the shit out of the compound. Anything to stop Thevetat from leaving the island. Gisela might be able to help coordinate the cleanup with the government and say it was a terrorist operation."

"You really believe Penelope will fail?"

"I can hope and pray that she doesn't, but I won't take the risk of not having a backup plan."

Marco held out his hand to the magician. "I'm in." Lyca shook it, and Marco felt the last of his law-abiding morals die.

TWENTY-NINE

THE DEEP TENSION in Alexis's bones eased as soon as he stepped back onto the dock at the Calle dei Cerchieri. He could feel the solid weave of his wardings around the city and the palazzo stronger than ever, and the buzzing of magic along his skin told him that everything was well. Which was why he was surprised to find broken crockery all over the kitchen and dining area, and Aelia and Phaidros red-faced and snarling at each other.

Penelope took in the wreckage with wide eyes. "What's going on?"

"Alexis and Constantine are back now, so you can go and cry to them about what a horrible person I am." Phaidros pushed Alexis out of the doorway and stormed off.

"Aelia?" She was shaking, but she wasn't in tears, so Alexis counted his blessings.

"All I did was try to talk to him about Caterina, and he lost his damn mind." Aelia huffed, and Alexis sensed this was a half-truth. She rested a hand on her cocked hip. "Well? Did you find the slut's stupid papers?"

"Whoa, is name-calling really necessary?" Penelope asked.

"It is where she is concerned."

"That's enough, Aelia. Go cool down, and when you decide to speak like a civilized person, you can return."

Aelia turned bright red, but Alexis was stern enough that she was smart enough not to push him. She stormed out of the kitchen, grinding the broken crockery into the tiles as she went.

Alexis watched her go. "I suppose we should count our blessings that they've remained peaceful this long."

"I'll find a broom," Penelope said.

"No need. I'll do it." Alexis held out his hand and let the pent-up magic inside of him trickle out. The fine grains of glass and porcelain lifted into the air, and the kitchen gradually remade itself.

Penelope gasped. "Wow."

"The high tide has its upsides, including frivolous magic use," Alexis said, her awe softening the sharper edges of his mood.

"Then that settles it. I'm not washing another dish until the tide goes down."

"Your wish is my command, Archivist." Alexis bowed.

"You're a genie at high tide too? This keeps getting better and better." Penelope squealed when he dragged her close and planted a kiss on her mouth.

"I know you're trying to distract me, naughty Archivist."

"Anything to stop you from frowning at lovers' tiffs that are *not* our concern."

"It'll become our concern if I can't get them to work together when the time comes."

"That time isn't now. Don't worry about it until you need to."

Alexis's eyes narrowed. "This coming from the biggest worrier of us all. Why are you in such a good mood?"

"Because I'm incredibly nosey and have a box of rare, precious documents to go through and scandalous secrets to uncover. Not to mention a whole bunch of books from Nereus's Atlantis collection. And I have a handsome man that I can kiss whenever I like," Penelope said and proved it.

"All excellent arguments, I must admit. Where would you like to start?"

"The Archives with the Vatican documents. I won't be able to concentrate on anything else until I have a look through them."

Alexis retrieved the box of papers from Constantine's arms minutes later. "Be careful of Aelia and Phaidros. They are at each other's
throats."

"Consider me warned. I'm more interested in talking with Lyca
and planning our invasion of Milos anyway. I was always better at war
than love."

Zo walked past them and headed for the staircase. "That's certainly what all the women in your life have said…"

Alexis moved away before another argument started. One was
enough for the day. If all else failed, he'd teach Penelope to lock them
out of the Archives.

THE WHOLE next day, Alexis was happily ensconced in Penelope's office, reading his way through Nereus's journals, using colorful
tabs to mark any places he noticed the strange, unreadable scribble. He
was eager for Penelope to translate them for him, so that he could study
them before she decided to test out any more of their suggestions. He
didn't mention it to her again, but he had a strange feeling that the
small annotations had been scribed by Poseidon. She was curled up on
the couch opposite him, reading a storybook about Poseidon.

Penelope's phone buzzed angrily on the small coffee table beside
her, interrupting the peaceful moment. She cast a glance at the flashing
name before sending it straight to voice mail.

"Someone you're avoiding, *mi amore*?"

Penelope turned back to her book. "It's Stuart wanting to be an
asshole. It's bad enough that Marco's been texting me about going to
the police to give a statement. I don't need my father grilling me too."
She stared at Alexis, as if expecting him to say something in her father's
defense, but he knew better.

"I'm sure you'll talk to Stuart when you're ready. Marco is right about the statement though. I don't trust the *polizia* to make the right judgment calls without your written explanation."

"They haven't asked me for one, which means they don't want it. Marco is panicking because he has too much time on his hands. Stopping Thevetat is more important."

Alexis couldn't argue with that. He was about to suggest they break for dinner when a ripple of magic rattled through the Archives.

Penelope glanced around. "What was that?"

"Stay here. I'll be right back." He portaled into the main foyer of the palazzo. If Aelia and Phaidros had progressed to using magic on each other, he was going to send them both for a dip in the lagoon to cool off.

"Alexis!" Aelia screamed from the courtyard, her voice full of terror.

He ran to find her. *Surely Thevetat wouldn't be so stupid to try to attack us here again.*

Aelia was panicking, clutching at her long hair with one hand, the other gripping the hilt of her gladius.

"What's happening?" Alexis demanded, and she threw herself into his arms. "Breathe, Aelia. Tell me what's wrong?"

"I g-got a call from my housekeeper in Vienna. She said there were people at the villa. She was s-so scared. I told her to stay hidden, but she started s-screaming. Then the line went dead." Aelia clutched her phone. "Please take me to her. Thevetat attacked Elazar. Maybe they know where my villa is too."

Cold settled along Alexis's bones. "We'll go. Let me get my things and meet me at the front door."

Minutes later, he found Penelope waiting with Constantine, who was holding Aelia, murmuring low reassurances to her.

"You were meant to stay in the Archives," Alexis said to Penelope.

"And let you go off on some crazy murder mission without saying goodbye? Unlikely." She folded her arms.

"How did you know—"

"I felt it through the *moíra desmós*. It went dead-still and very cold."

"Sounds like the killing calm," said Constantine.

Alexis glared at him, but he wasn't wrong. "Look after Penelope, and let Zo and Elazar know what's happened."

Aelia loosened her grip on Constantine and gave him a nod. "I'm ready."

Alexis kissed Penelope. "I'll be home soon."

"You'd better be."

Phaidros appeared, bow in one hand. "Don't try to argue with me, Aelia. I'm coming." He took Aelia by the hand, and she didn't shake it off. Alexis placed his hand on Phaidros's shoulder and released his magic, the palazzo blurring around them.

In Vienna, the sun was setting and the villa was in flames. They stood in Aelia's gardens as the supernatural fire ate through the main building. Aelia let out a cry of terror and raced inside.

"Aelia, stop!" Alexis shouted, but she ignored him.

"I'll follow her. Check the grounds for any escaping priests." Phaidros hurried after her.

Alexis swore in frustration. His yataghan appeared in his hand, and he went hunting.

PHAIDROS CAST a shield around himself as the burning walls surrounded him. The strange energy of Thevetat's power was tangible in the smoke and air.

"Aelia!"

He felt for her magic amidst the chaos. The rooms filled with ancient, beautiful instruments were burning to cinders. A high-pitched note echoed through the halls, and he latched on to the feel of Aelia's magic. He found her in the courtyard in the middle of the villa, clutching a bloody body and sobbing.

"Aelia…" He approached her slowly, despite the flames creeping from the front of the villa. He'd seen a cry from Aelia melt a man's brain with magic, and he wasn't about to startle her.

"We were too late. I'm always too late." Tears streamed down her cheeks.

Phaidros crouched by her side and studied the older woman in her arms. She'd been stripped bare, and her body was covered in the same carved and burnt glyphs that scarred Aelia's own skin.

"I'm sorry, love." He rested a hand on her shaking back, then looked up to see a message scrawled in bloody Atlantean symbols across the marble wall: *Slut to a dead god.*

"That's what Kreios whispered when he carved into me." Aelia's sobs were gone; there was only sadness left. She would resent him for trying to comfort her, so Phaidros pried the old woman's body from her tight grip instead.

"Let's get her out of here. They could still be close by, and you won't get your revenge sitting here weeping." He scooped the body up in his arms.

Aelia got to her feet and drew her sword. Her clothes were smeared in blood, and she looked as fearsome as a Fury. "This way. I'll cover you." She strode past the wall of abuse and back into the villa.

Phaidros spotted the figure moving amongst the smoke just as Aelia moved, cutting down the priest before he detected them. She lifted a small earpiece from the dead man and fitted it into her ear.

"They're meeting on the north side of the property. There are gardens there," she said.

The place was huge, and a part of Phaidros was sad that he'd never seen it before then. Outside the house again, they placed the housekeeper's body under a pine tree, where it would be safe from the ravaging flames. He unbuttoned his shirt and placed it over her, covering her nakedness as best he could. Aelia watched him, hollow-eyed.

"Thank you," she murmured, then turned on her heel. "We have to hurry before Alexis gets them all."

Phaidros followed her blindly through the dark gardens, checking the shadows for priests. A pulse of Alexis's power shuddered around them, and Aelia slid to a halt.

"What in Poseidon's name was that?"

"Alexis has just lost his temper." Phaidros ran to where the power emanated from.

A priest missing an arm stumbled in front of them, and Phaidros sank an arrow into her eye. The smell of burning flesh and blood grew stronger with every step. More dead littered the ground, and they followed the decimated bodies until they came to a small clearing, where a large stone fountain had been reduced to broken marble and spraying water.

Alexis stood in the middle of a ring of fallen priests, blue power simmering over him. He raised a bloody hand toward the burning villa, and wind rolled out of him. Wherever it flowed, the flames died. Alexis's head snapped to them, and Phaidros fought the urge to wet himself.

"Alexis, it's us," he said, his voice not nearly as strong as he wanted it to be.

Alexis swiped his sword down, shaking off the blood and gore that slicked it. "Kreios is here, and Thevetat too." His voice was far away and wreathed in power.

Aelia made a small sound behind Phaidros. He spun to find her violet eyes wide as a blade pressed to her throat. Phaidros trained an arrow on the tall figure behind her.

"Too slow, bowman." Red eyes gleamed in the shadows. It was a voice that echoed through his nightmares of blood and darkness and ash.

"Kreios," Phaidros said. He did not lower his bow.

Alexis stepped through the rubble. "Let her go. You can't take the three of us."

"The high tide works in my favor as much as yours, magician." Kreios smiled as he pulled Aelia back up against him. "You smell delicious as always, priestess. I can still detect my mark on you. There are some taints you can't wash aw—" Kreios shuddered and shoved Aelia at Phaidros. The knife in his hand lowered, as if invisible hands were dragging it down. His red eyes flashed back to his natural black. "Run, Aelia! I can't hold him back forever. Get out of here!"

Alexis tilted his head. "Gods, he's trying to fight Thevetat."

"Go, you insufferable bastard! He's got something planned for Penelope. I don't know what. You have to—" Kreios groaned, and the knife in his hand drove down into his thigh. He screamed, then lifted his head, eyes red once more. "Traitorous fool. You should know better than to force me away." He pulled the knife from his thigh and sliced it into his arms as punishment.

Phaidros was frozen in shock as Alexis grabbed him by the arms and his magic dragged him down.

THIRTY

PENELOPE STARED AT the space where Alexis had stood minutes before, the panic rising in her. It was why she automatically answered her phone without checking the name on the screen.

"Hello?"

"Penelope! Thank Christ you finally bothered to answer," Stuart Bryne said.

Penelope flinched, and Constantine gave her a quizzical look. "Hey. Sorry I've kept missing you."

"You could've made the time to call me back, at least to put your mother out of her misery. We've seen the footage from Florence. What's happening over there? What have you gotten caught up in, Penelope?"

Penelope took a deep breath and tried to keep her voice steady. "I haven't called you because there's been nothing to tell. There are ongoing investigations into the Florence attacks, but as yet, I haven't been questioned, nor am I under any suspicion."

"They are using your discovery as their rally cry! Of course you are going to be under suspicion. You packed up and left Australia to live with a group of strangers. Please tell me you aren't involved in this movement, even remotely."

Penelope couldn't believe her ears. "Are you actually asking me if I'm encouraging people to bomb each other? Do you really think so little of me?"

"I know you'd do anything to prove you were right about the damn stone tablet and your Atlantis theory. You might not even know that you're working with extremists. Have you accepted money from anyone lately to further your research?" If he hadn't sounded genuinely worried underneath his anger, Penelope would've hung up on him.

"Stuart, listen to me and stop jumping to ridiculous conclusions. I haven't accepted any private money to continue my research. I've always had people contacting me with crazy Atlantis theories, and I've never encouraged or entertained any of them—especially not ones that promote some messed-up sense of Aryan brotherhood, master race, neo-Nazi propaganda."

"You might not have realized that was their agenda. If the police find out you've had any contact with them at all, you could be tried as a terrorist, Penelope! All because you wouldn't let your bullshit about a myth die with Plato and get yourself a decent job in a respectable…"

Penelope let the rant wash over, numbed to her core by the fact that her own father would think she'd be involved—even remotely— with a mass killing. She didn't fight Constantine when he plucked the phone out of her hand.

"That's quite enough. Your daughter is one of the most intelligent, brave, and honorable people I've ever met, and I won't allow you to accuse her of such nonsense. As her father, you should know better and believe her when she speaks the truth. Shame on you, sir." Constantine hung up the phone and passed it back to Penelope. "I believe it's time for some fresh air. Let's go for a walk. I have a need to see the great saint's bones."

Penelope was horrified when tears began to fall down her cheeks. Constantine put his arms around her, and she bit back a sob. "There now, don't let him get to you." He rubbed her back. Though he didn't wield magic, her nose still picked up the scents that identified the uncanniness of his long life. Constantine's scent was like a holy war: parchment, temple incense, blood, and horses. She let him hold her until she'd calmed enough to speak.

"He actually thinks I'm a terrorist." She scrubbed at her cheeks with the palms of her hands.

"He's concerned, confused, and clearly terrible at communicating that correctly. I know you well enough to know that you're not about to let his lack of approval change your mind about anything."

Penelope sniffed and smiled at him. "You're right, and I do need a walk to clear my head and take my mind off worrying about Alexis."

They stepped through the blue door into the early Venetian evening. It was still warm, but the humidity had eased, replaced by a gentle breeze from the north. It took until the Accademia Bridge for the lump in Penelope's throat to recede.

Tourists lingered in small groups, and lights flickered on along the Grand Canal. The whole city was pale orange in the fading light. Venice was beautiful, and it was that beauty that always managed to soothe Penelope's ragged emotions.

"You really shouldn't worry about Alexis so much either." Constantine maneuvered around a group of Japanese tourists taking selfies on the top of the bridge.

"Yes, I should. He's throwing himself into danger, knowing that it's another trap of Thevetat's."

"Alexis has purposely walked into many traps before. Phaidros and Aelia will make sure he doesn't do anything too reckless, and if he does, they will be there to clean it up. Thevetat is attacking their emotions, hoping it will make them irrational. Alexis won't fall for it."

Penelope didn't want to argue with him about it. No one but her seemed to show any concern for Alexis. They all saw him as the Defender, with the exception of Nereus. *Protect him, Penelope. Whatever happens, protect him,* she'd said.

"Has your father always talked to you like that?" Constantine asked her.

"Pretty much."

"Any idea why?"

"Lots of reasons. I know it started because he didn't want children, but Mom got pregnant. He did his best, I suppose." There was a time, when she was much younger, that she looked up to him, but that faded when she refused to follow in his footsteps. She'd always been determined to carve her own path instead of treading on the smooth way made by others.

"Some people aren't cut out to be fathers. I would know; I'm one of them."

"I thought you had loads of children." So many, in fact, that the Roman Empire found itself in another civil war when his sons fought for supreme control.

"I did, and I failed them all in one way or another. The younger ones came too late, when I'd already stopped knowing how to love them or even trusted myself to do so."

"Why wouldn't you trust yourself to love your own children?" Penelope asked as they reached the still crowded Piazza San Marco.

"Because I didn't know how to be an emperor *and* a father. There came a time I had to choose between the two, and I made the biggest mistake of my life." Constantine looked over at her. "I thought Alexis would've already told you. It was the first—and most intense—falling out we ever had."

"What did you do?"

Deep, bitter sadness filled his eyes. "I killed my son."

Penelope let the noise of the piazza wash over her as she processed that statement, debating how much she could press him about such a personal matter. The Basilica San Marco rose up at the end of the square—a beacon to all who passed through Venice. Its iconic blend of Byzantine and Italian architecture never failed to fill Penelope with awe and reverence despite her lack of faith. It was stunning, from its great cupolas, stolen bronze horses, veined marbles, and mind-blowing mosaics.

Constantine stared at the building, looking a bit smug. "Do you know it was based on my design for the Church of Apostles in Constantinople?"

Penelope laughed. "Of course it was."

"It's true. I had plans to have the bones of all twelve apostles placed in it. In retrospect, I suppose it's a good thing I never succeeded, or their bones would've been scattered and destroyed when Constantinople fell. This one has Saint Mark, at least."

"You really believe it's him? I mean, it could be anyone's bones in there."

"I have faith that those intrepid Venetian merchants and Greek monks managed to sneak him out of his crypt in Alexandria and to safety. It's a fabulous story either way, and sometimes, a story can be just as powerful and holy as a saint's bones."

Instead of heading for the basilica, Constantine detoured around the lines of tourists outside of it and around the edge of the building. He stood in front of the purple-red, porphyry statues of the Tetrarchs and folded his arms.

"Speaking of terrible fathers, there are both of mine standing with my enemies," he said with a nod.

"Both of them?" Penelope sifted through undergraduate Roman history.

"Constantius wasn't too bad if you forget that he sent me to Diocletian's court as a damn hostage. Diocletian taught me a lot about running a court, but he and Galerius thought the best way to deal with me was to send me to fight barbarians and Persians." The expression on his face changed from amusement to a sneer as he whispered to the statue, "You thought the empire was too big for one man to run, and I did it for thirty years. I defeated all of you old bastards, and no matter how many years pass, the victory is still so sweet."

Penelope glanced around, hoping that no one else could hear him. An older woman wearing a pale yellow dress stared back at her, her dark brows knit in confusion. Something shivered along Penelope's skin—her magic and intuition warning her to move away before they drew any more attention.

"Stop abusing the statue, Con. People are starting to notice," Penelope said as the stranger tugged on her husband's sleeve.

"There are some pleasures that time doesn't diminish, and having a good gloat over your enemies is one of them." With that, he relented, and they made for the atrium.

Parts had been closed off to the public, and Penelope spied workmen and restorers repairing the warp on the mosaic floors. Above her, the golden tiles shone with the last moment of sun that lit up the Cupola of the Creation and the concentric bands, which told the story of creation in twenty-six scenes.

"This is the beginning of Genesis." Constantine pointed at the script that ran around them and whispered it to her in perfect Latin.

They went inside the cool, dark interior—a welcome reprieve from the heat. The susurration of people trying to be quiet as they pointed in excitement echoed through the space over the background music of church choirs. Penelope was full of wonder at the magnitude of artistic creation and history around her, and awkward at the same time, because she didn't know any of the Catholic rituals.

Constantine crossed himself before making his way to the candles. Penelope wondered who he would light a candle for when he'd lived so long and lost so many. Her thoughts automatically turned to Tim, and even though he would've made fun of her for doing it, she lit one for him and hoped that if there was an afterlife, he was enjoying it. She let the loss of him seep through her, hoping Constantine didn't notice the way her eyes filled again. *It must be the day for crying.* Constantine took her hand as he stared at the flames.

"The pain never goes away. If anyone tries to tell you otherwise, they are liars or haven't experienced true loss," he said, which only made her want to cry more.

They kept walking until they came to the Gothic iconostasis that marked the main part of the church from the presbytery, the statues of the apostles and the Virgin looking down on them. There was no evening mass, so they walked through the marble archway and sat down on an empty pew that looked on the sarcophagus of Saint Mark, sitting under its baldachin of green marble and alabaster.

Penelope leaned close to Constantine. "Can I ask what happened with your son?"

"I had a feeling you would."

"You wouldn't have mentioned it if you didn't want to talk about it."

The corner of Constantine's mouth rose in a wry smile. "You have a point. My firstborn was a special boy. He was the product of a love marriage, something my other children couldn't claim. I won't tell you about Minerva. I still hate talking about her death as much as I hate talking about Crispus. You only get the one today."

"I can understand that. You loved her?"

"Deeply. Then she died, and I married the daughter of my defeated enemy, Maximian."

"That's brutal."

"You have no idea. My mother tried to warn me, but it was done to regain some of the peace the civil war had caused."

"I can't imagine what that must've been like." The thought of being trapped in a marriage for political reasons horrified her.

"I wanted to be emperor more than anything else. There was nothing I wouldn't have done—that I didn't do—to secure that, including marrying a hateful woman like Fausta and making her give me heirs."

"How did she handle having a stepson around?"

"Well enough. Crispus was handsome and charming, like his father."

"I can imagine."

"He was becoming a competent leader with armies who were loyal to him. Fausta saw it too, and despite our years together and the children we'd had, she still had the taint of her father running through her veins. God, that woman grew spite like a rose garden grows weeds." Constantine's mouth thinned, stormy eyes growing cold. "I won't tell you the full, winding tragedy of it. It's too damn sad. When information came to me that Crispus was planning to use his influence with the army to overthrow me, I flew into a rage, filled with hurt and betrayal that cut deeper than any knife could. I acted too quickly in that anger—too decisively. I had him arrested and executed. I was emperor. I wouldn't allow another civil war to break out. Alexis had been on a mission for me in the Danube, keeping an eye on the restless barbarians. As soon as word reached him that Crispus had been arrested, he magicked himself to Rome, but he was too late. The deed was done."

Penelope didn't dare look at him, nor did she reach out to touch his clenched fists with gentle hands. She knew if she did, he'd stop talking, and a blind man could have seen the wound inside him needed lancing. The priests moved around the church, speaking softly with visitors and congregation members. Surely Constantine would be better off talking to one of them.

"The night Alexis returned, I honestly thought he was going to kill me. He loved Crispus like a son. He'd been one of his tutors and often fought with Lactantius on what to teach him. He couldn't—wouldn't—believe that Crispus would be willing to betray his family, even with the evidence we gave him. He swore he'd never help me again. Then, a few months later, he reappeared with a satchelful of letters and witness statements. Alexis had found proof that Crispus wasn't trying to start a civil war. It had been Fausta all along. She'd been trying her best to seduce him, amongst others, to gain favor and influence. Crispus had been trying to find how the conspiracy was connected before he came to me with it. I didn't even give him a chance to explain. I couldn't even *look* at him when I had him arrested. The order was carried out before my temper had cooled enough to think it through."

"And Fausta?" Penelope whispered, mouth dry.

Constantine smiled then—a sharp and deadly thing that sent goose bumps down her spine. "Alexis got Fausta. It would've been dishonorable for a husband to kill his wife, though God knew I wanted to choke the breath from her hateful body. Alexis drowned her with his bare hands, and even that couldn't satisfy his grief and rage at me. Not that I blamed him. It had been an ugly business, and he disappeared shortly after. He checked in occasionally, but it would be years before we spoke again."

Constantine unclenched his fist and took Penelope's hand. "Alexis and I have always argued, but I'm so happy that you've brought us all together again, Penelope."

"Even if we're all going to die because we're caught up in a prophecy?"

The coldness melted from Constantine's expression. "*Especially* because we all might die. Who knows—that damn prophecy might be the key to all of us being entangled together in these too-long lives. If we fulfill it, we might finally live and die as we should."

"Does that possibility frighten you?"

"No. I've been dead once already, and I have lived long enough as it is. I know all the magicians feel the same. Maybe Aelia would complain about the wrinkles, but that would be the extent of it."

Penelope muffled her laughter so as not to appear disrespectful. "You're right. She'd really hate that."

"Thank you for listening to this old man's confession."

"Thank you for trusting me enough to tell me."

"You're not repulsed by what I did? What Alexis did?"

Penelope looked up at the shining gold mosaics and saints above her, trying to formulate the best answer. "Who am I to judge? You seem to be carrying plenty of guilt without my sentence to make the load heavier. As for Alexis? He's all about justice. I know that. He's probably seeking his idea of it right now. It's who he is—a dark part of him, but a part all the same. I have to love that part with all the rest; otherwise, what I feel for him isn't really love. So no, I'm not repulsed by either of you. You wanted to talk about Crispus, and I'm a substitute for Alexis, because you don't really want forgiveness from your God or me, but him."

"You are as astute as you are beautiful, Penelope. Maybe Alexis is the god I need forgiveness from after all."

"Maybe don't refer to him as a god while we're in here. I don't need to be hit with a lightning bolt on top of everything else."

"If Alexis were a lesser man with a larger ego, he could've set himself up as a god. He can perform wonders and deal out justice with the best of them. It's probably why he's never felt the need to bend his knee to any deity. He knows there's something bigger and more powerful than himself in this universe, but there's no horror or paradise that can be promised that he hasn't already seen and lived through. Some people would say it's a hard thing to love a man like that."

"Some people are idiots," Penelope said before checking herself.

Constantine only laughed. "*Most* people are idiots. Let's continue our walk, Doctor Bryne. I require wine after that conversation."

They'd just made it out of the main doors when a woman screamed, "There she is! That's the bitch responsible for Florence."

Penelope's head whipped about. The woman in the yellow dress stood pointing, a crowd gathering behind her. A flash of hatred flickered through the woman's eyes before jumping to the person beside her, running through the crowd and making them angrier. Their voices rose as they spewed angry accusations in Italian and English.

Magic shuddered under Penelope's skin, trying to warn her of the danger. Constantine had moved her behind him, clearly not needing magic to see a fight brewing. He pulled a knife from somewhere, and the people shifted away from them.

"Back inside, Penelope," he said.

She pushed her way back through the exit. Constantine followed, and after a moment, the angry crowd did too. He put his hand on the small of her back, guiding her toward the altar. He spoke to a priest in rapid Italian, pointing to the crowd. The priest looked at Penelope in shock before ushering them behind the golden altar. Penelope pulled her phone out and rang Marco.

"*Buongiorno*, Penelope. What trouble have you gotten into now?"

"I'm stuck inside the basilica. Someone recognized me from the news and has stirred up a damn crowd."

"Is Alexis with you?"

"No, he's in Vienna. I'm with Constantine." She paced up and down the tiles. More priests had gathered, and Constantine was talking with them, his words quick and urgent.

"Stay where you are. I'll be there soon with some *polizia* to break them up. Don't do anything brave, Penelope."

Marco hung up. Penelope's finger hovered over Alexis's number, but he was caught up in God knew what, and contacting him now could endanger him.

"One of the priests has gone to fetch the *polizia locale* that usually patrols the piazza, and the others have gone to clear the church." Constantine joined her where she stood. "Don't worry, Penelope. We'll get you out of here."

"Marco was right. He told me to go give a statement before this escalated, and I didn't want to listen," she said, the angry faces still swimming in front of her.

Constantine lifted her chin. "Look at me. This is not your fault. These people only want someone to blame and take their pain and hate out on. They aren't going to lay a finger on you. Do you hear me?"

"Yes." She swallowed down her tears.

A short time later, raised voices inside the church announced the arrival of a pissed-off Marco and a group of uniformed officers. He looked relieved when he saw her and the big bodyguard beside her.

"Friend of Alexis?" Marco asked, staring at Constantine.

"Good friend," Penelope confirmed with a nod, fighting the urge to hug him.

"We need to take you to the station and get this mess sorted out."

"I'm coming with you," Constantine said. "Alexis would murder me if I let you go alone."

Marco looked the opposite of enthused. "Great, another overprotective man. Just what we need to stir up the media."

"If they ask, I'll tell them we're dating." Constantine gave Penelope a wink.

She glared at him. "You do, and I'll *let* Alexis murder you."

"Fine," Marco said. "He can come if it means we can get you out of here."

They formed a protective ring around her before stepping out into the night and into the shouts and flashing of smartphone cameras. Constantine had her by one hand and Marco the other as they escorted her to the waiting police boat. All she could do was follow their instructions and wish Alexis would hurry back to Venice.

THIRTY-ONE

IT HAD STARTED out as another peaceful day. Now he was back
at the station but not on duty, feeling out of place and unable to help
as Penelope was locked into an interview. Marco did manage to convince the officers on duty to let him and Constantine sit on the other
side of the mirrored glass and observe. It wasn't like Penelope was being
arrested. She was willingly giving a statement, and hopefully, the media
would get what they needed and back off.

"Thank the saints that Alexis is in Vienna." Marco chewed on his
lip and desperately wished for a cigarette.

"He'll be back soon enough," Constantine said without taking his
eyes off Penelope.

"Did you message him, at least?"

"Do I look stupid? Penelope isn't in any danger, and he'll panic.
Alexis isn't reasonable when it comes to her. You know that, don't you?"

"I do. He nearly lost her a few months ago—that would be enough
to send anyone into overprotective mode. Alexis is also…special." Marco
didn't dare say what Alexis actually was out loud in a police station.

"He is that."

"Are you?"

The big man gave him a wry smile. "What do you think?"

"If Alexis trusts you to be alone with Penelope, then I suppose you
must be." Marco ran a hand through his hair, watching as Penelope
calmly answered questions and the officer opposite her took notes.

"She should've come and done this a week ago, headed off the media and their lies."

"She's had more pressing matters to attend to. You can get the media to print something, can't you? Something official that will tell the public she's had no role in the bombings."

"I can try. The police will release a statement about it. Let's hope there won't be a repeat of this evening. Some of the witnesses said you pulled a knife on them."

Constantine didn't look the slightest bit worried. "They were worked up and distraught. It doesn't surprise me that they made up facts to make their own part sound less cowardly."

"Uh-huh. If you say so. Make sure it doesn't make an appearance while we're here, okay?"

It was almost midnight, and Marco was making another round of espressos when the hair on the back of his neck rose. The lights through the station flickered, and Constantine swore in something that sounded like Latin.

"What was that?" Marco asked.

"Alexis is here." Constantine nodded toward the main doors.

They opened with a bang, and a strong wind blew in just before Alexis filled the doorframe. Dressed in a neat suit, his face was smiling, but the look in his eyes when they landed on Marco made his pulse quicken. He'd only seen Alexis look that angry the night of the storm. Galenos came in behind him, also dressed in a suit and carrying an official-looking briefcase.

"Inspector Dandolo, I'm so glad to see that you are here." Alexis reached out a hand for Marco to shake.

Marco did his best to hold Alexis's eye contact. "I wouldn't be anywhere else at a time like this."

"What room is she in?" Alexis asked, not letting his hand go.

"Three."

"Galenos, go."

The tall magician gave Marco a sympathetic nod before hurrying past them.

"He's Penelope's lawyer—someone that should've been present before this interview started."

"She came willingly."

"That's not what I heard." Alexis finally let Marco's hand go and turned his fierce gaze on Constantine. "You were with her?"

"Every moment."

Marco whispered, "Your friend here thought it was a good idea to pull a knife on a crowd. You both should be grateful he's not in an interview room too."

"Is she hurt?"

"Not even a scratch, Alexis. I swear it," said Constantine.

There was a long pause before Alexis looked down at Marco. "Can I see her?"

Marco nodded. "Come this way."

He took Alexis back to the viewing room and away from the all-too-perceptive eyes of the other officers. Any time Alexis Donato decided to make an appearance was noteworthy. Marco could only pray that the younger female officers weren't on Twitter that very minute.

As soon as Alexis saw Penelope, the tension in him seemed to soften. She was talking with Galenos, a small frown on her face. Her hazel eyes swept up to the mirrored glass, as if she knew Alexis was there, and smiled. Alexis exhaled, his hands unclenching from their fists.

"I told you she was unharmed, Alecto," Constantine said.

"It shouldn't have happened."

"I agree. That's why I haven't shut up about Penelope coming in early for this," Marco said, unable to keep his irritation in check. "*Dio*, do you think I do it to waste my breath?"

"Thank you for being here, Marco. She would've been more frightened without you." All the anger was gone from Alexis's voice.

"She's family, Alexis. You know that. What happened in Vienna?"

"Are you asking as a friend or police?"

"Let's save it until we are back in the palazzo, shall we?" Constantine suggested. "Are Aelia and Phaidros unharmed?"

"Yes. Aelia is distraught, but she isn't wounded."

The officer in the room with Penelope put down his pen and gave the window a small nod.

"They are finished. You can go in, Alexis."

Marco and Constantine stayed where they were as Alexis opened the door to the interview room and knelt down beside Penelope's chair. She placed both hands on his cheeks while they whispered to each other.

"Have they always been this intense with each other?" Constantine asked.

Marco thought about the first time he'd seen them together. Penelope had been kidnapped and tortured by the Acolyte's thugs in a gondola shed, and somehow, Alexis had found her. They weren't even a couple then, and yet neither had been willing to separate from the other.

"Since day one." Alexis wrapped his arms around Penelope and was about to kiss her when Marco looked away. "We need to go get the boat ready. They don't need an audience."

Constantine smiled like he had the devil in him and banged on the glass, making Penelope jump and Alexis glower.

"Great idea. Piss him off more," muttered Marco.

"They'd be at it all night if I didn't motivate them to move. Come, *Signore* Dandolo, we need to get ourselves a drink."

Marco didn't like being bossed around, but he found himself falling in line and following the big man out of the station. He'd convinced Paulo, one of the other officers, to give him a cigarette and was about to light it when a hand appeared out of the shadows and snatched it from his hand.

"*Che cazzo!*" Marco huffed as Lyca glared at him.

With slow deliberation, she crushed the cigarette between her fingers, littering the ground with tobacco. "No," she said firmly.

"This is harassment! One occasional cigarette isn't going to kill me."

"No, but she will," said Alexis. He had an arm around Penelope and smiled in the direction of the few paparazzi lingering at the far side of the car park.

Lyca scowled. "Those vultures."

"It's okay. We need to be seen just this once," Penelope said, her voice tired from all the talking she'd done that evening.

They all climbed into the boat, and Lyca steered it out into the canals, silver eyes still glaring at the flash of cameras.

"Thank you for coming tonight," Penelope said to Marco over the rumbling engine.

"It's going to be okay. You know that, don't you? The public will settle down, and you won't have to fear leaving the palazzo."

She attempted a smile. "What's one more scandal in my illustrious career of scandals?"

When they arrived back at the palazzo, Marco waved them on as he secured the boat. He stepped through the blue door moments after them but didn't end up in the usual entry foyer. Penelope and the others were gone, and he was in a carpeted hall with gilt-framed mirrors on either side. By now, Marco knew the palazzo liked to shift around, but it had never placed him somewhere completely unfamiliar before.

"Hello?" he whispered, walking slowly toward a cream-and-gold door.

It opened with an angry yank, and there was Aelia, her face a tear-streaked mask of fury. The snarl on her lips died when she saw him. "Marco?" she said, then promptly collapsed in his arms.

"*La Dia*, what's wrong?" It was odd to see the impossibly confident woman upset about anything.

She let him go just as suddenly as she'd fallen into him and waved him inside. "I need another martini."

"Will you make me one too? It's been quite the evening."

"Of course, *amico*. I don't plan on drinking by myself."

Marco had never been in Aelia's wing of the palazzo. It was as chaotically beautiful as she was. Elaborate Murano glass chandeliers and a scattering of candles lit the room, and instruments from a variety of cultures and eras were scattered about. Expensive sound system equipment was set up in the middle of the room. The polished gladiuses she favored hung along one wall, and along others were portraits of herself done in a variety of styles. Brocaded cushions were tossed in piles, and stacks of jewelry and high heels were haphazardly abandoned.

"One olive or two?" Aelia asked from an antique sideboard covered in bottles, shakers, and used martini glasses.

"Two." Marco sat down on a chaise lounge, careful to avoid stepping on any of the sheet music arranged across the Persian carpet.

Aelia passed him his glass and sat beside him, then took his hand as if she needed reassurance.

"Tell me about your tears. Do I need to hit Phaidros where it hurts?" he asked.

"Those bastards burned my lovely villa, Marco. They murdered the kindest woman you could imagine." Her tears welled again.

He passed her his clean handkerchief, and she dabbed at her smeared mascara. "I'm sorry to hear that. Did she have any family?"

Aelia shook her head. "No. Only me. I've known her since she was a little girl. They killed her to hurt me, to lure me out so Thevetat could kill me too."

"Praise the saints he didn't get you." Marco drank a large mouthful of his strong martini.

"That's the problem. He *did* have me. Kreios was there, and...and he let me go." A sob escaped her trembling lips. "Oh gods, Marco, that man has haunted my nightmares for so long. I didn't want to believe Penelope when she said he was trying to help us. Before Abaddon got to him, Kreios was one of the eligible kings my father was pushing me to marry. I *liked* him when we first met. He was charming and serious and handsome. The next time I saw him, he was standing over me with a blade, ready and eager to carve sigils into my flesh."

Marco placed his arm around her shaking shoulders. "I met him only for a few moments, and it was one of the most terrifying experiences of my life. I can't imagine what you went through, *amica*."

"He had me tonight, and I froze. All my years of training meant nothing. He had a blade to my throat, and I was paralyzed by fear."

"You still got away from him, Aelia."

"Only because Kreios fought Thevetat's influence over him. He fought Thevetat so he could release me. For a moment, I saw a flash of that man I first met. I could see his humanity." She pushed a hand through her hair. "He's completely blown his cover with Thevetat. He's probably getting cut to pieces right now because of me. Do you know how much I hate this feeling? This guilt? My nightmare has now saved my life. What am I meant to do now?"

"You do as you planned: kill Abaddon and Thevetat. If Kreios doesn't survive his punishment, at least he did one good thing to atone for his crimes against you. You shouldn't feel guilty about that. You're here now because of him. You're beautiful and powerful and terrifying, and you'll get your revenge, *Dia*. Kreios has given you the chance to destroy them; don't waste it."

Aelia's violet eyes widened, and she leaned forward and kissed him.

Marco gently pushed her back. "*Bella*, no. Don't do that."

"Do what?"

He tucked one of her stray bronze curls back behind her ear. "Kiss me when you want Phaidros. I'm your friend, Aelia, but I know your lips weren't made for mine."

"Phaidros doesn't want me. For a moment, I thought we could get past our hurt and anger, but I don't know if we can. We're already at each other's throats again. I don't know how to stop him from hating me." She broke down into tears once more.

"If he hated you, he wouldn't have gone to Vienna. I doubt Alexis needed the backup. Phaidros was there for *you*. Talk to him, Aelia. Make him listen. Beat it into his stubborn head if you have to."

Aelia rested a warm palm against his cheek. "You're a good man, Marco. You know that, right?"

"I'm trying to be. I'll always be here for you, my friend. Will you show me the way back to the others? Penelope will want to hear what happened with Kreios."

Aelia drained her martini. "Give me a moment to fix my face."

Marco watched her in the mirror, wondering what he was doing caught up between gods and magic, love and war—and how a human like him was going to survive it all.

THIRTY-TWO

THE FOLLOWING DAY, the mood throughout the palazzo was quiet and subdued. Penelope had moved her box of Vatican research to the upstairs library and found a space on the upper mezzanine where she could keep an eye on Alexis and Constantine working beneath her.

Penelope could feel Alexis's anxiety radiating from him, even if he hadn't expressed it out loud. It was better for both of them to keep each other in their eyeline, if only just for the day. He'd held her firmly the night before as he told her about Vienna and Penelope spoke about the mob in San Marco. He'd scared himself—the amount of magic he used had decimated the priests that had attacked Aelia's home. He hadn't meant to cause such destruction, but the high tide was making his magic more unpredictable than it had in centuries. Kreios's warning that Penelope was in trouble had sent him over the edge and made him wild until he saw her safe at the police station. She'd never felt so loved, though his power frightened her as much as it moved her.

Penelope tore her eyes away from Alexis and back to the book in her lap. She'd planned on working through the box of documents methodically, but the overstuffed manuscript had called out to her. Like in Rome, it had a feeling about it, like an aura of magic that made the Living Language in her spark with interest.

Penelope had been flicking through the manuscript most of the morning. It was filled with recipes for beauty treatments and products like lipsticks, ways to help lactating mothers, and alchemy experiments. It was part diary, with notes and dates scrawled in the margins relating the efficacy of the recipe and sometimes who had given it to Caterina. In many ways, it reminded Penelope of Nereus's journals of magic; it wasn't pretty, but a private workbook filled with messy handwriting and diagrams. Penelope had no idea Caterina Sforza had been so into alchemy and science. She decided to take Carolyn's evergreen advice, opened her web browser, and Googled *Caterina Sforza Experimenti.*

"Okay, so you're the only one who didn't know she was an alchemist," Penelope murmured to herself as she scrolled through articles and book links.

By the end of the third article, Penelope had learned that the oldest version found of Caterina's *Gli Experimenti* was a copy made by a friend of her son Giovanni, which meant Penelope was holding the original.

"Oh my God," she whispered, looking back at the manuscript. The other known copy was part of a private collection, so there was no time to track it down to compare the differences in versions, but it had to contain something important for the original to end up in a box in the Vatican Secret Archive.

"What secrets are you hiding?" She leafed through the pages and soon found pages upon pages written in code. The Living Language had easily translated the Italian and Latin passages she'd read so far, but no matter how hard she stared at the code, it refused to translate. Penelope went back to the internet to see if the other copy had a code, and if some industrious scholar had cracked it for the benefit of all.

Within the hour, Penelope learned that someone had indeed solved it, but no key or help sheet had been published for public use. She also learned that Caterina had only written in code if the alchemical experiment or recipe was important.

Penelope groaned. "Great, so now I know for sure that it's hiding something."

"How goes it, *cara*?" Alexis called from down below.

"Caterina wrote in code, and the Living Language won't translate it because it's something she made up." She got up and walked down the twisted wrought iron staircase to join him.

Alexis's frown deepened as she showed him the pages and filled him in on what she'd discovered. "I'm as puzzled as you, Pen. You had no problem translating Poseidon's code in Nereus's journals."

"Penelope's magic was gifted to her by Nereus, who got hers from Poseidon, hence Penelope is wielding Poseidon's magic and knows his writing," Constantine said from his armchair. "This code is new, which is why she is unable to translate it."

"That's a remarkably insightful explanation coming from you," said Alexis.

"I'll try not to be offended by that. Did you think I wasn't paying attention during all your rants about magic over the years?"

"It still isn't going to help me solve this code, no matter how insightful," Penelope pointed out.

Alexis rubbed his chin. "You have no choice but to ask Phaidros, *cara*. He corresponded with Caterina for many years and through all of her marriages. They may have used this code with each other."

"I don't know if I should bother him. I don't want to start another fight between him and Aelia."

"He'll have to deal with it. This is more important than their lovers' quarrels." Constantine pointed to the far door. "He's been sunning himself out there all morning, and now is the time for him to make himself useful."

With considerable reluctance, Penelope gathered up her notebook and the manuscript and went to search for Phaidros.

PHAIDROS WASN'T as hard to find as Penelope thought he'd be. She only needed to follow the empty Peroni bottles that littered the lawn and gardens. He was lying face down on one of the white sun beds, and all Penelope could register was his bare, perfectly sculpted, golden ass.

Penelope squealed. "Jesus! Would you mind throwing a towel over it?" She used the books to shield her red face.

"You just wait until I roll over…" She could hear the lazy grin in his voice.

"Please don't do that. You have a lovely golden body, my dear Apollo, but I need to talk to you, and I don't need to have my eyes assaulted by your manhood the whole time."

Penelope waited behind her books while Phaidros let out a groan, sat up, and hopefully wrapped a towel around his waist.

"I'm presentable."

She peeked over the books to find him covered up and leaning back on the sun bed, sweating beer in hand. He looked like he was on a GQ shoot, unlike Penelope, who was already sweaty and uncomfortable. She sat in the shade and placed the books down beside her.

"What's all this homework you've brought with you? Don't forget to enjoy the summer and live a little. Beer?" Phaidros passed her one before she could object.

Penelope had a mouthful, and it was good after a morning with her head in books. "I need your help with something, and I don't know if it's going to upset you or not," she said, trying for diplomacy first.

"You know there isn't much that upsets me, Penelope."

Except for Aelia, she almost said but managed to swallow the words. "It's got to do with this manuscript we stole in Rome. It's written in code, and I'm hoping you'll understand it." She put her beer down and dried her damp palms before opening to the page she'd bookmarked.

Phaidros cracked one eye open and looked at what she was holding out to him. "I haven't seen this for a good five hundred years." He took it from her and placed it on his lap, his fingers gently running over the edges of the pages.

"As I said, some of it is written in a code I don't have the time to crack. Help me out?"

"Why do you need to know what's inside?"

"Because it's important somehow. Alexis, Zo, and I can all feel the magic on it. If the writing is personal, you don't need to tell me what it says. I only want to know if it's related to the ring of Solomon. Tim's visions led us to this. It must mean something."

"I'll help you if you stay out here and keep me company." He offered her a persuasive smile.

Penelope leaned back on her sun bed. "Fine, but you have to share your beers. You can make sense of that code, though, can't you?"

"Of course I can. Writing in code was about as close to privacy as you got in those days."

"I'm sorry if this gets you into more trouble with Aelia."

Phaidros's laugh was bitter and dismissive. "You'll soon learn that I'm always in trouble with Aelia. She has a very defined set of double standards I'm not sure we'll ever get past. It's fine for me to have to tolerate Constantine under my roof, but mention Caterina, and Aelia is ready to burn the world," he said, though his eyes remained on the writing in front of him.

"Aelia can't really hate a dead woman so much just because she loved you when she was alive."

"There are a lot of reasons, and none of them are worth bringing up. Suffice to say, Caterina was formidable and intimidating to men and women alike. Love and women are complicated, and I've never made it easy for myself by falling in love with someone with a gentle or submissive spirit. You don't need to look so concerned, Penelope. Aelia and I have fought worse than this. It was a good excuse for her to run into the arms of Marco Dandolo without a guilty conscience, so she got what she wanted. She always does."

The large number of empty beer bottles around him was starting to make more sense. Marco had told Penelope what happened between him and Aelia the night before, but Phaidros had seen the two of them together and jumped to all the wrong conclusions.

"Nothing is going on between Aelia and Marco. You don't need to worry about that. He's her friend and nothing more. He knows a lost cause when he sees it."

"I doubt that."

"Really? Because from where I'm sitting, all she wants is you, and you're both too full of your own bullshit to give it a chance." Phaidros looked astonished at her outburst, but she wasn't even a little bit done. "What? You think I'm going to act like Nereus and everyone else and stay silent and not call you out on your crap? We could all die fighting Thevetat. If we live, the magic maintaining your long life spans might give out, and you'll be mortal again. One life left, Phaidros. Is it really worth risking never being together because of your damn pride?"

"Zo always said you have ovaries of steel, Penelope. It seems—"

Something on the page caught his eye. He sat up and ran his finger over a line of code, his lips moving silently.

"What is it?"

"It's an experiment and part of a letter with one of her friends at La Murate. It was a nunnery in Florence that was well known for their healing remedies, amongst other things. They are talking about a ring of Girolamo's—"

"Do you think it's Solomon's?"

"Shhh, let me concentrate."

She leaned back with a huff as Phaidros lost himself in his dead lover's writing.

PENELOPE WOKE in the late afternoon, her journal on her lap. Alexis was now sitting on Phaidros's vacated sun bed, staring at the boats on the water. When he sensed her watching him, he reached over to trail his fingers over her arm.

She tucked a loose hair behind her ear. "I can't believe I fell asleep."

"Beer and sun will do that. I told Phaidros not to wake you. You needed the sleep."

"So do you."

He moved so he could crouch beside her and put an arm around her. The hardness that had been in his indigo eyes the past few days seemed to crack at whatever he saw in her face.

"What is it?" she asked.

"Sometimes, I still struggle to believe you're here, that's all." He kissed her gently. "You make me grateful even in an apocalypse."

"We haven't hit the apocalypse yet, my love." Penelope pulled him down to her, hand creeping under his shirt to touch his bare skin.

"If you two can wrap it up, I have something to show you." Phaidros moved Penelope's legs to one side and sat down.

"You really need to learn about personal space, Phaidros," Penelope complained as Alexis moved off her.

"Don't forget you're the one that asked for my help."

Alexis sat opposite them. "You'd better have something important to show us."

"As a matter of fact, I do. You were right, Penelope. It *was* the ring of Solomon." Phaidros passed her a stack of papers. "I've been translating the pages for you."

"Caterina had it, and you never noticed?" Alexis asked, dumbfounded.

"You knew Caterina—she was always working on something. Trying to keep up with her alchemy as well as her politics would've been a full-time job. She was always trading secrets and recipes with her friends throughout Europe. The nuns at La Murate would supply her with herbs and know-how. She wanted to be left alone to focus on healing and alchemy; that's why she retired there at the end of her life." Sadness crept into Phaidros's voice, but he seemed to shake it off as he opened to a page of *Gli Experimenti* where a letter had been pasted in. "This letter discusses the ring. Caterina knew Sixtus had given it to Girolamo from the Vatican collection and suspected its origins. She asked the nuns what they knew of its powers."

"Do you think it ever woke for her?" asked Penelope.

"It would seem that she was using it for different experiments. There is one here, a broth for bringing down a fever—she wrote a note saying that the healing properties of the broth were much stronger and faster-acting if she was wearing the ring when she brewed it." Phaidros flicked to another bookmarked page. "This one here tells of when she gave the ring to one of the nuns to wear when midwifing a woman through a difficult birth. She claims she observed 'a healing touch' when the nun massaged the woman's stomach and helped turn the child.'"

"Do you think that someone in the Vatican knew of these experiments, which is why the manuscript ended up in the secret archives?"

Phaidros shook his head. "The Vatican stopped interfering with Caterina after they refused to give her lands back. The simpler explanation is that Caterina left the book in Giovanni's possession, and he may have given it back to the nuns for their use and safekeeping. Caterina died and was buried at La Murate. The nuns were close confidants of hers, and Giovanni would have honored that friendship. Like Riccoldo, they could have entrusted the book to the Vatican at some point, and knowing its origins were tied to the Riario and Sforza family, it was filed with their other documents."

"I wonder if Caterina left the ring in the nuns' care too. It might be in the Vatican…but that doesn't make sense. Tim's visions stopped with it being in Caterina's possession." Penelope chewed her lip.

"Maybe it never left her," said Alexis.

"You don't think she was buried with it like Constantine?" Her heartbeat began to race.

"That's what Tim's writings implied, remember? *She was dying, and it refused to save her. She would take it to her tomb, for no man deserved to wield it.* If Caterina was buried at La Murate, it would've been a good place for the nuns to hide it, and if there was ever a real need for it, they could always take it from her sarcophagus and use it." Alexis's face fell.

"What's wrong?"

"Like much of Florence, La Murate was sacked by Napoleon and the French in 1808. The convent was turned into a prison in 1845."

"What is it now?"

"It was restored and reopened as a cultural place of interest a few years ago, but Caterina's sarcophagus would be long gone."

Penelope collapsed back on the sun bed and swore. Another dead end. She felt like crying. There were no more visions from Tim to help her.

"And what if the French never found Caterina's sarcophagus to sack it…" Phaidros said.

Penelope opened her eyes.

"What are you talking about? The French razed that place and took everything that wasn't nailed down to pay the army," said Alexis.

"I couldn't let them desecrate her. All of Florence was in turmoil, but I couldn't let them—" Phaidros pushed a hand through his hair. "I killed a soldier and stole his uniform. When they were busy with the chapel, I went out into the cemetery and used magic to…to steal her."

Alexis trained his gaze on him. "Where is she now, Phaidros?"

Phaidros hesitated for a long moment before admitting, "Her sarcophagus is in my garden in Santa Croce."

Alexis placed a hand on his slumped shoulder. "I'm sorry, Phaidros, but you know we need to open it to be sure."

Phaidros nodded. "Okay, but Thevetat obviously knows where our houses are, so we go with backup. We don't need Kreios or Abaddon jumping us just as we find the only relic that can stop him."

Penelope gripped her journal tightly in excitement. "Florence it is."

THIRTY-THREE

$\mathcal{A}$S THEY ASSEMBLED in the inner courtyard, Phaidros did his best not to act as uncomfortable as he felt. Aelia stood next to Penelope in tight leather pants and a black T-shirt, twin gladiuses strapped to her back, hair in warrior braids, and makeup-free. He didn't know who had told her, but she'd arrived downstairs and ready to go with them to Florence. She looked like a soldier, ready to kill every one of Thevetat's priests they encountered. The ferocity of her energy made him even edgier.

"I'm coming. Don't even try to argue with me," she said, meeting his gaze and throwing his own words back at him.

"Okay." He was tired of arguing with her, but he didn't know how they could ever stop.

"Are you ready?" Like Aelia, Alexis had geared up and made sure that Penelope had a dagger strapped around her waist.

Aelia's hand found his as they linked up, and Alexis's magic rushed around them.

The afternoon shadows were growing long in Florence. Alexis had placed them in the gardens at the back entrance to the house.

"I can't sense any priest's magic close by," he said, still gripping Penelope's hand. "We'll check the interior of the house. You two check the grounds, and we'll meet you at Caterina's sarcophagus when we're done." Alexis gave Phaidros a meaningful look behind Aelia's back. They were being given alone time.

"I'll follow your lead. I've never been here," Aelia said once Alexis and Penelope had stepped away. It was true. He'd never invited her to his Florentine home. He'd never even imagined her crossing its threshold unless it was to destroy it and him.

"We'll follow the wall and make sure the perimeter is clear." He headed down the white gravel path. He could feel the brush of her magic, a heady warm pulse behind him. He didn't dare think about their tumble in Venice all those weeks ago. They still hadn't really talked about it, and when they'd been close to broaching the subject, Caterina had come up to destroy whatever had been growing between them.

"This fountain is lovely." Aelia stopped in front of the gurgling marble figure of Venus, scrutinizing the sea creatures carved around the goddess's feet.

"Thank you." He scratched the back of his neck. "Uh, Salvi did it for me before he got commissioned to do the Trevi." Would he ever be able to talk to her and not feel like a fumbling teenager?

Aelia looked around at the trees and flower beds—anywhere but at him. "I don't feel any priests anywhere. Do you?"

"No. I'm hoping they've decided to leave this place alone. The sarcophagus is this way. I'll send a pulse to Alexis, and we can get this over with." Phaidros cut across the manicured lawn to a copse of decorative pine and cypress trees. Roses had grown and twisted around the pillars of the domed marble monument he'd built to shelter Caterina's sarcophagus from the weather. There was a small stone pew where he liked to sit to burn incense, drink, and remember her. He sat down on it and stared at the marble figure carved into the lid.

"Phaidros? Do I have your permission?" Aelia still stood on the steps.

"She's dead, Aelia. I don't think she cares that you're here." He said it more gruffly than he intended, but she still took it as acquiescence and joined him.

"God, I hated her," Aelia said, breaking their heavy silence.

"She hated you too. You know, you were both alike in many ways: clever, stubborn, ambitious, and beautiful enough to turn men into idiots."

"If she hadn't tried to kill me so many times, we may have learned to get along."

"Well, you did sweet-talk Cesare into invading Forli, so you couldn't expect a hand of friendship after that."

To his surprise, Aelia choked out a laugh. "Yes, I suppose that was me. To be fair, the Borgias wanted to kill her, and I convinced them to imprison her instead. I knew it would destroy you. Despite how much I hated her, I wanted to spare you that pain."

He'd always wondered why the Borgias had spared Caterina after the siege… "You only hated her because she had the courage to love me." It was bold of him to say, but he was tired of fearing how she would react.

"I know." Aelia shut her eyes and let out a long breath. "God, the way you looked at her used to make me wild. I'd only ever seen you look at me like that, on Atlantis, before everything went to hell. I knew you'd never look at me that way again, and it broke me down until there was only rage left."

"That's how I felt every time you were with Constantine." He shook his head. "We've spent so much time hurting each other, Aelia. Do you think we'd even know how to stop?"

Aelia's fingers were trembling when they found his. "I *want* to stop. I don't want to hurt you anymore. I never really did. I'm sorry, Phaidros, for everything."

He lifted her hand and kissed it. "I am too."

"I'll forgive you if you forgive me." A small, hopeful smile formed on her lips.

"We can give it a try and see how it goes." The tightness in his chest truly loosened for the first time in centuries. He didn't think the moment could get any more surreal, but he was wrong.

"Phaidros? You know I love you."

He turned to face her, unsure if he'd heard her right, breath caught in his throat. "What did you just say?"

"I love you," Aelia said. The edges of her violet eyes were silver with unshed tears. "It's okay if you don't feel the same anymore. I only thought you should know in case we all die horribly when we face Thevetat."

"What do you mean, *if I don't feel the same anymore?* Woman, I haven't been able to stop loving you for the last ten thousand years. Why the fuck would I stop now?"

Before she could change her mind, he took her face in his hands and kissed her with all the frustration, obsession, and love that had been eating away at him from the moment he first saw her at the Temple of Poseidon. Her hands tangled in his hair, her cheeks wet with tears and magic. He joined his energy with hers, and a wave of power shuddered out of them. It didn't make him stop kissing her. Thevetat appearing in the flesh in front of them wouldn't have made him stop kissing her.

Alexis and Penelope appeared, breathless with weapons drawn. "Damn it, you two! I felt the magic and thought you were being attacked."

"Your timing is terrible, Defender," Phaidros said and dropped his hands from Aelia's blushing face.

"Now you know how it feels to be interrupted all the time." Penelope grinned. "Every time you try to get alone time with Aelia, I'm going to be there to ruin the moment, just like you do to me and Alexis."

"You two took your time." Alexis smiled.

Aelia shrugged. "Better late than never."

"I hate to do this to you, but are we going to open this up?" Penelope's eyes fixed eagerly on the stone sarcophagus.

"I'm sorry, Phaidros. You know there's no stopping the archaeologist in her," Alexis said.

"No, Penelope is right. We have to open it. Ladies, if you would stand back?" Phaidros walked to one end of the marble slab, and Alexis moved to the other. Phaidros touched Caterina's marble cheek. "Forgive me, *amore*."

Using a combination of magic and man power, they slid back the lid with a groan of stone against stone and lowered it down. The shroud bearing the Sforza coat of arms was still mostly intact. Very slowly, Phaidros peeled back the fabric over her hands. Caterina's skeletal fingers were covered in golden rings of pearl and ruby, and on her left index finger was a ring made of bronze and carved carnelian.

"Oh God. That's it," Penelope whispered.

Phaidros carefully slid the ring off Caterina's shriveled finger and presented it to Penelope. "I believe you've been looking for this, Archivist."

Penelope took the ring from him, her face full of reverence and wonder for the tarnished trinket. Phaidros wrapped the shroud back over Caterina's jewels, arranging it as it had been before.

I hope you understand, and that you continue to rest in peace, he prayed.

When he looked up, Alexis's expression was worried and tense as he stared at Penelope's frowning face. The awe was gone from it, replaced with something more akin to despair.

"What's wrong?" Aelia asked.

Penelope paled. "The engravings—they aren't translating. I-I can't read it."

PART THREE

THE HEIR
OF GODS

*"The thing one must understand
about time is that it's not an
arrow, or a river, or something
with a beginning and end;
it is a state of mind. And like
all states of mind, it can be
changed and manipulated."*
— *Poseidon's Treatise of
Time and Its Functions* —

THIRTY-FOUR

P ENELOPE SAT ON the step of the canal entrance, her legs shin-deep in the salty, warm water. She held the ring of Solomon between her fingers, staring at the carved carnelian without really seeing it.

"It's definitely the real ring, Penelope," Constantine had assured her on their return to Venice. "It was on my finger for thirty years. I'd know a replica. It feels the same too. There's a low vibration running through it." His certainty had made her feel even worse. She'd threaded the ring onto her necklace with her Saint Mark medallion for safe-keeping, unable to part with it even for a moment in case it decided to translate.

Warm arms came around her waist, and Alexis's long legs dipped into the water next to hers. He rested his chin on her shoulder. "Talk to me, Penelope."

"We've spent months searching for this thing. T-Tim fucking died for it, and it's useless." Tears choked her as she tried to swallow them down. She'd done enough crying over things she couldn't change. Reliable anger surged up over her grief. "I feel like throwing it into the canal and being done with it."

"It's a magical object. They are notoriously temperamental."

"It worked in the memory. I saw it change! I don't know why it's silent now."

"Give it a chance. The prophecy said we needed to have it, so it has some part to play, but it's hardly the only iron in our fire. We'll find the way to sabotage Thevetat's ritual, and if not, Constantine's mercenaries are a little too excited by the prospect of attempting to blow up a demon." He stroked her cheek with his thumb. "We'll get our revenge for Tim and Nereus, one way or another, yes?"

"Yes." Penelope sniffed and leaned back against the solid warmth of his chest.

"Would you like to show me how to build a wave?"

"At your own risk of getting wet." Penelope's mouth twitched into the smallest smile. She could at least practice this side of her inherited magic. After tucking the ring back inside her shirt, she rested her palms on her knees faceup and closed her eyes.

Penelope let her breath deepen, focusing on calming her pulse and temper. She searched for the call, that whisper of the sea she'd heard last time she sat there.

After a fruitless five minutes, Alexis's hand settled over her heart. "Stop thinking so hard. Magic comes from the heart first and the head second. Imagine the connection that binds you to the sea until your intention becomes a reality. You've made the connection twice before. Your magic knows the way."

Penelope allowed the lapping water at her shins to calm her further until she tried reaching out like Poseidon's note had advised. She met a wall of resistance that held her back for a full minute before the warm caress of her magic rushed out of her. In that instant, she could feel the pull of the tide and the life in the lagoon shining like starlight in her mind. The water near her hummed, and she focused on manipulating it into the small wave she pictured in her mind.

"Open your eyes, Penelope."

The water swirled out from around her legs and formed into a small mound.

"Careful now. Feed it a little more of your magic and hold it."

Penelope did as she was told, and the mound grew up into a wave. Her magic sizzled silver along her skin, daring her to give it more and more. It whispered to her of what it could do at her command: topple boats, destroy cities, make the storms roll in. *No,* she replied firmly, though she wasn't sure who or what she was responding to. Sweat beaded at the base of her spine.

"Okay, *cara*. Let it go slowly," Alexis said.

She let the tide pull the wave back out into the canal. Blood rushed to her head, and she hung forward between her knees. "Oh, God. That's crazy."

Alexis rubbed her back. "Well done, Penelope. Very well done indeed."

"I can feel how the magic's changed. Grown. It's going to sound insane, but it was talking to me." Penelope struggled to explain. "I could've destroyed us all if I'd wanted to."

"It's the high tide. It's nearing its peak. That's why you're feeling that way. We are all going to have to be very careful from here on out."

"I barely have a drop of magic. I can't imagine what it must be like for you." Penelope wrapped her fingers over his ringed hand. "You'll tell me if it becomes too much?"

"I will. And I'll take myself to a cell if it is. I never thought I'd say it, but the magical high tide is the least of our worries at this moment."

"If everything else fails, I suppose I could just swamp Milos as best as I can."

"It's a better plan than relying on a holy relic."

Penelope leaned back in his arms. "You never trusted the ring would work?"

"Not in and of itself. I still want to find Nereus's experiments. I can understand and trust that because I'm a magician. Constantine, on the other hand, trusts his God, his sword, and not much else. Three elements to one plan. We can't rely on any one to work on its own."

Penelope clutched the ring that hung between her breasts. "I trust Poseidon wouldn't have tied our fates together without good reason.

He strikes me as a man that enjoys the last laugh, so I doubt he'd have set us up to fail."

"Let's hope that means I'll find Nereus's experiments soon. The last lot we retrieved from the astrolabe was interesting but not what we're after."

"Do you want to take another trip into the astrolabe? I'm sure it'll let you in without me."

"I suppose I have to try. Though this is nice too." He pressed his lips to the top of her head.

Penelope turned in his arms. "It is. Unfortunately, sitting here all day won't help us defeat Thevetat."

Alexis let out a sigh. "After Abaddon is dead and Thevetat is gone, I plan on having a lot of lazy days with you, Doctor Bryne."

"We will. I promise." She kissed him to seal the deal.

DOWN IN the Archives, Penelope gawked at the mess that littered her office. "I swear, I'm never letting Constantine or Phaidros in here again."

The Archives usually cleaned up after her each day, and yet papers were now scattered over chairs and both of their desks, books sat in piles, and wineglasses had been abandoned on the floor.

"At least their mess was productive for once. Are you sure the astrolabe will let me in without you?" asked Alexis.

"I don't see why not. I'm going to start translating all of Poseidon's notes that you've found and see if I can build a list of different ways to use my magic following his instructions." Penelope tapped the pile of books on her desk.

Alexis opened the astrolabe. "If I get stuck in here, you had better rescue me."

"Five hours, and then I'm coming after you." Penelope leaned down and whispered to the astrolabe, "Listen to him."

Alexis's eyes shined with amusement. "Do you think that will help?"

Penelope shrugged. "Can't hurt." She stepped back as Alexis pressed the sigil and disappeared, leaving her alone amongst the mess of her office and emotions.

She stared at the completed wall of research, Tim's words printed and stuck on, drawn over with notes and covered with photos. It was a visual map of the madness of his final days, along with months of her own efforts to manically decode it so she didn't have to deal with the guilt and grief gnawing at her. Bile rose up in her throat, and she reached for one of the sticky notes and pulled it off the glass. Her vision clouded with tears, and she tore at the wall until shredded paper and crushed photos littered the floor like confetti.

"Spring-cleaning?" Zo asked, and she jerked in surprise. Constantine was with him, and both were dressed in workout clothes and armed with swords and daggers.

She turned away to hide her tears. "No point in it staying up now."

"What has Alecto done to upset you?"

"Nothing. He's busy in the astrolabe hunting something that's actually going to help us, like he should've been doing from the beginning instead of wasting time with me and my own pointless hunt."

"Ah, she's having a tantrum because the ring wouldn't give up its secrets," Constantine said to Zo.

"I'm not having a tantrum. I'm cleaning up—"

"Definitely a tantrum." Zo folded his arms. "You know, for someone who was so determined on finding not only Atlantis, but the ring of Solomon, you give up remarkably easily when it comes to magic. You don't know the first thing about relics or magic."

"Then you should go tell Poseidon to choose another heir if I'm so hopeless at everything."

"Those are your words, not mine. You're not hopeless—"

Penelope pulled the ring out of her singlet. "This was the only thing I had on Thevetat. I have no real magic. I thought this stupid trinket would mean I could actually be useful in this fight. I'm not a magician. I'm not a warrior. I'm a fucking archaeologist!"

Constantine closed the space between them, and before she could react, he picked her up and flung her over one broad shoulder.

"Maybe that's not such a good idea, Con..." Zo cast a nervous glance at the astrolabe.

"Put me down this instant, you Neanderthal!" Penelope shouted as she wriggled in his grip.

"No. You said you don't want to be useless. Well then, let's turn you into something else." He carried her through the stacks, only laughing when she gave him a tongue lashing. When they reached Lyca's training area, he dumped her on the sparring mat. Red-faced and furious, she took a swing at him. He dodged it as if he'd been expecting it.

"Do you have any training in a martial art?" he asked.

"Only Krav Maga for some self-defense." Penelope straightened her singlet. She turned to walk away, only to find Zo blocking her path. "Get out of my way."

"Make me," he said, but then his expression softened. "Even Marco has been training to handle Thevetat's priests. Alexis can't be watching over you the whole time we're on Milos. You need to learn to handle a dagger, at least."

"I recall it was me who put a knife in Kreios."

"Kreios *let* you put a knife in him. It's quite a different thing, Penelope. You and Alexis will need to get close to Abaddon and Thevetat during the ritual. You need to be able to watch his back. Otherwise, he'll end up as dead as he was during Carnevale."

Penelope's eyes narrowed. "Using Alexis as a bargaining chip is a low blow, Zotikos."

"Not if it works," Constantine said. "What do you think, Zo? We could get her using a pugio in a few days if she stops bitching."

"I'm starting to see why everyone calls you a prick."

"Sticks and stones, Doctor Bryne. I wore that ring for most of my life, and I could never read its inscription, but you don't see me crying about it. You're disappointed—I understand that—but you really need to ask yourself if giving up is a part of your nature or not. If not, then you'll leave the books to Alexis and train every day until we go to Milos."

Penelope wanted to lash out at his arrogance, but it didn't make him less right. She couldn't force the ring to give up its secrets. She couldn't make magic easier to use. She *could* get a refresher on self-defense and learn how to use a dagger.

Her stubborn streak forced her spine straight and her shoulders square. "If you're so confident you can turn me into a soldier, do your worst."

Constantine's reply was a smile as cold as a wolf's right before it goes for the throat.

THIRTY-FIVE

INSIDE THE ASTROLABE, Alexis touched the blue leather spine of another book and sent his magic inside of it. He searched for any reference that could be helpful to him. He didn't approve of cheating, but he was running out of time.

They all were.

Away from Penelope, he could let his own frustrations show. She was feeling bad enough that her translation magic had failed her. She didn't need to see how disappointed he was as well. Alexis hadn't lied when he said he'd never believed the ring of Solomon would be the absolute answer. All gods could be fickle when bestowing favors, and relying on them to defeat Thevetat and Abaddon was no kind of plan.

"Nereus, if you foresaw all of this, you could've made the process easier on us by cataloging your books." It was like the whole room was designed to frustrate him. He wasn't always the tidiest of people, but at least his chaos had order. Plus, the books were all full of magic, and that was the most distracting element of all.

Alexis picked up another book and placed his palm over the cover. It dealt with brontology and biology, so he put it aside and reached for another. He didn't know how much time was passing in the outside world, and he did his best not to think about anything beyond the astrolabe, but he was worried about Penelope more than ever. She hadn't grieved properly, and now that she didn't have the ring to search for, he could see all the pain she'd buried rising to the surface.

Focus! Penelope is a grown woman.

Something rattled on the next shelf over, and a small, black leather journal fell forward. As soon as Alexis touched it, pain and loss and despair raced through him. He dropped it in surprise and shook out his hand.

Those emotions were not mine. He looked around, even though he knew he was alone. There was no strange magic in the air either. Alexis cast a protection over his hands before reaching down to pick up the book once more, then sat down on the lounge chair and opened it. Each page was filled with Nereus's handwriting, but it wasn't the neat, disciplined script he was used to reading. This was haphazard and angry, pain and frustration in every stroke and dash of the Atlantean characters.

The whole of Atlas stinks of funeral incense, people burning sacrifices and showing their respect for someone they didn't know. They knew the king; they never knew the man. They never saw him walking through the villages, giving money and advice, stopping storms that would've decimated crops, or smiling as new colts played in the fields…

It was a journal, and even without dates on the entries, Alexis knew she was talking about Poseidon's death. His cult had already risen and was well-established by the time Alexis was born, so he'd never imagined what Atlantis was like before that. Nereus had known Poseidon as the magician, not the god-king. She'd rarely talked about him, only to correct Alexis on assumptions of his divinity.

"He was a powerful magician, but he wasn't a god like they claim. Always remember, Alexis, no matter how powerful you get, what wonders you work, we are men, not gods. We are only more advanced because we live longer to learn from our mistakes," she'd told him not long after he mastered his first piece of advanced magic.

Poseidon had given up his crown at least a hundred years before his death and had rarely been seen by the public. His sons had ruled in his place, and Poseidon had gone wandering.

"Perhaps he went searching for his heir that Penelope told him about," Alexis mused. He turned the pages tentatively, conscious of invading Nereus's privacy while she was grieving her mentor and lover. Despite that, he had a feeling somewhere within the pages were the answers he sought.

Abaddon, the worm, came to the citadel again today. This time, he brought Atlas's men with him and demanded that I go to the king. Atlas isn't a fool, but for a king, he's too easily led by lesser men. If I'd known what madness Abaddon was whispering in his ears, I'd have watched over the king more carefully. Resurrect Poseidon! Didn't he do enough for them? He made Atlantis into a great nation, protected it like a father does a child. His shade deserves its rest...

Gods help me, they've removed his body from his tomb, and the priests have been working to restore it. Where did Abaddon find this magic? I fear that in my efforts for peace, and by letting him into the citadel library, he's found this horrible power in my own house. I can't defy Atlas and put the citadel in danger, and fighting the enemy within his own walls is easier than outside of them...

"Now we're getting somewhere." Alexis tried to turn the next page, but there was a wad of them stuck together. No matter how he tugged at them, they wouldn't part. "Gods damn you, Nereus!"

His magic poured through his hands and into the book. The black leather swelled and wriggled in his grasp, radiating magic. It pulled itself free from his hands and lifted into the air before it burst open, pieces of paper exploding out and showering down on him. Then the journal shrank back to its usual size and dropped into his lap.

Alexis picked up one of the loose sheets. It was a made of different paper than that of the journal, thin as onion skin. He unfolded it, smoothing it out on the small table beside him. At first, his mind couldn't make sense of the tiny writing and diagrams. He turned the page around and around.

"A puzzle." He hurried to smooth out another sheet. He studied it, excitement blooming inside him. Not only had Nereus figured out a way to counteract whatever magic Abaddon planned, she'd also made sure that no spy would ever find it. And if they did, they would've spent a lifetime trying to work out the answers. Nereus and her games were something that Alexis was familiar with. As he'd progressed as her apprentice, Nereus had created such challenges for him to solve.

When the war had broken out, she'd often send different magicians a single page, and it wasn't until they were all together that they'd be able to put the message together.

Alexis didn't have time to assemble it in the astrolabe, so he set about gathering all the loose pages that had flown about the room. Powerful, strange magic pulsed once, and something clanged behind him. Sitting on top of the fallen journal was something he'd not seen in nine thousand years.

"It can't be." There was a tube made of orichalcum, carved with magic characters that kept it from being opened by anyone but its intended recipient. A strip of aqua blue cloth, embroidered with golden tridents, was wrapped around it and sealed with Poseidon's golden insignia. *A royal missive.*

Alexis picked it up and studied the seal more closely. *THE HEIR OF GODS* had been stitched into the aqua fabric as the missive's recipient.

"Penelope," he whispered. Quickly, he gathered up the last of the pages, the journal, and the missive. He had to get to her. He had to get to his tower to study the pages. He had to find out what the message from Poseidon said.

"Please return me to the Archives." For a moment, he thought the astrolabe was going to ignore him, but then he was being dragged back through the device and into Penelope's office.

Alexis couldn't sense her in the Archives, so he portaled to his tower. The sun had set outside, and he knew he should probably find Penelope and something to eat. Instead, he cleared one of his worktables and started to smooth out the pieces of paper he'd collected. Nereus had left him a magical riddle, and his mind could focus on nothing else until it was solved.

A SHIFT in the *moíra desmós* told Penelope that Alexis had come out of the astrolabe. When he didn't come down to eat dinner, she put a tray together and headed for the tower. Her body ached from the hours of training Zo and Constantine had put her through, but it was the good kind of tired that hopefully meant she'd sleep the night through instead of staying up riddled with anxiety. The physical exertion had also improved her mood and beaten back the despair that was trying to claw her insides to pieces.

At the top of the tower, Alexis was bent over his worktable, deep in thought and murmuring under his breath. Magic glimmered under his skin, and Penelope took a moment to watch him work, his long fingers sketching symbols in the air while his eyes followed some writing on the page in front of him. She was growing used to being around the magicians, but occasionally, she was still struck dumb by how beautiful Alexis was, dressed in another of his entari robes—wine red with golden hieroglyphs—and lost in work that he loved. He looked exactly like ancient, mad magi from another time, and she wanted to kiss him just because she could. *You got it so bad,* Carolyn's voice echoed at the back of her head.

"I thought you might have found something interesting," Penelope said softly so she didn't startle him.

He straightened. "I'm sorry, *cara.* I was going to come down…"

Penelope waved away his apologies and placed the tray down on a spare table. "Don't worry about it. Constantine and Zo have kept me busy by kicking my ass from one end of the Archives to the other."

Alexis's smile faltered. "They did what?"

"Not literally. Well, sort of. Come and eat, and I'll tell you. Then you can explain what it is you're working on." She sat down in one of his armchairs and poured him some mint tea. He relented, coming to sit down opposite her, so she told him about Constantine's boot camp.

"As much as I hate the idea of you being caught in the conflict, it's wise to prepare you for it."

"He's a good teacher, even if I only want to learn so I can kick his ass when he gets too arrogant." Penelope sipped her tea. "Find something good in the astrolabe?"

Alexis leaned back in his chair, a smile playing about his lips. "Many somethings. I believe I've found the magic that will stop Thevetat's ritual. The only problem is that it's broken up into pieces, and I need to solve how to put it together before I can attempt to use the magic itself."

Alexis explained how he'd come across Nereus's journal, and how he'd felt when it relinquished all the plans hidden within it.

"Nereus always did like to make me work for answers." He rested his chin in his hand, watching her thoughtfully. "I also found something for you. Or rather, it found me." He reached into his robe and took out a slender tube as long as her forearm.

"Is that orichalcum?" Her hand drifted down to touch the cuff on her wrist.

"It is. This is a royal missive, and it's addressed to you. There is only one heir of gods." Alexis offered it to her, and she took it eagerly, running her fingers over the engraved metal.

"Are you sure? I thought I was only Poseidon's heir."

"You carry Poseidon's magic in your blood and a gift from the hand of Yahweh around your neck. That's two gods who have decided to involve themselves in this business." Alexis didn't look particularly pleased about it, but he couldn't hide his curiosity either.

Penelope used her thumbnail to break the golden wax that sealed the top of the tube. There was no magical reaction, so Alexis gave her a nod, and she unscrewed the lid and tipped the tube upside down. When no scroll fell out, Penelope lifted the tube to her eye.

"That's weird. There's nothing—" Aqua and gold magic flew out of the tube and shot into her third eye. Alexis shouted as gold light clouded her vision and the magic took hold.

Penelope saw images of white beach sand and blue water. Poseidon smiled at her as he walked to the edge of the waves. His mouth was moving but Penelope couldn't hold his words in her mind or understand them. With one hand he traced something onto her forehead, magic moving through her with a searing brand. Before she could scream, it was gone. Poseidon cupped her cheeks with his strong hands.

"Good luck to you, my little heir."

The magic lifted, and Penelope came back to herself, gripping the arms of her chair and breathing in panicked gasps. Alexis was kneeling in front of her, hands on her knees.

"Wake up, Penelope!"

"I'm here." She toppled forward into his arms and breathed in his cinnamon-and-firecracker scent, his warm body grounding her. "I'm here. I'm not hurt," she repeated to assure herself more than him.

"What did you see?"

"Poseidon on a beach. He—he did something. Oh God, Alexis. It's gone. He showed me magic, and I can't remember it!"

"Shhh, *cara*. I'll have a look." Alexis moved back so that he could touch her forehead. The familiar warmth of his magic moved over her skin. "He's done…something. I can feel his magic locked in your mind."

"Like a tumor?"

"More like a pocket of power. I'm not sure how he's done it."

"It's the spell," Penelope said. "I can't remember what he did, but I know how his magic felt when he worked it; it was like my bones were going to melt. What's the point of putting it there if I can't remember the damn thing? He put a magical bomb in my head!"

"He wouldn't have done it if it was going to hurt you."

"We don't know that. One life to stop Thevetat from getting into a body and having the power to release more demons? Poseidon might just see me as a suicide bomber."

Alexis shook his head. "I refuse to believe that. I've seen magicians use such spells before, and what's in your head isn't malicious in the slightest. It doesn't have the structure to kill."

"How can you be sure?"

Alexis's expression shifted and she could see all the pain, years, wars, and death in his eyes. "Because I've had to use that kind of magic before, and no, I will not tell you about it," he replied. "Those kinds of stories aren't worth repeating, and it's something magic should never be used for."

Penelope rested her forehead against his, her heart pulsing with so much love for him and fear for their future. She didn't know how she would contain it. "I trust you, Alexis, even if I don't trust Poseidon."

THIRTY-SIX

THE FOLLOWING WEEK passed in a blur of magic, sleeping, and eating. Alexis worked in a haze, focused solely on the magical code that Nereus had left for him. Penelope was caught up in training with Constantine, Marco, and the other magicians, who each had strong opinions on what techniques she should be learning. Alexis stayed out of it, his mind too occupied. Plus, Penelope had no problem dealing with them on her own.

He checked the pocket of magic in her mind every night and morning. It hadn't grown, and it wasn't hurting her, so he was beginning to agree with Penelope's assumption that it was a spell. Whether it helped or hindered when it went off was yet to be seen. He refused to entertain the idea that it might kill her when it did.

"Alexis? Hello?" Phaidros stood in front of him and snapped his fingers.

"Sorry, what were you saying?"

"I came to make sure you weren't going crazy up here." He leaned over the papers. "Ah, Nereus. Still a pain-in-the-ass teacher."

"I'm not crazy. Please don't touch anything."

Phaidros frowned, leaning closer to study the original diagrams and pages of Alexis's decoding. He ate some of the grapes from Alexis's untouched breakfast. "This spell is energy-driven."

"What?"

"These are all energy workings, and this formula is backward." Phaidros moved the order of pages. "This is not only necromancy, but necromancy through energy exchange. Think Frankenstein's monster needing the lightning bolt. With this"—he lifted a sheet of paper at random—"they are going to use the magic of the high tide as the lightning bolt. I'd say the hotels Duilio was building as magic traps would've been used to give life to the bodies for the other demons Thevetat wants to summon."

Alexis laughed, surprised and utterly dumbfounded. He grabbed Phaidros into a fierce hug. "You are brilliant."

Phaidros struggled until Alexis released him. "I've told you this for years."

"If you weren't so ugly, I'd kiss you. Show me what you're talking about. Work with me, so we can understand this."

"You know, this could've been solved days ago if you'd gotten out of your own head long enough to ask for help."

"I know, I know. You're here now, and here you'll stay until we can work this out."

Phaidros groaned. "I should've stayed in bed."

Alexis dragged up his chair. "Too late now."

"Firstly, let's get these pieces in the right order. Seriously, Alexis, have you been drunk all week?" Phaidros reorganized the pages, and Alexis smiled, even though it was at his own expense. It seemed so obvious now that Phaidros had pointed it out. With any luck, he'd also be able to decipher the way to corrupt the spell, and then they'd be one step closer to ending Abaddon and Thevetat forever.

Two hours later, Phaidros and Alexis had pieced the spell together and theorized how they could interrupt the ritual.

"Penelope won't like this," Phaidros pointed out.

"I know. That's why we can't tell her."

"Alexis, you have no idea what will happen if they pull your magic into this ritual."

"We need bait, and this time it'll be me. If the ritual siphons my magic, we can make sure that it siphons the disruptor spell at the same time. You know they won't give me the chance to cast anything. Making them think they have me down will make them drop their guard. They won't stop to analyze what magic they are taking from me; they will want all of it to fuel Thevetat's resurrection." Alexis dropped his hands in his lap. "It's the best idea we have."

"And what about the ring?"

"We can't know for sure that it will work, and who knows what the spell Poseidon put into Penelope's head actually does? If they work, that's great, but I'm not going to rely on either of them as a guarantee. Too much is at stake. I know this isn't a good idea, but it's the best of all our options." Alexis didn't *want* to be caught up in any magic of Thevetat's, but he didn't know how else to stop the ritual. Nereus had been a part of the ritual when they'd originally attempted it, and he'd have to be as well. As much as he didn't like keeping things from Penelope, she didn't need another thing to worry about, and she would definitely have opinions about Alexis using himself as bait.

Phaidros threw his hands up in surrender. "Okay, this is what you'll need to do."

PENELOPE HAD lost track of how many times she'd ended up flat on her back. After a week of training, she'd moved past the muscle aches and was now speckled with bruises from the wooden daggers she'd been training with. Zo was making it up to her by cooking her favorite food, and Elazar had been coaxed to tell stories every night.

"You're still hesitating before you strike," Lyca said from the other side of the mat.

"I don't mean to." Penelope groaned as she dragged herself back to her feet.

"You're learning fast—much faster than Marco did. You need to *want* to attack. I notice you don't hesitate when you're sparring against Constantine."

"That's because he's a jerk." She was only half-joking. She liked him immensely, but he knew precisely which buttons to press to set her off.

"A jerk who's going to be very helpful. Constantine has always been irritating because he's insightful. Dinner should be ready soon. Let's call it a day." Lyca slid her training weapons onto the rack.

"I wonder if Alexis made better progress than me today."

"Phaidros has been locked up with him for a few hours. He'll drag him down to dinner and force him to be social, I'm sure." Lyca gave Penelope an encouraging pat on her shoulder. "You really are getting better. Don't worry. I know that you won't hesitate to protect Alexis should a priest get in the way."

"Thank you," Penelope said, strangely touched that Lyca had bothered to compliment her at all.

Upstairs in her rooms, Penelope pulled off her sweaty work-out clothes and headed for the shower. She was finding herself torn between the citadel rooms and her own, and she was reluctant to leave the tower. *Maybe the palazzo will move them if I ask.* She would make it a priority when they returned from Milos.

Every day for the past week, she'd written down something she wanted to do in the future. It was a small gesture, but it was a way of keeping her anxiety locked safely in its box. She didn't want to consider for a moment that they could all die within the next month. There were still so many things she wanted to do with her life, and for every one of those things, she could see Alexis beside her.

Penelope stepped out of the bathroom and was about to drop her towel when a voice cleared behind her.

She squealed. "Fuck, Aelia!"

The magician was lounging on a chaise, dressed in black silk harem pants and a black-and-gold crop top, looking like she'd wandered out of an *Arabian Nights* harem. "Go ahead. I've seen you naked before."

"What are you doing in here?"

"I've come to have a girl chat."

Penelope grabbed clothes from her wardrobe and went back to the bathroom to change, Aelia's amused laughter following her. By the time Penelope was dressed, Aelia had produced a bottle of limoncello from somewhere and was sipping it from a delicate china glass the size of Penelope's thumb.

She passed her one. "Drink this and let your feathers unruffle."

Penelope sat down in her armchair with a sigh. "Okay, Aelia, what do you want?"

"Why do I need to want anything other than your company?"

Penelope sipped her tangy liquor and waited.

Aelia let out a huff. "Oh, very well. I wanted to thank you."

"For what?"

"For...everything. You coming to us was a good thing despite Thevetat rearing his head at the same time. Your presence shifted things, changed all of us, for the better," Aelia said, as sincere as Penelope had ever seen her.

"The tide is getting higher every day. We might be running out of time to say the things we know we should. You brought us together again. You are the glue we needed. You're one of us." She reached out to take Penelope's hand. "I don't want you to think for a single moment that you don't belong here with us."

"Thank you, Aelia. I appreciate that." Penelope swallowed the unexpected lump in her throat, not knowing what else to say. "You all drive me crazy, but I love you. Even Con, when he's not acting like a dick."

Aelia's laughter filled the room with magic. "I knew he'd win you over."

"If I'd known sex with Phaidros would bring out your sweet side, I would've convinced you to do it months ago," Penelope said, with a grin.

"If I'd known how good it would be, I would've done it centuries ago." Her smile turned sly.

"Stop. I know what you're thinking, and no, I absolutely don't want details."

Aelia gave them anyway, and by the time Alexis and Phaidros came down, Penelope was bright red and Aelia was in a fit of giggles.

"What are you two talking about?" Phaidros asked with narrow eyes.

Penelope was unable to look at him when she said, "Nothing," just as Aelia said, "Sex."

"Is that so? I'm starting to think I was hanging out in the wrong part of the tower." He gave Aelia a look that made her ears pink.

Alexis tapped his journal on Phaidros's head. "Enough of that. We didn't spend all day solving magical riddles so you could get distracted now."

This earned a scowl from Phaidros. "Really, Penelope, I don't know how you put up with him."

"You solved Nereus's spell?" Penelope reached for Alexis. "Show me!"

"That's how she puts up with him. They both have a one-track mind," Aelia pointed out.

Downstairs, with everyone sprawled out on couches, Alexis and Phaidros explained the magic of Nereus's spell. The magicians and Elazar all nodded and asked questions, while Penelope struggled to follow the complexities and Constantine looked bored. After ten minutes, she gave up trying to understand and simply trusted that the important thing was that it made sense to Alexis. Penelope sent a text to Marco, letting him know that the plan was progressing.

Constantine refilled his wineglass. "You get used to being confused when they talk magic.

Give me something tangible I can attack any day over this mumbo jumbo."

"Spoken like a true Roman."

All talk suddenly ceased, and a shudder of power ran through the magicians. Penelope's mouth tasted of sea salt and Atlantean flowers. In her pocket, the astrolabe vibrated, and she struggled to pull it out. It pulsed with blue light. She opened it, and the tolling of bells echoed from it.

"What is that?" Penelope asked over the din.

The magicians looked at each other.

"The citadel bells," said Galenos. "It's high tide."

PENELOPE SAT on Alexis's balcony, watching the boats in the canal below. He was asleep after a tense night, but Penelope's own restlessness had dragged her from his arms. The astrolabe was quiet now, its metal warm in her hands. The alarm had finally died away, leaving the whole palazzo strained. The high tide meant Thevetat would be getting ready to perform the ritual. Time was up. She needed to talk to Kreios.

Penelope slipped the silver ring that kept her bound to her body from her finger and shut her eyes. The sounds of the night closed in around her, and she fell into them, letting the meditation settle over her. She focused on Kreios: the way he stood, his dark eyes and wry smile, the feel of his presence. Her heart raced as she felt a dragging sensation, and then she heard ocean waves lapping against stone. It was dark in the cave, the only light coming from a guttering torch. The clinking of chains made her turn, and in the gloom was the broken form of a man. Shackles were secured on his wrists and bolted to stone; the sand he sat on was still damp from the tide.

"You shouldn't be here, Doctor Bryne."

"Kreios?" Penelope went to him, kneeling down to brush the hair back from his bloodied face. He was covered in lacerations. "What happened to you?"

"Punishment...for helping Aelia," he said from between busted lips. His black eyes glittered with rage and pain. "Don't look so worried about your enemy. I've had worse."

Penelope was going to be sick. "We'll stop them. We'll save you."

"I don't need saving, Penelope. Thevetat won't let me die. He only wants me to suffer before he takes over my body and heals me. Abaddon needs my help with the ritual. Otherwise, my punishment would've been a lot worse than this." He shifted, the chains clanking against stone. "I hope you have a plan."

"We do, but you understand why I can't tell you."

"Very clever of you."

"It's high tide," she said, not knowing what else to say. She'd always have nightmares about being locked in the tombs of San Zaccaria but looking at him reduced to nothing but meat and pain, she couldn't stop the tears running down her cheeks.

"You have two days, until the night of the full moon. That's when it will all begin. I suggest you don't waste that time." Kreios looked up at her, and the rage in his black eyes softened. "Go, Penelope. Don't let them find you here, even in your astral form. Save your tears for someone who actually deserves them. Don't pity this monster."

Penelope touched his cheek—the one place on his body left whole—then let her body call her back to Venice. She leaned over the railing of the balcony and vomited.

Alexis's hands came to her shoulders. "What did you see?"

"Kreios. We've got two days to get to Milos."

THIRTY-SEVEN

THEY LEFT VENICE the following morning on a charter flight heading to Paros. It was the first time in a thousand years that the palazzo in Venice had been emptied of Atlanteans. Only Elazar remained to watch over its halls. Lyca had tried to convince Galenos to stay behind too, but he'd blatantly refused. Penelope didn't blame him. Who would want to be the last magician standing—or the one left behind with nothing to do but wait?

"I'm an old man, Penelope. I'd only get in the way," Elazar had said when she'd voiced that opinion. He'd cast a fond glance in Zo's direction. "Besides, Abba would worry too much about me, and you're going to need him by your side and at his best. Protect yourself, dear Archivist. I'd hate to keep your books all to myself."

Penelope had kissed both his cheeks, knowing that if the worst should happen, her books couldn't find better hands to look after them.

The lagoon and terra-cotta roofs of Venice stretched out beneath her, and Penelope silently wished it another goodbye, just as she had earlier that morning, her feet in the water, her magic connected to it.

"You'll see Venice again." Alexis lifted their interlocked hands and kissed her fingers.

"Undoubtedly," Penelope replied with a bravado in her voice that she fought to be believable.

"Reitia will watch over the city in our absence. If she accidentally damages the hulls of a few cruise ships while we're gone, all the better."

Penelope laughed, the coiled tension within her easing a little. She hadn't been to Greece since she found the corner of the Atlantis tablet, and once again, she felt like she was being pulled full circle. She leaned back against Alexis and tried not to think of Kreios suffering in his dark cave. After she told Alexis what she'd seen the previous night, the magicians had launched into action. Weapons and equipment were packed, and Marco was summoned. He was talking with Zo a few rows away and seemed far more relaxed about his role in the upcoming conflict than Penelope was.

Five hours later, Penelope shielded her eyes against the glare of the burning sun on whitewashed houses. The port at Paros was crammed with boats and busy with fishing locals and sunburnt tourists. Penelope thought the magicians were the most conspicuous bunch of tourists by far, but none of them seemed concerned that Thevetat had spies on the island. Galenos had provided them all with forged identities, so even if Thevetat had some of his followers watching flights, they'd be none the wiser about their movements.

After finding their hotel, everyone scattered with promises to catch up at sundown for dinner. They all had jobs to do: Galenos would be busy checking his surveillance of Milos; Alexis and Phaidros were still working at the magic they'd use to disrupt the ritual, and they'd also be going over invasion plans with Constantine and Lyca; Zo and Aelia were in charge of gleaning gossip from the locals at the bars. Marco and Penelope ended up at a table on the beach, shaded by a bright umbrella, cold beers in hand.

"You can't say you never got to have your holiday," Penelope said, peeling a pistachio and offering it to him.

"I'm starting to understand their appeal. Isabella almost packed my bag for me; she was so keen to get me out from under her feet."

"I don't suppose I would have any chance of talking you out of coming with us tomorrow night and into staying here instead?"

Marco laughed. "About as much chance as I would have convincing you to do the same. We've both come too far, and I need to know

that this is over either way. I'll be on the other side of Milos. You don't
need to have a single worry for me. Save it for yourself. You'll be the
one going to slay the monster. Who would've thought that you'd cause
me so much trouble the day you walked into my police station back in
March?"

THE NIGHT was balmy, and their dinner was loud. They ate outside under the trees and sprawling bougainvillea, which were strung
with lights. Phaidros and Aelia sat together, holding hands like shy
teenagers, and Penelope had to admire Constantine's resolve not to
get upset or offended. If their positions had been reversed, Penelope
wouldn't have handled seeing Alexis with another woman so well. Zo
kept Constantine distracted. They were thick as thieves, bantering
about classical Greek poetry and how the world needed more writers
composing epics, before the art was only studied and not practiced.

Alexis was quiet as the others ate, joked, and told stories. Penelope
didn't have to ask to know that he was still thinking about magic. When
she took his hand under the table, his eyes refocused and landed on her.

"Let's get out of here," he whispered in her ear.

The others paid little attention as Penelope and Alexis slipped
away. They crossed through back alleys and down to the beach.

"Are you okay?" she asked once they were truly alone.

Alexis placed an arm around her shoulders as they walked bare-
foot across the sand. "I am. I know how to disrupt the ritual's magic,
but I feel so horribly unprepared. It seems too last-minute, and my
mind won't stop running over the steps I'll need to do to build the
magic. It's complicated, and even with the extra power of the high tide,
it'll be draining."

"At least you know what to do. I have a ring that won't translate and
a spell I don't know what to do with. I have to rely on faith—something
I've never had an overabundance of—to see me through. If all else fails,
we chop off Thevetat's and Abaddon's heads and hope for the best."

This earned a laugh from Alexis. "Constantine is rubbing off on you."

They reached the surf, and Penelope wriggled her toes in the cool water. Poseidon's magic shivered as it reached through her and connected with the ocean. It felt different than it did in the lagoon in Venice. There was something else—something buried that called out to her. *Paros is at the heart of the islands that made up the Cyclades Plateau,* Penelope realized. It was in the same stretch of ocean that Atlantis had been destroyed.

"What is it, Penelope?"

"Can you feel that? There's something underneath the water. It feels like…" She couldn't find the words. She took his hand and tried to share the sensation through the *moîra desmós.* Alexis sucked in a breath as she reached for the power under the waves.

"It's home," Alexis said. "It feels like Atlantis did—or parts of its magic, at least. I've never felt it like this in the water."

"Maybe because it's the high tide? No wonder Thevetat chose Milos for his base. If there's still power left in the scattered rubble of Atlantis, he might be tapping into it as well."

"It's possible. I had no idea so much magic still lay in what was left."

"You never tried to find any artifacts or anything?"

"No." Alexis shook his head. "In part, because it would've been too much like digging in a graveyard. Also, the technology wasn't advanced enough back then, and Nereus was determined that we all move on and not look back. There was nothing to return to. I was always concerned that something magical would wash up on a beach and cause havoc, but there was no way I could control or police that. That's one of the reasons I always investigated magic wielders—to be sure that they hadn't learned from any survivors or found something left over from Atlantis that could hurt them or others." He pulled her close. "Thank you for sharing that with me, for letting me know it's still there."

"You want to feel more?"

"Yes," Alexis whispered.

As they stood in the breaking waves, Penelope reached out with her magic again until she could feel the pulse of Atlantis. To anyone walking past, they would've looked like lovers embracing in the moonlight. How could she ever explain what it felt like to anyone but Alexis? She didn't know if it was Poseidon's magic or the part of her that had always known Atlantis had existed, but Alexis was right—whatever source she was connecting to felt like home. Full of magic and emotion, Penelope stood up on tiptoes and kissed Alexis. He was home and love and magic, and if she died tomorrow, he'd be right beside her. Instead of making her feel vulnerable, that thought filled her with a strength she didn't know she was capable of.

"Whatever happens, we'll be okay, *cara*." He cupped her cheeks between his palms, and his expression brightened. "I'm going to show you a memory tonight."

"That sounds promising."

"We'd better do it off the beach, or people will think we've lost our minds."

They headed back up the beach and to their hotel room. When Alexis pulled her down on the bed beside him, Penelope asked, "What are you planning?"

His expression heated as he brushed the stray curls from her face. "Stop looking at me like that, or I'll forget all about showing you memories and focus on making some new ones."

"I promise to make you a memory you won't ever forget afterward."

Alexis gave her a filthy smile, then kissed her. Penelope fought temptation and shut her eyes as Alexis's magic pulled her under.

WHEN PENELOPE opened her eyes, she was standing next to a marble column in a bustling marketplace. Alexis was beside her, but it wasn't the Alexis she'd curled up in bed with. This one had gold in his hair and at his wrists, and was dressed in a maroon tunic threaded with gold and belted at his waist. Her Alexis came to stand on the other side of her.

"Gods, was I ever that young?" He stared at himself.

"You still look exactly the same." Penelope gave him a devilish wink. "I'm all for you bringing this look back."

"Good to know." Alexis laughed, and the younger version of himself disappeared into the crowd.

"Where are we?"

"I thought I'd show you one of Poseidon's feast days. You shouldn't only see Atlantis at war. I want you to experience some of its beauty too, in case I'm not able to show you again." He took her hand. "Welcome to Atlas, *cara.*"

"Alexis…" Penelope was so touched she pulled him down to kiss him quick and hard. "Thank you. Show me everything."

And he did. For a day, they walked hand in hand through the city. He showed her the main agora, where politicians and philosophers argued. Priestesses of Poseidon threaded their way through the crowds in their deep aqua chitons and veils, with golden tridents painted on their foreheads. There were stalls selling everything from jewelry to cured squid.

Penelope let the mad energy of the place pull her under its spell as Alexis acted as her tour guide, showing her the bull dancers and temples, the palace, and lastly, the strangely tall and imposing tower that was the Citadel of Magicians. It was a spike of marble, its triangular roof painted gold and blue with an orichalcum statue of Poseidon on top of its walled gates. They passed underneath his stern gaze, and Penelope shivered, feeling the magic of the place even in the memory.

"This place is amazing." She tilted her head back to stare at the arched windows that wound their way in a spiral all the way to the top.

"It was. There were usually about two hundred magicians under its roof at any one time."

They crossed through the marble pillars and inside the tower. Alexis showed her various rooms where magicians could work different elemental magic. She peeked in at magicians working earth, water, air, and fire magic. As they walked, she realized that the inside of the tower was vastly bigger than the outside, and she said as much to Alexis.

"The palazzo in Venice is much the same. Too much magic made the citadel sentient as well, and it kept growing to accommodate the magicians that came to learn. Nereus could never determine for certain if it was an original spell of Poseidon's or if it was too much exposure to raw magic. There are levels upon levels of books beneath us, like the Archives, so either theory is possible."

Next, he showed her the library, and Penelope felt like crying at the thought that so many books now lay at the bottom of the ocean. Standing on the ground floor, Penelope could stare up at the levels upon levels above her, and down at ones that fell away into the darkness beneath. Light streamed down from the top of the tower, reflecting off carefully positioned mirrors of glass and crystal. They bounced the light from one to another and filled everything with warm light. It was the most breathtaking place she'd ever seen, and she hung onto Alexis, unable to find the words.

"I would've never left," she said eventually.

Alexis had a happy, melancholy look on his face as he held her. "Before you ask—no, you won't be able to pick out a book and read it unless I read it in the past. Still, it is nice to come and visit."

IT WAS long past midnight when Alexis pulled them out of the memory and back into their bed on Paros. Penelope opened her eyes, surprised to find they were filled with tears.

"Thank you so much, Alexis."

"You are very welcome, *cara*. Thank you for making those memories good for me again. I stopped venturing into them because of the pain they caused. You have healed me in so many ways—*saved* me in so many ways." His grip on her tightened. "You're a miracle and a blessing, and I want nothing more than to spend whatever time I have left with you. It doesn't matter if the curse of our long lives breaks tomorrow or not; I'll be here with you for as long as you'll have me."

"I wouldn't want to be anywhere else but by your side—tomorrow, when we face Thevetat, or in a hundred years, when we will undoubtedly be hunting another mystery. It would seem Carolyn was wrong: there is a man in existence that comes before my hunt for Atlantis." Her smile widened. "You're my true love, after all."

"And you are mine," he said, moving on top of her. "Now, Doctor Bryne, I believe you promised me a new memory I'll never forget."

THIRTY-EIGHT

MARCO WAS DOING his best to play the role of curious tourist with too much money as the chartered helicopter dropped him off at the Milos airport. He'd come hours ahead of the others and felt strangely exposed without them. Galenos had rented him a car in advance, and Marco went through the motions of picking it up in Adamantas, going shopping for trinkets, and eating at one of the restaurants. He killed time until his phone alerted him at 3 p.m., after which he drove to the Catacombs of Milos.

Marco joined the scattered groups of tourists, reading the informative plaques with feigned interest. The catacombs were dated from the first to the fifth centuries, with speculation that they predated the necropolis of Rome. Apparently, Saint Paul himself had been shipwrecked there on his way to Athens after teaching on Crete. Also, over two thousand Christians were buried there.

Marco stepped out of the hot sun and down the stone steps into the cool, dark gloom. The hair on the back of his neck stood up as the hush of the place settled over him. He wasn't superstitious, but the place had a morbid holiness. He crossed himself before forcing himself farther inside. A helpful-looking tour guide told him that the catacombs would be closing in fifteen minutes, and he assured her he would be out by then.

Marco tried not to look hurried or suspicious as he moved deeper into the catacombs, thumbing the coin-sized metal discs in his pocket.

"You only need to place three of them down and then get out of there. If you see any priests, don't engage with them, and don't look at them for a second longer than you need to," Lyca had warned him. Then she'd taken his face in her hands. "Don't get killed unnecessarily." It was the only pep talk he'd received from her, and it was, quintessentially, Lyca.

The catacombs had three sections, and in a shadowed corner of each one, Marco placed one of the small black metal discs carved with glyphs. He didn't understand how a tiny piece of metal could stop Thevetat from drawing on the power of the dead. Galenos had tried to explain, but Marco glazed over within seconds. All he knew was that they would somehow activate when the time was right and wouldn't alert Thevetat until it was too late.

Marco followed the line of tourists out of the catacombs and headed to the car park. Two men passed him, and even though they looked like any other tourists, Marco's skin crawled when he caught the scent of incense and death on them. It smelled like the cave in the Bahamas. He looked down at his phone, pretending that he didn't want to vomit.

No one seemed to notice as the men took a bundle of keys offered by the tour guide before they slipped back into the catacombs. Marco climbed into his car and gripped the steering wheel until his knuckles were white. He had the urge to stop them before they began any horrible magic, but that would give him away, and then their whole plan would be ruined. Fighting his policeman instincts, he started the car and drove back to Adamantas. Constantine's friends would soon be arriving at their hotel—if they hadn't already—and Marco was meant to join them before they settled in to wait.

AT DUSK, Phaidros, Aelia, Constantine, Lyca, Zo, and Galenos were dropped off by helicopter on the south side of Milos. Phaidros didn't know how many favors Constantine had called in to get them their own private helicopter, but he wasn't about to complain, because approaching the villa on the cliffs would've been a lot harder by automobile. This part of Milos was sparsely populated, and the only roads in the area led to Thevetat's compound.

Zo, Lyca, and Galenos disappeared into the trees, heading for the north side of the villa, while Phaidros, Aelia, and Constantine would approach from the west.

"This is starting to feel like old times," said Constantine cheerily. He pulled out a dagger. "Now, remember, you two: no using magic. If they sense it, we're all dead."

"Not our first time, Con, darling." Aelia's violet eyes flickered to Phaidros. "Are you ready?"

Phaidros kissed her once. "Okay, now I am." He told himself it was for luck, but the truth was, he wanted to get one more in just in case they all ended up dead.

They crept through the trees, hunting the small groups of priests that patrolled the borders. Constantine grabbed one priest around the mouth and slid his dagger across the man's throat before he could register what was happening. Aelia was a golden shimmer in front of him, taking out the priest's companion with a blade through the ribs. She took the comms earpiece from the dead man and slipped it over her ear, then froze as Phaidros shot two arrows over her shoulder. Another guard fell to the dusty ground.

"Watch your back," he whispered.

"That's what you're here for."

Constantine came out of the darkness, hands bloody. "Where is everyone? The satellite images from the last week has had this place crawling with people."

"Galenos will be able to tell us as soon as he gets into their surveillance."

Aelia waved them silent, tapped her earpiece, and hurried through the trees. They scattered as another three priests approached down one of the roads.

"Is that blood?" one asked, the beam of his torch hovering over the dark stain on the ground.

Phaidros loosed three arrows just as Constantine came up behind the group on the other side.

"Now you're showing off," he said.

"You were taking too long. Where's Aelia?"

A yelp sounded through the trees, and he ran toward it. He shouldn't have worried—Aelia's gladius shone silver in the moonlight, and she was surrounded by bodies.

"Will you boys hurry up?" She flicked the gore from her blade. "I just saw Lyca go into the villa. We should be clear to move."

"Right behind you," said Constantine.

They left the scrubby trees and reached the manicured gardens surrounding the monstrosity of a villa. The dark ocean spread out in front of them.

"It almost seems a shame to destroy it," Phaidros said.

Aelia snorted. "Consider shopping for a holiday house that hasn't been tarnished by demons."

They followed Constantine up the marble steps of the main entrance, and Phaidros did his best not to step in the pools of blood. He'd seen Lyca kill during the war, and she'd lost none of her savageness over the years. There wasn't a single priest left whole.

"Galenos?" he whispered.

The shadows shifted in an empty doorway, and Lyca appeared. "The surveillance room is this way, but I can show you where all the other priests are hiding." She waved them through the house.

Zo stood in the shadows of the balcony. He wore fury on his face and had death in his eyes.

Phaidros joined him. "What is it?"

Zo pointed to the strip of beach beneath them. Every few meters, a sacrifice had been pegged in the sand illuminated by burning torches. They all led to a cliff farther up from them and at the base was a cave mouth. Between them and that cave were at least two hundred people; priests and mercenaries.

Constantine rested his hand on the hilt of his gladius. "How nice of them to meet in one place for us."

"My thoughts exactly, Emperor." Lyca smiled.

"Six of us, two hundred of them. I almost feel sorry for them." Aelia's eyes narrowed at the line of sacrifices. "Almost."

Galenos cleared his throat behind them. "I do hate to interrupt, but I've got what I need from their servers, and the bombs have been set."

Lyca turned away from the balcony. "Excellent, my love."

They hurried from the house, heading back through the gardens and out of the blast zone. A wave of nausea rolled over Phaidros, and he stopped in his tracks, breathing heavily as aura colors shuddered over his field of vision.

Aelia stopped too. "What's wrong?"

After pulling in a deep inhale, Phaidros straightened. "Thevetat's pulling on the energy and magic of this place. It's all heading toward the caves. The ritual has started."

"Excellent. That means we can do this." Zo pressed the button of a detonator. A resounding boom echoed through the trees, and they all staggered when the shock wave reached them. Plumes of smoke and fire lit the night sky. "Damn, Galenos. How much power did you use?"

"Enough to make sure the job was done properly."

Phaidros drew his sword and looked to Lyca. "Following your lead, General."

Her smile was a slash of white in the darkness. "Now, we get our revenge for Nereus, Tim, and what they fucking did to Atlantis."

The thick, dark shadows of her magic unleashed, and the screaming began.

THIRTY-NINE

PENELOPE WATCHED THE villa on the cliffs go up in flames. She heard the explosion from the beach on Paximadi. Alexis stood beside her, face cold. He was dressed in his armor, his chest plate repaired from where it had melted saving Elazar. Swords hung from his back, and knives were strapped to his forearms. He'd settled into that calm, killing place Penelope couldn't understand or reach.

That morning, Lyca had surprised Penelope with a set of daggers and a chest plate of her own and had shown her how to strap it in place. It had the trident and book of Poseidon engraved into the front, and she could sense the protections that had been hammered into the metal. When she'd thanked Lyca, the other magician had knocked her knuckles against it.

"One of us now," she'd said and then groaned as Penelope hugged her.

Penelope was now thanking any gods that would listen for Lyca's gift. She brushed her thumb against Solomon's ring on her index finger. *Please work.*

"Are you ready, Penelope?"

"As I'll ever be." She stared up at Alexis, her heart full of love and fear. "I love you."

Alexis kissed her—a brief press of lips, warmth, and reassurance. "I love you too. Let's end this." His magic burned brightly under his skin, and he took her hand and portaled across to Milos.

It was like being dropped into Hell. The beach was a chaotic scene of blood and screaming, the magicians and Constantine slicing through the priests of Thevetat. Penelope kept her eyes firmly on Alexis, running after him as he followed the line of sacrifices. A wave of magic poured out of him, and one by one, the bodies went up in smoke, reduced to ashes in seconds.

Alexis had made Penelope promise she wouldn't engage the priests unless she was forced to, but seeing him now, she wondered why he was worried in the first place. Alexis was death personified. He cut away any priest that dared to face him. It took all her effort to stay out of his way but also follow him closely enough not to be separated.

Behind them, more bombs went off, sending Penelope to the sand. She glanced behind her in time to see the back ranks of priests swing about and open fire on her. Alexis grabbed her by the arm and pulled her to her feet, then threw up a shimmering shield of light between them and the enemy. Bullets struck it, then fell in piles on the sand.

"We're almost there. Don't stop," Alexis shouted to her over the noise and pointed to a cave in the distance. He kept the shield between them and the priests as they ran across the bloodstained sand.

As they drew closer to the cave, Penelope could make out Abaddon and Kreios standing in a circle of torches. In between them was a clay body on a stone altar. Thevetat's magic hit them, and Penelope was knocked back. The noxious power ripped Alexis's swords from his hands.

"You just can't stop interfering, can you?" Kreios said, eyes glowing red.

Penelope tried to reconcile him with the broken and bloody man she'd seen a few days ago. Kreios was right—Thevetat had only wanted him to suffer temporarily. He'd healed his wounds as soon as he took over his body. Alexis cast a bolt of magic at them, only for it to deflect off an invisible field inside the circle.

"Such childish tricks, magician." Abaddon shook his head. "You're as bad as your precious Nereus. She never could understand where true power lies."

"Thevetat will never share his power with you, Abaddon," Alexis said. "Once he gets what he needs, what use will he have for an old man with no magic of his own?"

"Magicians—only good for one thing." Thevetat spoke through Kreios's body, and upon the last word, dark power knocked Penelope to the sand, and her mouth filled with blood. Alexis screamed as magic was ripped from his body.

"Start the ritual now, Abaddon," Thevetat demanded.

Abaddon spoke in a language that sounded like Atlantean but became harsher and more guttural with every word. Penelope struggled against the invisible power holding her down.

"Alexis!" she shouted, trying to reach where he writhed in the sand.

With one pain-filled eye, he winked at her. Was this a part of his plan to disrupt the ritual? He wasn't faking the next scream that tore from him. Pale blue light rushed from his body and was dragged into the circle where Abaddon and Kreios chanted. Penelope reached inside for her own magic, trying desperately to call the water to her. Pain split her head, and the spell that Poseidon had placed inside her detonated.

PENELOPE STUMBLED into Piazza San Marco. The sun shone above her, and children ate melting ice creams. A silver-haired woman sat feeding the pigeons, and she turned as the bells of the Torre dell'Orologio began to chime.

"Nereus?"

The old magician's face went from shock to joy. "So it'll be you then. Doctor Bryne—I might have known. Alexis isn't going to be happy to learn you're the heir. How many years have we got?"

Disorientated, Penelope remembered the words in the first letter that had dropped into her lap on the plane; *I foresaw my death five years ago as I sat feeding pigeons in Saint Marco's square...* Nereus had said she'd seen her death, that she'd *seen* Penelope. Penelope had thought it was a premonition, she never thought it was literal.

"F-five years," she said. "How is this happening?"

"Poseidon, I imagine. He told me about you."

"I told him about you too."

Nereus clicked her tongue. "He was the craftiest magician I ever met to pull this off. Out with it, girl. Tell me how I die and how I can set you on your path."

The words came tumbling out of Penelope: Nereus's death, the letters, the citadel rooms and incense, how she'd met with Poseidon and the magic he'd placed in her head.

Nereus cackled with laughter. "It's certainly his magic doing this. How terribly unnerving for you. Oh well, can't be helped. You'd best go and stop that fucker Abaddon once and for all." She gripped Penelope's hands. "I'm so glad it's you. Kiss them all for me."

"I will. Thank you, Nereus."

"No, thank you, Heir of Gods." Nereus pressed two fingers to Penelope's forehead. "Get out of here."

PENELOPE WAS back on the beach in Milos in the blink of an eye. She climbed to her feet; whatever Thevetat was using to hold her had melted away. Kreios was slumped beside the stone table, and the clay body atop it unleashed a scream in a language no human tongue could have spoken. Its arms jerked as it sat up. Abaddon continued chanting as the clay began to glow red.

"*No*," Penelope commanded, and time slowed. The world lit up around her. The lines of magic that bound Alexis to the ritual were visible in the air. She waved one finger toward him, severing the ties and freeing him. Hot, silver magic streaked out of her and into the ocean at her back. She gripped a wave and pulled it up the shore.

Abaddon's chanting slowed to a distorted groan as Penelope walked toward them. The clay figure's red eyes burned with fury as the ocean wave wrapped around it and the infernal heat was put out.

"You can't stop this with your water tricks," Thevetat hissed through muddy lips.

The ring on Penelope's hand glowed as she reached out and took Thevetat by his clay face. The glyphs on the ring shone and shifted, and Penelope could read it at last.

Penelope stared at the sacred Word that had the power to remake all of creation if only she asked it. Thevetat screeched only once as the Word tumbled from her lips. Time normalized, and the clay body exploded into a million pieces under her hand. Her wave dragged the pieces back into the ocean, scattering them in the tide.

The magic released her, and the ring's glow vanished. She turned and stumbled across the sand to where Alexis lay.

He groaned. "P-Penelope."

She brushed the bloody hair from his face. "You're okay. I have you."

"You did it, *cara*." Alexis kissed her. "You did it."

"It helps to be the heir of gods. I honestly don't know how much of that was Poseidon and how much was me." She steadied him as he got to his feet.

Abaddon screeched. "What have you done?!" On his hands and knees, he clawed at the slick mud, all that was left of Thevetat.

"Stay down!" Constantine and the other magicians raced up the beach.

The priests of Thevetat that were still breathing were being herded into groups by men in black tactical gear behind them. Penelope breathed a sigh of relief when she spotted Marco's curly hair amongst them.

Kreios got to his feet. "Doctor Bryne, I knew you'd do it."

Abaddon wheeled on him. "What are you talking about? You betrayed *me* to this woman?"

"Yes, I did, you piece of shit who dragged me into this hell ten thousand years ago, stealing my will and life from me." Kreios pulled a gun from his belt, and before anyone could stop him, he shot the old man in the face. He tossed the gun to the sand and went down on his knees in front of Aelia, hands laced behind his head. "Now, you may do to me as you wish."

Aelia's gladius was at his throat in a blink, her bloody face streaked with tears. "Why should I be the one to judge you?"

Kreios's black eyes were sincere. "Because it was you who I did unforgivable things too. I should've married you and protected you. Instead, a demon forced me to rape you and cut you to pieces. I forfeit my life to you, Princess."

Penelope held her breath as Aelia's blade wavered at Kreios's throat. "It's okay, Aelia. Do it." Kreios shut his eyes.

Aelia gripped his long black hair to yank his head back. She pressed her blade to the skin of his throat. "No. I won't have your death on my hands today. You were under Thevetat's control, and as much as I've dreamed of causing you the same pain you caused me, I won't do it. I'm better than Abaddon. I'm better than you." She let him go with a shove, and he fell backward onto the sand. "Your life is yours once more, but if I ever see you again, I'll fucking kill you."

Kreios ducked his head and placed one fist to his chest. "As my princess commands."

THE SUN'S first rays streamed across the sky as Alexis joined Penelope at the water's edge. Poseidon's power still called gently to the waves, but it lay quiet and dormant under her skin. Alexis took her hand, and they watched the sunrise.

"We survived," she said, needing to say the words aloud to make them real.

"We did, and my great plan to interrupt the ritual didn't work a single bit."

"You mean your great plan to let Thevetat pull your magic out of you and with it a disruption spell? When I have the energy, I'm going to give you the lecture of your life for trying something so damn foolish."

Alexis's smile widened despite her tone. "I'll take whatever punishment you see fit, but first, tell me what happened."

"You're not going to believe this…"

She told him about Poseidon's magic taking her to Nereus, the wave of power inside her, and how she could finally read the Word. She couldn't remember what it sounded like, but she knew how it had felt. With every word, Alexis's grip on her tightened. Tears of exhaustion and relief were streaming down her face by the time she finished. He kissed them from her cheeks, and she tasted the salt on his lips as they found hers. They shook as they held on to each other.

Up the beach, the other magicians were seeing to their wounds and arguing about something she couldn't hear. They were damaged, but they were whole, and now that Thevetat was gone, they were safe.

Alexis brushed a thumb over her cheek, his indigo eyes full of love and magic as he stared into hers. "Tell me, Doctor Bryne, what would you like to do now that you've saved me and the rest of the world?"

Penelope smiled wide, and the lost magic on the ocean floor began to pulse.

EPILOGUE

IT WAS ANOTHER sunny day, and the Aegean shone like a clear aqua gemstone. Penelope pulled her wet suit on, the material cool against her skin, and made sure her seams were straight. Her phone beeped, and a photo came through of Aelia and Phaidros, half-naked on a beach somewhere, with strict instructions not to work too hard. Penelope smiled and ignored the advice, just as Aelia knew she would.

It had been two months since the magicians clashed with Thevetat and Abaddon, and they had all scattered to recover and deal with the ongoing high tide. Alexis and Penelope had gotten on a sailboat and hadn't left the Greek islands for the last month. She couldn't remember ever being so relaxed.

She'd received one message from Kreios since, and while she didn't know if they would ever get to the point of being friends, she was reluctant to abandon him altogether after everything they had been through.

Alexis came up on deck. "I swear, if I get one more message from Zo asking me about paint colors for the kitchen in the palazzo, I'm going to change my number."

"Just do what I do and give him such horrible suggestions that he stops asking."

The Greek sun had tanned Alexis's skin and streaked his hair with gold, and he was looking more and more like a corsair she'd run away with and less like the scholar in his tower.

He zipped up her wet suit and planted a kiss on the back of her neck. "What are you smiling about?"

"I'm starting to see the value of holidays in the Greek islands with incredibly handsome men."

"*Cara*, you are diving for Atlantis relics. You're still working."

"That *is* my idea of a holiday."

"I know. Don't worry. I'm not complaining. I'm stress-free and alone with a beautiful woman where I can't be interrupted by meddling magicians."

"Does this mean I've stopped giving you gray hairs already?"

"I wouldn't go that far. I still have valid concerns that you're going to stumble across a magical relic down there and get yourself into trouble."

Penelope put her arms around his neck. "But if I *do*, you can come rescue me, and you love doing that."

"Stop trying to distract me from being worried about you being in danger," Alexis said, even as his arms went around her, drawing her close.

"Why? It's working." Penelope went up on her tiptoes to kiss him.

"I'm serious, Doctor Bryne. Remember the rules."

"I haven't forgotten our deal, my love. I get to look for Atlantis relics on the proviso that you get to study anything magical I discover, and then I get to write papers on anything of a safe and mundane nature that I find," Penelope recited and crossed her heart.

"Don't you forget it, *cara*. You've got that gleam in your eye that tells me Poseidon's magic is picking up on something."

"It woke me up last night, so I just *know* it's going to be something good." Penelope bounced on the balls of her feet.

Alexis laughed at her enthusiasm. "I can feel that new gray hair already. Your tank has three hours of oxygen left, so don't forget to set your watch."

"I won't. It's not going to take me three hours to find it—it's so *loud*."

Penelope put the rest of her dive gear on, and Alexis gave her a final kiss. "I love you. Be careful."

"I love you too, and I'm always careful. You know me." Penelope laughed, then flipped off the back of the boat and into the sea before he could argue.

She let the blue waters drag her under before she reached out with her magic and sent out her command: *Show me.* As the current pulled her through the water, a thrill ran up her spine. There was a pulse, an answering call of strange power that she could only identify as *Atlantis*.

Penelope smiled around her regulator and sent it a reply: *I'm coming for you.*

ABOUT THE AUTHOR

Amy Kuivalainen is a Finnish-Australian writer who is obsessed with magical wardrobes, doors, auroras, and burial mounds that might offer her a way into another realm. Until that happens, she plans to write about monsters, magic, mythology and fairy tales because that's the next best thing. She enjoys practicing yoga and spending time in the beautiful city of Melbourne.